CRIMSON
REIGN

CRIMSON REIGN

AMÉLIE WEN ZHAO

DELACORTE PRESS

Visit us on the Web! GetUnderlined.com
Educators and librarians, for a variety of teaching tools,
visit us at RHTeachersLibrarians.com

Library of Congress Cataloging-in-Publication Data
Names: Zhao, Amélie Wen, author. | Zhao, Amélie Wen. Blood heir trilogy ; 3.
Title: Crimson reign / Amélie Wen Zhao.
Description: First edition. | New York : Delacorte Press, [2022] | Series: Blood heir ; book 3 |
Audience: Ages 14 . | Audience: Grades 10–12. | Summary: Anastacya Mikhailov's
blood Affinity was stolen from her during the battle in Bregon, and even though
every day without her Affinity brings her closer to death she is determined to
return to Cyrilia and prevent the Empress Morganya from obtaining a legendary
ancient power that will allow her to rule the whole world; the only allies she has left
are the navy she recruited and the courage of her friends, but she is absolutely
determined to liberate her people from Morganya's reign of darkness.
Identifiers: LCCN 2021020902 (print) | LCCN 2021020903 (ebook) |
ISBN 978-0-525-70787-5 (hardcover) | ISBN 978-0-525-70789-9 (ebook)
Subjects: LCSH: Magic—Juvenile fiction. | Good and evil—Juvenile fiction. |
Ability—Juvenile fiction. | Imaginary places—Juvenile fiction. | Friendship—Juvenile
fiction. | Fantasy. | CYAC: Magic—Fiction. | Ability—Fiction. | Good and evil—Fiction. |
Fantasy. | LCGFT: Fantasy fiction.
Classification: LCC PZ7.1.Z5125 Cr 2022 (print) | LCC PZ7.1.Z5125 (ebook) | DDC [Fic]—dc23

The text of this book is set in 11.35-point Adobe Caslon Pro
Interior design by Ken Crossland

Printed in the United States of America
10 9 8 7 6 5 4 3 2 1
First Edition

To Clement—
for showing me the hope in revolutions
and for being the forever to my story

PART I

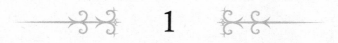

1

THE CYRILIAN EMPIRE

The moon was red tonight and the ocean looked like blood, glistening a deep, clear crimson. Anastacya Mikhailov leaned over the railing of her ship and breathed in the sharp, ice-tinted scent of her empire.

Throughout their journey over the past fortnight, she had watched the waters shift from the lovely cobalt blue of Bregon's coastal shore to the pale, vicious waves of Cyrilia. The humid ocean air of the south had turned stark and dry as they traveled north, the wind whipping at their sails.

The Cyrilian Empire was carved of ice and snow, and she its daughter, born and raised.

"An hour till we make land," came a voice.

Ana turned. Daya of Kusutri strode toward her. She'd donned a thick fur cloak over her Bregonian tunic and leather shoes as they journeyed north and the weather grew colder. Her captain's pin flashed, and tonight, even Daya's easy grin was absent in the place of sobriety as she sidled up and leaned against the railing by Ana's side.

"Crew's up and ready for . . . well, whatever we find out there," Daya finished, tipping her head forward in a grim gesture.

Whatever we find out there. Ana gripped the railing, her jaw tightening as she gazed unflinchingly ahead.

It had been over a moon since she'd been forced to flee her empire, abandoning her people to a scene of slaughter—all in search of a deadly weapon that, if obtained by Morganya, would cause the demise of not only Cyrilia but the entire world. Siphons enabled their bearers to steal powers from Affinites and had been part of a larger, decades-long plan by Alaric Kerlan and the Bregonian government to further exploit Affinites. Morganya, of course, had sought out the two existing functional siphons to gain power for herself.

"There's only one person we're searching for," Ana said quietly.

"You think she's out there?" Daya murmured, nodding in the direction of the shores.

Their quarry: Sorsha Farrald, Ramson's half sister and former Lieutenant of the Blue Fort. The girl who had betrayed her own army and kingdom from the inside on a quest for revenge and destruction.

The girl who had stolen both siphons.

Sorsha had used one siphon to steal Ana's blood Affinity for herself, storing it and channeling it at will in the searock band that she wore on her wrist. The other, she'd sworn to bring to Morganya before she'd disappeared.

It sickened Ana to know that her power would be used by a girl obsessed with wrath and ruin—and it was only the first example of the devastation the siphons would unleash upon the world. The exploitation of Affinites would continue at the hands of humanity. The wheel of power and powerless, oppressor and oppressed, would continue to spin.

Unless Ana found the siphons and overthrew Morganya's reign of terror.

Her eyes narrowed a fraction. "I know she's out there," Ana replied. "We just have to find her before Morganya—"

A fit of coughs overtook her and she lurched over the railing, feeling, not for the first time, that there was something inside her that was wrong, an emptiness that was scraping her raw.

She felt Daya's hands on her shoulders, steadying her. "Feeling all right?" A pause, then: "Have you eaten today?"

Over the past two weeks aboard Daya's *Stormbringer,* Ana's appetite had diminished—something she had blamed on seasickness. But the insomnia, the bouts of dizziness, and the coughing fits—it was clear to anybody who paid attention that those were side effects of something much deeper.

The effect of having one's Affinity torn from them.

She'd heard stories from her friend and ally, Linn, who'd witnessed it firsthand in the Bregonian research dungeons they'd broken into. A girl, Linn had told her, looking more like skin and bones than human. Gold hair thinned and falling out in clumps. Face sunken to the point of being skeletal.

Ana had examined her own reflection in the looking glass Daya kept in her captain's cabin, imagining her cheeks hollowing out, her thick dark hair that she'd inherited from her mother thinning to strands.

Every day, she told herself that King Darias of Bregon was spearheading research on destroying siphons and reversing their effects. That he would send word to her immediately should he find anything new.

Ana straightened. "It's nothing," she said, avoiding Daya's eyes.

Her friend patted her back. "Probably seasickness. You'll feel much better once we're on land." Daya smiled and gestured. "It's a Blood Moon tonight. You know what that means?"

Ana followed her gaze. "I believe Cyrilian legends call it the Winter's Fire," she said. "But I do rather like 'Blood Moon.'"

"According to my gods, it heralds war and bloodshed," Daya said, leaning her head to mirror Ana's pose. She brushed a coil of braided black hair out of her face. Her teeth flashed white in the dark. "With a thousand Bregonian troops behind us, I'd say I rather like our chances."

At the thought, Ana turned from the prow. Behind her, phantomlike in the moonlight and lunging to the skies like daggers, were the sails of her warfleet, one thousand strong, lent to her as an alliance between her and King Darias. They flew silver sails with the Bregonian seadragon entwined with the Cyrilian roaring tiger insignia—only, instead of stark white, this one was bloodred.

Red Tigress.

It had become the symbol for her party, for her revolution. The symbol for a new Cyrilia: an equal, balanced land free of oppression, where Affinites and non-Affinites walked side by side.

As to what that held for her, for the future she'd once dreamt of as the heir of an empire, she wasn't certain.

A gust of wind knifed past her, whipping her cloak behind her in a scarlet trail. Not for the first time, Ana wondered what the ghosts of her family would think of her now. She could so clearly see the cold disappointment in her father's eyes, the muted sorrow on her brother's face. Yet Papa, Luka, and now, Morganya . . . one by one, the previous rulers of the Cyrilian Empire had proven the dangers of a monarchy unchecked as their failures led Cyrilia further and further down a spiral of darkness, of corruption, of oppression.

She gripped the railing tighter, knuckles whitening. The dead were dead; she had to focus on the living, on what was best for her empire, her people.

"Speaking of," Daya said, "I should rouse the crew. We'll be arriving within the hour."

A cry came from the crow's nest. "Snowhawk!"

Ana looked up to see a pale shape descending upon them in the night, heading straight for her. She held her arm up and it alighted, its claws digging into the thick fabric of her crimson cloak. In its beak it held a clump of fabric embroidered with small gold flowers.

She recognized it immediately: the sleeve of a kechyan she had worn back at the Salskoff Palace.

Ana gently stroked the bird's beak, prompting it to release the kechyan. Folded neatly inside was a single piece of parchment. Ana held it between trembling fingers.

Kolst Imperatorya, we await. Yours faithfully,

A. Markov

Daya leaned in. "Confirmation?"

Ana nodded, her throat stuck.

Here it was, her plan in motion, her people still loyal to her, waiting to rally to her name.

She'd sent a Bregonian seadove to her trusted confidant at the Palace: Kapitan Markov, the old guard who had watched over her throughout her childhood, and who had helped her escape death at Morganya's hands two moons ago. She'd asked him to leave the Palace with all troops loyal to her to meet her by the seaside fishing village of Balgorod, two days' travel south of Salskoff, where she would assemble her forces and begin her march upon the Imperial Court.

He'd replied, each time with a token that only they knew about, to verify his identity.

"Well, then," Daya said, straightening and clicking her heels together. "I've never done this before, but I suppose I'll be readying a thousand Bregonian troops for battle."

Ana looked at her captain, her *friend*, who just weeks before had been a stray sailor looking for business in the southern ports of Cyrilia. "Daya," she said. "You don't have to do this. The Bregonian fleets have their own commanders. I . . . I could drop you off in Balgorod, where you'd be safe, and find you once the war is over."

The truth was, she couldn't bear it if anyone else that she cared about got hurt fighting for her.

Daya tilted her head. "You know," she said, and there was a rare sobriety to her tone. "Before all this, I was some cast-out sailor scraping by for a living. Wasn't sure what I was doing with life, just focusing on getting by day after day. And now . . ." She drew a deep breath, gesturing around them. "Now I'm captain of a ship. I'm allies with the girl who leads an entire army—an entire *movement*. All this has become much more to me than just coin, Ana."

"Don't let Ramson hear you say that." The words were out of Ana's mouth before she could stop herself. Her breath caught, and a sharp pain cracked in her heart—perhaps the worst kind of all. In the darkness of the night he seemed to materialize, sandy hair sparkling and hazel eyes curved in a ghostly smile. *Witch.*

She'd allowed her thoughts to drift toward Ramson—Ramson *Farrald*—during the long nights, when spasms of coughs and bouts of sleeplessness kept her awake. He'd remained in Bregon to hunt down the remainders of Alaric Kerlan's criminal empire and root out whatever information was still hidden beyond the waters of Bregon. She'd recalled that morning, the sky a halcyon blue, when she'd leaned against the railing of this ship and gazed back at Bregon and all that she was leaving behind.

Wondering if she would ever see him again.

Ana blinked and the phantoms of memories swirled away like smoke before she could dwell on them. This was the cost of war, of choosing to fight for an entire empire and an entire people. Yet she would choose the same sacrifices, over and over again, if that meant saving Cyrilia.

"Of course, I'll still be waiting to dive into your imperial coffers at the end of it all," Daya was saying. "But I'm a non-Affinite, Ana. What do you think happens to me and people like me under the current regime? I know I could leave—sail away to another kingdom, but . . . I've seen what happens if Morganya succeeds. Look at what nearly happened to Bregon." Across the deck, her eyes found Ana's, earth-brown and hard. "If the world falls, the last thing I want is to know I could have fought and made a difference and chose not to."

Daya's words lingered for a moment in the salt-tinged winds, heavy with meaning and sharp with consequences—the consequences of what the world might become if Ana failed.

A reminder of what she fought for.

Ana nodded. "Thank you, Daya."

Daya tapped two fingers to her forehead in a mock salute before hopping onto the ratlines and scurrying up several rungs. "*Stormbringer* crew!" she shouted. "Attention!"

Ana turned to the prow, letting the ocean spray surge against her cheeks, drinking in the cold of her empire. She'd missed it. The southern Bregonian weather had been warm and mild, but she felt a part of herself becoming reinvigorated beneath the snow-tinged skies of the great northern Empire.

But there was something . . . *different* about her empire to-night. Something sharper, something *off,* the pine-scented wind and snow bladed with a tang of blood and steel. There was more than ice to the air; there was a sense of hostility from the way the waves lunged at their hull to the way the clouds roiled fast over-head. As though the land itself knew of the war awaiting.

The crew set about their preparations; a sound Affinite, one of the many they had rescued from Bregon's cruel research dun-geons where they had been waiting to be tested on the siphons, carried Daya's instructions across the rest of the fleet following behind.

Their ships sluiced forward in the night. The glow of the red moon was now covered by snow clouds, and a mist had ap-peared over the waters. The crew gathered on the decks, watch-ing in tense silence as they approached. Daya's lips moved as she counted down the seconds, a bronze pocketwatch held in the palm of her hand.

A sailor near the edge of the ship gave a soft exclamation. "Ruselkya," he said.

Ana leaned over the railing. From here, the waters lapping at the hull of their ship were black, tinted with a faint red hue. It resembled blood.

Gliding beneath the surface were long, spectral shapes, threading between waves. It was only when they turned, tails flashing silver, that Ana caught sight of their torsos, and their long hair streaming behind them.

Daya came to stand next to her. "Are you familiar with the sailors' myths about ruselkya?"

"They bring misfortune," Ana said, thinking of the storybooks she'd read of the water spirits in the past. Whereas ice spirits— syvint'sya—ranged from gentle to malicious in nature, ruselkya were believed to be remnants of vicious, darker magic left in this world by the Deities.

Daya nodded. "I've heard stories from sailors who went to the farthest corners of the Silent Sea and found themselves in the ruselkya's grasps. But I've never seen them this active, nor so close to land." She was silent for a moment, a troubled expression crossing her face. Then she shook her head and barked a laugh. "They're all just stories. What's real is the thousand-strong Bregonian fleet behind our backs. You still have that charm I gave you?"

Ana reached for the amulet at her neck: a pendant in the shape of a sun, no bigger than the tip of her pinky finger. It was made of garnet from the Kingdom of Kusutri, Daya's home. Daya had gifted it to Ana as a good-luck charm, saying the bloodred hue of the stone matched her better. *For when you get your Affinity back,* the sailor had said.

Ana stroked a thumb over the gem's smooth surface. "I'd never lose it."

"Good," Daya said. "Now, come with me—I'm making rounds to check that all is in order. We're a quarter hour to shore."

Ana was about to follow when something caught her attention. She blinked, looking over the railing, across the midnight-black expanse of sea, wondering if it had been a trick of the Blood Moon's light.

But there it was again: a flare of light, piercing the fog, small, but growing larger.

"Daya," she began, but then the night around them lit up like day.

The first explosion slammed Ana into the wooden deck, her bones jarring and her teeth rattling in her skull. Heat gusted in her face. The sky and sea reeled all around her as she lifted her head, vision blurring in and out of focus. Flames licked at the wood, rising with the wind to engulf members of the crew and splinters of debris strewn across the floor. The entire midsection of the *Stormbringer* had been torn off; a hole gaped in the railing, and water was beginning to fill in.

The second explosion plunged her into the water.

2

KINGDOM OF BREGON

The foyer was dark, and the man in the shadows was dying.
Captain Ramson Farrald stepped over the threshold into
the liminal space between darkness and light, his steps muffled
by the dust-covered carpet in the house. Even from here, he could
make out the skeletal form of his mark, slumped over in the arm-
chair. Only the slightest rise and fall to his chest, the tip of his
head, and the gleam of his rimmed spectacles in the watery sunlight indicated that he was alive at all.

The mansion itself was in almost as much neglect. Colloqui-
ally named "the Nest," it was rumored to be the headquarters
where the remnants of Kerlan's forces were gathered. Ramson
wasn't sure what he'd expected when he'd arrived—something
akin to a shabby version of the Kerlan Estate, perhaps, oozing
with unnecessary opulence, or a simple wooden shack packed to
bursting with mercenaries and ex–Order of the Lily members.

Not a man, dying alone in an empty house, surrounded
by nothing but scrolls of parchments, books, and binders of
papers.

Ramson held up a leather-gloved hand, signaling for the
Bregonian Navy soldiers in his squad to wait outside. Then he

stepped forward, drawing his misericord. "Seems I've finally found you," he said quietly, "Scholar Ardonn."

Just weeks ago, Ramson had wrested the Kingdom of Bregon from its spiral of corruption at his father's hands and restored the rightful King and the Three Courts into governance. Yet the war was far from over. Alaric Kerlan was dead, but the roots of the criminal empire he'd planted—in both Cyrilia and Bregon— ran deep. King Darias of Bregon had appointed Ramson under a secret task force to dig out the remnants of Kerlan's criminal network.

A fortnight's search had led Ramson here, to the north- ernmost tip of Bregon, where it was rumored the remnants of Kerlan's forces were gathered at a headquarters referred to as "the Nest." According to King Darias's sources, the Nest and the last of Kerlan's forces could hold the keys to knowledge about the deadly weapons with the power to steal Affinities: siphons.

A single candle burned on the table before the scholar. Up close, he looked nothing like the Royal Scholar who had worked with Alaric Kerlan to develop siphons—the one that Ramson had once glimpsed aboard the ship where Kerlan had conducted his experiments. Where Ramson had seen, with his own eyes, a former colleague named Bogdan wield the powers of a siphon and the Affinities it had stolen.

Ramson took in the sharp edges of his quarry's face: sunken cheeks, hollowed eyes, ash-gray beard falling out in tufts. Instead of the turquoise-collared white robes he'd once worn as a sym- bol of knowledge and power, he had on a commoner's tunic and pants. He looked like a portrait left exposed too long in the sun, fading fast.

Yet the sight sent a thrill shooting through Ramson's veins.

Here was the man who might hold the keys to all the information they needed about the siphons—where they were, how to destroy them, and, most importantly, how to reverse their effects.

Scholar Ardonn gave a long, low chuckle. "So you're the bastard son."

The words would once have twisted in him like a knife, opening a wound that had never fully healed. But now, Ramson found only a passing sadness, the stir of his father's memory.

He tilted his head. "I am. But I'm a different breed of bastard from you, Ardonn."

The skeletal man turned his bulging eyes to Ramson. "So, which of my dearest former associates blabbed? Was it one of the Cyrilians?"

"They were all quite eager to sing once I applied some tried-and-true methods of persuasion."

Ardonn chuckled. "Seems you've quite a bit of Alaric Kerlan left in you, eh, *Quicktongue*?"

Ramson's grasp tightened on his misericord. "It appears so. King Darias has issued a royal decree to have you escorted back to the Blue Fort for trial."

The scholar rasped a laugh. "Trial," he repeated. He drew the candle closer to him, fiddling with the handle of the holder as he huddled over its warmth. "I have no intention of going back to the Blue Fort for *trial*, boy."

"I quite agree. You'll see I've left my men outside to wait. If we can settle matters here just between the two of us, I've no intention of taking you into captivity." It was far from the truth, but Ramson had never been one to feel guilt over his lies, so long as he got what he wanted.

And what he wanted was, in reality, quite different from what

King Darias had wanted when he'd sent Ramson out here with a full squad of Bregonian naval officers.

He shoved aside those thoughts. His mind focused, sharp as the tip of the misericord he pointed at the scholar's throat. "Where is she?"

Scholar Ardonn blinked. "I haven't the faintest idea who you're talking about."

"Then let me make it clear to you," Ramson replied, applying pressure on his weapon. The scholar winced, the candlelight in the room flickering as he tensed. The flame had eaten halfway through the wax. "Sorsha Farrald, former Lieutenant of the Royal Guard and Kerlan's ally. My *darling* half sister, who took both the siphons and disappeared during the Battle of Godhallem. *Where is she?*"

Scholar Ardonn shook his head. "I don't know. I haven't seen her since the evening before the Battle of Godhallem. I'd heard rumors she was dead."

Ramson narrowed his eyes. His sister danced with madness, but she was also one of the strongest and most ruthless warriors he'd encountered. It wasn't fathomable to him that she'd simply . . . died after that night. No, his gut instinct—a cruel sort of brother-sister bond—told him she was still out there, unrelentingly clawing toward her goal. Ruin, revenge, and a complete upset of power over the men who had made her this way.

Scholar Ardonn chortled, which turned into another fit of coughs. "I know why you're really here," he said softly, his words burrowing into Ramson's mind. "I was there when Kerlan spoke to you that night on the boat; I've heard rumors of what happened during the Battle of Godhallem." His grin turned sharp. "You want to know what'll happen to Cyrilia's blood princess."

And, just like that, no matter how long he'd steeled himself, Ramson's thoughts scattered. Against every ounce of his will, a face flashed in his mind: fawn skin and dark hair, sharp cheekbones and chin, and most of all, eyes that pierced like they could see straight through every single one of his façades.

His knuckles whitened against the hilt of his weapon.

"All right, then. Let's cut to the chase." His voice scraped, and something stretched taut inside him. He felt as though *he* were the one with a blade pressed against his throat. This scholar was his last hope; it was his last bid to find out what happened to someone whose Affinity had been siphoned. "I want to know everything about the siphons. How to destroy them. How to restore the stolen Affinities to their original owners. And . . . what happens to those whose powers were stolen."

"Why should I tell you anything?"

Ramson tipped his head. "I'm a man who speaks the language of bargains. Scratch my back, and I'll scratch yours. I can't promise the Blue Fort will be as accommodating."

It wasn't the truth, yet it wasn't exactly a lie, either. It was a hedge—a promise that if Ardonn wasn't willing to take the bargain the Blue Fort offered him, then Ramson was an alternate choice.

A better choice.

He couldn't help it; as much as he owed King Darias for his current circumstances and the Bregonian Navy squad assigned to him, Ramson had been brought up a con man, a mastermind of his own plans. He was used to working alone, against authority. His Navy squad tolerated no talk of treason or disloyalty, yet in Ramson's opinion, words were just words; what did they matter as long as he got a confession or bargain out of their mark?

Scholar Ardonn grinned, showing a mouth of missing teeth. "What makes you think I have anything left to bargain for?"

It was the first time in their conversation that his words gave Ramson pause.

"You think Kerlan left without ensuring that none of us would survive to expose his secrets?" Ardonn continued. He raised a hand. In the lowlight, it was no more than skin on bones. "Ever heard of the poison ricyn?"

Ramson lowered his misericord. "He poisoned you." The realization came too late.

Of course Kerlan would have devised a cruel way to protect his secrets. Before he'd fled Cyrilia, he'd murdered every one of his former subordinates in Novo Mynsk, with the help of Bogdan's now-widow, a poison Affinite named Olyusha. It was Olyusha who had alerted Ramson to Kerlan's trafficking scheme in a desperate search for her kidnapped husband.

He could almost hear her throaty chuckle in the room now. *You've gotten rusty, Quicktongue.*

"Ricyn," the scholar repeated, "is a unique type of poison found only in a rare type of Cyrilian flower. The antidote comes from the roots. Kerlan fed the poison to us every day while we were employed under his service. He would give us a large enough dosage of the antidote so that we were safe. And now that he's dead, he's carved out the same fate for us." Ardonn tilted his head to Ramson, skin stretching across hollow cheeks as he smiled. "Sounds like our master, doesn't it?"

Ramson lunged forward to seize the scholar's shirt. The man inhaled sharply, but his gaze was steady. The candle in his hands quivered, wax splashing over Ramson's hands in bright bursts of searing pain. "Then you'll tell me everything I need to know, *right now,* or you'll wish the poison was what took you."

Scholar Ardonn barked a laugh. It cut off quickly as Ramson shook him hard enough to break bones.

"How can the siphons be destroyed? How can we return the Affinities stored within to the original owner?" He paused, and pushed the last question from his lips. "And what happens to those whose Affinities were siphoned?"

Scholar Ardonn's shoulders were shaking, and Ramson realized the man was giggling. "I have a fortnight to live, if I'm lucky, and I have no plans to die the slow, painful death that ricyn promises." He waved the candle, dripping wax on the carpets. "Look around you, Quicktongue. You see that dust on the carpets? Smell something strange about them?"

Ramson froze. He could smell it now—something metallic mixed in the fusty, wet-wood scent of the mansion. He recognized the aroma now, too late: a highly flammable powder developed by the Bregonian Navy, used in the explosives that their rigs fired. It was one of the reasons the Bregonian Navy was the preeminent navy in the world.

One spark, and the entire mansion would go up in flames.

"That's right," Ardonn chortled. "Red powder."

And then, with a maniacal smile, he turned and flung his candle to the floor.

Time seemed to slow. The candle arced through the air out of Ramson's reach, flame flickering, hot wax dripping in a smooth curve.

Ramson turned and leapt for the scholar.

He reached Ardonn just in time. He heard the muffled thump

of the candle landing, the fizz of flame as it came into contact with the explosive powder that coated the carpet.

Ramson pressed the scholar between him and the wall and arced his back.

The mansion lit up in a blinding, searing maelstrom of whites and reds and oranges. The explosion hit Ramson so hard that black spots smothered his vision. From a distance, he heard shouts, the bark of a dog. Smoke—there was smoke, acrid and bitter and asphyxiating, choking his throat and coating his tongue with bile.

Ramson fought against the darkness closing in on him. He pushed off from the wall, gritting his teeth against a scream as the flesh on his back seemed to split.

Ardonn was wedged between him and the wall; besides a bloodied nose and spectacles knocked askance, he was unharmed. The man's confusion turned to fear as Ramson seized the front of his shirt, ignoring the pain in his arms, and drew the scholar so close that he could feel his stale breath on his cheeks.

"You forget," Ramson gritted, spitting each word, "that I, too, am a man with nothing to lose. And I'll do *anything* it takes to get what I want." He lifted an arm, the sleeves of his new Navy doublet seared into his flesh, his skin a raw, red, glistening mass. Behind him, flames continued to lick at the walls and the floor; a part of the ceiling had collapsed, and he could hear shouts as his men continued to try to break through. It would only be a matter of time.

The smugness in Ardonn's expression turned to fear.

"If I'm willing to do this to myself," Ramson panted, holding his burnt arm so that the scholar could see every bloody inch of it, "what do you think I won't do to *you?*"

A series of loud thumps from behind them, the cracks of wood splintering and orders barked.

"Even if you save me," the scholar rasped, flames flickering in those hollow eyes, "the poison will kill me. There's nothing you can do."

The smoke was overwhelming now, the world growing fuzzy. But Ramson held himself between the scholar and the roaring fire, even as heat seared streaks of white, burning pain down his back.

There was a loud smash, and he heard the shouts of his men as they finally broke through the debris barrier. There was the hiss of liquid dousing flames as one of their water magen went to work.

"Over here!" someone bellowed. Ramson recognized that voice—First Officer Narron, Ramson's deputy.

Ramson shrugged off his squad's hands as they swarmed around him. "Take the scholar," he gasped, his voice like sandpaper against stone. "If anyone touches a hair on his head, I'll skin them myself."

They stepped out into bright daylight. The midday sun hung halfway across the sky, reflecting from the cobalt ocean like shards of glass.

Ramson inhaled lungfuls of fresh, salt-sprayed air. The healer of their squad was already rushing over; Ramson held up a hand, wincing as his burns screamed. He hobbled to Ardonn and knelt on the sand next to him.

Leaning very close to the scholar, Ramson said: "Here's my offer. Your life, for the information I want."

Ardonn's face was streaked with soot, his cheeks sweaty and

hollowed. Yet his eyes were cunning as they turned to Ramson. "The information *you* want, or the information the Blue Fort wants?" he wheezed.

The crash of waves rolled over his words so that none other than Ramson could hear them. Something tightened painfully inside him, as though the scholar had slit open his chest and seen through to the deepest parts of his raw, beating heart.

He and the Blue Fort were aligned in their goals, if not by their motivations. Together, with the team of scholars King Darias had assembled at the Blue Fort, they would wring all the information there was to know about siphons from Ardonn.

Ramson straightened, his lips curling. "You'll be singing soon enough at the Blue Fort," he said.

The scholar's laugh was soft, his words barely audible. "The poison'll kill me in a little over a fortnight, anyway," he said. "What makes you think I have anything left to sing for?"

"You worked for my father," Ramson replied tonelessly. "You know his methods of interrogation. I can promise you that I am, in some ways, my father's son."

A flint of recognition in the old scholar's eyes, and then Ardonn gave a long sigh, his breath whistling faintly. "I could tell you, boy," the scholar said, "but you won't like it. In fact, there's a lot you won't like about what I could tell you."

"Speak clearly. If there's one thing I hate, it's a man who equivocates."

"You think destroying the siphons will put an end to all this? Think again." The scholar's eyes were dark, and Ramson wondered what secrets this man hid. "What you're seeing now—the siphons, the sickness that they spread in Affinites and non-Affinites alike . . . it all started a long time ago, when we began using blackstone against them. You see, this didn't start with the newest Empress of Cyrilia, or even with Alaric Kerlan." There was a raw, hollow tone to the scholar's words. "These weapons of magek—they're about something bigger than you, or I, or emperors or empresses. They're a test on humanity. On our nature, on how far we're willing to go to gain power. On the bounds of our cruelty, and the depths of our selfishness. I'm a man of the gods as much as I am a man of science, Ramson Quicktongue, and I believe these remnants of magek were left to us to see what choices we would make. Whether we would come together in harmony . . . or whether we would tear one another apart in our quest for power."

The man was spiraling into madness. Ramson turned away and gestured to the healer on his squad. "Iversha," he said briskly. "Tend to the prisoner with the utmost care."

"But, Captain," she protested, her gaze roving over the burns on his back, the strips of his doublet that were peeling and bloodied from his skin.

"That's an *order*," Ramson said. The healer saluted and, without another word, rushed over to where Ardonn lay on the sand.

Ramson turned to the rest of his squad. A decision he had been mulling over hardened in his chest, with more certainty than ever. They were at the northernmost tip of Bregon; the Blue Fort was a half day's journey away by boat.

Half a day seemed like a long stretch when time was in short supply.

Ramson looked out to the ocean, to where the sky met the sea. To the Navy squad that King Darias Rennaron had entrusted to his command. He had the urge to drop everything and sail away to Cyrilia right now.

The last time he'd seen Ana had been a little over a fortnight ago, when she'd left for the great Northern Empire again. He remembered the wan complexion to her skin, the dark circles beneath her eyes and the slight hollowing to her cheeks.

King Darias and the Three Courts were intent on finding out more about the siphons to understand how Morganya might use them to become invincible and to destroy the balance of their world.

And as always, Ramson's reasons were far from noble. Selfish, just as he'd always been.

Ramson wanted to know what happened to the Affinites whose powers were siphoned.

He wanted to find out what would happen to Ana.

He closed his eyes briefly, listening to the crash of waves over the shore. King Darias had committed the full resources of the Blue Fort and its renowned scholars to researching the siphons. Leaving now would mean abandoning all of that; leaving now meant destroying everything Ramson had begun to build up for himself here in Bregon and betraying the trust he'd brokered with his king.

A soft wind brushed his face with the briny scent of the sea, bringing back echoes of a yesterday long past, the words of an old friend who had told him to live for himself.

Your heart is your compass.

Ramson wasn't sure he fully understood what that meant anymore. His heart pointed in a completely different direction than his mind, than what made sense.

"Officer Narron," he said, and the young officer stepped forward with a salute. "Search the rest of the mansion. I want all books and papers and parchments that survived the fire to be loaded onto our ship."

"Yes, sir."

"We set sail for the Blue Fort within the hour."

It was only when his Navy squad turned and headed for the scarred, smoking remains of the Nest that Ramson loosed a breath. The pain pulsing in his back and his arms crested suddenly, and it was all that he could do to limp over to where Healer Iversha was tending to Ardonn.

The scholar was staring at Ramson, his lips opening and closing. As Ramson drew closer, he caught what Ardonn was trying to say.

". . . wanted to know . . . about the blood princess."

The world tipped. Ramson knelt on the sand, ignoring Iversha's protests as he seized a fistful of Ardonn's shirt. "What is it?" His voice was a rasp. "What do you know about her?"

Scholar Ardonn's face was ashen; a sheen of sweat covered his forehead. His eyes fluttered as he began to slip into a drug-induced slumber. But Ramson heard the last words he uttered, like the sigh of wind combing through waves.

"I'm afraid . . . it won't be a happy ending . . . for your blood princess."

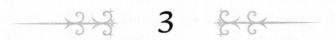

3

THE JADE TRAIL

The fog was thick, but Linn had dreamt of a night like this for years.

She sat on deck, listening to the sound of silence as their ship sluiced through the midnight waters. Each slosh of a wave against the hull, each *whoompf* of the sails against a cool breeze, felt like a small sign of magic.

For tonight, Linn was on her way home.

She'd left here eight years ago, alone and afraid yet determined, in pursuit of a brother stolen by Cyrilian traffickers. She'd endured horrors many would never see during their entire lives, and she'd survived the brutality of a broken system.

Now, she returned as Ambassador of Cyrilia to the Kemeiran Empire to recruit forces in the Aseatic Isles on behalf of the Red Tigress, Anastacya Mikhailov. Preparing for a war that would end the system she'd been subjugated to.

For as much as this was Ana's war, this was also *Linn's* fight.

King Darias had commissioned this brig for her, replacing the Bregonian navy-blue sails, painting over the symbols of stallions, eagles, and fish, and hand-picking a crew for it from the Blue Fort. Now, the colors they flew were gray, the shades of clouds and wind and everything in between, punctured by the sigil of a Bregonian seadragon entwined with a red roaring tiger. It was a sigil significantly different from that of the Cyrilian Empire— with which the Kemeiran Empire was formally in a state of war—and yet it was one honest and true to Linn's cause: to make peace between Cyrilia and her homeland, and to convince the Kemeiran government to support the Red Tigress in her fight against the current monarch.

From far off, the ship was no more than a slip of a shadow in this weather. A phantom, just the way she liked it.

Her favorite gift, though, was the translucent fabric that she kept draped over her shoulders. It stretched down to her hands, roped gently around her wrists.

Her chi, which meant *wing* in the Kemeiran tongue, was something she kept on her at all times. She slept with it, and during the days at sea, she'd leap off the crow's nest and fly, soaring over clouds and dipping over the waves to the song of ghost-whales. Her arm, which Alaric Kerlan had shattered during the Battle of Godhallem, was healing nicely; with every passing day, she found that she could move it a little more, use it to adjust her balance a little better. With a cast for support, she was able to fly for longer and longer periods of time, working the muscles that had atrophied during her injury.

It had been over a fortnight since she'd set out for Kemeira, and they were close. Linn closed her eyes against the cool ocean air, the evening breeze wrapping around her. She could practically *smell* it, the subtle shifts in the air currents, the crisp, wintry coolness different from both Cyrilia and Bregon, stirring memories buried deep in her heart. She'd watched silently earlier as the sun set across the seam between sky and sea, glowing deep orange like the tangerines of her childhood that had burst sweet and tangy over her tongue. A knot had formed in her throat, and she found that even if she'd wanted to speak, she had no words to describe this feeling.

The feeling of coming home.

The fog continued to roll across the waves, silent and gray, stretching infinitely in all directions until it was swallowed by night.

Linn frowned, leaning on the railing. The weather had taken a turn for the worse in the past hour; visibility was now so poor, she could barely make out the end of her ship. Not to mention, there was something different about this fog. It felt too thick, too heavy.

"I thought I would find you here."

Linn turned. She could just make out a silhouette between the ghostly tendrils of mist—the steady slope of his shoulders, the cords of muscles.

Kaïs came to stand by her side, his footsteps light as a cat's despite his heavy build. He'd ditched Cyrilian and Bregonian armor for a simple black tunic and dark cloak, drifting lightly over him as he shifted. It suited him.

"We are close," Linn said. "The captain said we would alight at midnight."

He was silent for a few moments, their breaths mingling comfortably in the cold ocean air. "Do you feel nostalgic?"

There was a wistfulness to the deep, steady bass of his voice. Like her, Kaïs had been stolen from his mother and brought over the border to Cyrilia at a young age, where he was enlisted in the Imperial Patrols due to his special ability to sense and control other Affinites. His kind was called yaegers, or *hunters* in Old Cyrilic, used to keep regular Affinites under the Empire's control.

Kerlan had kidnapped Kaïs's mother and used that as a threat to control him during the Battle of Godhallem. Yet Kaïs's last-minute change of heart had helped Ana and Linn win the battle—but potentially cost him the opportunity to ever see his mother again.

If I return now, Morganya will know what I did, the traitor that I am, he'd told Linn. *The only way to protect my mother is for them to believe that I am dead.*

I must become a ghost.

Standing before her, weaving in and out of sight between the ever-shifting clouds, he seemed to have become that. His eyes were silvered by the moonlight, and in them, Linn thought she could see land and sea, mirrored yet never meeting.

Over the course of the fortnight, she'd mulled over their plan in Kemeira. The ache of wanting to return to her village and see her mother was almost physical—yet her home village lay in the opposite direction of their destination, Bei'kin. There, the Emperor of Kemeira resided in his Imperial Palace built atop the highest fortified mountain of the city. And in the city center was the revered Temple of the Skies, housing the greatest Temple Masters in all of Kemeira.

If the Emperor was the head of Kemeira, then the Temple Masters were its heart, serving as invaluable counselors to the Emperor and implementing governing policies through the network of Temple Masters that stretched across all provinces and regions like the veins of the country.

It was the approval of those two governing bodies Linn

sought. It was they who could launch Kemeira's forces, the deadliest and most well-trained wielders—the Kemeiran term for Affinites—in the world.

No matter what, she knew what her Wind Masters would have told her.

"Duty first," she said. "We must make for the Northern Capital, Bei'kin, to appeal for the Emperor's and the Temple Masters' help. After that . . ."

She'd given a lot of thought to the seemingly impossible task before her. The Kemeiran Empire had been in a state of war with Cyrilia for longer than she'd been alive, over their disagreements on how Affinites were treated in the Cyrilian Empire as well as the clandestine trafficking of Kemeiran wielders to the Great Northern Empire, which Cyrilia had admitted no involvement in yet had taken no measures to prevent.

Would the Kemeiran government take the chance to stand behind a different empress? One who would abolish the current regime and make good of her empire? Or would they watch their longtime enemy, the other great empire in this world, burn?

Linn's trail of thought broke as something stirred in the winds that she always kept with her in the back of her mind.

She looked out sharply. The waters were empty, darkness looming in the silver mist. Why did she have a sense of foreboding, that something was waiting for them out there beyond the fog?

That was when a shout rang out from the crow's nest.

"Flare!"

The footsteps aboard the deck stopped as all her crew members craned their necks to the skies, searching. Linn squinted, and *there*, between the swirls of fog and shadows of night, was the faintest glow. It was a warm color, like orange, or . . .

Every nerve in Linn's body stretched taut. It couldn't be. By her side, she sensed Kaïs's outline tense. "Color?" she demanded of her barrelman.

"Red!"

Alarm bells pealed in her head. Red, the distress signal. Linn had learned enough to understand that the red flare signal opened your waters to foreign ships for assistance. It was the most desperate of signals.

What could have caused a ship to send this type of a signal?

"What colors does the vessel fly?" she called.

"I can't see!"

Of course. The fog.

Linn gathered her Affinity, roping it over the still air weaving between the fog. She pushed, and a gust of wind cleaved apart the mist. For a moment, the silhouette of a ship, lit up in an eerie crimson glow, loomed out of the fog. And then the flare faded, the fog rolled back in, and the darkness swallowed whatever had been out there.

But Linn had seen all she needed. The webbed sails fanning behind, in perfect imitation of the wings of a dragon. There was only one kingdom that flew those sails.

"Kemeiran!" came the cry. "A Kemeiran ship, Ambassador!"

Unease tightened her chest. Why had a ship from her homeland come out in the dead of the night, to send out a red flare?

Strong, warm hands gripped her shoulders. She blinked, and Kaïs was in front of her, his eyes steady as they held hers. "Linn—"

Footsteps sounded, approaching. Kaïs pulled back, stepping

neatly around her so that he stood by her side to face the new-comer.

"Ambassador." The slender, straight silhouette of her captain cut through the swirls of fog. The pommel of his sword glimmered at his side, light lancing off from the lamp in his hand. "Distress signal identified. Your orders, please."

The lamplight cocooned the three of them in a small circle. "Head in the direction of the flare," Linn replied.

The captain hesitated. "With all due respect, Ambassador, I would advise against. We have extremely low visibility and are inadequately stocked to handle a rescue mission. Not to mention, our primary mission is to get you to Kemeira."

Linn hesitated. She had no wish to endanger the lives of her crew. And yet . . . "Captain, we are the only ship within the vicinity. If the ship is in trouble, should we not help?"

"It would also be prudent to understand why a distress signal was sent from a Kemeiran ship, especially as we are about to dock," Kaïs said. A rush of gratitude filled Linn at the sound of his voice, so steady and sure.

The captain nodded. "Very well. I will send a seadove back to Bregon to alert them of this."

"Thank you." Linn watched him turn back and disappear through the fog. She heard his orders as though from a distance, heard the crew scrambling as they made preparations for rescue.

A dark shape cut through the mist to the sound of wingbeats. One of the messenger seadoves had been dispatched to report this to Bregon.

The ship plowed forward. The water sloshed. The fog breathed.

Suddenly, Kaïs tensed. "I sense something."

Linn opened her mouth, intending to ask him what it was. But at that moment, the fog parted and gave way to clear air, and stole the words from her.

Linn looked out and saw a graveyard.

The ocean before them was littered with wreckages of ships, their broken hulls jutting out of the sea like rib cages, torn sails trailing the black waters like hair. Linn had the impression that they were looking at rows upon rows of tombstones.

There was utter silence from onboard their ship as the crew processed this. Only, far off, there came a strange, whistling sound, cutting through the wind, steadily growing louder.

A second shout rang out from their crow's nest. A shout that made Linn's blood freeze.

"CYRILIAN SHIP! TAKE COVER!"

Linn had just turned to Kaïs when a bright light shot across the waters before them.

Their ship exploded. The ocean was infinitely colder and darker than Linn remembered. The impact drove nearly all the air from her lungs, sucking her into an abyss black as night.

Under here, there were no stars.

Time seemed to slow. Linn twisted, and in the depths, she found phantom flashes of sight: the night lighting up in sparks of fire, the crack of wood splintering, the groans of their entire ship as it sank. The blur of sky and flames and sea as she was flung into the night; the slap of her body against water.

There was a sharp, consuming pain in her left leg. Her lungs felt pinched; she needed to swim, to breathe.

Linn kicked, but with one arm still recovering from her injury, her balance was off; she veered wildly in one direction, then another, unable to gain control.

Linn struck out again, pulling herself forward with broad strokes of her good arm as the Water Masters had taught her as a child. *Move with the current.*

But this was the open sea, and the currents tossed and turned around her in all different directions, battering her like a leaf in a gale. She had no idea which way was up and which way was down, and there wasn't the slightest sliver of light here to guide her.

Linn called to her Affinity, searching, searching for her winds. Yet here, buried deep beneath the waves, she was a whole world away from them. Suffocating slowly.

No, Linn thought, still grasping for a hint of her winds. She had not endured so much and survived for so long just to drown at the shores of her homeland, on the precipice of a war she still needed to fight.

Her world was growing fuzzy, her tether to her Affinity slipping from her mind. There was pressure around her chest, as though something had cinched around it. She was feeling lighter. Her world seemed to grow bright—and then it burned, flaring shades of ugly orange and searing reds.

The world tumbled back in all its messy, swirling colors, the sharp rocking of waves and screams of dying men.

"Breathe," commanded a deep voice by her ear, and Linn suddenly found that she was vomiting water, then gasping in breaths, gulping down lungfuls upon lungfuls of cold, acrid air, choked with smoke.

She knew that voice. Shaking, she turned to its owner, his silver gaze reflecting the flames of their sinking ship.

"I'm going to swim," Kaïs said. "Can you hold on to me?"

She clung to his shoulders. The water was like ice, the cold squeezing Linn's muscles with every passing second until she was numb. Behind her was the fading orange glow of their ship, its light dimming until it flickered out. Then it was just her and Kaïs, making their way forward in the dark. She was pressed against him, their hearts beating the same prayer, the rhythm of their breaths blending into the sound of the sea.

She could sense the fatigue in each stroke of his powerful arms, in the way the ocean easily knocked them back and forth.

Something loomed out of the sky before them. Beneath the ghostly light that seeped through the clouds overhead, the shape of a ship emerged.

Linn thought she would weep from relief. "Kaïs," she croaked. "A ship."

"Something's wrong." He spoke softly, as though not wanting to be heard.

In that moment, the moon slid out from behind the clouds. Its light swept over the pale blue of the sails, the sigil of a roaring white tiger fanning out from multiple ships anchored silently in the bay.

Cyrilian ships. Not just one—but an entire fleet.

For a few moments, Linn forgot to breathe. She sensed Kaïs's shoulders tense beneath her palms, heard his intake of breath. The barrelman aboard their ship had called out to them with this information the second before they were attacked.

What were Cyrilian ships doing here?

Her mind was numb; it latched on to hope. That Ana had arrived in Cyrilia and sent reinforcements to Kemeira.

But—no, that wasn't possible. The timing was off. Ana would have barely reached Cyrilia by now.

Linn was so distressed that she didn't notice the shoreline until Kaïs grunted and stumbled. They fell, splashing between the waves and cold sands, shivering to their cores.

"Why?" Her teeth chattered. "Why are there Cyrilian ships in Kemeira?"

Kaïs knelt next to her. He had shed his cloak, revealing his tight-fitting black tunic and leather boots. His hair was plastered across his cheeks and curled at the nape of his neck, dripping ocean water. "Linn. You're injured."

She looked down at her leg and finally found the source of the throbbing pain. The flesh on her left calf had been split open; she thought she saw the pale gleam of bone amid muscle and sinew. Blood already darkened the sand where they sat.

She heard rustling, the clinking of jars, and realized Kaïs had somehow salvaged his survival pack and was looking through it. "I'm going to sew it shut," he said. "Drink this. It's a sedative."

She took the vial he handed her. The liquid was bitter—an alchemical concoction for injured soldiers. It burned all the way down to her stomach.

Within moments, warmth tingled through her limbs, and the pain began to ease. The world began to slip from her, her thoughts running groggy.

How had it gone so wrong? One moment they'd been on their ship; there'd been a bright light, and the next thing she knew, she was on the shores of a kingdom she'd left eight years ago, bleeding out from an injury. Her ship, her crew, everything she had for her mission had been destroyed.

And an enemy navy pressed at the doorstep of her homeland.

Sluggishly, she watched Kaïs rattle a globefire; heard the sharp crack of glass, saw him hold a needle to the flame. His hands were astonishingly gentle as he knelt at her leg and began to sew, the needle points eliciting no more than strange pricks and tugs against her skin as thread slid through flesh. The waves swirled, the roar turning dull in her ears.

Kaïs took off his cotton shift and tore it into long, thin shreds. With militaristic precision and efficiency, he began to wrap the makeshift bandage over her wound. When he was done, he slipped on his tunic again. Then he wrapped his arms beneath her shoulders and knees, pulling her close to him, and stood.

She let her head lean against Kaïs's shoulder, keeping silent as he walked. Wet sand turned into mud and rock; salt spray and ocean air gave way to the musty smell of leaves and the crackle of brush. Moonlight filtered through the trees, their branches so gnarled and different from the straight, sleek conifers of Cyrilia.

At last, Kaïs stopped beneath an outcrop of rock that stretched over their heads, in some semblance of shelter. Gently, he deposited Linn on the moss.

"Give me your chi," he said, and she unstrapped it from her wrists. He walked a few steps away and wrung it out. It was still damp when he returned it to her, but she immediately fastened it back onto her wrists.

Kaïs disappeared again, and she heard rustling as he shucked off the rest of his clothes, water splattering the leaves as he wrung them out. Dully, she surveyed her surroundings: the uneven edges of rock overhead, barely peeking out over vines and ferns; the smooth lichen beneath her feet; the occasional chirps of birds and bugs echoing in the forest. The air slowly warmed her skin, gentle and humid in a way that it had never been in Cyrilia. Back there, the wind had cracked, sharp and dry and cold.

Bushes rattled; Kaïs appeared by the mouth of their cave. He prowled over and sat down across from her. Without further word, he took her injured arm and began to unravel the sodden, torn bandages of her cast, replacing them with fresh ones. The air swirled with unsaid thoughts and unspoken questions.

Linn broke the silence first. "Were we attacked?"

"Yes. Likely by Cyrilian Affinites, judging from the fire damage."

"The rest of the crew," she whispered.

He shook his head. "I don't know what happened to them. I only sensed you calling on your Affinity and found you."

Even now, his voice was steady, calm, the anchor to her turbulent world.

Linn shut her eyes briefly. Pale blue flags, flying insignias of a Cyrilian Deities' Circle with a crown in the center. "Those ships bore imperial Cyrilian flags."

"Yes." Kaïs kept his voice level, but she heard the tightness to it. "It appears Morganya's forces are here."

Why? It was the question that had haunted her since the very moment they'd seen those ships. What could have drawn Morganya to Kemeira, an ocean away from the Cyrilian Empire?

The answers lay with those ships docked out in the darkness.

But not tonight.

Her head spun; she felt light from blood loss. Linn wrapped her arms around herself and drew several deep breaths. "We rest,"

she said, sounding more certain than she felt by far. "We eat, regain our strength. And in the morning . . ."

Her gaze caught on her leg. It lay stretched out in front of
her, wrapped in bandages soaked red. There was the faint tingle
of pain, countered by the woozy fog of the sedative he'd given her.

"In the morning, we go and gather information on those
ships," Kaïs finished matter-of-factly, as though the deep gash
in her leg did not exist. As though he hadn't had to save her and
carry her from the ocean to here. He stretched out next to her.
"Stay close to me. It's the best way to preserve the heat in our
bodies."

Linn curled up in the crook between his elbows and his torso.
His chest was warm and solid, and the steady beat of his heart
calmed her. She felt him smooth out her chi, draping it over her
shoulders like a blanket.

Beneath it, though, Linn was wound tight as a spring. In
one night, her plans had been blown to pieces. Kemeira, once
a safe haven in her mind, had been swept into the bloodshed
and violence that Morganya had inflicted upon Cyrilia, and then
Bregon. And if Morganya's ships had reached even the Kemeiran
Empire's shores, then Bei'kin and the Temple of the Skies might
not be safe from her clutches.

Linn's hands fisted. She had endured too much, come too far,
to back down.

This was her war.

This was her *home*.

And she would not let Morganya win.

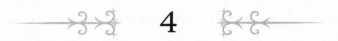

4

Ana woke to a gentle, lulling rhythm, the squeak of wagon wheels, and the muffled thud of hooves against snow.

She inhaled sharply, eyes snapping open. It took a moment for her to orient herself. The last she'd known was the searing cold of icy waters, blinding darkness, vicious currents buffeting her this way and that until there was no up or down, no sense of where the water ended and the sky began.

The floorboards beneath her rocked—that was not her imagination—and all around her there was the creak of wood and nails. She was in a carriage, moonlight pouring red through the bars of a window across. It was still night, yet the moon had sunk low over the other end of the sky; she must have been unconscious for hours after her ship was hit.

Her ship.

Ana tried to sit up from the pallet, only to find that her hands and feet were in chains. She lifted a wrist, examining the dull luster of her binds, as though light itself did not reflect from them. She knew the material: blackstone, a substance that inhibited Affinite powers. The sight of it drew bile to her throat, and she remembered all too well the feeling of nausea that came with it, the draining of her Affinity as though she'd lost one of her senses.

Yet now, she felt nothing from the chains save an unpleasant chafing and a coldness where they touched her skin.

There was movement in the corner. Ana looked up sharply as a figure peeled from the shadows.

Relief filled her as the man stepped into the light of the Blood Moon beneath the window. "Kapitan?" Her voice was a hoarse whisper. "Kapitan Markov?"

It was him, in the flesh, dressed in an immaculate suit of gray armor, his hair flecked with grays like salt and pepper: the old guard who had watched her grow up, who had told her stories to tide her through the worst of her nightmares back at the Salskoff Palace, who had stayed by her side all along. She recalled each weathered line of his face as one would the contours of a map, and she noticed with tenderness that there were new creases to his forehead, his cheeks, around his mouth.

Yet his eyes . . . the warmth in them was gone, like a fire put out in an empty hearth.

"Kapitan." She was beginning to shiver. She was still wet, the chill of the ocean water seeping into her bones. "What's going on? Where am I?"

Kapitan Markov only continued to watch her with that haunting gaze. She noticed he wasn't chained, and his sword was strapped to his hip. One gloved hand rested against its hilt.

"Kapitan." Her relief had dried into cold fear. "Unlock me from these chains at once. This is an order."

Yet a creeping realization was beginning to twine its grasp around her as she looked into the face of her guard and one of her most trusted confidants. It was as though someone else wore his skin, so vastly different was his expression, the way he looked back at her without seeing her.

She'd encountered this once before in her life. She'd seen this type of hollow gaze in the eyes of her brother, Luka, during the last days he'd spent under the mind control of Morganya, forced to take a poison that slowly killed him and left the throne to their aunt. In the face of her father, who'd suffered the same fate unbeknownst to the world.

Ana pressed herself against the wall of the wagon, chains clinking as she folded her hands together to stop their trembling. Outlined against the window, the body that belonged to Kapitan Markov stood stone-still and silent, watching her.

The light outside was beginning to flicker: yellows and oranges mingling with the eerie red glow of the Blood Moon. It was torchlight, Ana realized.

Beyond the darkness of a Cyrilian winter night, there came the gleam of distant fire. As they drew closer, the outline of a town unfolded: the uniform rise and fall of roofs, the spires and steeples of a cathedral. The firelight grew brighter as their carriage pulled up to a cobblestone road.

A crowd was gathered at the town square around a stage. Ana caught sight of the gray-hued gleam of armor and the colorless cloaks of Imperial Patrols lined up beneath a wooden scaffold. Onstage, a figure paced back and forth.

Even from here, Ana recognized her aunt's poise and elegance. The Empress Morganya was dressed in a resplendent gown of silver that reflected crimson in the night, her gestures sweeping and grand. She held an otherworldly aura, as though she were a Deity reincarnate. As she spoke, her words indiscernible from this distance, the crowd shifted like a puppet beneath her strings.

A sickening feeling gripped Ana's stomach as she watched her aunt, the Empress she was meant to dethrone. Ana had only been gone from Cyrilia for a little over a moon, and the last she'd seen of it was her empire burning under a mad empress's reign.

Yet . . . as they drew nearer, the scene shifted, the sounds of the crowd drifting to Ana through the barred window. What she had taken to be cheers began to change to jeers and boos. Among the torches raised, she could make out banners and posters lifted, pointed aggressively at the stage.

Banners and flags . . . with the sigil of a red tigress on them.

Ana drew herself up, lunging against her chains to gain a closer look. Before she could, the wagon came to a sudden halt, throwing her to the floor. Pain seared in her arm as her bindings stretched taut, chains clinking. In the corner, Kapitan Markov continued to stare at her with unseeing eyes.

The doors to her wagon were flung open. "Well done, Kapitan," came a familiar voice that slithered serpentine. "We couldn't have done this without you."

A voice that plunged Ana into an old nightmare.

She lifted her gaze.

Vladimir Sadov, the Imperial Consultant, brought his steepled pale fingers to his curled lips. "Little Tigress," he said softly. "Or, should I say, *Red* Tigress now?" Her title was a mockery in his mouth. "How long I have waited to see you."

She could sense his Affinity to fear settling over her like a thin veil, quickening her heartbeat and moistening her palms. A part of her reaction, though, was genuine. She'd spent years of her childhood in the dungeons of the Salskoff Palace, strapped to a table at this man's fingertips, being pried and prodded at as he toyed with her Affinity, pretending he was trying to find a nonexistent cure. The familiar panic now crawled up her throat; her heart thudded painfully in her chest; the wagon walls seemed to shrink.

"You," Ana choked. She glanced behind her at Markov's hollow expression, then back to Sadov. "What have you done to him?"

Sadov's smile widened. "I see it's all coming together for you," he said, a hint of glee to his words. "Did you really think the Empress wouldn't find out about your correspondences with dear old Kapitan Markov? She was, after all, your beloved mamika for all those years. Always watching you, and those who cared to linger around you."

Bile rose to her tongue.

"All it took," Sadov continued, "was some mind control, which our Kolst Imperatorya is quite adept at." He glanced at Markov, standing statuesque in the midst of their conversation, gaze blank. "The poor old fool never knew it was coming. Turning your pawn into our pawn was a brilliant move by our Kolst Imperatorya. We gained access to your communications. We tracked your movements. We planned for this day."

Ana's throat closed as she beheld the guard. She wasn't sure she could bear it if someone else she loved ended up hurt or dead because of her.

"Kapitan," she whispered. "I'm so sorry."

Kapitan Markov continued to look ahead serenely.

"Enough of sentiment." Sadov snapped his fingers, and an Imperial Patrol stepped in—one who bore the new insignia of the Empress on his chest, a Deys'krug with a crown in the center. He wore armor that was paler than the blackstone-infused mail of regular Patrols. He was an Inquisitor—an Imperial Patrol with an Affinity—one of many whom Morganya had begun recruiting after her ascension to the throne, to solidify her own power and grow her army.

The Inquisitor unhooked her chains from the wall of the wagon and grabbed one of her arms. Kapitan Markov took her other one.

The move itself wasn't painful, but Ana's chest ached as Kapitan Markov began to haul her from the wagon. The Markov she'd known had been like a father to her when her own had turned away. He'd been the one to carry her to bed on nights when her Affinity spun out of control.

Ana closed her eyes and thought of the gentleness of his arms, the way they'd steadied her like a rock in a storm-tossed sea.

Yet as she stepped out from the wagon, a realization swept over her.

She was on shore.

She was *home.*

The icy soil of her empire cracked open her heart; the sharp winds breathed life into her, and she grounded herself with one thought. There was nothing she wouldn't do to save Cyrilia.

She was escorted inside a mansion, down a dark hallway, and thrust into a room. As Ana took in her surroundings, it began to dawn on her that she was truly and firmly trapped. The room was windowless and sealed. A single blackstone chair sat in the middle of the floor like a perverse rendition of a throne. Ana had a fearful suspicion of what it was used for.

The thought had barely occurred to her when Kapitan Markov and the Inquisitor thrust her into the chair. They tightened the chains around her chest and strapped her wrists to the armrests.

"Dry her up," Sadov commanded when they finished. Carefully, he hung a snowglobe lantern to the doorframe. Its light spilled into the jagged corners of the room. "We wouldn't want our guest to freeze to death just yet."

The Inquisitor nodded and raised his hands. She felt his water Affinity begin to pull out the moisture from her clothes, the droplets coalescing in the air and flowing toward him. Within seconds, her Bregonian cloak and tunic were dry, crusty with salt from the ocean.

Ana took these few moments to pull herself together. Escaping now was not a feasible option, with blackstone chains binding her arms and legs. There was no way for her to send a message to Daya and her troops—if, Ana thought with sickening dread, they had survived the attack. The Bregonian Navy was the best in the world; Ana could only trust that Morganya's forces would be outmatched when it came to naval warfare.

The one thing Ana could do right now was to gather information. Negotiate her way out. If they'd wanted her dead, she wouldn't be here right now.

At that moment, footsteps sounded outside, down the corridor. The doors to Ana's chambers opened; two rows of Imperial Patrols stood outside, their livery painting them ghostly in the lowlight.

Then, like the parting waves of an ocean, they stepped back.

Morganya stood in the doorway, looking even more ethereal than the last time they'd met in the seaside trading town of Goldwater Port, before Ana had fled for the Kingdom of Bregon. Her skin was the dusk-gold of statues and crowns, and embedded like gemstones were the pale green of her eyes, the ruby-red slash of her mouth. Her hair had been sculpted into a glistening black wreath beneath a jeweled crown of white diamonds, split in the middle by the sign of a Deys'krug. Her imperial kechyan, too, spilled from her shoulders to the floor in pristine white, silver filigree glittering as though the Deities themselves had draped it around her.

There was something different about her face, about her *eyes*, though. Once, Ana had looked into them and seen kindness, gentleness, the love of an aunt. Those had been farcical. The ravaging anger and ruinous wrath that had spilled through during the Coronation when Luka had appointed Ana as his heir had been shocking, but truer to who Morganya might have been.

Those emotions, at least, had been human.

Now, those eyes stared out, and in them was something profoundly hollow, as though in place of her soul, there was nothing left.

Morganya waved a hand. "Leave," she commanded her Imperial Patrols. "No—you stay, dear Kapitan."

A sharp fear pierced Ana's chest. *Leave. Don't listen to her,* she thought, looking to Markov, but he remained by Sadov's side, a puppet on strings.

The door clicked shut, and at last, Morganya turned to Ana. For a moment, they looked at each other.

The blow came out of nowhere, slamming into Ana's face so hard that she saw stars.

"You little *bitch*," Morganya hissed. "I ought to *kill* you for what you did in Bregon."

The second blow filled Ana's mouth with the metallic taste of blood, hot and foreign where her Affinity might once have stirred at its scent. Her head spun, but in the fog of pain, a realization cut through like the blade of a sword.

Blinking the black spots from her vision, Ana focused on the Empress's wrists. They were covered by the sleeves of the kechyan she wore, but Morganya's fury could only mean one thing.

Both siphons were still lost—for the moment, at least. Sorsha had disappeared since the Battle of Godhallem over one fortnight ago; if she was indeed alive, it seemed she hadn't reached Morganya yet.

As though thinking along the same lines, Morganya clenched her fingers around Ana's throat. Her nails gouged into Ana's flesh, sparking pinpricks of pain. "Where is it?" Morganya hissed. *"Where is the siphon that was meant for me?"*

It was the first time Ana had seen Morganya in such an unbridled state. As she took in her aunt's wild eyes and savage snarl, Ana realized just how deeply the cracks ran behind Morganya's façade of control and domination.

And, as Ramson would have said, cracks were weaknesses, to be used as leverage. Better yet, Morganya had just confirmed the greatest advantage Ana held against her: that Morganya was only aware of a single siphon's existence where, in reality, there existed two.

Ana split her mouth in a grin. Warmth dribbled down her chin. "What's wrong, mamika?" The moniker, once used as a gesture of affection, tasted like rot on her tongue. "Things aren't going as well as you'd planned?"

Morganya's face paled. For a moment, she looked nearly unhinged. Then her gaze shuttered, and she gave a laugh. "You know, I wanted to kill you, at first," she said softly, her voice velvet poison. "Just like, at the very start of it all, I tried to fight you. I sent my forces from town to town, searching for you. I thought that if I got rid of you, I would secure my place as Empress. That if you were dead, the people would turn to me." Her eyes flicked up, and in them was an old cruelty, an ancient wisdom.

"But, even as my soldiers marched across the Empire, rooting out traitors and filthy non-Affinites, the rebellions didn't stop. And a movement began to spread from town to town. The *Red Tigress.*" Her lips curled into a sneer and she spat the words. "You see, Anastacya, the people weren't in love with *you*. They didn't believe that *you* would lead them to a better future. No—they were enamored of the *idea* of you. That you were a savior, a rebel, a revolutionary. It was their ideology that was corrupted, that I needed to change.

"I have spent years of my life dedicating myself to the study of history. And what I've found, Anastacya, is that most wars are not won on a physical level, but on an ideological level. The people are no more than sheep, their thoughts malleable to misdirection. And I, as their divine shepherd, must guide them the right way."

"By controlling their minds?" Ana croaked. "That will never last." She thought of the jeers and boos of the crowd earlier; of the ordinary people she had met in Goldwater Port, downtrodden and powerless, yet still fighting. Still resisting. "You cannot seize power, just as you cannot force loyalty. Both must flow from the people themselves."

Morganya's sharp laugh rent the air. "'Flow from the people'?" she repeated. "The people see what they are told to see. Whether history writes us as monsters or heroes has never been up to the *people,* Anastacya. It is up to us. And when the time comes, I will be the one narrating the tale."

Monsters or heroes. The words washed over Ana with chilling familiarity. Hadn't she once thought herself the monster? Hadn't she questioned every single one of her actions, weighing the benefits against the costs, wondering if bloodshed was merely the means to an end, a necessary precursor to justice and good?

And yet . . . throughout it all, she had never sought to take her people's free will. Whether they viewed her as a monster or a hero in the end, she had always left it to the people to judge.

"You see, Little Tigress," Morganya continued, "we are on the precipice of a great change—one of the greatest revolutions of humankind. I speak not of the battle between us, nor of the mundane cycle of dynasties that we wheel through every few centuries." She waved a hand. "No, Little Tigress. With the siphon, I am going to restore the balance of the world."

Ana gazed at her. The words sounded familiar—she had heard Linn speak of the harmony of the world according to her Kemeiran Wind Masters. And she had heard these words spoken by a dying man in Bregon—a scholar named Tarschon who had been responsible for inventing the siphons. *The siphons . . . can be . . . destroyed,* he'd whispered just before he'd stopped breathing. *Restore . . . the natural . . . order . . .*

"Wielding the siphon will *destroy* the balance of the world," Ana rasped.

Morganya was gazing at a spot over Ana's shoulder, and when she spoke, it was as though she was barely aware of Ana's presence. "When I took the throne, I knew I had far more work before me than any of the previous monarchs. I am an Affinite, and the order of our world seemed to have been made *against* people like me. Yet I wondered: Why is it that we, Affinites, born more powerful than any regular mortal, have suffered for so long? Just like the syvint'sya and the Deities' Lights, we are created with the touch of the Deities; our Affinities are remnants of the gods themselves."

The Cyrilian Empire had long forgotten these sayings, be-lieving Affinites to be demons—yet it was Morganya who had first told Ana of this tale. Ana recalled the times she'd found her aunt praying in the temple behind the Salskoff Palace, her tea-green eyes a pale puzzle.

And you, Kolst Pryntsessa, her mamika had told her back then, *were chosen by the Deities to fight the battles that they cannot in this world.*

The words drew out another memory: Scholar Tarschon, out-lined beneath a ceiling of holy paintings in the Great Scholars' Library of Bregon. *Long ago, the gods parted from our world. Yet they left traces of magek in their wake . . . in us, in the magen.*

"I threw myself into the study of our Deities, of all the folk-lores and myths and legends recorded in our lands," the Empress continued. "And I found traces of what we know as alchemical power—but what I believe to be *magic,* left over by the Deities. Ancient powers, left to us to use, to control. First: blackstone, to suppress Affinities in the case that we grew too powerful."

Cyrilia received the gift of blackstone, Scholar Tarschon had whispered.

"Yet when humans discovered it," Morganya said softly, "they began to abuse it. They used it to control Affinites, to exploit us, because they *feared* us, dear child. Humans will always fear the things they do not understand." A malignant hatred, something rotten and fetid, twisted Morganya's features. "When you speak of *destroying* the natural order, remember this: The unbalancing of our world began long ago, when humanity discovered black-stone and began to use it against Affinites."

Perhaps that was true, Ana thought, keeping silent. Per-haps the world had already been unbalanced long ago, when the oppression of Affinites began at the hands of non-Affinites through blackstone. And she, born into a world like this, had simply accepted it as the natural order, the way things were meant to be.

"And then," Morganya continued, "the Deities left us searock, an element with powers naturally absorptive of alchemical magic. It took Alaric years to create siphons out of it so that we could use it on the alchemical power in *humans*. In the wrong hands, it can be used to take away Affinities. In the right hands—in *Affinite* hands—it is used to gain more power."

And Bregon, Scholar Tarschon had said, *we received searock.*

"Why leave us this magic," Morganya murmured, "if not for us to use it? Why create Affinites in their shape if not to have us rule? The Deities have left us remnants of their powers so that we can *become* them, Anastacya. I now understand that it is my duty to fulfill that destiny, and to bring balance back to this world."

"You once spoke of liberating Affinites, of bringing equality to this world," Ana said. "Yet you have freed Affinites from one type of servitude only to force them into another." She spat the last words. "Into servitude for *you*."

"For me?" Morganya laughed, as though she genuinely found this amusing. "Darling girl, don't you see? I am *restoring* the balance of the world. I am putting power *back* into the hands of Affinites. All I need . . . is for them to believe in my cause, first. You see, people want to think they have a choice, yet you take that choice away, and they will begin to realize that everything I'm doing is right, that everything I'm doing is for *them*. Then, I can create the perfect world I envision. I will dictate who is deserving of power and punish those who are not. I can dispense justice upon this land, unencumbered. I can re-create this world as it should be."

Ana thought back to a conversation that bore chilling echoes of this one—a conversation she'd had over a moon ago, in the darkest corner of Novo Mynsk, with a boy made of shadows. Seyin, the deputy of the rebel group the Redcloaks, had questioned the monarchy, questioned the idea of a world with a benevolent ruler.

"You're not doing this for the people," Ana said quietly, "you're doing this to play at being a god. Look at the riots outside. And look at you. You're so afraid of losing power that you would stop at nothing to take it all. To remake yourself in the form of a Deity."

Morganya's expression held such cold fury that Ana thought the Empress would kill her, right there and then.

But the Empress only bent forward, her eyes turning understanding, her face holding a glimmer of the quiet, kind aunt Ana had once thought her to be. "My dear Anastacya," she whispered, stroking Ana's face, each touch of her hand sending shivers of revulsion down Ana's spine. "Why do you resist? You and I, we are the same."

Against Ana's will, Seyin's whispers came back to her. *Tell me, what is the difference between you and Morganya? You are, after all, both Affinite empresses promising a better world for your people.*

Ana wanted to shut her eyes. But Morganya held her in place, her gaze boring into Ana's.

"I grew up as the only Affinite in my small village," Morganya said. "They called me a witch, a deimhov, an abomination." Her expression had become distant, clouded in memories; her fingers had fallen still against Ana's face. There was a sadness in her expression, so faint that Ana might have missed it. "I swore to myself, then, that I would do whatever it took to take my revenge. To rid the world of people like that: those who inflicted cruelty, and those who stood by doing nothing as they watched.

"And then I came to Salskoff Palace. I watched as your father mistreated you, as he made the mistakes only a foolish emperor who'd experienced nothing of what his people were going through would make. I knew I had to take things into my own hands and remake this world as it should be. A world where a little girl born with a strange power might not think herself different, might not wonder herself a monster."

It was as though Morganya had pulled out the whispers inside Ana's own heart and spoken them from her lips. As Ana stared into her aunt's face, looked over all its familiar edges and curves, she couldn't help but feel as though she were looking into a cruel reflection of herself.

But—no, *no*, she thought, struggling, Morganya's Affinity on her body resisting her attempts to turn away.

Morganya had murdered Mama, then Papa, then Luka, and hundreds, if not thousands, of other innocents without even batting an eyelash. And now, she planned to use and manipulate the very people she was sworn to protect . . . to grow her own power.

But Ana . . . Ana had always remembered the very first thing her brother had told her. A whisper from all those years past. She closed her eyes, summoning his image, the bright green eyes sparkling against fawn skin, the smile that had lit up her world just like Mama's used to. *Your Affinity does not define you,* he'd told her. *What defines you is how you choose to wield it.*

Ana lifted her gaze to her aunt's. "No one is born a monster," she said quietly. "We become monsters because of our choices."

The empathy on Morganya's face vanished. "My Affinity is spent from our earlier speech," she snapped, turning to Sadov. Exhaustion lined her face; sometime throughout their conversation, dark circles had appeared beneath her eyes. "I cannot exercise adequate control over her mind."

Realization washed over Ana like cold water: Morganya had been trying to use mind control on Ana. It was the more insidious aspect of her Affinity to flesh and the makeup of one's body: Over the years, Morganya had trained herself to be able to reform the matters in people's minds, shaping the nebulous spaces where thoughts were born and twisting them to her way.

Yet there was always a cost to using one's Affinity—a cost with which Ana was intimately familiar. She knew, all too well, the feeling of weakness, nausea, and fatigue that came after expending one's powers.

Morganya had overused hers—perhaps in an attempt to control too many people.

Sadov's reply came from the shadows. "Soon, my Divine Empress, your power shall be unfettered."

There was something in his tone that drew Ana's attention. Something she wasn't understanding, just yet.

The Empress turned back to Ana. Her expression was stoic, almost businesslike. "I thought persuading you to change your mind might be the kind way out," she said softly, and lifted a slender hand in Kapitan Markov's direction. "One last chance, Anastacya. Tell me where the siphon is, or your Kapitan dies."

It was as though she'd knocked the breath from Ana. "No." Her voice shook. "You can do whatever you wish to me. Just don't hurt him."

Her aunt laughed, a silken sound. "If I know you at all, it is that you have one great weakness, Little Tigress. I have learned that hurting you will achieve nothing. But hurting the ones you love?" Her lips curled triumphantly, and she flexed her fingers. "The siphon. Last chance."

Ana's stomach twisted; she wrenched against her chains so hard that she felt a searing pain across her arm, blood spiraling down her skin. "I . . . truly don't know where it is, mamika," she choked out.

Morganya's gaze was flat. Then, she exhaled. "I tire of this," she said, and slashed her hand down.

Time seemed to slow. There was Markov, swaying where he stood, blood pouring from his neck. He blinked and his face shifted, as though he'd jolted out of a long slumber. His gaze came to focus on Ana.

Slowly, he fell onto the floor, blood pooling under him and running along the wood, steam curling into the winter air. His hands—those hands that had protected her since she'd been born—shook as they tried to stem the flow of blood.

It felt like a lifetime before he grew still. His eyes, the sword-metal gray she'd known her entire life, stared out at her, his mouth open.

Someone was screaming. No, *she* was screaming. She was dimly aware of someone shaking her shoulders, of a gag being stuffed in her mouth.

Sadov stood over her, teeth glinting in the semidarkness as he spoke. "Kolst Deys'va Imperatorya, shall I take over?"

Ana heard Morganya's reply. "Yes. Break her, Vladimir, as you so excel at it."

Sadov's smile stretched, his long white fingers tapping together as he settled into the chair.

The Empress swept past Markov's body without a second glance. The door shut with a clang, and Ana was left with a pale-fingered monster in the darkness and the still-cooling body of her faithful guard.

Sadov leaned forward. "Let's begin, shall we?" he said softly. And then the nightmares descended, flooding her mind and body.

Ana doubled over in her chair, screaming even as tears carved tracks down her cheeks like blood.

5

The Blue Fort looked as it always had: regal, powerful, and impenetrable. Sitting atop high cliffs that faced the ocean with a zigzag path of waterways, its searock walls gleamed beneath the setting sun: a symbol of Bregonian might, overlooking the Four Seas.

Ramson leaned against the mast of his ship, watching as they drew closer to the wide marble steps that led to Godhallem, the meeting hall of Bregon's Three Courts. It still felt strange, almost unnatural, for him to be here. Less than one moon ago, he'd returned to the kingdom of his birth after spending an eternity away.

Gazing at the cobalt waves of his birth home, he couldn't help but think of a different shore. A land scraped raw by winter, frozen beneath layers of ice and snow, and imbued with its own wild and untamed beauty.

A land that had come to mean something to him.

A land that held someone who had come to mean something to him.

He let out a sharp breath and glanced behind him. Five of his officers were preparing to escort Ardonn into the halls of Godhallem, directly to the King and the Three Courts.

The scholar hadn't yielded a single word throughout the course of their half-day journey. For the entire afternoon, Ramson's squad healer, Iversha, had tended to him, clearing the smoke from his lungs and feeding him tonics meant to soothe the harsh effects of the ricyn poison. But when Ramson visited his prisoner's quarters belowdecks, the man had lain stone-still, staring at the ceiling.

I'm afraid it won't be a happy ending for your blood princess.

He gripped the railing tighter, then pushed off to walk to the front of the ship to disembark. A seadove had been sent ahead; the King and the Three Courts would be expecting their arrival.

Royal Guards lined the marble steps. They clicked their heels together and saluted as the gangplank was lowered and Ramson disembarked trailed by his squad, marching tightly in formation. The supply wagons with Kerlan's documents would be unloaded; in the meantime, Ramson had selected samples to be brought to the King. First Officer Narron hurried at his heels, several thick tomes balanced in his arms.

Ramson had spent the boat ride poring over the documents rescued from Kerlan's Nest. He'd known all too well what they were; he'd spent years keeping similar records for Goldwater Port. The papers were trade ledgers, some containing transactions between Cyrilia and Bregon, others between Kerlan and his suppliers across the Kingdom of Bregon. Most troubling were the ledgers that had contained not goods, but *names*. It was evident that the global Affinite trafficking network—which Kerlan had been a part of—stretched much farther and much deeper than Ramson had ever known.

Once upon a time, he might have averted his gaze, returned to his own business. But today, the discovery had left Ramson feeling sick. He'd perused those lists, faces swimming in the back of his mind: a child with ocean-colored eyes and hair like waves, a solemn-faced warrior with a gaze like blades. May and Linn had once been on a ledger just like the ones they'd found. An entire human being, a *life*, reduced to a few letters and a sum on a long list.

"Captain Farrald." A voice jolted him from his thoughts. Lieutenant Ronnoc of the King's Guard stood before him, giving a sharp salute. "This way."

In just the two weeks that he'd been away, Godhallem—and the rest of the Blue Fort—had undergone remarkable repairs. Most of it had been destroyed during the battle against Alaric Kerlan. The last time Ramson had seen the place, wooden beams had been erected and crates of stone and supplies were piled everywhere.

Now, the marble steps had been reconstructed, and the newly painted doors opened into the hall of gods.

Most of the searock in Godhallem had been replaced by regular stone, creating intersections of the undulating turquoise material and gray rock. On either side of the hall sat the Sky and Earth Courts, more of their seats now filled with new faces. The Sea Court occupied the far end, where the walls opened to cliffs that plunged down into the sea. A veranda had been built, complete with a balustrade. Gossamer curtains billowed gently in the breeze, and sunlight streamed through, pooling in the middle of the chamber.

King Darias stood in the center of the hall. In just weeks, the boy, who was several years Ramson's junior, seemed to have grown into his crown. He carried himself with gravitas, his smile weighing heavy but kind as he shook hands with new courtiers bearing the seals of the Three Courts.

He looked up, a strand of black hair escaping his crown. At the sight of Ramson, his face broke into a boyish grin.

Ramson knelt before the man-made line of water that separated the aisle of the throne from the rest of the hall. Several light steps, and he was looking into the polished leather boots of the King.

"Rise," laughed King Darias as he stepped over the water line. Ramson did. "You never disappoint me, Ramson Farrald. Two weeks it has been, and you have sent back scores of Kerlan's spies, dug out most of his network, and found the scholar holding the legacy of his work." His eyes narrowed a fraction. "Perhaps, now, you'll consider joining my government officially?"

King Darias had been pressing for him to accept an official appointment within the Bregonian government—still without success. Ramson inclined his head and gestured at the new courtiers gathered throughout the hall. "You are too generous, Your Majesty. I see the People's Elections seem to be progressing extremely well."

King Darias nodded. "We are in the process of filling seats in the Three Courts. I took a survey of our population and divided the seats according to income and geographical region. There are magen here, as well."

Ramson swept a gaze over the seats, half still sitting empty. For some reason, the mention of magen—the Bregonian term for Affinites—stirred a faint emotion in his chest.

Ana would have wanted to see this. Harmony between Affinites and non-Affinites, equality from the government down to its people . . . those were ideals she had been seeking to build since they had first met.

"I'm reforming the system to ensure accurate representation of our people," King Darias continued, looking thoughtful as he studied his courts. "Previously, my father and his ancestors chose only those with power and money. It was impossible for those without to get anywhere in the ranks of our government . . . which is wrong."

Gazing at the King, at his ink-black hair and bright eyes, Ramson couldn't help but think of another boy. His childhood friend and sea brother, Jonah, an orphan who had been brought into the Naval Academy as a Navy recruit, had seen the same issues. The system of old had neglected the hopeless and down-trodden and, at worst, punished them to preserve itself.

Jonah had died as a result of the broken system.

Ramson pushed those thoughts away and changed the subject. "An interesting choice of construction," he said, gesturing at the floors and walls around them. "I'm sure it wouldn't have been difficult to mine more searock to complete the reconstruction."

"We are a nation of metal and stone," King Darias remarked. "It won't do to forget our origins . . . or our history. This hall shall serve to represent the scars we carry." He paused. "Besides, I've ordered all remaining supplies of searock to be purchased by the Royal Treasury, and banned new mining activity."

Ramson nodded. Searock was one of the key materials that went into constructing the siphons, and upon further study by the Bregonian scholars, it was found to possess the power to absorb the properties of magek that resided in magen.

"Not to mention," King Darias continued, a slight frown creasing his brows, "our economy has suffered heavy damage with the war. I've received reports from many regions over the past two weeks that trade routes with Cyrilia seem to have collapsed."

A tinge of cold unease trickled through Ramson. "I may have answers for you on that front, Your Majesty."

"Oh?"

"As you know, my squad and I tracked down the scholar to a northern village of Denner. There, we found what we presume to be the hub of all Alaric Kerlan's activity. We believe to have uncovered a massive operation of illicit trade between Cyrilia and Bregon, which Alaric Kerlan has facilitated for decades. This includes . . . magen trafficking networks." Ramson motioned at Narron, who was standing at the doors. The young man clicked his heels together and hurried to Ramson's side.

King Darias's gaze sharpened. He held out a hand; Narron slid a tome into his fingers. The boy king flipped through several pages, his expression tightening. Ramson watched, the feeling of foreboding growing with each passing moment. These trade ledgers spanned years, *decades,* even, all perfectly preserved. There were sums on these pages indicating fortunes, and Ramson couldn't help but wonder how many lives were contained within these lines, how many families destroyed to satisfy the rapacious greed of cruel men.

At last, King Darias leaned back. He drummed his fingers along the sample tomes. "This is sickening," he muttered.

"I would concur, Your Majesty," Ramson said.

King Darias steepled his fingers. "The Kingdom of Bregon will continue our fight against the illicit and abhorrent trade of human lives, as we always have," he said. "Kerlan's sinister practices infiltrated our kingdom only because he had someone on the inside working for him." His fist tightened.

Ramson inclined his head. "In whichever manner you decide to remedy this issue, my sword is yours."

At this, the King's eyes sharpened on Ramson. "There is something I've been thinking," he said, and his tone gave Ramson pause. "Our Courts suffered heavy losses in the wake of the battle, as you know; currently, the post for Ambassador of Trade and Commerce in the Earth Court is still open." He leaned forward. "I wish to nominate you."

Ramson shouldn't have been caught off-guard—the boy king had proven to have more than his share of brains and deviousness. It took Ramson a moment to gather his thoughts. "Your Majesty," he said, clasping a fist to his chest. "Thank you. It is an honor."

The King studied him for a moment. "But?" he asked.

Ramson licked his lips. "My work of rooting out Alaric Kerlan's criminal network is not finished," he said. "Especially in light of the new information we discovered. The global network of Affinite traffickers remains strong."

"And you could work to prevent them here, in Bregon. The surest way to catch these criminals is through stringent inspection of trade ships, which the Kingdom of Bregon has upheld for centuries."

"Bregon is not the centerpoint for these networks." Ramson gestured at the ledgers Narron carried. "You saw from the paperwork that the trafficking organizations have their strongest foothold in the Aseatic region." He wasn't even sure why he was debating this. The King had offered a wonderful proposition—one that gave him everything he'd wanted: riches, status, and the opportunity to pursue his dream of owning his own port and trade routes. Before, he would have jumped at the chance.

But for some reason, he kept thinking back to Linn, to her frightened gaze, the way she'd looked at him like a trapped animal when he'd approached her that night in Kerlan's Playpen. Of May, the earth Affinite Ana had rescued from her indenturement in Cyrilia, her eyes bearing a jaded wisdom that did not befit her child's body.

King Darias waved a hand, leaning back. "No matter. We'll table this for later. My scholars have assembled for the interrogation." He raised his voice. "Lieutenant Ronnoc, secure the hall and summon the scholars. Captain Farrald, have your squad bring in the prisoner for questioning."

Ramson's attention shifted. From the side doors, beneath open-air arches, a group of scholars filed in, their white robes flashing in the sun. Scrolls of parchment and papers fluttered as they settled in a circle around the dais. Without further word, King Darias swept up to the dais and took his seat. As the Three Courts settled, Ramson's squad marched in. They held Scholar Ardonn between them.

Lieutenant Ronnoc chained the man to a chair in the middle of the hall.

King Darias nodded at Ramson. "Captain Farrald, if you please."

Ramson cleared his throat and stepped forward. "King Darias, Scholars," he said. "I'd like to introduce the former Scholar Ardonn, who was caught assisting Alaric Kerlan in his studies of siphons and transfer of Affinities."

There were sharp intakes of breath from the scholars and courtiers all around them.

King Darias leaned forward, chin resting against his knuckles. "Former Scholar Ardonn," he said. "Would you like to speak for your crimes?"

Ardonn lifted his head at last. A smirk spread across his face as he surveyed his former colleagues and his king, his gaze coming to land, at last, upon Ramson. "You're wasting your time," he croaked. "I have nothing to say."

"I am sure you will," one of the scholars retorted. Her hair was snowy white, her mouth set in a somber line. Ramson recognized her as Scholar Hestanna, the lead scholar that King Darias had appointed for the siphon task force. "We would prefer not to use other methods to coerce you, Ardonn. Remember that you have committed a crime, and that you have a chance to correct it."

Ardonn gave a rasping laugh. "I'm one step from my deathbed. Besides, the balance of the world has shifted; it's too late to reverse it."

"What do you mean by that?" King Darias demanded.

"Magek," Ardonn said, flicking a glance at Scholar Hestanna.

Ramson suppressed a long sigh. Scholars were known to speak in riddles. He had no gods-damned interest in the principles of alchemy. He only cared for answers, and a solution to destroying the siphons.

Time was running out.

Scholar Hestanna's lips tightened, and she turned to King Darias. "According to the principles of magek, studied by thousands of scholars over the history of our kingdom, there is a balance to the forces of this world. Those inclined to religious worship believe that the Three Gods left traces of themselves in this world; those inclined to scientific study believe that a source of power—what we refer to as magek, the Cyrilians as alchemy—manifests in magen and various other elements.

"What we know is that traces of magek can be found in certain places around the world. In humans—as magen; in spirits, such as our gossenwal and their ice spirits; and in some elements. First: blackstone. And now"—her eyes raked back to Ardonn, dagger-sharp—"searock, which our recent studies show may absorb magek. The act of taking this natural element and twisting it into man-made siphons to absorb the magek in *humans* is an abomination in itself. The transfer of Affinities is unnatural, unheard of, and the very existence of siphons is a poison to this world."

"Always at the top of your game, Hestie," Ardonn drawled.

"We have seen, with our own eyes, the atrocities committed using these siphons," King Darias said, addressing his team of scholars. "The key question, now, is how we can find and destroy them."

Scholar Hestanna gave a curt nod. "Ardonn, cooperate with us," she said. "There's nothing left in this for you. Tell us all you know about these siphons—their creation, the extent of their power, and how they can be destroyed—and King Darias will issue a pardon to your crimes. You could spend the rest of your days living in a cottage by the sea."

Ardonn chuckled. "Seems the young bastard son here has left out some details," he said, casting a glance at Ramson. "Throughout the years, Kerlan regularly injected his scholars with poison to which only he held the antidote—his way of keeping us in check and our mouths sealed, you see. Now that he's dead, the

antidote supply's run out. I've two weeks left to live, Hestie—
three, if I'm lucky." He leaned back in his seat. "You'll see why I'm
less than tempted by your wonderful offer."

"And you can choose either a quiet, quick death with a seaside
view, or to die painfully, tortured in this very hall beneath the eyes
of our gods," Darias interjected. There was nothing boyish about
his face anymore. The lines of his eyes were hard. "Now, answer
my question. Can the siphons be destroyed?"

The smile had dropped from Ardonn's face; he stared at the
King, expression tight. "You're far cleverer than your father ever
was, I'll give you that," he said at last, and there wasn't a trace of
ridicule to his tone. "A siphon can only be parted from its bearer
if the bearer is killed. But even then, the stolen magek is stored
in that siphon. In the history of our research, we have only ever
created two perfectly functioning siphons—and neither has been
destroyed yet." He shrugged. "Therefore, there is no proof they
can even be destroyed."

Ramson felt a sudden rush of blood in his ears. *No proof they
can even be destroyed.*

Dimly, as though from a distance, he heard Scholar Hestanna
say: "But in theory, the effects of both blackstone and searock are
temporary in nature. The founding theory of searock is that it can
only borrow the properties of that which it steals from. Therefore, there is no permanence to their effects. And that means—in
theory—their damage is reversible."

Ardonn's pause seemed to last a lifetime. "In theory," he said
at last, and Ramson loosed a breath. Hope—there was hope.

"So the mageks stored within the siphons," Ramson cut in,
earning some surprised glances from the scholars, "those can be
returned if we reverse or destroy the effects of the siphons?"

"Yes," Ardonn said. "The newly created magen we experimented upon were unfamiliar with their magek. They made mistakes, couldn't control the magek in the siphons. In all the cases where the siphons broke from being created improperly, the magek returned to the original magen."

Relief crashed over Ramson.

This question had haunted him ever since that night, during the Battle of Godhallem, when Sorsha had siphoned Ana's Affinity. Ana had collapsed, and when she had woken, something in her had shifted. In the days after, her voice had become quieter; her cheeks had hollowed; dark rings had appeared beneath her eyes, and an empty look sometimes overtook her gaze.

It had been a little over two weeks since he'd seen her, yet she remained in his thoughts nearly every second of every day.

Yes, there had been another, deeper reason for him to hunt down the remnants of Alaric Kerlan's Order members, to dig out the roots of the siphon research his former master had planted in Bregon nearly decades ago.

If there was a way for him to destroy the siphon holding Ana's Affinity and restore her power to her . . . if there was *any* remote possibility of it at all, even in theory, Ramson would find it.

He was so deep into his thoughts that he almost missed the next question Scholar Hestanna posed.

"And the magen," she said, looking down at her notes, "the ones that you experimented upon, who had their magek siphoned. What happens to those who never get their magek back?"

Ramson's head snapped up.

All the prayers to all his gods could not have stopped what came out of Ardonn's mouth next.

"They die."

6

Linn awoke to the trill of birdsong, the hum of cicadas, and the faint rush of a stream. A cool breeze blew in, carrying with it the scent of fresh rain. For a moment, she was ten years old again and back in her hut, listening to the sound of rain through the bamboo doors, tucked under the scratchy hemp blankets of her pallet. Ama-ka would be in the back room, steaming rice and salting radishes for them to break their fast.

As long as she kept her eyes closed, everything would be all right.

But the cold and the damp seeped in, and she lay not on smooth pine floors but on hard, uneven ground, parts of it digging into her back. Linn shifted, but for some reason, it was difficult to move.

And then the real world came crashing back. The Cyrilian ships. The fire. A dark ocean, an ally, blood on her legs.

Her eyes flew open and she shifted herself into a sitting position. The frantic pounding of her heart calmed slightly as Kaïs emerged from between two pine trees outside. He pushed aside the dangling moss that partially obscured the entrance to their cave. In his hands, he held a dead rabbit and a clump of crown-daisy stalks.

He paused as his gaze settled on her. "Are you all right?"

She let out a breath and nodded.

Kaïs sat down by her side. Gently, methodically, he set his catch aside and dumped an armful of kindling between them. "I saw movement down by the beach. I believe it is the Cyrilian ships we saw last night." He withdrew a piece of flint from his tunic, unsheathed a small dagger, and began to strike. The *tchik-tchik-tchik* sound somehow calmed Linn. "We will need to hike up higher into the mountains later to see them. You will need to fly."

She looked at him, but he continued to focus on the fire, each strike of his blade cutting precise movements through the air. Again, she marveled at how well he understood her without her needing to say anything. Soldier to soldier, he'd known that the only way to keep her grounded was to keep pushing forward, to keep surviving, and to keep fighting.

"Sounds good," she said, nodding, more to herself than to Kaïs. "We will find out what those ships are here for. And then we make a new plan." Her eyes narrowed. "If they are Morganya's forces, I highly doubt they are here on friendly terms."

Kaïs raised his eyebrows, turning the rabbit over the roasting spit. "That woman's name and the word *friendly* should not be spoken in the same sentence."

In spite of everything, her lips curled. "Was that a joke?"

He looked up for a brief moment and matched her smile. "Not at all."

Linn trailed her finger in little swirls on the ground. Thinking.

"If they are attacking Kemeira, we must find out why. And once we find out why, we must go to Bei'kin to warn the Temple Masters at the Temple of the Skies." She thought back to the ships she had seen in the night. Perhaps it had been the darkness, but . . . "I did not see a large number of ships."

"Neither did I."

"If Morganya wanted to invade, would she not send a larger fleet?"

"I don't think she is here to invade." Kaïs examined the cooked rabbit, put it back on the spit. "Morganya has just lost a battle in Bregon. At least a large part of her navy was destroyed. Not to mention, Ana has sown the seeds of resistance back in Cyrilia." He frowned. "It would be unwise of her to attempt an invasion so far across the seas."

Linn felt a hint of relief loosening her muscles. If he was correct, her home was safe from Morganya's clutches, it seemed—for the time being.

Her appetite opened as Kaïs handed her half a cooked rabbit. They tore into the meat hungrily, juices running slick down their faces and hands. When they finished, they doused the fire and packed the few belongings they had, using moss and mud to smear out any traces that they had been there. Then Kaïs carried her to the stream they had heard gurgling near their cave.

She sat by the water, scrubbing her legs in the soft currents. Her left one was still purpling from internal bleeding, her wound swollen and puckering with angry red welts where Kaïs had stitched it back together. She wasn't sure how she would be able to walk, like this. She needed to find a healer—soon.

Not wanting to dwell on it, Linn looked up. The conifers and cypresses of the mountain wound higher and higher between threads of gray mist until, at last, they disappeared. She had once run in these pine forests—*song'lin,* in her native tongue—with Enn by her side, plucking berries from branches and listening to the songs of birds.

Today, the mountain was silent.

Kaïs strode over to her. His hair glistened black with water. "We go," he said, and reached out a hand. "May I?"

She let him slip one arm around her waist and one under the bend of her knees, wrapping her good hand around his neck as he lifted her.

Kaïs was tall and powerfully built; next to him, Linn was barely a slip of shadow. Even so, they made slow progress. The mist grew thicker as they climbed, the air colder, and Linn had the impression that they were walking through clouds. The air was heavy with impending rain.

Once or twice, Kaïs stopped to catch his breath. They were utterly alone in these forests, and Linn could not stop looking all around them, trying to discern from the shape of a leaf or the pattern on a bark where in Kemeira they might have landed. They had been sailing for Ton'hei, the easternmost harbor, before everything had gone wrong. Hopefully they had not landed too far from there.

She would find out.

The forests here seemed endless, but soon, Linn felt it: a tug of wind against her senses. She reached out with her Affinity— and there, a dozen or so steps ahead, churning and roiling with breezes from high to low, was a large stretch of open air as far as she could feel.

"To your right," she said to Kaïs.

The trees parted, and *there,* right in front of her, was Kemeira, just as she remembered. Jagged mountains rising through weaving gray mist, crooked pines dotting the landscape as far as she could see. The winter sun, a distant white in overcast skies. The scent of rain, mud, and leaves dancing in harmony with the winds.

Gingerly, Kaïs dropped her to the ground. Linn stood for a moment, balancing her weight on her uninjured leg, simply drinking in the sight of the land.

They set to securing the straps of her chi. Finally, Kaïs drew back. "I will track your Affinity as far as I can."

His words were simple, the unspoken trust in them speaking volumes. No doubt, no questioning, no coddling. This was the soldier's way. The *warrior's* way.

Linn nodded. With Kaïs's help, she turned to face the cliff's edge.

Her musty boots clung to moss and dirt; beyond that, there was nothing but wind and cloud. The fog below wove like a river, a living thing, swallowing the mighty mountains all around. In this moment, she remembered how very much *alive* the world was, how the wind moved in harmony with the mountains and mist around it. How small a part she played in the vastness of existence.

Here, she was a girl with wings.

Linn spread her arms and summoned her Affinity.

And the mountains answered.

As the wind crescendoed to a triumphant roar, her chi bloomed behind her like sails. With a jump, she was airborne, soaring like a bird. It became instinct for her to tug on the winds as one might tug on the strings of a lute, each shift a note weaving an endless, beautiful melody.

A feeling of pure joy blossomed in her belly, working its way up through her chest.

She could sense Kaïs's grasp easing in her mind as she took control. Linn pulled her winds and turned back. She spotted him, a small figure below her, half-visible in the mist.

She flipped and twisted in a sleek loop so that he could see.

His Affinity tightened on hers for a brief moment—a mental nod—before it retracted.

And then she was on her own.

Linn pulled on her winds, and they bore her eastward, to the harbor.

As she flew, the currents around her shifted, bringing with them the scent of the sea. Briny, salty, yet so different from that of Cyrilia: Kemeira's oceans were gentler, sweeter, almost. They were home.

The clouds began to thicken. The small white dot that had been the sun in the sky disappeared, and the air grew cold.

Linn began to descend. Wetness seeped into her clothes, and the world around her grew gray as she dipped into the clouds. When she burst out of them again, the scene below her had changed.

In Kemeira, the mountains spilled into the ocean, their bodies hulking over shores and plunging into turquoise waters. Yet today, crouched in their shadows were ships. She counted six. Their sails stood pale and stark, almost bleached of color in contrast to the cool teal waves of the Jade Trail.

From up here, the ships were no larger than her thumb, but the sight seemed to expand before Linn's eyes until she could no longer hold the images flipping through her mind, faster and faster like the pages of a book:

Enn, soaring before her, hair and chi billowing like the feathers of a black sparrow.

Enn, falling, the wind whistling so *wrong* in the gash that had torn through his chi.

And those bone-white sails with the sigil of three lilies of the valley, leaves and stems sharp as waiting daggers.

Linn gasped. The wind slammed against her, the breezes growing erratic. Her chi rippled in protest; her momentum stalled.

For a moment, she fumbled through the air, a tangle of fabric and limbs and hair.

And then she began to plummet.

Joy dissipated beneath the shadows of fear like the sun sliding behind clouds as she fell, dream shifting to nightmare.

Her Wind Masters had always told her: The higher one flew, the harder one fell. All it took was the smallest slip of concentration. The tiniest mistake.

Linn thrashed, a scream trapped in her chest. She pulled on the wind, but it had gone all wrong, the tune to a song lost in discord. The downforce was too strong—her arms were pinned against her body and her chi flattened, her winds whistling past. She was dropping like a stone. Her stomach emptied with the uncontrollable feeling of free fall.

Through watering eyes and a blur of sky and sea and trees, Linn *pulled*.

The wind beneath her gave way. It slipped into a slanted stream, catching her and slowing her fall. Another tug, and she managed to propel herself sideways. Only now—

The trees loomed out from the mist, so suddenly that she didn't have time to react.

Linn crashed into the forest of Kemeiran pines.

The world went black.

 **7**

Ana was awoken by a whisper in the dark.

She pushed herself up, heart thumping as a key turned in the lock and the hinges to her door squeaked. A light cracked across her vision, so bright that she threw her hands over her eyes. Bile rose in her throat, and through the blurred mist of fear from her earlier session with Sadov, one thought cut through: that they had come back for her, that they would torture her until she was broken and her mind shattered.

But the boots that scuffed across the floor were different, hushed as though their wearer were deliberately trying to quiet them.

"Kolst Imperatorya."

Her breath caught. She knew that voice; it was there, buried in the recesses of her memories. The last she'd heard it was in the dungeons of the Salskoff Palace, the lowlight of a torch flickering like her last hope.

"Lieutenant Henryk?" she whispered.

The world came into focus: the flare of a globefire illuminating the rough-hewn walls around her, the figure that stood in the doorway.

Lieutenant Henryk had aged since she'd last seen him. Stubble grew on his chin and cheeks, and his once-youthful blue eyes were now sunken and somber. She remembered him mostly from how he'd followed Kapitan Markov around in Salskoff Palace, boyish-looking with a snubbed nose and freckles peppered across his cheeks. Now, it was as though she looked at an entirely different person.

Something twisted in her heart at the memories. Somewhere out there, Kapitan Markov's body lay cooling.

"Your dinner," Lieutenant Henryk said stiffly, and deposited the tray he held onto the floor with a clatter. Ana's chest clenched. What if Morganya had done the same thing to Lieutenant Henryk as she had to Kapitan Markov?

But Henryk did not draw back. Instead, he leaned forward, lowering his voice so that only she could hear. "Kolst Imperatorya," he murmured, and there was a tremor to his tone.

Nausea stirred in her stomach and she pulled away. "What do you want?" she whispered.

"I'm not under Morganya's control," he whispered, holding up a placating hand. "Look at me—please, I don't have much time. Markov and I made sure to distance ourselves, in case something happened to one of us." His voice grew thick; he looked away sharply for a moment, hands fisting.

It was this subtle motion that broke her. Ana leaned forward; Henryk reached for her at the same time, and then she was in his arms, clinging as tightly as though he were her anchor in a storm, silent sobs racking her body, nails digging into his shoulders.

Holding on to the only piece of her past that she still had, in this moment.

His voice was thick with tears. "I'm going to get you out, Kolst Imperatorya. I have to go now, but I promise I'll be back."

Don't go, she wanted to beg. It took every ounce of her self-restraint to pull back, to gather her thoughts and drag herself from the fog of fear that was closing in again. "When?"

"Tonight," he whispered. "When they order you to be taken to the interrogation chamber. There's someone who wants to see you. There are other Affinites imprisoned here, did you know that?" From the corridor outside came the sharp clang of blackstone doors, the clicks of footsteps echoing.

"Who?" Ana asked. "Why?"

"I must leave." He was still holding her hand; gently, he squeezed it before letting go, the cold swarming in to take the warmth of his touch. Ana wrapped her arms around herself, hugging her knees to her chest, already beginning to shiver. "Wait for my word, Kolst Imperatorya. I won't be long."

"Lieutenant," she whispered. He paused before the door. "Call me Ana."

In the lowlight of the globefire, he glanced back at her, koffee-brown hair framing his wearied face. His eyes softened for a moment; he nodded. "Ana," he murmured, and with that, he was gone, the blackstone door clicking shut behind him, the darkness swallowing her once again.

Lieutenant Henryk's visit had been a lifeline. Even as she leaned over her cot, shivering and feverish, to throw up whatever cold kashya porridge she'd managed to eat, even as she sweated and screamed in the liminal moments between consciousness and nightmares, she thought of her old friend and his reassuring whisper that he'd be back.

She wasn't sure how much time had passed when she saw him again. There was the clank of keys against her door, and when the guards entered, she caught sight of his face. Through the squadron of Whitecloaks, Henryk's blue eyes found her. He gave a nearly imperceptible nod.

Ana let the guards unchain her from the wall and escort her from her room. It was the first time since she'd arrived that she was stepping outside. The hallways were empty and devoid of windows, torchlight dripping from the sconces on the walls.

They came to a stop before a pair of nondescript doors—blackstone, and carved with the sign of the roaring Cyrilian tiger. The sight called to mind the dungeon doors of her childhood, the darkness that clung to her body like oil, the mounting fear as Sadov turned to her with spindly pale fingers and a wan smile. Ana fought to keep her breathing steady as Lieutenant Henryk's hands held her shoulders: a comforting touch, a reminder that he was here, with her.

The door before them burst open and a pair of Imperial Patrols exited, holding a prisoner between them.

It took Ana several moments before she realized that she wasn't hallucinating.

Shamaïra's face had thinned to the point of skeletal, her once-full cheeks now sagging like parchment over brittle bones. Her hair, which Ana remembered to be lustrously black, was streaked with gray and caked with blood and grime. She had always looked so fierce, crackling with energy and spirit, but now—and this terrified Ana the most—she looked empty. Fragile.

Broken.

Somewhere in Ana's throat, there was a scream: trapped in horror and in pain at what Morganya had done to her friend over the past moon. Anger at herself, for not being able to save Shamaïra.

Yet in that emaciated face, there was something Ana recognized. Shamaïra's eyes: those electric orbs of the lightest blue, the color resembling the heart of flames and glaciers.

They sharpened.

Before anyone could react, Shamaïra burst forward with speed and strength unimaginable for someone her size. The Imperial Patrols, caught by surprise, lost their sense of balance, and Shamaïra slipped from their grasp.

Drooling and snarling like a feral animal, she threw herself at Ana with enough force to knock her off her feet. They crashed to the floor together, skidding several feet across the stone-tiled floors.

There were shouts in the air as Henryk stepped neatly in front of the onslaught of Imperial Patrols, tripping them and using the momentary confusion to buy Ana time. Ana almost didn't realize Shamaïra was speaking to her until she saw the woman's lips move.

"You must stop her," Shamaïra whispered. If Ana had thought her mad just moments ago, there was no question of her sanity now, from her rapid-fire words to the fierce lucidity of her gaze that cracked like blue lightning. "Once she has the siphon, Morganya will seek the Deities' Heart. *Stop her—*"

The Deities' Heart. Ana drew a sharp breath, two questions crystallizing in the maelstrom of her thoughts. "The Deities' Heart?" she repeated, and then: "Have you seen the future, Shamaïra? Does she get the siphon?"

"The half sister," Shamaïra continued, her fingers clawing at Ana's collar. Her bloodshot eyes narrowed a fraction. "She will arrive in Salskoff in precisely seventeen days. You must stop her—"

Ana's chest tightened. She knew exactly whom Shamaïra referred to.

Sorsha Farrald.

Before she could say anything more, the Imperial Patrols were on them, pulling them apart. Shamaïra's screams echoed in Ana's mind long after they took her away.

The Imperial Patrols shoved Ana into the interrogation chamber, and even as they strapped her down to a blackstone chair—just like the one in her own cell—her heart was pounding, her thoughts swirling with what had just happened.

She will arrive in Salskoff in precisely seventeen days. You must stop her—

Ramson had told her Morganya had captured Shamaïra; Kaïs had almost been coerced into betraying them because of it.

The reason for the capture had eluded her until just now.

Shamaïra's rare Affinity to time gave her the ability to glimpse fragments of the future. Should Morganya siphon Shamaïra's Affinity, the Empress would have a pulse on the flow of events. On what was to come.

"A little scuffle out there?"

She jerked her head up. She'd been so deep in her thoughts that she hadn't even noticed Sadov's presence. Today, instead of the rod-straight posture he always adopted for these sessions, he slouched slightly. There were faint bags under his eyes.

The familiar fog of fear threatened to descend upon her—but now, a sharp ray of hope pierced through like sunlight. She wasn't helpless anymore. Henryk was here; Shamaïra was here.

Movement—a flicker of light—drew her attention to the mullioned window in the back. The glass was fogged from condensation inside, and haloed against it was the flickering glow of torchlight somewhere distant.

"I was told you were friends with her," Sadov continued. "Well, with what she once was—before I broke her. Did you know she had a son in the Imperial Patrols? Oh, how easily minds can be shattered when pressed with fears for ones they love."

Fury coursed through Ana. With great effort, she wrested her expression into careful blankness.

Sadov steepled his fingers. "Now, Little Tigress," he murmured. "Won't you tell me where the siphon is?" He smiled again, and those white teeth morphed, and the visions began.

For Ana, they always started in the middle of a dark, cold dungeon. Her heart beat so hard she thought her rib cage would burst; cold slicked her veins like liquid mercury, and sweat wet her shirt and her hair.

There were things in the pitch-blackness: bodies, their blood bright bursts, their limbs a pale tangle. The dead came first: Mama, then Papa and Luka and May, now Markov.

Then, the living. Linn, lying in a broken heap, daggers limp in unfeeling hands. Kaïs, splayed on the ground with a sword pierced through his chest; Daya, expression blank, braids drifting in a watery tomb beneath the wreckage of her ship. And Ramson—light gone from those quick hazel eyes, sandy hair tangled over a bloodied forehead, lips parted and half-curved as though he'd been about to speak her name.

Stop, Ana sobbed, but the word echoed in the prison of her mind, of her own emotion. *Stop stop stop stop STOP—*

"STOP!"

White fingers against dark velvet. Teeth, bared in that same smile.

"Had enough?" Sadov whispered.

It took her moments of gulping in rapid breaths, feeling as though her heart were about to explode, for her mind to piece itself together again. Who she was. How she had gotten here.

What Shamaïra had just told her.

"Just tell me what you know about the siphon," Sadov crooned, "and all this will end."

"I don't," Ana croaked, "know. Where the siphon is."

Sadov's fingers twitched again. Visions danced across her eyes—only this time, they were different: flickering shapes in the faintest oranges and yellows, reminding her of . . . fire.

It was the firelight from earlier, she realized, blinking away her tears and squinting at the windows.

Sadov stood, moving past her to the two windows overlooking the town square. Her back was to them, but Ana heard him mutter, "What . . . ?"

Ana blinked. The light was growing brighter—approaching too fast, at a jagged pace . . . like the fireball that had demolished Ana's ship. On the wall opposite her, shadows danced.

Sadov gave a sudden yelp and dove past her, wrenching open the door. She'd barely heard him yell, "We're under attack!" when the wall behind her exploded.

The entire room rocked; the force knocked Ana's chair to the floor. Time swirled into a slow trickle as the scene before her faded in and out. She was lying on the stone floor, still strapped to the blackstone chair. As her sensations began to return, she felt pain in her head, the stickiness of blood against her face.

Before her, the wall was engulfed in flames. There was a hole where something had blasted through the blackstone, but the flames licked closer with every passing moment. Gusts of hot, acrid smoke billowed over her, and all she could do was squeeze her eyes shut against the searing brightness of fire just steps from her. The place was burning; the heat was unbearable. She was beginning to feel the exhaustion that she'd long held at bay seeping into her bones. She'd spent so long resisting Sadov.

She was so, so tired.

Breathe. She couldn't breathe.

Her body was weightless. Light.

Was it her imagination, or did shouts echo somewhere nearby?

Shadows flitted across the warm orange of her eyelids; dimly, she sensed someone kneeling by her. A hand placed on her shoulder. Gentle.

"A prisoner," an unfamiliar voice said. "She's chained to this chair. Lil, give me a hand—or a dagger . . ." Footsteps; someone else dropping to their knees. Within moments, there was a *crack*, followed by a strange relief spreading over Ana's shoulders as the chair broke and her arms fell to her sides. The blackstone chains were still tight around her wrists.

Someone pressed a hand to her neck. "Non-Affinite," said the same voice—a boy.

"A non-Affinite?" This time a girl spoke, her voice high and sweet. Somehow, it sounded familiar. "Then why is she bound with blackstone?"

Ana opened her eyes a sliver. Through the tangles of her hair, she could see two figures bending over her. One—a boy—reached over to brush her hair aside, and her eyes fluttered shut again. She heard him let out a soft swear.

"What?" the girl said, and then she gasped. "Deities."

"It's . . . it's her," the boy whispered, awe and fear coloring his voice. "What do we do?"

"What do you mean?" the girl snapped. "We save her!"

"But we're meant to rescue the Affinites Morganya has imprisoned here—"

"Well, she's definitely an Affinite. They don't call her the Blood Witch of Salskoff for nothing."

The boy sounded uncertain. "I can't sense her Affinity, Lil. And it's not the blackstone on her wrists."

"We take her to my brother." The girl's tone brooked no argument.

Ana had the sensation of being lifted, of several unsteady footsteps, and then they were outside. The winter air caressed her face.

Sensation flooded back into her limbs as she drew lungful after lungful of fresh, clean air—ice-tinged and winter-scented, just like her empire.

Ana forced her eyes open.

Flames rose from the square they were in, blazing higher and hungrier than any fire she'd seen. The midnight sky overhead churned orange, choked by a mixture of clouds and smoke. Flakes twirled down gently, and it wasn't until they landed on her cheeks, small blooms of delightful cold, that she realized they weren't ashes.

They were snow.

The boy's steps slowed, and he deposited Ana by the brick wall of a dacha in the square. "Lil," he called. "Can you bring him here? I can't carry her much farther."

Ana hated that she couldn't even stand; could barely even summon enough energy to open her eyes.

Her savior knelt before her, watching her with open curiosity. He was a boy several years younger than her, Southern Cyrilian by the looks of his sandy-brown hair and tan skin close to her own. His eyes were a warm shade of gold. They reminded her of liquid honey.

Ana swallowed, pushed her voice past her cracked lips. "Who . . . are you?"

He cleared his throat, blinking and averting his gaze, and then drew a circle over his chest. "Konstantyn Yerdev of the Northern Crimson Forces," he declared. "You can call me, um, Kons. Like my friends. Except you're not . . ."

He trailed off as Ana squeezed her eyes shut, pain lancing along her skull. "Northern Crimson Forces?" she repeated.

"Yes." He nodded, and then as he spoke next, his words were broken by the sound of approaching footsteps. "Of the Redcloaks."

Shock jolted through Ana. She blinked, taking in the boy's outfit for the first time: plain tunic and breeches and cheap commoner's boots, all wrapped beneath a dark cloak with a bright red interior. The Redcloaks were a revolutionary group that had risen against the Empress Morganya, intent to overthrow the monarchy and hand over power to the people. Their uneasy relationship with Ana had collapsed when one of their members—their deputy, Seyin—tried to assassinate Ana in order to destroy the last living member of the fallen Cyrilian monarchy.

The knife wound had hurt less, though, than the knowledge that the Redcloaks were led by none other than Ana's childhood friend, Yuri, once a servant at the Salskoff Palace.

A shadow fell over them. Someone stood behind Konstantyn.

The boy turned and jumped. "Commander!" he exclaimed, saluting as he scrambled aside, revealing the figure behind.

From her vantage point, sitting against the corner of a dacha wall, he looked even taller than the last time they'd met. Flames swirled in the square behind him, eating away at the wooden scaffold and curling into Morganya's flags until they crumbled to ash. With his back to the fire, his face was swathed in shadows, but it was one Ana would have recognized anywhere.

"Red Tigress," Yuri Kostov said. There was no trace of mercy, no glint of forgiveness, nothing of the boy she'd known, in his steel-gray gaze. "I'm glad they found you." From the scabbard at his hip, he drew a blade and lifted it into the air. "This way, I can end things with my own two hands."

"No!"

The cry came sharp and clear. A figure darted out from behind Yuri, stopping between him and Ana.

As the ripple of her cloak settled, Ana saw the outline of a familiar profile: freckled cheeks and gray eyes as fierce as Yuri's, glaring back at him. She was the voice Ana had heard earlier, and Ana now realized why it had sounded so familiar.

Liliya Kostov held up her hand, her mouth a firm line, her eyes narrowed. Her red hair, which had once been tied in two girlish pigtails, now hung at her chin, cut in a clean line at the bottom.

It was as though, in a moon, she had aged years.

Surprise flitted across Yuri's face. "Liliya," he gritted. "Stand aside."

"She's your friend!" Liliya refused to move, her face set in defiance that rivaled Yuri's.

"She's our enemy," Yuri shot back.

Leaning against the wall, head aching and limbs still recovering from the blast, Ana only felt a dull sorrow somewhere in her chest. The last time she'd seen Yuri had been in Goldwater Port, at his family's café, where she'd met his mother and his sister, Liliya, one moon past.

The memory felt like years ago. They had parted on conflicting terms, with Yuri convinced that the Cyrilian monarchy was to be overthrown . . . and Ana unable to swallow that bitter pill.

She needed to speak to Yuri. She needed to tell him . . . to tell him that he was right.

"She saved your *life* during the Goldwater Port Inquisition," Liliya snapped back. "I know you blame her for Mama—"

"Don't." Yuri's voice cracked, and the cold hatred returned to his face. It was such an unfamiliar expression, so jarring on his features, that Ana felt as though she were gazing into the face of a stranger.

She'd sent him a message by seadove one fortnight ago, before she'd begun her journey back from Bregon, across the White-waves. *Prepare for war. The Red Tigress returns.*

It had been a sign from her, a suggestion that they could be allies, that they *needed* to be on the same side in order to bring down Morganya.

Looking into his eyes, she realized the message had been futile.

Ana exhaled. Slowly, she straightened from her slumped position, using the wall for support. It took the last of her strength to sit up, but she clung on. "Yuri," she began. "I understand—"

"You understand *nothing*," he snarled, raising his dagger and pointing it at her. "You've always stood against everything we work toward."

"Listen to me—"

"I'm *done* listening to you, Ana," he snapped, and she heard it, then: the smallest crack to his voice. "I should have listened to Seyin all along."

Cold squeezed her heart. Ana pushed to the single lucid thought that she'd kept throughout all this.

"Yuri," she said. "Shamaïra is here."

His eyes widened; his grip on his dagger turned white. "Where?"

"I don't know, but they have her, and—" Ana drew a deep breath, trying to quell her rising panic and gather her frantic thoughts. Shamaïra. Henryk. They were both still in there, and Henryk had told her Morganya held other Affinites prisoner. "There are Affinites imprisoned here, Yuri—if we don't get them out, then Morganya—"

"Why else do you think we're *here*?" Yuri growled. "The Red-cloaks have been conducting rescue missions all over the Empire, trying to save lives, and all this time *you've* been sailing across oceans—"

The words twisted sharp in her chest, but at that moment, Konstantyn cut in.

"We should go," he said. "I can sense Affinites—over a dozen of them, closing in from all directions." He swallowed. "I can sense Affinites—Inquisitors, over a dozen of them. . . . They're headed our way."

Yuri looked up at the burning scaffold, the wood beginning to collapse on itself. "The rest of the Northern Crimson Forces, have they completed the rescue?"

Konstantyn hesitated. "We were only able to free a portion of the Affinites before Inquisitors were on our tails. Lil and I caused this explosion as a distraction, to lure the Whitecloaks away."

Yuri looked to Konstantyn. "How many Inquisitors did you say are headed our way?"

The slightest pause as Konstantyn closed his eyes to count. "Seventeen."

"Shit." Yuri's voice cracked, and he looked desperately at the mansion, one of its walls broken through and rapidly being swallowed by flames. *"Shit!"*

"Bratika," Liliya cut in, her tone sharp in a way that suddenly reminded Ana of their mother. "If you try to rescue Shamaïra now, we all die."

"Inquisitors," Konstantyn chimed, a tremor to his voice.

But Ana was watching Yuri, the firelight enveloping him like a halo. If there was still one thing they had in common, it was that they both loved fiercely, and would rather die than see their loved ones be hurt. Henryk would be fine, he'd continue playing the part of a loyal Whitecloak, but . . . "Yuri, we *must* come back for Shamaïra—if not today, then another day. What Morganya's planning to do to her—" Her voice caught.

In the stalemate between her and the Redcloak commander, Liliya broke through. The girl swooped forward, looping Ana's arm over her shoulders. "Run now, talk later," she snapped, glaring at her brother.

Yuri let out a sharp breath. His eyes darted from Ana to Liliya, and then to Konstantyn and the fire that raged behind them.

And then he exhaled and jerked his chin at Konstantyn. "Help her. Keep close."

8

Ramson heard very little of the remainder of the questioning. His mind sifted through the words, the scholars diving into alchemy and theories of magek, yet one single sentence echoed through his thoughts like a cruel refrain.

They die.

A numbness had descended upon him—his body's defense mechanisms kicking in, perhaps. He anchored himself somewhere between the present and the past, focusing on steadying his breathing.

In the midst of it, his mind lurched forward.

He needed to—he *wanted* to—no, Ramson didn't even know what he wanted. In the white fog of his thoughts, a single face surfaced.

Fierce brown eyes beneath a sweep of dark lashes, a boldness to the curve of her jaw, and courage to the pout of her lips. She sometimes came to him standing beneath a curtain of softly falling snow; sometimes in the midst of a tempest, her hair wild and wet and tangled, rain running down her face like rivers.

The rational part of him had thought he might never meet

her again. But somewhere deep in his heart, he'd held on to something Ramson Farrald tended to avoid.

Hope.

And as he stood there, watching the scholars finish their interrogation and the Royal Guard escort Ardonn to the dungeons of the Blue Fort, two other words began to circle in his mind.

In theory.

In theory, the siphons' damage could be reversed. And once a siphon was destroyed, the Affinities held within would return to their original owners.

Ramson was one of the last people to go off theories and wild-goose hunts; he had never believed in chasing uncertainty, a deal that wasn't sealed.

But today, right now, in this moment . . . *in theory* would have to do.

The side doors to Godhallem swung shut, Ardonn disappearing through them, small and thin between the bulky livery of Bregonian Royal Guards. He was a dying man, and he'd looked it: defeated, shrunken, the light to his eyes dulled.

What makes you think I have anything left to sing for?

And just like that, a spark flared in his mind. The first rule to negotiating: You had to have something to give. Find the other party's weaknesses or desires and use them. He'd made many a Trade this way in his days as Deputy of the Order of the Lily and Portmaster at Goldwater Port.

Ramson stared at the newly built stone doors where Ardonn had vanished, the wheels in his mind turning fast. Ricyn—a poison found only in the roots of a flower in Cyrilia. He racked his brains, drawing a blank. Olyusha would know, he thought irritably.

Then, he froze.

Olyusha would know.

And just like that, an idea—a plan—bloomed in his head. A risky, dangerous one that might destroy everything he had begun to build up for himself here in Bregon and betray the trust he'd brokered with his king.

"Ramson."

The voice tore him from the midst of his reveries. King Darias was motioning to him from the throne.

Ramson approached. "Your Majesty."

The King's eyes were heavy, the lines on his young face much deeper than his fourteen years of age. "Ardonn gave us much to consider—and for that, I must thank you."

Ramson inclined his head. The motion felt stiff.

"My scholars are discussing; we will continue the interrogation over the course of the next weeks."

Ramson blinked. "Your Majesty?" he said cautiously. "With all due respect, Ardonn himself revealed that he has been poisoned by ricyn. He has a little over a fortnight to live."

"And before his death, we must extract as much information out of him as possible. My scholars will use the knowledge to further their research on magek and siphons. I fully trust that my scholars will understand how to reverse the effects of the siphons." King Darias's eyes pierced Ramson like daggers. "Then, we'd know how to save Ana. Isn't that what matters most to you?"

Once again, Ramson was caught off-guard by the boy king's astuteness. He cleared his throat and looked away. "It is something I care about, Your Majesty."

But his mind raced. By the time they finished interrogating

Ardonn on the details . . . by the time the Blue Fort's best scholars completed their research and located whatever artifact it was
that would balance the effect of the siphons . . . it might be too
late.

They die.

The words clinched tightly around Ramson's heart, refusing
to let go. He felt as though he held an hourglass, the sand trickling from the cracks of his fingers like water. Like blood.

The siphons themselves had taken decades to perfect. Ana
did not have the time to wait for a group of scholars to complete
their research. And if they let Ardonn die, the last source of information on the siphons and all the experimentation Alaric Kerlan
had done . . . would be gone forever.

Darias was speaking again; it took every ounce of Ramson's
willpower to wrench his focus back to the present. Away from the
plan that continued to unfurl in his mind.

"Have you given more thought to your appointment as Ambassador of Trade and Commerce?" the King asked.

Ramson hesitated. Lies swirled at the tip of his tongue; he
could easily spin a falsehood to please the King, earn his trust.
And yet . . . Darias was different. Ramson respected the boy.

He *wanted* to work with Darias, in some ways.

King Darias's lips curled in a wry smile. "I would have thought
someone would be more enthusiastic about being given an appointment at the Blue Fort."

Ramson had never expected to feel so conflicted when handed
everything he'd ever wanted, on a silver platter. *Ambassador of
Trade.* There it was, that feeling of fate, of destiny, reaching out
to him. The memory of a sun-filled sky, a fishing boat, and a boy

with raven's eyes. *Thing is, Ramson, you can achieve everything in this world, but if it's for someone else, it's pointless. Figure out what you want to do in this life. Live for yourself.*

His vision of his future had always held a variation of this: returning to Cyrilia, taking back Goldwater Port, resuming trade and doing what he was best at: brokering, bartering, and bargaining.

The offer stretched before him, gleaming in the sunlit room.

And yet . . . over the course of the past moons, everything had changed with a girl. A girl who'd seized the broken wreckage of his heart and held the direction of his compass stubbornly, unyieldingly.

They die.

He knew what he had to do.

Ramson inclined his head. "Would you allow me some time to think it over, Your Majesty?"

The King leaned back in his throne, chin to knuckle, storm-gray gaze lingering on Ramson. Then he sighed and broke into the first boyish smile Ramson had seen all day. "Of course, Ramson," said Darias. "I look forward to hearing your answer."

Ramson bowed again, long and low, before he turned to leave.

Allow me some time to think it over. In a negotiation, one should always be as specific as possible. Ramson hadn't lied, nor would he break his promise to his king.

He would think it over, very carefully.

He simply had a few other plans of his own he needed to see to first.

Ramson marched out, leaving the King sitting on his throne in a pool of fading sunlight, blue banners of Bregon waving over his gleaming crown.

* * *

The moon was just rising, silver light brushing through the whisper of alder trees and water when Ramson set off across the courtyards of the Blue Fort. King Darias had set him up in the Navy's wing. Ramson had walked this path a hundred times in his childhood, and it always ended up the same: before a tall stone building, gazing through a latticed window or from the shadows, trying to catch a glimpse of his father.

Ramson would never trace these footsteps again.

It was dinnertime, and most of the Blue Fort would be taking their suppers in the meal halls, winding down for the day. In the distance, outlined against the violet canvas of night, were the silhouettes of supply wagons and boats leaving the Blue Fort.

Ramson had spent the evening making preparations, methodically moving every piece of his plan into place. Now all that was left was to execute.

Someone was waiting for him in front of the door to the healer's wing.

"Captain Farrald, sir?" In the semidarkness, First Officer Narron looked immaculate in his Navy uniform, rapier strapped to his hips. He pressed a hand to his chest. "I've pulled out our squad from the mess hall, per your orders, sir."

Ramson jerked his head toward the healer's wing. "Follow," he said briskly, and strode forward, pulling the doors open.

The medic's ward weighed heavy with memories for him, his footsteps sounding loudly on the stone floors. He still remembered the last time he'd been here, after the battle against Kerlan's forces. Ana had been with him. She'd looked exhausted, bloodied, and bruised—but she had been here, by his side. Everything had felt surreal, even hopeful, like the shocking blue of an open sky after a rainstorm.

Torches flickered along the rough-hewn stone walls; there was a distinctly antiseptic smell to the air, the scent of chemicals and alms. Narron's footsteps echoed dutifully behind him; if the young officer had questions, he asked none. This was one of the reasons Ramson had appointed him as First Officer, and why he relied on Narron for his plan to work.

Two Royal Guards were posted in front of the healing chamber doors. They straightened slightly as they took in the flash of his badges, his Navy captain's uniform. "Captain Farrald, sir," they chorused, pressing their fists to their chests.

Of course they recognized him; word must have spread around Bregon that Captain Ramson Farrald was the one who had brought back a highly important prisoner and ward, earning the King's favor.

Power was currency.

Ramson threw them icy looks. "Did the King's message not reach you?" He could sense Narron stiffening behind him.

The guards glanced at each other. "No, sir," one replied. "Apologies, sir."

Ramson let the ensuing pause drag on for several moments. Then he snapped, "Well? Must I ask you to open the doors?"

The guards practically jumped for the brass door handles.

As soon as they were inside and the doors were shut behind them, Narron asked, "Captain Farrald, sir—"

Ramson held a finger to his lips. "Stay there," he said, lowering his voice, "and make sure nobody comes in."

Narron hesitated. Ramson's muscles stretched taut, his hand

grazing against the hilt of his misericord. This was his one chance. He wouldn't let anyone jeopardize it.

It was a testament to how much Narron trusted him, then, that the First Officer only pressed his lips together before turning and taking a position by the door.

Ramson's heartbeat steadied as he turned to face the sickbed. Beneath the latticed window, Ardonn's face was all sharp edges and pale skin, carved in monochrome by the moon. A shadow of a cross fell over his white patient's gown as he slept.

Ramson leaned close to Ardonn's ear. "Wake up," he whispered, then clamped a hand over the man's mouth to smother his cry.

Ardonn thrashed for a few moments, then tensed as Ramson brought his other hand to his lips, motioning for silence. The scholar's eyes flitted wildly between Ramson and the door, pupils dilated.

"If you make a sound, I'll kill you," Ramson said. Slowly, he removed his hand.

Ardonn licked his lips, his breaths coming shallow. "You mean you haven't come to murder me?"

"If I'd really wanted you dead, you would never have made it this far." Ramson folded his arms, and at last, he unspooled the words that would begin to weave together his plan. "I'm here to make you a deal, Ardonn."

The scholar rasped a chuckle. "What deal can you still make with a dying man, boy?"

Ramson finally allowed the edges of his lips to curl. "What if I told you I could save your life?"

All traces of mirth vanished from Ardonn's face. "You should know better than to bluff with that," he said quietly.

"I never bluff. I can get you the antidote."

Ramson knew the look of a man hooked. Scholar Ardonn's gaze lingered on him for several moments, as though attempting to decipher truth or lie from the lines on his face.

"How?" he said at last.

"You remember Bogdan," Ramson said. "The reason I came to Bregon to hunt down Kerlan was because his now-widow tipped me off." He paused, deliberately taking his time. "Olyusha's a beautiful woman. Her laughter can light up the room, and her insults sting as much as her poison."

Ardonn's chest stilled for a beat. Then he exhaled, staring as Ramson continued.

"She's a poison Affinite. Had a gift with plants and metals that made up the worst poisons. But . . . she always had an antidote." Ramson leaned forward. "Let's make a Trade, Ardonn. Surely, you've heard of this term before, under Kerlan's tutelage—a Trade is a sworn bargain between two members of the Order of the Lily. I get you the antidote, and you tell me—in extensive detail— everything about your research on siphons and these . . . *theories* on how they can be destroyed."

The scholar's eyes flickered. "Do I have a choice?"

"You do. You can spend the next fortnight en route to saving your life under my squad's best care. Or you can spend it in agony, being tortured and interrogated at the Blue Fort until your very last moments. One way or another, Ardonn, I'm getting that information from you, and I'd prefer if we worked on the same side."

Ardonn gave a long sigh, his breath whistling faintly. "Risky of you, to gamble so much on . . . theories," he murmured. "Either this girl matters more to you than everything that you've built for yourself here, or you're not the man Kerlan warned us you were."

Ramson's breath stilled. The man was goading him, trying to pry out information that might prove to be useful to him. In a negotiation, one never showed their hand.

He leaned forward with a smile like a wolf's. "I should warn you now that should I find you have overpromised and underdelivered on your grand theories, I'll make Kerlan's worst torture sessions feel like bedtime massages."

The threat rolled off his tongue easily, but inside, every inch of him held taut as he looked into the man's filmy eyes. This was the moment of truth: the indirect way to squeeze out an affirmation from Ardonn that the siphons could be destroyed.

That Ana could be saved.

An affirmation . . . or a denial.

Ardonn's reply seemed to take forever in coming. At last, slowly, the man said: "You should know that our former master taught us to know better than to overpromise and underdeliver. Let me be clear: These theories—on destroying siphons, on the principles of magek—exist, yet as it stands, no scholars in this world bear any empirical evidence that they may succeed. But . . . all that said, there are ways. Ways to allay the effects of a siphon, ways to prolong a siphoned magen's waning life . . . and, most importantly, a theoretical way to save the blood princess, should you wish to pursue it, Ramson Farrald."

Relief surged through Ramson, so strong that he might have knelt and kissed the man's wasted hands right there.

Ramson held Ardonn's gaze. "Then I shall be first to prove those theories true," he replied. "Well? Do we have a deal or not?"

The moment Ardonn accepted, Ramson would be putting in motion a plan that ran directly against the wishes of his king, one that could be considered treason. They had one chance to leave the Blue Fort without arousing suspicion, and that was within the next hour, before the last of the supply wagons and boats set off and the Blue Fort closed its gates for the night.

Ardonn shut his eyes. Even in his emaciated state, wounded with burns, a faint smile drifted over his face. "I'm a scholar, boy. My life's work has been to gather knowledge to advance humanity, and I admit I have an unhealthy penchant for curiosity. If I have the chance to see this saga to its end—whether blessing or tragedy—then I accept."

Ramson held out his hand. "Trade up."

His tongue curled against those words—words he'd said so often while he'd led a different life under a different moniker, as Alaric Kerlan's Deputy. He wondered whether there was a part of him that would always be Ramson Quicktongue, con man and crime lord—whether the monster he'd spent years creating had irrevocably shaped his heart. He brushed a hand against his left wrist, tracing his tattoo of a flower with three bulbs and razor-sharp leaves. The Order of the Lily had indelibly left its mark on him.

So had his father.

So had Ana.

He'd been searching for himself, for the direction to his ship, for so long, yet perhaps the answer lay not solely in one of his identities. Perhaps he didn't have to choose between con man or crime lord or captain. Perhaps he could carve a path different from those ordained for him by his father or Kerlan or Darias.

"Narron," he said, straightening and turning to the young officer. "Help me escort Scholar Ardonn. We're relocating him."

Narron hesitated, confusion and wariness scrawled across his face. To the First Officer's credit, he pressed his lips together briefly and brought his fist to his chest. "Yes, Captain." Then, he stepped forward and, without another word, bent to sling Ardonn's arm around his shoulders. Ramson took Ardonn's other arm, and in lockstep, they made for the doors. The two Royal Guards stationed at the door straightened as they exited, clicking their heels together and saluting.

Ramson tapped two fingers to his head and winked at them.

He'd left a letter in his chambers for King Darias to explain his plan—and to ensure that when it came down to it, he would be the one to take all the blame.

"Captain," Narron said as soon as they stepped outside the healer's wing. "With all due respect, sir, explain yourself."

Ramson exhaled, counting the distance between where they were and the waterway, where his ship would be anchored and waiting. "Narron," he said. "You were there during the interrogation. King Darias plans to let this man—the only man who holds all the keys to understanding the siphons—die. And I'm going to save his life."

There was silence apart from their boots scraping against the stone paths as Narron quietly processed this. "You're going to the Cyrilian Empire," he said at last. "That's why you asked me to prepare the ship and assemble the squad."

Ramson's lips curled at the edges. They were passing the Livren Skolaren now; Godhallem was just within sight, and beyond that, the waterway. "I knew I'd made the right choice appointing you as my First Officer, Narron," he said. "You remind me of myself, when I was younger, with all that quick thinking." A pause. "I've left a letter for King Darias in my chambers to let him know that you and the men in my squad were coerced into this. Of course, I'd appreciate your help on this mission, but

I understand if you're uncomfortable—and if I have to sail to Cyrilia by myself, I will."

Godhallem loomed high over them, a shadow of turrets and crenellated walls carved against the night, pockets of light spilling out from its mullioned windows. Laughter drifted out on the cool evening breeze, between the whispers of alder trees and the murmur of water. It would be so easy, Ramson thought, to step away right now and follow the cobblestone path to the doors, into the warmth and golden firelight. He'd accept his position as Ambassador of Trade and Commerce, reshape with his own hands the system that had taken everything from him once, live out a comfortable life in the King's favor. It was everything he'd ever wanted.

Once.

"I suppose, Captain, it would be impossible for one person to man a ship." Narron spoke lightly. "Besides, if you're going to fire me, sir, I'd have to face the wrath of my mother."

Ramson's smile stretched. He'd known he'd made the right choice when he'd appointed Narron as his First Officer. "Well, now," he said. "We wouldn't want that, would we?"

He could swear he caught the ghost of a grin on Narron's face. "No, sir."

They rounded the bend to Godhallem's main waterway. Outlined against the ink-black canvas of the night sky was the mast of his brig, seadragon sigil roaring silver in the moonlight.

When Ramson had instructed Narron to ensure that the ship was loaded, he'd requested that some specific items be packed. Supplies aside, this included an entire roost of seadoves. He'd also put in a special equipment request. "The blackstone armor and weapons are onboard?" he asked Narron, just to be sure.

"Aye, Captain."

Ramson gave a grim nod. "Good. The magen in Cyrilia are . . . something else, altogether." *Especially,* he thought, *those whetted into weapons and cruelty by their mad monarch.* He'd make sure his squad was briefed and fully trained to face Morganya's Imperial Inquisitors—powerful Cyrilian Affinites trained to fight in her army.

Ramson's squad stood waiting for him, shadows lined in silver against the river of the waterway. They clicked their heels together and saluted as he boarded. He inclined his head and gestured at Narron.

Ramson escorted Ardonn to the captain's cabin. The scholar looked drained even from their brief walk across the Blue Fort just now; with a grateful exhale, he lay down on the bed and shut his eyes, his breathing whistling in the silence of the confined quarters.

"Thank you," the man whispered hoarsely, "for taking a chance on me."

Ramson looked down at the emaciated figure without pity. "I'm not taking a chance on you," he said. "I'm giving you the chance to right just a few of the wrongs you've made in your life."

He left and locked the door, then went to lean against the mizzenmast and watch his First Officer brief their squad on the mission. Narron was telling anyone with a morsel of reluctance to jump overboard now, before it was too late.

The boy would make a fine con man, someday.

One by one, Ramson's men turned to him and pressed their fists to their chests.

An entire squad, following him to the ends of whatever this mission brought them. Twelve men on a wild-goose hunt.

Ramson kept his gaze on the horizon as the gangplank was pulled in and the anchor hauled. The sails bloomed, full-bellied in the wind, the sea began to move beneath them, and the clouds began to retreat. He remembered the feeling of standing at the shores of his kingdom after Ana had left, staring out at the waves that seemed to push and pull at the land in an endless rhythm, at a horizon where the sky reached for the sea in all eternity.

He could never live with himself if he simply stayed in Bregon and waited for Ana to die. No matter what their story would be, no matter how it would all end, he wasn't going to make the same mistake of watching the shadow of her ship disappear over the skyline.

His heart was his compass.

He simply had to follow it.

9

Cool orange light across her eyelids, flickering tendrils of shadows. Cold air on her cheeks. And . . . pain.

Linn awoke to the scent of smoke.

She was trapped between the branches of a Kemeiran pine, draped like a piece of cloth. The pine needles jutted into her arms and legs, but besides a few scrapes on her cheeks, her skintight shirt and breeches that King Darias had gifted her as a uniform had absorbed most of the damage.

With a few wriggles, she extricated herself, swinging into a crouch to untangle her chi.

Only, a large branch had torn through it. The fabric bore a huge gash across its center, gaping like an open wound. Linn winced. Like her daggers, this chi had become an extension of herself. She'd kept it strapped to her person since Kaïs had gifted it to her when they'd escaped the Wailing Cliffs together. With it, she'd learned to fly again. With it, she'd found herself.

Without it, she felt . . . incomplete.

Linn freed the contraption from the tree anyway. Strapped it to her, tangled fabric and snapped wood and all. A part of it was for practicality—she couldn't risk leaving any signs that she'd been here—but for the most part, it was for sentimentality.

She'd lost all sense of time and direction from her fall, but it appeared as though an entire day had passed; the sun now slanted over the thick canopy and the breeze had cooled. Her leg, too, was hurting, the pain pulsing. Growing.

She needed to find shelter, and medicine, before nightfall.

Linn turned and began to limp in the direction of the smoke. It came in drifts with the wind, growing stronger, until at last, she found the source.

Against a twilit sky, a dark column of smoke wound into the clouds.

The forest parted before her to reveal a village. Through the thinning tangle of branches and leaves, Linn could make out the gray-shingled roofs, tiles ridged like the scales of a fish, curving at the ends. Clay walls flashed pale between the trees, yet as she approached, she saw that parts of the homes had been singed black.

Closing her eyes, Linn wound her Affinity through the forest and into the dirt roads of the village, between buildings that stood as no more than shadows to her wind.

No movement. Whoever had done this was long gone.

Linn ducked out through the thicket. A mud road appeared beneath her boots, wet from the mist. The village, she now saw, was no more than a cluster of clay cottages and straw huts, tucked between the folds of this mountain.

She pulled on a piece of fabric dangling from her chi and held it over her nose and mouth as she walked through. Burnt pieces of debris and rubble littered the path. Entire structures had collapsed, and the village was still as death.

She wasn't far from the sea, where earlier she'd seen the

Cyrilian ships docked, sails glistening pale as fish bellies in the water. She had the strongest feeling they had everything to do with the ravaged town before her.

Linn heard it before she felt it. A groan; at the same time, the smallest intake of breath against her winds. It came from the inside of a half-collapsed hut.

She hobbled forward, ignoring the sharp streaks of pain up her injured calf. The entrance of the hut had caved in on itself, leaving only a small hole. Gritting her teeth, Linn began to dig. She scrabbled at the rubble until, with a gasp, she freed the last piece.

She leapt through.

In the darkness, there was only the smell of smoke, and a gentle pulsing in the air: the push and pull of breathing.

Linn touched a hand to the hilt of her dagger strapped to her hip. She'd barely taken a step forward when she heard it. A man's voice so soft, so hoarse, it might have been the rustle of the evening breeze.

"Shik'shei tai?"

The words drifted through her mind like wisps of smoke, the sounds so familiar, the syllables curling in a way she hadn't heard in nearly ten years, the vowels lilting in a pattern that was song.

Who is there?

She swallowed. Wetted her lips. "Ke'mei'ra rin," she replied. *A Kemeiran person.* Her tongue twisted clumsily around her home language. It tasted bittersweet, sharp with nostalgia. "I am here to help."

A pause. And then: "I beg you." *Kui'kui-nen.*

Linn approached. It was difficult to tell in the darkness, but it seemed a wooden beam from the roof had fallen, pinning the man beneath. It was a miracle he'd survived at all, she thought as she felt along the structure.

"This may hurt," she advised, bending and wrapping a firm grip around the pole. Then she heaved.

Her calf seared with pain as the muscles clenched; she thought she felt warmth dripping down her breeches anew. With every ounce of her strength, she pushed.

The wooden beam moved. Slowly, painstakingly, it yielded.

Linn staggered, clenching her teeth against the pain in her calf. Cold sweat broke out over her back. Her leg was screaming.

She leaned forward and felt in the darkness for the man. Her hands closed around a skinny arm, and then a second. She pulled, and then, slinging the man's arm over her own aching shoulders, stumbled out of the hut.

The twilight had shifted to true night. Between the clouds, the moon poured silver onto the earth, turning the world monochrome. White was the mourning color in Kemeira, and looking around at the bleached cottage walls, black burns dripping down them like blood, Linn thought the Kemeiran gods might be remembering the dead.

She turned to her rescue. Small but lithe, he sat in the middle of the mud road. His hair was the color of clouds flecked with snow; he looked old enough to be a grandfather, an elder. He clutched his midriff, where a dark stain crept across a coarse cotton robe.

"What happened here?" Her voice was quiet, but it cracked like a whip in the stillness around.

The elder looked up. "They came," he said simply.

"Who?"

"The pale-faces. Hair yellow as straw." For a moment, he

looked distant, as though caught in a memory. "On ships with sails like clouds."

"Cyrilians."

His head still tilted to the sky, the man gave a nod. "They took the Temple Masters," he continued in a rasp. He massaged his abdomen with a hand, eyes closed. "And they ransacked the bookhouse."

"What for?"

This time, the old man's gaze turned to her. Though he bore the placid expression of a Kemeiran god, his eyes were the steel of daggers, midnight-colored like her own. She hadn't realized how long it had been since she'd gazed into a face like hers.

"Whose Daughter are you?" he asked instead. It was the Kemeiran way of saying, *Who are you?*

"Kemeira's," Linn replied steadily. "Daughter of Hu'kian, born to Ko Innen."

It felt strange to say her village name, her mother's name, as normally as though this were an exchange on her way to the fish market. Never mind that there was an eight-year gap in between.

"Then why," the old man said, "do you wear foreign clothes?"

How was she to condense a decade of her life into a single sentence? "It is complicated."

His eyes narrowed. "You know why this old man didn't die back there, when the roof caved in, Daughter?"

A sliver of impatience bit at her. The sky had grown dark; Kaïs would be worrying about her. She needed to find a way to send word to him—or even better, find a chi. She needed to understand why the Cyrilians had burned down an entire village, ransacked its bookhouse. And she needed medicine for her wound, which had begun throbbing in pain again.

But Linn looked at the elder and swallowed her fretfulness. "Pray tell."

"This old man wields flesh and specializes in the art of healing. He kept himself alive by regenerating his own organs." He bared his teeth. His hands stopped moving in circles over his wound. Linn suddenly noticed that the bleeding had stopped; there was only a faint trace of blood on the palm of his hand. "And he could just as easily take yours if he finds you dishonest or a traitor to the kingdom."

The shock of his words froze her for a moment. A Temple Master—he was a *Temple Master.* The order of elite warriors that protected Kemeira—the ones her Wind Masters had belonged to. The position that most wielders in their lives sought to achieve. When she was growing up, the Temple Masters had governed her village, tasked with ensuring stability and prosperity across all aspects of societal life and serving as the representative liaisons between their local village and the central government.

Linn dropped to her knees. Her hands shook as she splayed them out on the ground, pressing her cheeks to the mud. "Shi'sen," she gasped. *Master.* "Forgive me for my disrespect. Eight years ago, my brother was taken by Cyrilian traffickers, and I boarded their ships in hopes of finding him." Her voice cracked. "I have returned home."

There was a long silence as her words hung in the air. Linn might have remained like this, prostrated before the Temple Master for an entire night, as was custom for some apprentices in other Temples.

She felt him stir, the movement coursing through her winds. His hand, steady and strong, came to rest on her head. "Rise, Daughter."

She did; his eyes remained on her for several moments until, at last, he clasped his hands together in a salute. "A Daughter of the Wind, it seems." Her eyes widened; his face broke into a smile that wasn't unkind. "Well met, Ko Linnet. This old man is Gen Fusann. He suggests taking a look at that leg first—and that old injury on your right arm. Come."

She stretched out her left leg and right arm—the one Kerlan had broken, which had still not healed properly. Now that she'd gotten over the emotion of meeting a Temple Master, the pain had returned: a constant feeling that the flesh of her calf was aflame.

Gen's hands were gentle, and each touch of his fingers—quick, light, like a dragonfly skimming over water—sent ripples of relief through her nerves. Barely a minute had passed when he nodded and folded his hands over each other. "The leg wound is gone. Your arm should feel better. Best to rest for the moment."

With incredulity, she realized that the laceration across her calf was utterly sealed, the skin over it nearly as smooth as it had been, bearing the tiny stitch marks that Kaïs had sewn for her. And her arm . . . Linn held it up to the moonlight, her mouth dropping open as she flexed her fingers. Slowly, she removed her cast. The bandages fell in strips onto the ground.

The Temple Master gave a rough chuckle. "Ever heard of the expression 'a peasant girl sees gold for the first time'?"

Linn blushed, lowering her arm to her side. Still, she tapped her fingers against her legs, marveling at the return of their dexterity. "I left in search of my brother before I finished my training. I have heard of the prowess of the other Temples, but I have never seen it."

Something like sympathy flickered in the man's eyes. "The

Temple Masters became aware of the Cyrilian traffickers and began to fight back. But the Kemeiran way is to harmonize, to heal. Kemeirans are fierce fighters, yet their values teach them forgiveness and restraint." His lips thinned. "That is not the Cyrilian way, it appears."

Linn straightened. "Please," she said. "Do you know why they are here?"

"This old man believes they seek knowledge. They ransacked the local bookhouse, kidnapped the Temple Masters. Gen faked his own death . . . and they left him here."

"Knowledge?" Linn repeated. "What kind of knowledge?"

"Only the gods know, Daughter. But word must be sent to warn the next villages . . . if that is not already too late. Word must be sent to Bei'kin, before they arrive."

She swallowed her excitement. "Shi'sen, you make for Bei'kin?"

"Indeed. Old Gen shall walk. And he must start now. It is two weeks and a few days' journey away."

One week. If these Cyrilian ships were the same ones that had attacked hers . . . then they must have just docked. Linn wasn't far behind.

And yet . . .

Kaïs.

A small bud of panic bloomed inside her as she thought of him, standing over the bluffs, watching the skies for her. Would he still be waiting for her? Or would he have gotten worried, and left to search for her?

"Gen shi'sen, where are we?" she asked.

"Shan'hak Village," came the reply. *The Village Beneath the Mountain.*

Linn had no idea where to place it on a map. "If there is a way to find messenger pigeons, I would like to send a message. I have been separated from a friend."

Gen gave a wheezing laugh. "If you can find a carrier pigeon in this village that did not flee from the fire, you may use it." He slapped his knee and stood. "Old Gen cannot afford to wait. He will not stand to see one more Kemeiran life lost to those pale-faces."

Linn's thoughts scattered like a flock of small birds. *Kaïs is waiting for you,* whispered one part of her.

But another, larger part of her realized how important this was: that she'd found a Temple Master who had survived the Cyrilian attacks and had some information as to why Morganya's forces were here. Not to mention, he was on his way to Bei'kin, the northern capital, where Linn's ship had been headed before they were attacked.

Bei'kin was where all the answers lay, where the greatest wielders of the Kemeiran Empire ruled from the Temple of the Skies. Bei'kin was where she needed to go, to broker an alliance between Kemeira and Cyrilia and convince the Temple Masters to fight with the Red Tigress.

Now, with Morganya's forces on their doorstep, Bei'kin lay vulnerable . . . and Gen Fusann could be the key to saving their empire. At all costs, she needed to ensure that he reached Bei'kin to deliver a warning.

Gen put a fist to his palm in a salute, a gesture of thanks. "This old man owes a debt to the Daughter of the Wind for saving his life. It will be paid."

He turned to leave.

Linn shifted her fingers against the hilt of her dagger, frozen in indecision as her heart pulled in two different directions.

At the end of it all, though, she was Kemeiran: born and bred to sacrifice self over the greater good, to protect her kingdom and her people no matter what the personal cost.

I am sorry, Kaïs.

Linn sprang to her feet and raced after the man.

"Gen shi'sen," she said. "Let me come with you."

10

Ana and the Redcloaks made their way through winding streets, the darkness of night cloaking them, the steadily falling snow muffling their steps. They'd drawn far away enough from the mansion where Morganya and her Inquisition stayed that they could no longer hear the shouts or see the flicker of fire churning against snow clouds. The town was empty, a shell of itself, as most towns ravaged by the Imperial Inquisition tended to become. Dilapidated road signs announced Iyenza, a town that Ana recalled was in Northern Cyrilia, about three days' ride from Salskoff.

Her stomach tightened. Her body was battered, bruised, and utterly exhausted, but for the first time in the past few days, Ana felt hopeful. She was out of Morganya's imprisonment, she was alive, and as long as she was alive, she could keep fighting.

At one corner, Yuri turned in to a stable, where three valkryfs awaited them: pale horses with milk-white eyes, their sharp clawed hoofs perfect for travel through snowy mountains, their muscles carved for speed.

Yuri mounted one. "The others'll be on their way to camp," he said to Liliya and Konstantyn. "The wagon's gone."

"Think we provided enough time for a distraction?" Konstantyn asked, untying his own steed.

Liliya gave a sharp nod. "The fire drew them all out. Yesenya and her team had plenty of time to free the Affinite prisoners." She turned and held out her hand. "Ana, ride with me."

If Yuri had any objections to this, he said nothing, only turning away as Ana mounted Liliya's valkryf and settled behind her in the saddle, clutching her waist. The blackstone cuffs jangled awkwardly around Ana's wrists, and she wondered whether Yuri had instructed Liliya to leave them on. Of everyone in the world, he was one of the people who had seen, firsthand, the destructiveness of her Affinity.

Not that it mattered any longer. Under Morganya's imprisonment, the illusion of power was all that Ana had had to defend herself with. Yet with the Redcloaks, who had always viewed her as a threat . . . perhaps her best option was to tell them that she, as of now, was at their mercy.

They burst out into the night, riding at a full gallop, and it wasn't long before the darkened streets of town fell away behind them, shifting to the ice-covered conifers and snowy forestland of the Syvern Taiga.

They rode on throughout the night, Yuri leading the way with a fire flickering in his palm. It wove before them like a syvint'sya snow spirit. They spoke little, their ears attuned to the sounds all around them, alert for any unwelcome intruders.

Dawn was but a wisp of gold between the trees when Yuri slowed. They had reached an outcrop of rock, surging upward in a formation that resembled flames. Trees grew in a tight line before it.

Tossing her hair back, Liliya gave three short, high-pitched whistles. The sound echoed between the trees, fading, easily mistaken for the call of a bird.

From nearby came a response. A figure emerged from behind a tall conifer, pulling down a fur hood to reveal brown braids and fawn skin, cheeks and nose tinged pink from the cold. Ana recognized her—the snow Affinite, Yesenya, who had come with Yuri to rescue her from the Ossenitsva Cross one moon ago.

The girl nodded at Yuri as he passed, flicked a small smile at Konstantyn, and then reached up with a fist and tapped her knuckles against Liliya's. Ana caught Liliya's grin as they passed between two tight rows of conifers. Glancing back, she saw Yesenya's pupils flash white as she turned to the trail they had left. Pinching her thumb and forefinger together, she blew.

Snow swirled from around the girl in drifts, sweeping over their valkryfs' hoofprints until there was nothing left but a blank white expanse. As suddenly as she had emerged, Yesenya retreated behind her tree, falling still.

Branches scraped across Ana's face as they pushed deeper into the thicket. When they broke through the line of trees, the rock formation stood within hand's reach—only, instead of a solid surface, it was split in the middle by a crevice just large enough to fit a single-file trail of riders.

The Redcloaks dismounted, and Ana followed suit. Liliya shot her a smile that wasn't unkind. "Camp," she told Ana.

Ana ducked through the crack in the stones. They were in a tunnel, the walls and ground strangely smooth, as though someone had scraped them. Yuri walked ahead, flame clutched in the palm of his hand, lending light as it had for their entire journey.

"We built this," Liliya whispered to Ana. "We planted the trees, and our stone Affinites made this tunnel."

Gradually, pale light filtered in from somewhere ahead, growing brighter and brighter until Yuri extinguished his flames. A gentle dawn met them, and almost as suddenly as it had started, the tunnel ended, and they were standing in the open on the other side of the rock formation.

Ana couldn't believe her eyes.

They were in a basin, surrounded on all sides by ridges of rocks that rose into mountains, looming between silver-gold expanses of sky and beneath lingering snow clouds. Trees dotted the landscape, and in between them were tents. People were beginning to wake, smoke rising as they lit fires and began to cook meals.

Liliya grinned. "Welcome to the settlement of the Northern Crimson Forces," she said.

Ana looked around them, at the looming mountains. The cold here was deeper, sharper; her breath crystallized in tiny droplets of ice in the air.

"Chilly, right?" Liliya said. "We're near Leydvolnya."

The Ice Port, Ana thought with surprise. It was old Cyrilian folklore that the area around the Ice Port was cursed; the surrounding settlements had been abandoned after villagers claimed malignant spirits haunted its waters, which bled into the Silent Sea of the North.

Yuri turned to them, his mouth a tight line. "Take her to the War Room," he instructed.

Liliya rolled her eyes. "She can barely stand, Firebraids—"

"I told you not to call me that," Yuri gritted out.

"—and besides, what do you think she's going to do?" She

waved at Ana's blackstone cuffs. "Her Affinity's all locked up, and—"

"It's gone," Ana said quietly.

They all looked at her.

Ana summoned the last of her strength, forced herself to speak. "My Affinity," she said, her voice barely louder than a whisper. "It's gone."

She was looking at Yuri, and he was staring back at her. Something flickered in his eyes, like the ghost of an old memory. "What do you mean, gone?" he asked.

"It's what I wanted to talk to you about," Ana said. "It's why I went to Bregon, Yuri—to find out and stop what Morganya's planning. What she can do. What she could do to . . . to Shamaïra."

Yuri clenched his teeth. Shamaïra's name seemed to stir something inside him; emotions flashed across his face. "I need to check on the others who were dispatched to Iyenza—make sure they're all right." He nodded to Liliya. "Lil, bring her to my quarters. I'll be there in a minute." His gaze turned to her, searing. "You'll tell me everything—about your Affinity, Morganya's plan, and Shamaïra. No more hiding the truth, Ana."

Liliya's cheer seemed dampened as she led Ana through the camp. The girl kept glancing up at Ana, as though she might break apart at any moment.

The Northern Crimson Forces were slowly waking, people emerging from their tents sleepy-eyed and barely glancing at them as they passed by. There were entire families here, Ana noticed, and she couldn't help but marvel at how easily Affinities were used, as though they were a part of daily life. Here, a water Affinite was shoveling snow into a cauldron; with a touch of her fingers, the snow turned to water, which she distributed between her siblings to drink. There, an earth Affinite taking clumps of rock and spinning them in his palms. When they grew still, they had become gleaming, glass-like figurines, to the delight of his children.

There was so much unbridled joy in their freedom, and the scenes roused an old ache deep in Ana's chest. May would have fit in so well here. She could imagine her friend sitting on the ground, a gaggle of children gathered around her as her small hands fluttered like butterflies, weaving magic and making flowers grow from nothing but mud.

Liliya caught her looking and beamed, perhaps eager to divert the subject. "It's amazing, isn't it? A lot of them have never been able to freely use their Affinities throughout their entire lives and are just learning. Konstantyn's been holding sessions to teach them. He's a provyod—a yaeger," she clarified, "though, here, we call them *provyods*."

Provyod, thought Ana. *Guide*.

It was a lovely and symbolic gesture, more conducive to the nature of their powers, which consisted of the ability to connect to and influence other Affinities. Kaïs, a yaeger who had taught her much of how to use her Affinity, would have fitted this description better. Their original name, *yaeger*, meaning *hunter*, had been popularized by the Cyrilian Imperial Patrols.

"Provyod," Ana murmured. "I like that." She turned to Liliya, and this time she had the strength to muster a tired smile. "I like this place."

Liliya's grin was tinged with pride. "This camp is proof that

Affinites and non-Affinites can coexist peacefully," she said. "Yuri's been working on the philosophy of the Redcloaks and our revolution"—she crossed her eyes and waggled her brows— "which are *really* boring when he gets into one of his lectures, but the camp here managed by the Northern Crimson Forces is basically the kind of world we want to make."

Her words rang heavy in Ana's head, along with a budding realization: This was the type of world *she* wanted to make, too. One where a small earth Affinite could sit on a sidewalk and grow flowers. Where a young blood Affinite could look at her own two hands and realize the tremendous amount of good she could do with them, instead of seeing her power as something wicked, an abomination she would spend years trying to bleed out of her body.

Ana looked away, shielding her eyes against the brightening sky. "How did you come to join the Redcloaks?"

Liliya's smile slipped slightly. "Goldwater Port was taken over by the Imperial Inquisition the day you left. Mama sent me and Yuri away before they closed off the city. We were going to lie low for several weeks, and she was going to send us a snowhawk once things cleared up. But . . ." She swallowed and turned away. "They killed her."

The sentence knocked the breath from Ana's lungs. She remembered the cheerful yellow wallpaper of the Kostovs' family restaurant; the feel of Raisa's sturdy, firm hands as they'd helped bandage a wound; her bright laughter as she'd told Ana stories from Yuri's childhood.

"I'm so sorry, Liliya." The words fell from her lips, small, inadequate, a drop of water in an ocean.

The girl blinked rapidly, staring ahead. "That's why I joined the Redcloaks. Because this?" She exhaled and swept a hand before them. "This is the world I would have wanted to live in with my mama and my bratika. Yuri left us so young only because he was an Affinite and he was safer apprenticed at the Palace. I'm here so that will *never* have to happen with another family again."

The words sounded so familiar, Ana could have spoken them herself. She swallowed at the ache in her throat as she watched two Affinite children chase each other around, one shooting puffs of air from her hands while the other sent small blades of green grass whirling from her palms.

"But I think what happened with Mama affected Yuri the most," Liliya continued quietly.

Ana's attention snapped back. "What do you mean?"

"He was the one who saw her body. He'd gone to Novo Mynsk on a scouting mission. When he came back, he was . . ." She shook her head, frowning. ". . . different. Darker. I can't really explain it. But he's my bratika—I felt it."

Ana thought of the way he'd looked down at her as one might a piece of dirt on their shoe, the passion and emotions he'd once worn so clearly on his face hardened to something cold, unfeeling.

As they walked, the tents around them began to turn from small sleeping quarters to larger ones, some even installed with windows of sorts. The casual clothing and fur cloaks around them shifted to the livery of Redcloaks: black boots and black cloaks that flipped bright red on the inside. They had to be nearing the command quarters of the campsite.

Liliya slowed. "We're here."

They'd reached a large tent somewhere at the center of the camp. A black-haired boy leaned against a conifer, his facial features smooth, resembling those of the Aseatic kingdoms. He straightened as they approached.

"This is Lei," Liliya said. "He's a silver Affinite and our resident lockpicker." She gave Ana a rueful smile. "He's going to get those awful chains off you."

Tentatively, Lei took Ana's wrists, careful not to touch the blackstone. In his hands, he held a clump of silver. He squeezed his eyes shut and the metal began to morph like liquid, twisting like a silver serpent. It flowed from his palm into the keyholes in the cuffs, filling them.

Then it hardened.

With two neat clicks, the blackstone chains fell away. Ana flung them to the ground, rubbing her wrists, which had been chafed red and raw.

"Thank you," she said quietly, and turned to Liliya, clasping the girl's hands in her own. "And thank you, Liliya."

"Just promise me one thing," Liliya said seriously, those light-gray eyes so similar to Yuri's. She leaned closer, and a conspiratorial smile broke on her face. "I'm trying to start this campaign of having all the kids around here call Yuri 'Firebraids.' Promise me you'll help out?"

Ana laughed out loud. It had been so long since she'd felt this kind of joy, the sound came as a surprise.

At that moment, amid the people bustling around them, Yuri strode into sight. His hair was mussed, gleaming red in the sunlight, and he looked harried but somehow even more energized as he finished a conversation with a few other Redcloaks.

He glanced up as they approached, and his expression grew dark.

Liliya looked to Ana, her grin fading slightly. "I'm off on other duties," she whispered. "Good luck. If my brother bullies you, you let me know, and I'll show him who's boss." A wink, and then the girl turned and wove through the tents, disappearing from sight.

Ana's smile dropped as she turned to follow Yuri toward his tent.

If only it were that simple.

The interior of Yuri's tent was large, crammed to bursting. Trunks were heaped at the edges, overflowing with tomes. Crates had been turned into makeshift chairs and tables, and on them were an array of scrolls and charcoal pencils. Fireglobes, both used and new, littered the place. In one corner was a roost of snowhawks, their pale plumage sleek in the firelight where they rested. They chirped softly, awaiting letters to be sent.

Yuri took a seat at one of the crates. He followed her eyes, his face turning at once defensive. "Sorry it's not Salskoff Palace. We're not exactly overflowing with funding at the moment."

"I didn't say anything," Ana replied shortly.

"I know what you're thinking."

It was this assessment of her character, the implication of their closeness, that unmoored her. A reminder of what they had once been, and what they had become.

Yuri motioned at one of the other upturned crates. "Take a seat." He was shuffling papers on the makeshift table, drawing out space for them, doing anything but meeting her gaze.

Ana sat, studying the snowhawks at the other end of the room as she waited. The birds cooed softly and stirred, blinking intelligent eyes, and as she watched, one soared in through the tent flap with a rolled-up scroll attached to its leg.

She turned her gaze to Yuri and said nothing. When, at last, he looked up at her, he paused. They hadn't had the chance to be this close to each other in so long, and she watched him take in her face, the bruises on her cheeks and scratches on her flesh, her new sickly pallor and the rings beneath her eyes.

Yuri let out a breath, and something in his expression melted. "Deities, Ana. What happened to you?"

She attempted a smile. "If you've ever wondered what happens when someone loses their Affinity." The joke struck hollow, scraping against her chest, and she was once again reminded of the abyss inside her where her Affinity had once been.

Yuri frowned. "I don't understand."

She began recounting to him her discoveries in the past moon, of how the Kingdom of Bregon had been embroiled in a decades-long scheme to reproduce siphons, deadly weapons capable of transferring Affinities, and how Morganya had planned to seize that technology, unbeknownst to Bregon. Then, she delineated her journey to Cyrilia, her capture by Morganya, and what she had learned during her imprisonment.

"And now, the siphons are still missing with Sorsha Farrald," Ana finished quietly. "If they reach Morganya . . ."

"She'd be invincible," Yuri finished. She could see thoughts warring in his eyes: that they *shouldn't* be conversing in strategy, that they were meant to fight on different sides of a war. Yet curiosity won out, and he asked: "Is there a way for you—and the other Affinites—to get your powers back?"

It was the question she'd asked herself in the stretches of sleepless nights. The one that drifted back to haunt her thoughts when she found herself unoccupied for a moment.

"I don't know," Ana admitted. "But this is related to what

Shamaïra told me last night." Her heart clenched at the thought of the friend they'd left behind. They had been so close, yet not close enough. "She seems to believe the siphons will make their way to Morganya. And that if that happens, Morganya will not hesitate to siphon Affinities—Shamaïra's, and those of other Affinites—to make herself infinitely powerful."

And once Morganya had the siphons, she would search for the Deities' Heart—whatever that was.

This, however, Ana kept to herself.

Yuri stood and began pacing, speaking his thoughts aloud. "We rescued a number of Affinites from her holding cells in Iyenza last night—it was why we were there in the first place. They told me the Imperial Inquisition was preparing to transport them to Salskoff in the next few days." He looked up at her, understanding dawning on his face. "Our scouts reported that Morganya's been arresting all Affinites found to oppose her and her regime."

The news was chilling, confirming her worst fears. "She wants to siphon their Affinities, growing her power while destroying her enemies in a single blow," Ana said quietly. "She could take the power of all those who oppose her and bestow it upon those who are loyal to her. She could take as many Affinities as she wanted, without limit."

Yuri's hands fisted. "So we must find the Farrald girl." His gaze sharpened, the fire returning to those familiar coal-gray eyes. He was focused intensely on her, his stance leaning toward her, hanging on to her every word.

This was her chance.

Ana nodded and began to unspool the threads of her strategy.

"King Darias—the Bregonian monarch—is currently recovering the research done on these siphons. He is meant to provide an update soon." She watched Yuri cautiously, taking in every shift in every line of his face. "The King put together a task force of scholars dedicated to unearthing the research that was done on these siphons in the past decade."

Yuri frowned at her. "So?"

"We need to cooperate with the Bregonian government. I returned with a thousand of their troops under my banner, before Morganya attacked." She did not mention that they might all be lost—that the only thing she had left of them was the garnet amulet Daya had gifted her, hanging around her neck. "Help me reach them, Yuri, and we'd have an army to help us seek out the siphons—and put a stop to Morganya's plans before . . ."

She trailed off. Yuri's expression had shifted, his eyes narrowing. "*Your* forces," he repeated. "You want me to help you reach your forces—forces you secured with the backing of the Bregonian *King*—so, what, you can attack the Northern Crimson Forces and destroy us to take the throne? Another monarch, stepping on our backs to wear your gilded crown?" He stood, his jaw clenched, and in his eyes, Ana saw a shadow of the man who had drawn his dagger to kill her back at Iyenza.

I think what happened with Mama affected Yuri the most. Liliya's words echoed in her mind. *He was . . . different. Darker.*

He blames me, Ana thought with sudden clarity. In his eyes, it was the monarchy's fault for the way the world was. For the suffering of Affinites, for this war and the casualties it brought.

And she was its very last living and breathing symbol, still sitting before him, alive, where his mother was not.

The thought stung, that someone who had once meant the world to her could despise her with such passion. And if she could not win him over right now, all was lost.

Ana leaned forward. "Yuri," she said, her tone softening. "I'm not fighting so I can take back the throne."

He blinked.

"Shamaïra told me that Sorsha Farrald will reach Salskoff precisely two weeks from now. We will need to stop her from handing a siphon to Morganya, at all costs. And for that, we need an army." She paused, forming her tone to soothe. "If I can reach my troops, then together, we can stop Morganya before it's too late. And if we can stop Morganya, then we can work to begin building a world we want." She shifted, leaning to draw back the flap of their tent. "A world like this, right here."

The inferno in Yuri's expression calmed to flickering flames. He looked away and exhaled deeply. "I want to believe you, Ana—"

"Then believe me," she said earnestly.

Yuri folded his arms across his chest, and she suddenly noted how corded they had become, the skin on his hand crossed with new, raw scars. "You want to know how I really feel, Ana?" he said at last. "I resent you."

For a moment, she couldn't breathe.

"I resent you, and what you've done to our empire," Yuri continued. "If you hadn't been so intent on taking back the throne, we could have worked together from the start. We could have stopped Morganya from launching the Imperial Inquisition. Our empire needn't have burned. And my mother needn't have died." His jaw clenched for a moment, and he drew another deep breath. "It's all too little, too late, Ana."

She would rather have taken a knife to the ribs than listen to him speak like this. The air was suddenly frigid, piercing, her lungs turned to ice.

Everything he said was true.

"I know," she whispered, and her voice broke. "I resent myself for that, too."

Yuri looked up, the inferno of his expression calming to flickering flames.

The room blurred, her eyes stinging and an ache rising deep in her throat, but Ana kept speaking. If she didn't, this tentative moment between them would fade, along with her chances of convincing Yuri.

"You remember May," she continued. The ache in her chest welled. "She was the first friend I learned to love. Besides you."

Yuri was silent. The pause between them was soft as a held breath.

"There was once when I woke early in the morning, and she was gone from my bedside." Ana closed her eyes, pulling on the memory, gently, gingerly, lest it crack and all the pain and sorrow she had kept buried beneath come pouring out. "We were sleeping in an abandoned dacha, and it was cold—in the middle of the winter. I panicked, of course, but when I looked outside the window, there she was." She could remember the image so vividly, so indelibly was it seared into the deepest parts of her heart. "Sitting outside on the fresh-fallen snow. She'd brushed some aside and cupped her hands around the smallest seedling that had sprouted from the ground. And the plant was growing, right before her hands—the leaves turning green, the buds blooming into flower." She drew a sharp breath, and the words slipped from her lips: "It felt a little bit like magic, watching her."

There was so much she would give to return to that quiet morning, when the sun was but a silver whisper across the horizon, its light so distant that it felt as though the entire world had fallen away but for her and May and the magic of that flower.

Ana opened her eyes, the memory dissipating. "I want to make that world," she said, and she found that she was no longer crafting her sentences to convince Yuri. She turned, and found him staring at her, that crease between his eyebrows, that golden-red glow to his hair. "I want to make a world where a small earth Affinite can sit on the sidewalk and make a flower grow. I owe it to her."

They looked at each other from across the table, and the tent with all its open books and messy parchment and makeshift furniture seemed to fade before them. A gentle breeze stirred in from the open tent flap, bringing with it the sound of laughter and song.

It tasted like hope.

Yuri loosed a breath. Ana thought she glimpsed the shine of tears in his eyes as he stood and began pacing the perimeters of his tent. She pretended to look away as Yuri swept a hand across his face. He'd known May; when she had been held prisoner by Alaric Kerlan as part of his Affinite trafficking scheme, Yuri had worked with her to free the Affinites and destroy the Playpen.

May had been the girl to spark this revolution. Now, she was gone.

It was up to Ana to finish what her friend had started.

"All right," Yuri said. He stepped back in front of her, hands clasped behind his back, conflict blazing in his eyes. "The Redcloaks will work with you to intercept Sorsha Farrald and take these siphons back. But that's it. You'll be at our mercy. You'll obey every instruction I give you. And you won't speak of your movement—of the Red Tigress—while you're with us."

The proposal was bittersweet, but it was a start.

Ana stood and held out her hand. She noticed Yuri's gaze drifting to it as he reached forward, likely taking in how the bones jutted on her wrist and how wan her skin had become. A shadow of emotion flitted across his face, there and then gone. He pressed his lips together and said nothing as he shook her hand.

Then, as quickly as though she were the one who held fire in her hands, he let go.

"All right, then," he said grimly. "Two weeks for us to form a plan and get to Salskoff. We stop Sorsha, and we rescue Shamaïra."

The sun was bright and high in the sky when she stepped outside.

Ana tipped her face to the heavens and sent a prayer, not to the Deities or to any gods.

This is for you, May. I'm going to finish what you started.

11

With every day that passed, the hope of finding Kaïs again diminished. Linn walked in silence with Gen, through bamboo forests and stretches of pine trees that had once rung with birdsong and the hum of cicadas.

The birds had fallen silent, the cicadas still.

Gen made quick progress through the mountains, sturdier and nimbler on his legs than a Kemeiran mountain goat. Linn had thought herself fast, but she found herself admiring the Temple Master's steps, the way he never misplaced a single toe. He would stop and squat on the ground, swiping fingers across mud, patches of grass, and leaves, and bringing them to his nose. Sometimes, he licked them and muttered to himself.

On the third night, they happened upon another abandoned village. Charred black. Linn's throat knotted as she passed the crumbling houses, knowing full well what had happened. Knowing full well what lay within those walls.

Gen stopped to inspect certain buildings. The Temple Master kept his eyes closed, his hands clasped in meditation before him. Searching, Linn realized, for any living victims of the destruction the Cyrilians had wreaked upon this village.

Gen grunted. "We draw close to the invaders."

They stopped by a house that had completely burned. He bent to the ground and picked something up. A tome, miraculously unscathed amid all the destruction.

Gently, the old Temple Master dusted it off. The pages fluttered silver in the moonlit night. "They came to our bookhouse first, too. They took our Temple Masters." His eyes narrowed. "It is clear they seek information that Kemeira stands to protect."

Linn thought of the Temple Masters that Gen said the Cyrilians had kidnapped from his village. "Then we had better hurry."

The night wore on. Gen walked silently, his hand held before his chest in the same meditation pose as earlier. Every now and then, he glanced up at the stars, holding his hands before his eyes in a measurement of direction.

They came upon the camp suddenly. One moment, Linn was focusing on placing her feet over an extremely slippery patch of mud; the next moment, she felt stirrings in her wind ahead. She froze in place, tuning in to the vibrations like a spider on a web.

Ahead, Gen, too, had stopped. The Temple Master's eyes were closed, his hands clasped before him.

Linn's hands went to her daggers. She sensed figures cutting through the air, moving in the vicinity ahead. She counted. "Twenty-six people," she breathed. "About thirty paces ahead."

Gen cracked open an eye. His lips arced in cunning; he shook a finger at her. "Twenty-nine, Daughter. You are losing your touch."

Heat crept up Linn's neck. She was rusty, her training having been cut off at a young age. Her wind-wielding skills were nothing like they should be.

"Can you tell," the Temple Master continued, "how many soldiers?"

Linn closed her eyes, blocking out all other senses. Focusing, as her Wind Masters had taught her, solely on the movement of air. The currents. The breezes. How some of them curved against the figures, delineating sharp edges and hard armor, others soft cloth rippling gently in the night. "Four Masters," she said at last. "Twenty-five soldiers."

When she opened her eyes again, Gen was grinning at her. "Good," he said. "Now, follow."

They stopped when they were near the edge of what appeared to be a clearing in the forest. A small glow came from between the trees. Linn recognized it: the light of globefires—an invention unique to Cyrilia. She crouched, watching the shadows flicker, listening to the voices that drifted to her.

From their vantage point, they could make out a circle of soldiers dressed in the ubiquitous livery of the Cyrilian Imperial Patrols: glittering gray armor with tomb-white cloaks. Their backs blocked Linn's view, and it was only when one of them shifted that Linn realized what they stood around.

In the center of the circle were four Kemeiran elders: two women and two men. They were dressed in plain cotton robes, adorned with a black silk belt at the waist. Blackstone collars gleamed around their necks.

Temple Masters.

A Whitecloak stepped forward and prodded one of the women with a foot. Anger stirred in the pit of Linn's belly. "Are you going to talk, or are we going to have to make you?" he growled.

Ana had always spoken the Cyrilian tongue with an air of grace, the lilting and rounded vowels falling like song from her lips. When this Whitecloak spoke, however, the language sounded oily, covered with slime in a way that made Linn's stomach twist.

He leered down at the Temple Master, a small woman who might have been Linn's mother's age. Tufts of her long gray hair had escaped her braid, and a blue bruise was blooming on her left cheek.

"The yellow dogs don't speak our language, Myroslav." A woman spoke; her hair glimmered gold in the globefire light, her armor silver. "Let the translator handle it. It's why the bastard's here."

Linn's fingers wrapped tightly around her knives.

Gen shi'sen watched her. "This Daughter speaks their language?"

Linn nodded. "They speak of an interrogation." She paused to listen. In the clearing, a Kemeiran man had stepped from the ranks of the Cyrilians. And as he began to speak in Kemeiran, she realized exactly what he was: a trafficking victim, brought back here to serve as their translator.

It was like looking into a mirror, watching the young man's Kemeiran features remain stone-dead as he murmured to the Temple Masters, then turned to the Whitecloaks. He switched seamlessly into Cyrilian, but she could hear it: the smallest edge of an accent that the Northern Empire hadn't managed to wipe away.

Just like hers.

She frowned. The words barely made any sense to her. "They ask about . . . relics . . . of the Deities—the gods. The center . . . no, the core . . . of the gods, I believe." Her Kemeiran was rusty; she stumbled over the big words. "The Temple Masters do not yield."

Gen's face shifted as quickly as melting water. "The Heart of the Gods?"

Linn's head snapped to him. "Yes," she said in surprise. "You know it?"

The old Temple Master's expression shuttered, like a shadow falling over the sun. "That is troubling."

Linn had found that whereas Cyrilians and Bregonians tended to exaggerate in their speech, Kemeirans reveled in subtlety and understatements.

Her chest tightened. "Why? What is it?"

Gen turned to look at her, and this time, his expression was dead-eyed and calm, the sharp blade's edge of a warrior. "Listen carefully to me, Daughter. No matter what happens here tonight, you must promise Gen one thing. Go to Bei'kin. Warn the Temple Masters that these Cyrilian invaders seek the Heart of the Gods."

"But is the Heart—"

A cry rose from the clearing. Linn snapped her head back. The gold-haired woman had grabbed one of the female Temple Masters and splayed her hand on a rock. Without hesitation, she raised her dagger and swung it down. Linn heard the crack echo across the clearing, saw red spurt across the stone.

The Temple Master bent over, teeth gritted and face twisted in agony.

The gold-haired Cyrilian stepped back, wiping her face in disgust. "Deities curse them," she spat. "Getting blood all over my cloak."

Linn's hands shook on the hilts of her daggers.

"Are you ready, Daughter?" Gen whispered. His eyes shone, dark as the deepest circle of hell. "Are you ready to dance with Gen?"

Linn had only a moment to process her confusion before Gen moved.

Quick as a viper, the old man uncoiled and sprang forth. He clasped his hands behind his back and, to her horror, walked right into the middle of the clearing as though he were going for a morning stroll. Linn bit down a cry, frozen in indecision as she watched.

The Whitecloaks didn't notice him until he was several steps from them. And then one of them looked up, stared at Gen for two, three seconds, before addressing him.

"Oi! What in the—who are you?"

In response, Gen's weathered face cracked into a smile. He lifted his hands, and that was when Linn understood what he meant by *dancing*.

When Gen began moving again, he looked completely different. It was as though the old man Linn had encountered had been only a shadow of the soul inside. Shoulders straight, arms out, muscles corded, graceful as though guided by the touch of the gods themselves, Gen stepped forward like a snake shedding skin.

The first Imperial Patrol he came across sliced a sword through the air with enough strength to sever a man's head. Linn blinked, and Gen had bent backward, his expression placid as he watched the blade curve harmlessly overhead. In an extension of that same move, he swung round.

The Wind Masters had taught Linn that fighting was the act of wielding and giving—the pillars that founded Kemeiran culture and principles. Action and counteraction. Harmony.

Gen's arm lashed out like the head of a snake, whipping across the Imperial Patrol's neck. A single bite, so fast that it was a blur.

The Imperial Patrol fell to the ground, his sword clattering uselessly to his side.

There were shouts from the other soldiers as they drew their weapons.

The Temple Master moved through them like water past rocks, weaving and wending, giving and taking, never striking first, always standing last. Time seemed to slow as he spun in a dance of his own, and as Linn watched, her disbelief turned to incredulity. At least four decades her senior, and the old man moved twice as fast as she.

Between the flash of blades, Gen shot Linn a smile. He raised a hand and beckoned at Linn.

Are you ready to dance with Gen?

Linn swept her fingers over her knives. They leapt into her palms as she began to run, her feet flying into a blur beneath her, the wind whistling in her face and whispering at her back.

Linn burst from the clearing and leapt into the fray. For a brief, glorious moment, she was airborne, a mere slip of a shadow in the night as the Imperial Patrols continued to fight below her.

And then she was landing, her knife sinking into its first mark, parting flesh and spilling blood as red as cinnabar. She'd leapt away even before the soldier crumpled, already making for her next opponent. Dodge. Swipe. Duck. Stab. Tuck and roll.

She leapt up, her back to Gen, knives out as they circled together, yin and yang, in perfect harmony. Linn was panting, sweat beading at her temples. Behind her, she could sense Gen's chest rising and falling faster. They had taken out ten thus far. More closed in; an ocean of gleaming gray armor and pale white cloaks.

Gen moved with her with a seeming instinctual sense as to where the blades were and where each soldier stood. This was true mastery of his ability, Linn thought, to be able to detect movement of exposed parts of the Imperial Patrols' bodies—faces, necks, and hands—that were not encased in a thick layer of blackstone.

Then came a sharp swipe out of nowhere. A slash of pain across her cheek. Warmth, dripping.

It threw Linn off-rhythm. She stumbled. The half second cost her; another blade came out of nowhere, cutting across her abdomen.

She hissed in pain, jabbing back, her dagger finding its mark. Bodies of Imperial Patrols lay before her, but still, they closed in . . . still, there were too many. . . .

"Shi'sen," she gasped. "You must go, without delay. I cannot expect to hold them much longer."

"Listen carefully," Gen said from behind her, his words coming fast, urgent. "In the Bei'kin Bookhouse, there lies a tablet carved in jade. It holds the secret to the Heart of the Gods. It must not fall into their hands. Understand?"

"Gen shi'sen—"

"Gen told this Daughter to prepare to run. Now . . . *run*."

"No! I cannot leave you—"

A Whitecloak appeared out of nowhere, his sword arcing toward her arm. Linn heard the whistle of metal through air, saw its glint in the torchlight, too late to dodge—

"Stop."

She sensed the blade's cold kiss against her neck. Poised, like a scorpion's sting. Waiting to strike.

"No, we don't want to kill them," that same female voice continued. "Question her and the old cur. Ask them why they're here."

Linn kicked out, but multiple sets of arms and legs pinned

her down, the cold armor crushing her painfully. She blinked, and a face swam into view: pale skin, framed by hair like spun gold. Eyes colder and crueler than ice.

"You yellow cur," hissed the gold-haired Imperial Patrol Linn had seen earlier—the kapitan, by the looks of the badges on her armor. "You cost me half my team."

Linn spat in her face.

The blow came sudden and harsh. The world spun; she saw stars, and when she blinked the blackness from her eyes, the kapitan had drawn out a sword. "You slit-eyed deimhovs better learn to behave," the kapitan crooned. "I take particular pleasure in the pain of your kind."

Linn's stomach twisted. She'd known these types of people— barely human, reveling in the pain of others. Her traffickers— they'd looked at her like a slab of meat, like a pig to be used and abused, slaughtered at their whim or fancy.

Out of the corner of her eyes, she saw Gen lying on the ground. A long sword impaled his abdomen, rising into the night like the marker of a grave. Around him lay the bodies of the other Temple Masters, their pale robes fluttering like phantoms in the night.

Horror crept through her veins, freezing her like ice. With Gen dead, she didn't have a chance against these soldiers. She would never know what this unit of Imperial Patrols had come to her land for; she would never find out what the Heart of the Gods was. It might have been a crucial piece of the puzzle to Morganya's plans—and it would die here, with the two of them.

"Ask her who sent her," the kapitan snapped at the Kemeiran translator, who stood to one side, fear bright in his eyes. They were expecting her to be a Kemeiran spy, perhaps an apprentice to the Temple Masters. The truth, though, they would likely never believe.

At this, Linn laughed. That laugh turned into a scream as the kapitan brought her heel down on her hand and ground it into the dirt.

In the mist of her pain, Linn felt cold steel against her neck. "You slit-eyed deimhovs are all the same to me," the kapitan snarled. *"Worthless."*

A stroke of her sword and she would have proved her point right there and then—if not for the deep voice that rang out across the clearing.

"I would not do that if I were you."

A shadow shifted in the trees. Then, out of nowhere, a dagger hissed through the air. It struck a Whitecloak who stood right next to the kapitan; Linn felt the thud of his body on the ground.

The kapitan raised her sword, and in that moment, Linn acted.

Summoning the last of her strength, she tucked and rolled, grabbing the daggers strewn on the floor. She pivoted and struck out. The close brush with death had cleared the fog from her brain, focused her energy. Her mind was sharper than a sword, her entire body strung together in perfect harmony as she whirled. A dance. She was dancing. Action, counteraction. Yin and yang.

The other half to her song was across the clearing: carved like the statue of a god, hair ink-black under the moon, eyes lethal as blue flames.

Kaïs.

The clearing had become a graveyard of bodies; Kaïs was engaged in combat with one of the last remaining Whitecloaks. From behind his back, though, a silhouette stole toward him.

The kapitan had her sword out, lifted to kill.

Linn sprang.

She caught the kapitan in midair; they tumbled to the ground, a tangle of limbs and sharp metal. Linn rolled to avoid being cut by the Whitecloak's blade. With a back kick she'd learned from her early days in training, Linn rolled over the kapitan.

She pulled her elbow back and gave the woman a solid punch on her cheek. Her knuckle connected with bone; she heard a crunch, saw the splatter of blood and what resembled a tooth on the ground. *This is for Gen,* Linn thought. *For the Temple Masters you tortured. For the innocents you slaughtered.*

The kapitan knocked a hand into Linn's face and shoved. She was heavier and bigger than Linn; the impact sent Linn wobbling.

Linn shifted tactics. She somersaulted to her feet, clutching her knives in both her hands. She was battered, bruised, and bleeding freely from the wound on her abdomen inflicted by the Whitecloak earlier—but no matter. As long as she had her blades, she could not be stopped.

"You bitch," the kapitan snarled. "Do you know who I am?"

"No," Linn replied in fluent Cyrilian. "And I do not particularly care."

"So it speaks," the Imperial Patrol sneered. "Well, I'll have you know that you face First Kapitan Karinya of the Cyrilian Imperial Patrols." She paused and spat out a mouthful of blood. "No need to ask where a creature like you came from."

Linn only gave her a cool look. She'd worked for these types of pale-faces back in the days she'd spent under indenturement; they were all the same. Born with faces like marble and hair like gold, and they thought they all wore crowns on their heads and were entitled to palaces.

"Pitiful deimhov," the First Kapitan continued. "I have the Deities on my side. I will wipe you from the face of this world like the stain you are."

Linn lifted her own daggers. They were small, but they were sharp. "I do not need your gods," she replied, surprised to find her voice so steady. "I am human, and I have strength enough."

The First Kapitan pounced. And Linn thought of everything her Wind Masters had taught her, of how she'd watched Gen dance earlier.

She yielded to the woman's sword, shifting ever so slightly to step out of harm's way. And then, in an extension of the same movement, she kicked out.

The woman screamed as Linn's foot slammed into her stomach.

Linn knelt over the First Kapitan, holding her blade against the woman's neck. "What is the Deities' Heart?" This time, she used the Cyrilian words she had heard them say earlier.

The First Kapitan's face cracked into a bloodied smile. "You'll never stop us," she leered. "You think we're the only unit deployed here? Think again."

Linn hesitated, her blade hovering over the woman's skin.

A silhouette flashed; pain exploded in her side, and she slammed onto the mud. Linn struggled to her feet as another Whitecloak lifted his weapon to her head—

—and a tall, burly figure stepped in her path. Kaïs's sword made a sound like a knife slicing through fruit. The man expired in his arms.

Several paces away, the First Kapitan was crawling, reaching for her sword. Kaïs stalked toward her. Before Linn could call out, he slashed his blade through the woman's back. The First Kapitan fell to the ground and lay still.

Linn pushed herself to her feet. "No," she gasped. She stumbled; Kaïs reached out and caught her. "You should not have . . ."

His expression was tight as he wound a hand around her back to steady her. "She deserved worse."

"She had valuable information we needed," Linn choked out.

A pause. "I'm sorry," Kaïs said. She remained silent, staring at the body of the kapitan and the information she'd held that was now lost to them forever.

Linn closed her eyes briefly. "The fault was not yours," she said, and pushed away from him.

Before them: a clearing of cooling bodies, Cyrilian soldiers and Temple Masters alike. In their midst was Gen, silver hair fanned out over the mud.

Linn knelt by the fallen Temple Master. Somehow, even in death, he looked graceful. His robes were pale, nearly white in the flickering lowlight, and Linn thought again of how white was the color of mourning in Kemeira.

Her eyes pricked. He'd saved her life; he'd been the only connection she'd made in her homeland. She touched a hand to his cheeks, the skin papery and cooling beneath her fingers. "I am sorry, shi'sen," she whispered.

Gen had known of the Heart of the Gods . . . the Deities' Heart . . . whatever it was that Morganya's forces were here for. He'd needed to protect it so badly that he'd given his own life.

Linn closed his eyes. Pulled the sword from his chest. Folded his hands over the gaping wound. Her fingers brushed against something hard.

A lacquered wood token fell out from his palm: smooth, worn from age, with an intricate carving of a multistory building. A scroll was engraved on the flip side, Kemeiran characters written in beautiful, sweeping strokes. *Bei'kin Shiu'gon.*

"Bei'kin Bookhouse," Linn murmured. The pendant was attached to two red threads, presumably which Gen had used to fasten it to him. Linn stared at those red ribbons for several moments, her vision blurring.

No matter what happens here tonight, you must promise Gen one thing. Go to Bei'kin. Warn the Temple Masters that these invaders seek the Heart of the Gods.

Kaïs took her injured hand and began wrapping it in a torn cloak. "You worried me," he said. "I began searching for you two hours after you did not return. When I found your tracks, and subsequently saw the Imperial Patrols' tracks, I thought they had taken you." He paused. "Why were they here?"

She tilted her head, the lacquered wood token clutched tightly in her hand—the one Gen had healed. "Have you heard of the Deities' Heart?"

A shake of his head.

"Me neither," she sighed. "I believe they were searching for it. They were torturing the Temple Masters for information." She thought to the First Kapitan's words. "And there are more of them coming."

Kaïs's eyes were slightly narrowed. "I studied the tracks on my way here. This resembles guerrilla warfare. Small units of twenty or so soldiers dispatched in secret."

Linn met his gaze. Her mind hurtled forward, even as the adrenaline in her body began to dissipate. "Might it be . . . something related to the siphons, in that case? Did they mention anything to you . . . back then?"

It was still a tender memory, the fact that Kaïs had nearly betrayed them in Bregon. He'd been coerced into it by Sorsha Farrald, who had been working with Morganya all along; they had captured his mother, Shamaïra, and tried to use her against him.

Kaïs shook his head. "No. But that does not preclude the possibility that this is related to the siphons." He exhaled. "I am sorry, Linn, for killing our lead."

"You saved my life. Besides . . ." She raised the lacquered token. It gleamed in the moonlight. "I know our way forward. Have you heard of the red threads of fate?"

"No."

Gently, Linn began to fasten the pendant around her neck. "In Kemeiran culture, we believe all fate is woven together by red threads. That a red thread connects the hearts of those who were fated to meet. That the cord may stretch or tangle, but it will never break." She drew out the knot. The pendant came to rest on her breastbone, warming to the beat of her heart. Linn lifted her gaze to Kaïs, who was watching her, eyes bright. They flicked to her throat, where the red cord dipped into her shirt. "Gen shi'sen's fate is connected to mine. Mine is connected to Ana's. I think . . . I think it is all woven together, Kaïs. Across time and distance and possibility. And it all leads to . . . to Bei'kin."

In the Bei'kin Bookhouse, there lies a tablet carved in jade. It holds the secret to the Heart of the Gods. It must not fall into their hands.

Linn unstrapped her chi from her back—her beautiful, broken chi that had accompanied her through so much. It would serve no purpose now, but she could at least give a bit of the respect due to Gen shi'sen, the master who had saved her life.

Gently, she draped the fabric over his body, smoothing it out. It settled over him like a layer of snow, the color of death.

After kneeling over the other slain Temple Masters to say a prayer, Linn set out with Kaïs. The night was not half over yet, and Bei'kin was still about two weeks' journey out.

Shan'hak had been where the mountain met the sea. Now, they began the steady trek through Kemeiran pine forests along the shore. They spoke in hushed voices as they walked, theorizing on the Imperial Patrols' objectives and the Heart of the Gods, and discussing the next steps of the plan.

"This must be knowledge unique to Kemeira," Kaïs postulated. "Morganya would not send forces across two oceans if not."

"Gen shi'sen knew," Linn agreed. She touched a hand to the pendant pressed against her chest. "The Bei'kin bookhouse should have the answers we seek."

"Let us hope so."

Linn forged forward in heavy silence. Her head was light from fatigue, but she stubbornly plowed through her thoughts, trying to puzzle out the bigger picture. Did Ana know about this? Was she aware that Morganya had sent troops across the oceans in search of an ancient knowledge so powerful that the sages of Linn's land would die to protect it?

Linn knew, in her heart, that she had chosen this path for a reason. It had felt like chance that day when, on the Blue Fort balcony overlooking the Four Seas, she'd accepted Ana's offer as ambassador between their homelands.

Now, Linn recognized with more certainty than ever, fate had guided her hand.

Go to Bei'kin. Relay the message. Protect the jade tablet.

She could only hope she was not too late.

12

The ocean grew hungrier, its waves more violent, the closer they drew to the Cyrilian Empire. With each passing day, Ramson leaned over the mast and watched the water turn paler, the aquamarine leaching out of it as though color were slowly fading from the world. The wind began to tear at the ship with an errant malevolence, battering them long into the night with the silence of blades, and Ramson thought he could begin to understand where the tales of Leydvolnya and the Silent Sea of the North had stemmed from.

His crew was growing restless, and himself, too. The days crawled by, and each morning, he woke only to count down another day. One fortnight was a long time when someone was dying—someone who had come to encompass his world. He thought also of Darias and the Blue Fort, wondering whether the King would ever forgive him.

Ramson made the most use of his daytime hours reading copies of reports that the scholars of the siphon task force had put together, which Narron had obtained for him back at the Blue Fort prior to their escape. There wasn't much in them that he didn't already know: A siphon could accumulate a number of mageks—Affinities—within it, allowing the wearer to wield as many as it held. The mageks remained in the siphon even after its bearer died.

Until, he knew, the siphon was destroyed.

The question as to *how* remained. Ardonn's health continued to deteriorate with every passing day. Iversha's balms and concoctions restored some semblance of life to Ardonn's cheeks, but the man had sunk into a half-comatose state, breaths rattling each time Ramson went to visit him in his stale-smelling quarters. Any attempts at extricating information about the siphons and theories to their destruction was only met with delirious mutterings.

As they drew closer to their destination, Ramson found that instead of the dozens of plans he typically thought out, this time, he had only one, and it was woefully simple. Reach Olyusha, cure Ardonn, find Ana.

Destroy the siphons.

He'd never been on a mission with so little information and so many unknowns. Whether Olyusha had received his seadove. Whether she would meet him at Leydvolnya, whether she would have the antidote. Whether Ardonn would be able to find a way to reverse the siphons' effects. Whether they would even find the siphons in time to save Ana.

One morning, Ardonn coughed out blood. Ramson knew from Iversha's look that the man had barely days left to live.

They were running out of time.

"Land!"

The cry came on the fourteenth day, at the cusp of twilight, from the crow's nest. Ramson had been leaning against the mast, sharpening his misericord; at the call, he straightened, running to the prow. His crew crowded around him, peering over the railings, anxiety and anticipation thick in the evening air. They'd donned their new blackstone-infused armor and strapped blackstone broadswords to themselves, having spent the past fortnight practicing with the new weapons to acquaint themselves with the different weight and texture.

The moments trickled by between held breaths. Then, in the falling darkness of night, they heard a sound, drifting to them from the silent stretch of sea beyond. At first, Ramson thought it was the howl of the wind. Narron stiffened by his side.

Ramson frowned. "You hear that, too?"

It sounded like a widow's lament, rising and falling over the sound of the waves, eerie yet haunting. Almost like a song, only sharper, more ancient, and more ethereal.

More voices rose, and the keening grew into a chorus, a wild melody with no tune but that somehow made sense.

And then Ramson saw the lights.

He'd seen the Deities' Lights in Cyrilia, shimmering over the Syvern Taiga; he'd encountered syvint'sya snow spirits in the deepest parts of the forests. But he'd never seen them this close. They danced over the ocean just beyond the horizon, soft ephemeral blues that sifted like sand in a slow, sensual spiral. They crested and dipped, sometimes falling so close to the water that they disappeared from view for several moments.

In the ocean, something, too, was stirring. Ghostly gleams at first, growing brighter until the entire sea around them was alight in an unending ripple of blues and phantom silvers. The lights flickered with shapes that swam alongside their ship like fish.

Only . . . they weren't.

"Sirens," Narron breathed, leaning over the railing. "I thought they were old legends."

"Old legends tend to surface in these parts of the world," a more seasoned soldier chimed in. He gave them a significant look. "Near the Silent Sea, that is."

Ramson had only heard of the Silent Sea in myths. Bregonians thought it to be a place where the magek of the world gathered—gossenwal, spirits, wassengost, and the souls of their dead before Sommesreven, the Bregonian Night of Souls—but barely anyone who visited had lived to tell the tale of it. Kerlan had once bought a piece of shimmering, iridescent rock rumored to be from the depths of the Silent Sea, small enough to fit in the center of his palm yet expensive enough that its price might have fed a midsized Bregonian city.

He straightened. Magek or not, they were nearing Leydvolnya, and they would need to navigate the waters with all the skill of a dozen Bregonian Royal Navy sailors combined.

"Focus," he instructed his crew, though he, too, felt gooseflesh rising on his arms at the sound of that eerie, bodiless chorus.

They anchored quietly beneath a set of cliffs out of the vantage point of any passersby. A soldier remained on deck to watch the ship; the rest of them descended from the gangplank.

The shores of Leydvolnya were black, the sand coarse and rough, sticking to them like ash. The Whitewaves lunged mercilessly upward, surging onto the cliffs and sending spray into the air. Pale waters raked against black sand, turning a deep shade of gray. Nicknamed the Ice Port, Leydvolnya had once been Cyrilia's northernmost port. Over time, the vicious weather and superstitions had driven residents away, leaving it abandoned—and a haven for smuggling.

The moon was but a ghostly smudge at the edge of the sky as they set out. The cold of the great Northern Empire pierced like ice in his lungs; he'd forgotten just how unforgiving this land could be.

They moved on foot, the new, heavier blackstone livery sinking into knee-deep snow. The fire magen in their squad, Torron, kept by Ramson's side, the light from the flames in his palm lancing over the trees and throwing jagged silhouettes. Narron and the rest of the squad carried Ardonn on a stretcher. The scholar was swathed in thick furs and blankets, his head lolling from side to side. In the lowlight, the man resembled no more than a skeleton.

Ramson kept silent, holding his compass tightly in his hands; only he knew the way to their destination. He'd asked Olyusha to meet him at an old Order of the Lily hideout in the vicinity. It would serve as a temporary base for his squad.

He slowed suddenly, pulled from his thoughts by what seemed like movement up front, between two tall conifers. He heard the crunching steps of his men fade, the intakes of breath; sensed the tightening of muscles as their hands strayed to their weapons.

Ramson squinted. There . . . he saw it, a shadow darker than dark . . . something was watching them.

He drew his misericord and pressed forward.

One of his men made a strangled noise.

The light of their flame had fallen upon the figure, and Ramson immediately recognized it for what it was: a man whose face had bloated beyond the point of recognition, his cheeks purple, spittle trailing a pale line down his face. Someone had propped him up against a tree, tying his hand to a branch in a macabre greeting.

Ramson knew exactly whose work this was. He raised a hand to his men. "Nothing to worry about," he called.

"I don't know, sir," Narron said, eyeing the corpse. "That looks exactly like something to worry about."

"The killer's on our side," Ramson said breezily.

"I wouldn't be too sure about that," came a husky voice, and the next moment, a silhouette appeared behind the corpse.

The past moon had not been kind to Olyusha. Her curls, once golden and lustrous, had been cut to chin-length and tied up with a ribbon; the furs across her shoulders showed signs of wear and tear. Her face had thinned significantly, and there were dark circles under her eyes. Back when Bogdan had been alive, she'd been a woman with laughter that rang gold as the sun; now, her lips were pressed in a straight, narrow line.

Still, Ramson couldn't help the relief that flooded him when he saw her. "Olyusha," he said, stepping forward. "It's good to see—"

The slap sent him reeling. Ramson stumbled back, hand against his cheek, blinking the stars from his eyes.

"One moon I don't hear from you and you expect to waltz back to ask for my help?" Olyusha snarled. She lifted her hand and Ramson flinched, but he saw that she held a piece of parchment—the letter he had sent her prior to departing Bregon. "'Meet me at the old hideout in Leydvolnya. I trust that you'll take care of any less-than-friendly intruders should any still lurk there.'" She flung the letter into the snow. "Give me one good reason why I shouldn't poison you right here, right now."

Ramson thought fast. "I'm here to tell you about Bogdan," he said. Not a lie—he hadn't known how to write her to deliver the news until now, and he'd been deliberately vague in his letter to her.

As he'd expected, the fire in Olyusha's eyes fizzled out. She loosed a sharp breath. "Tell me," she said.

Ramson massaged his face, his skin still stinging from her slap. He was suddenly painfully aware of his entire squad of soldiers watching, slack-jawed, their swords drawn, eyes darting between him and Olyusha as though awaiting his command. Olyusha ignored them, fixing her gaze on Ramson and crossing her arms as she waited.

Gods be damned, this was embarrassing.

"I'll tell you," he said, "after you administer the antidote to the scholar, as I requested."

Olyusha's expression darkened; her features twisted horrifyingly fast. Suddenly, she lashed out at him again. Ramson felt a sharp prick on his neck, then the heat of something spreading through his veins.

"What—?" he started, but then his throat began to close.

"Bastard," the poison Affinite snarled, and Ramson caught the tip of her fingernail, sharpened to a knife's point, reddened with blood and a second clear, glistening liquid. "We made a Trade, Quicktongue. I tell you everything I know about Kerlan's scheme in exchange for you to bring Bogdan back to me. And now you're asking for more, you cretin?" She spat at his feet. "Tell me now, or I'll let the wolfsbane poison take you."

Ramson's chest was beginning to seize; he sank to his knees. Behind, he heard his men make to move for him. He held a hand up, and they fell still.

"Captain," Narron began, but Ramson shook his head.

"Olyusha," he rasped. His larynx was rapidly swelling, his voice disappearing as his vocal cords cramped. Soon, he wouldn't be able to breathe. "Please. The scholar . . . knows . . . Bogdan . . ."

A flicker of uncertainty lit in her gaze. She hesitated. Ramson caught sight of the worn hemp sack she carried with her, saw the twitch of her fingers toward it.

So she did have the antidote to the poison coursing through Ardonn's veins. It had to be in that bag.

His chest constricted, and he finally let himself slump over on the snow. His mind was muddying; he knew the effects of wolfsbane, knew that he would begin to convulse and that everything would be over within seconds.

Dimly, he heard Olyusha swear at him; sensed her shadow fall over him as she stepped past his body to where his squad was gathered. Black spots were beginning to crowd in his vision; air was a distant luxury, and his arms and legs had started to tremble uncontrollably.

Then came an uncomfortable sensation: something sharp pinching his chest, a slow draining of warmth from his body. The cold began to seep back in.

Ramson groaned. A pair of big blue eyes blinked at him and then drew back. "He's alive," he heard Olyusha declare flatly. She straightened, wiping her hands on a handkerchief and glaring down at him in utter fury.

Ramson shot her a weak attempt at a smile. "I'd forgotten how fast wolfsbane works," he mumbled. "Thanks, Olyusha."

"You're getting rusty, Quicktongue." She *tsk*ed. "All right, you bastard. I'll administer the antidote. And then you'll tell me where my husband is."

Ramson crawled to his hands and knees, rubbing his throat.

His head spun. His limbs were weak. "Bring Ardonn forward," he managed.

There was a scuffle from the back, and Narron and three others hauled the scholar's stretcher to the front of the squad. Olyusha pursed her lips as she ran her gaze over Ardonn. The scholar looked as though he was clinging to life, his breath barely misting before his chapped lips, frost clinging to skin that had turned a disturbing shade of white.

"Deities," the poison Affinite grumbled as she hoisted her sack open and began to rummage inside. "How did he get to this state?"

She drew out a delicate bundle of a plant with bulbs covered in scarlet spikes, bright as blood. Ramson and the entire squad of Navy soldiers watched as she leaned over the plant, splitting one of the bulbs to reveal three koffee-colored, patterned seeds inside. With deft fingers, she plucked them out and closed her eyes.

A translucent liquid began to seep out from the pods, pooling against her skin. It was the first time Ramson had seen Olyusha at work, and he couldn't help but share the inhale of astonishment from his squad.

Olyusha deposited the liquid into a small glass vial from her bag and set it aside. Then, she rubbed her hands against the snow and began to draw out liquid from the stalk. "The antidote rests in the stem of the ricyn plant," she said. "But one must first draw out the poison in the pods first, or it contaminates the antidote."

Ramson watched as she lifted a hand to Ardonn. Without waiting for permission, she pressed her finger to his mouth. The flicker of the firelight stained the droplets of antidote orange as they slid down Ardonn's chapped lips.

Olyusha straightened, swiping her hand against her hand-kerchief again. "I'll need to administer the antidote on a daily basis to revive him, until the poison is cleared from his system." She wheeled to Ramson, the little vial of ricyn poison she'd extracted flashing between her fingers. "Now. Where were we?"

A weight fell on Ramson. He remembered the scene so clearly: the hull of a ship, the lantern swaying, the damp smell of wood . . . and the bar of gold that spun above Bogdan, its light refracting on him and spreading on his skin like fissures, as though he were splitting apart from the inside.

Bogdan was dead. And Olyusha . . .

Ramson pushed himself to his feet, careful to keep his expression blank. "Let's talk inside, Olyusha."

The hideout was generously sized: a sprawling dacha with room enough to fit them all. Olyusha had spruced up the inside, Ramson noticed as he and his squad trailed her through the doors. There was an entire pack of globefires and candles, a good supply of firewood sitting by the fireplace, and even some dry crackers and deer jerky that they happily distributed.

Within moments, his men had unfurled their packs and were drying their boots by the fire that Torron had lit, taking turns to use the wash closet. Ramson installed Ardonn in one of the separate bedrooms on a wooden cot with a lantern for light and fire. When he turned around, Olyusha leaned against the doorframe, waiting for him.

In spite of her attempts at nonchalance, Ramson caught the tightness to the edges of her eyes, the way she worried her lips as she studied his face. "Well, Ramson," she said quietly. "You owe me an answer."

"Olyusha." Ramson drew a deep breath, exhaled. "Bogdan's dead."

He wasn't sure what he'd expected—for her face to fall, for her to crumple to the floor—but it wasn't this. Olyusha's eyes narrowed and she nodded, pursing her lips. Through the pain lining her gaze, she threw her hair back and jerked her head at Ardonn. "And that's the bastard responsible?"

"Kerlan was responsible," Ramson said. "He needed to test out a type of weapon. It transfers Affinities, taking them from Affinites and storing them so that the bearer of the weapon can wield them. Bogdan was a test subject. And this man here was a scholar on Kerlan's team conducting the research. He was there the night Bogdan died."

Olyusha kept looking at Ardonn, her jaw clenched. There might have been the shimmer of tears in her eyes, or it might have been the reflection of the torchlight. "So he knows what happened to my husband," she said.

The scholar's chest rose and fell steadily, his face hollowed out to a frightening degree—yet there was finally some semblance of peace to his expression, his brows smoothed out and the edges of his lips relaxed. For a brief moment, Ramson thought of how terrifying it was that a single human being held the keys that could alter the course of thousands of lives—of the entire world.

"He doesn't know everything, but he's the closest we've got to what Kerlan was orchestrating," Ramson said. "Look, Olyusha, I'm sorry. About . . . about Bogdan. And thank you for everything you've done and, well, for not murdering me up until now."

"I was close," the poison Affinite snapped. "And I still could, so don't bother thanking me yet, Quicktongue. I'm not done with you, or with him." Olyusha propped her hands on her hips. "What's with that expression? You thought I'd just let my husband's murderer dance off into the sunset? Do you even know me?"

There was a moment during which Ramson was stunned into silence at this unexpected new development. And then the gears in his mind were turning again, this time recasting his plans with Olyusha—a former Order of the Lily member and a powerful Affinite—in them. He gave a rueful sigh. "Olyusha, I don't know what to say."

"Deities, could it be?" Olyusha rolled her eyes and pretended to wipe a tear from her cheeks. "Ramson Quicktongue, getting all sappy on me? Nay, I recognize that scheming look, you cretin." At this, Ramson chuckled. "I'm not making a Trade with you this time. I'm going to find the answers from that bastard if it's the last thing we do." A pause, and her expression softened. "Bogdan deserved it."

Ramson hadn't exactly been friends with Bogdan—more like uneasy acquaintances, as was commonly the case when working with a gang. You could only afford to look out for yourself. The man had been greedy, pompous, stingy, but Ramson had known worse men, crueler men. The love between Bogdan and Olyusha, it seemed, had been real.

Olyusha drummed her fingers against the doorframe, lifting a fine eyebrow. "So, what's the plan?"

For the first time, Ramson realized the full impact of what he was doing and what he might accomplish. The siphons were a part of Morganya's plan to turn the tides of the world, and as he stood there looking at Olyusha, the consequences were no longer far away. He was looking into a mirror of his own pain: another human being who'd lost someone they loved to this war, to a mad monarch's wild lunge for power.

Who knew, perhaps he'd actually do something good for once in his life.

"We cure Ardonn day by day," he said, "which provides us leverage to force the answers from him."

And Ramson—Ramson would begin his search for Anastacya Mikhailov, Blood Witch of Salskoff and Red Tigress of Cyrilia.

13

The days passed in a whirl of activity as Ana began to work with the Redcloak leadership to put their plan together. Yuri had set her up in a tent next to his commander's quarters—which, Ana noticed, was always crowded with Redcloak guards. They avoided her gaze, but she could feel their eyes on her, always watching. With the loss of her blood Affinity, she was no longer a threat to the Redcloaks—yet the guards never allowed her a moment alone.

And for good reason.

Beneath the façade of cooperativeness she put up, Ana was planning a way to send a letter to Daya and her Bregonian Navy forces—using one of the snowhawks that were kept in Yuri's commander's quarters. She simply needed a chance to get in and out without being caught.

Yet the commander's quarters, the focal point of the camp, remained heavily guarded and bustling with movement even when the night deepened and fires burned bright. With each passing day, Ana felt her chances at kicking her plan into motion slipping through her fingers, her worry for her friend and her forces gnawing incessantly at her. Whether they were safe, whether they were looking for her, whether they had run into trouble.

Whether they were still alive.

Yuri continued to avoid asking her about her Affinity and her health, but Ana noticed small comforts allotted to her tent that others seemed not to have. Her bathwater was always heated by a quiet fire Affinite so that she could soak the cold from her bones at the end of each day; her pallet had a thick bundle of furs; and she'd woken up several times to find the fire in her pit still blazing, with new logs added.

Given Shamaïra's prediction on Sorsha's imminent arrival, Yuri had scouts sent to the nearby ports of Northern Cyrilia to watch for her; several even awaited in Salskoff as a precaution.

"We should leave for Salskoff three days before her predicted arrival," Ana said to Yuri one night over a crackling fire. They slumped against the table, bowls of kashya scraped empty, papers strewn everywhere from a long day of planning. "Shamaïra's visions can change; she can see fragments of time, but it's dependent on a number of different paths. If one of them changes, then the entire vision shifts. We must account for that."

They agreed to split the team in two: one, comprising their most powerful Affinites, to waylay Sorsha and provide a distraction, and the other, the same team that had conducted the rescue back in Iyenza, to break out Shamaïra and the other Affinites Morganya still kept imprisoned. Ana had told the Redcloaks of the secret tunnel to the Palace dungeons located across the Tiger's Tail river—the very one from which she had escaped two moons ago, with the help of Kapitan Markov and Lieutenant Henryk.

On the last night before their intended departure, Ana took supper with the rest of the Redcloaks at the meal pit near the living quarters, letting laughter and conversation wash over her in warm waves. The Redcloak cook had pulled out all the stops today, and Ana couldn't help but see traces of the Salskoff Palace in the dishes: hot kashya, roast venison, grilled beef shashlyk, even sweet chokolad.

It felt like the calm before the storm, sitting before a fire and watching the merriment all around her. Ana took her first bite of food—and that was when she realized it had no taste.

Frowning, she picked up the shashlyk skewer and pulled off another chunk of beef, closing her eyes and focusing. It might have been made of ash.

Bile coated her tongue; she snapped her eyes open, her heartbeat quickening, as she tried to sense if her throat was closing. Nobody else around her had reacted to the food. Across the fire, Liliya tipped her head back and roared with laughter at something Yesenya said; Yuri was deep in conversation with the younger fire Affinite, gesturing animatedly with his hands.

The loss of her sense of taste and her appetite was one of the symptoms the Bregonian medics had warned her of—a sign that having had her Affinity siphoned was slowly taking its toll on her body. She could feel faint ebbings of hunger swirling in her stomach, but the thought of food made her sick.

She stood, glancing at the guards assigned to watch her this evening. They were gathered by the sunwine table, tankards flashing, backs to her.

Platter in hand, Ana turned and made for her tent. She was grateful for the quiet and darkness inside, where she hadn't the need to hold up any fronts for anybody. Where she could sit and close her eyes and be herself—whoever that was—for just a little while: tired, and alone, and vulnerable.

The fire in her firepit was out; everyone was at the feast, with the remainder of guards on periphery duty. When she opened her eyes, she could see Yuri's commander's quarters through the half-open flap of her tent, just twenty paces away. It was dark, silvered only by the moon.

Empty.

Before she could think twice, she put down her platter of food, grabbed a spare globefire from her pallet, and made for the commander's quarters.

Ana lifted the tent flap, holding her globefire before her. In the back, the snowhawks' sleek plumage shone coral, reflecting the lowlight from her globefire.

She stepped inside and let the flap fall as she crossed over to the table. The surface was littered with half-used scrolls and charcoal stubs from their brainstorming sessions. Ana snatched a piece of parchment and charcoal and began to write.

The note was three sentences long, detailing the most important information. Once finished, Ana crossed the room to the roost of snowhawks. The bird she selected cooed softly as she stroked its feathers. She bound her letter to the length of string already attached to its leg for deliveries, then reached back and unhooked the garnet necklace she wore at all times.

The one Daya had gifted her.

"Here," she whispered, lifting it to the snowhawk's beak. The bird regarded her with curious, intelligent eyes and tilted its head to scent the necklace. Snowhawks were marvelous creatures— magical creatures, some said—able to track down prey for long distances by smell. The bird took the necklace in its beak.

Carefully, Ana coaxed it onto her shoulder and brought it outside. The snowhawk rustled its feathers as a sharp, icy wind blew into them. With another coo, it spread its wings and took off, its talons digging briefly through Ana's cloak.

Blood roared in her ears as she hurried back to her tent. The Redcloaks had started singing; she caught drifts of distant song as she ducked inside her tent, the melody soothing and mournful at the same time.

Someone was already there. Ana bit back a cry as Yuri turned to her, the fire he'd lit in her pit lancing sharp and crimson over his features, his eyes searing. "Where were you?"

Ana forced the guilt out of her voice as she said, "I wasn't feeling well, so I left." She gestured at the plate of food she'd set down by her cot. Ramson had once told her that the best lie was one that hinged on the truth. "I can't taste anything anymore, Yuri."

His expression softened. He took a small step forward and held out his hands to her, and it was then that she saw what he carried in them: a small plate of koffee-colored cubes, cut open to reveal creamy insides. Ptychy'moloko: bird's milk cake.

"I saved them for you because I knew they were your favorite," Yuri said quietly. He was silent for a moment, staring down at the cakes. "But I suppose you wouldn't be able to taste them anymore."

Ana moved toward him, grasping the edge of the plate. She took a piece, turning it over in her fingers. It was roughly made, the chocolate bumpy and the cream lumpy, nowhere near the delicacies she'd had back at the Palace. Slowly, she closed her eyes and bit into it. She tasted nothing, yet the gesture reminded her of a Palace she now only frequented in her dreams, of a boy with that smoldering gray gaze who had once guided her across the storm-tossed waters of her trauma and anchored her world.

When she opened her eyes, he stood before her, watching her. Friend, stranger, and enemy in one. Cocoa powder coated the tips of her fingers.

"Thank you," she said.

"So what happens?" Yuri asked. "After we find Sorsha Farrald and take the siphons from her. We stop Morganya. What happens to . . ." He trailed off, gesturing at her.

"I don't know." She'd told herself to focus on stopping Sorsha from getting the siphons to Morganya. But now that they were so close and the preparation work was complete, the inevitable question of what came next weighed heavy on her.

"Ana," Yuri said, and she looked up at his tone. His expression was one of helplessness, of uncertainty, of anxiety, all of which made him appear much younger and much more vulnerable. It was one he'd worn on the many nights he'd sat by her door, watching her cry, her arms raw and bleeding from her attempts to claw out her Affinity.

The one she wanted to remember, at the end of all this.

"Yes?" she said.

Before he could respond, the flap of the tent opened and a cold wind swept in. The shadows in the tent lengthened; the fire flickered, dimming.

"Red Tigress," came a voice, cold and dark as a starless night. "I thought we'd meet again."

Ana spun round. Even in the light of the flames that Yuri had lit, shadows seeped into the corners of Seyin's figure. His hair had grown longer, darker, if possible, hiding his eyes as he watched her. The last time they'd met, the Second-in-Command of the Redcloaks had attempted to murder Ana.

At the sight of his face, a deep fear, cold as the slice of a blade, gripped her chest. Ana pulled instinctively at her Affinity—only to scrape the hollow space where it had once been.

She steadied her breath and held his gaze. "I don't think you expected to see me ever again, Seyin."

He tilted his head. "Indeed," he said. "But things have changed since the last time we met. I was given certain *orders*." His gaze cut to Yuri's, flashing like daggers.

Yuri's expression hardened; the flames in the hearth burned brighter. "Seyin—" he began, but the other boy interrupted.

"I've had a long journey from my station in Salskoff, Commander. Imagine my surprise when, upon my arrival at camp, my shadows sense an intruder in your quarters." Seyin's lips curled as he turned back to Ana with the look of a predator who'd cornered prey. "Tell me, *Red Tigress,* what were you doing in our commander's quarters, all alone?"

The room seemed to hold its breath as the two Redcloaks regarded Ana, one with grim satisfaction, the other with a sudden wariness. Options ran through her head as she looked at Yuri, even as guilt churned in her stomach. Shamaïra's words came to her as though from a distant dream. *A day will arrive when you will be asked to sacrifice that which you hold dearest for the good of your empire.* She could see the Unseer's eyes burning into hers, a fierce, piercing blue that had cut to her soul. That *is the choice you must make: which of the Anastacyas you shall be.*

She was no longer simply Ana, the girl who'd cried herself to sleep, who'd tried to scratch her own Affinity out of herself and clung to the kindnesses of her brother, an old guard, and a Palace servant who was her friend—for that girl was long gone.

She was Anastacya Mikhailov, Red Tigress of Cyrilia.

She had to be.

"You lie," Ana said calmly, meeting Seyin's gaze. "I know it is the last thing you wish, to work with me, Seyin, but telling false-hoods to ruin the goal Yuri and I are working toward will jeopar-dize the good of this empire, this world." She paused, lifting her chin. "I suppose I shouldn't have considered it beneath you."

"The only thing jeopardizing the good of this empire," Seyin said coldly, "is you, *Princess*. I should have put an end to it when I could."

"That's enough, Seyin," Yuri said quietly.

Ana turned to Yuri. "You would keep someone who tried to assassinate your only ally in a position of power?"

Seyin's eyes were unfathomably black; the shadows at his heels rippled suddenly. "You conniving—"

"I said that's *enough*, Seyin," Yuri snapped. He drew a deep breath as the other Redcloak fell silent, but the open look to his gaze was gone, replaced by the caution with which he'd beheld Ana for so long. "We are in an alliance with Ana until we find the weapons she speaks of; my word is final. Now tell me, what news of Salskoff?"

It spoke to the power and trust Yuri held with the Redcloaks that Seyin, jaw clenched, turned to him and, without another word, gave his report. "Morganya's Imperial Inquisition was seen crossing Salskoff's borders several days ago, returning to the Pal-ace. I came as soon as I could."

"Just as the Affinites we rescued told us," Yuri said. "Very well. We keep our plan to set out for Salskoff tomorrow."

There was a beat during which Ana and Seyin glanced at each other. They both spoke at once.

"Yuri, is *he* coming with us—"

"Commander, surely you don't mean *she*—"

"Silence." Yuri held up a hand. The fire in his gaze brooked no argument. "We proceed as planned. Seyin, you will work with the rescue team to retrieve Shamaïra and any other Affinites imprisoned within the Salskoff Palace. Ana will work with me to waylay Sorsha Farrald and retrieve the siphons at all costs."

Seyin's features twisted. "But—"

"*Enough,*" Yuri snarled. "I'll not let your personal vendettas affect our mission. As a shadow Affinite, Seyin, you are crucial for our undercover rescue missions. And you, Ana, with your knowledge of siphons and all that happened in Bregon, are a valuable resource to us. I'll need the two of you to work together for the greater good."

Ana looked at Seyin. There was nothing in his expression that promised fair play in consideration of the greater good.

"Now that *that's* clear," Yuri said, straightening and turning for the door, "I must get back to supper before it ends; they're waiting for me to make a speech." He barely glanced back at Ana, tilting her head in her direction as he added: "Try to finish your food. You'll need the strength. And rest early tonight."

Then, he was gone, and Seyin with him, the firelight steadying and the shadows seeping out, leaving Ana utterly alone.

Ana slept fitfully that night, her dreams plagued with knives glinting in the darkness, of siphons writhing and exploding into a thousand snakes that choked her until she lost consciousness.

She woke to a voice by her ear and to someone shaking her shoulders roughly.

"Ana. Ana, wake up."

There was the flicker of a flame near her face, its warmth spilling over her cheeks. She huddled beneath her furs for a moment, fatigue casting a sluggish net over her. Then, a face crystallized before her: glittering gray eyes and hair bright as fire.

"Yuri?" Her voice was hoarse. "What's going on?"

Yuri's jaw was clenched. He was dressed in full battle gear, with blackstone-enforced armor that he'd obtained for their group of Redcloaks. Ana had specifically requested it, knowing iron would not work against Sorsha Farrald. "A scout has just sent word from Leydvolnya," he said. "They've found Sorsha Farrald."

She dressed quickly as Yuri waited outside. The indigo skies held only the faint promise of dawn as they crossed the short distance to the commander's quarters.

Inside Yuri's tent, the torches were lit; a group of Redcloaks, most of whom Ana recognized by now, huddled over the makeshift table. They'd joined in her briefing and planning sessions with Yuri: There was Lei, the silver Affinite; Yesenya with her snow Affinity; the young fire Affinite; and a lightning Affinite, among others.

"One of our scouts witnessed an unknown Affinite destroying a village en route to Salskoff." Yuri spoke quickly to the group hunched over the map he'd spread out. "The report says . . ." He paused, his frown deepening. "The report says she was wielding multiple Affinities." A chill of certainty wrapped around Ana, just as Yuri looked up, straight at her. His voice was low. "It seems everything Ana told us was accurate."

She gave him a grim smile.

Yuri exhaled and straightened, rolling up the map and tucking it into a rucksack. "Our scouts are tracking her progress. They'll send snowhawks with updates. Ana, you'll travel with me by valkryf." He looked around the table, the torchlight carving shadows under his eyes. "This is it. Let's move out."

14

Ramson pressed his misericord to Ardonn's throat. "Rise and shine," he crooned, and with his other hand, he tore open the moth-eaten curtains that hung limp and dusty over the window. Outside, the Syvern Taiga was but a smudge of silver, morning little more than a dream in the dark of the Cyrilian winter night.

The scholar stirred. In just one night, Ardonn's complexion had improved tremendously: Color had seeped back into his skin like a painting restored, his previously wan complexion regaining what resembled a healthy Bregonian suntan. His eyes fluttered open; he drew a sharp breath, the muscles in his neck tightening. "Pleasant as ever, eh, Quicktongue?"

"That's my job," Ramson replied. Behind him, Olyusha slammed the door shut, her hemp bag slung over her shoulder. She held a new stalk of ricyn in one hand; in the other, she spun the vial of poison she'd drawn the day before. Ramson switched to the Cyrilian tongue for her benefit as he addressed Ardonn. "And what you tell us today will help dictate just how pleasant I am to you."

The scholar swallowed, turning his gaze to the ceiling rafters.

"How am I to know you won't simply leave me to die if I tell you everything I know?" His Cyrilian was rough and halting, the vowels drawing sharper and consonants harsher.

"You can't. But I can tell you now that I will most definitely leave you to die if you *don't*. So." Ramson bared his teeth in a grin. "What'll it be, Ardonn? I want answers on the siphons. On how to destroy them. On all the *theories* you mentioned back in the Blue Fort under interrogation."

Ardonn gave a long-suffering sigh, his eyes darting to Olyusha, who tapped her razor-sharp nails against the glass of her vial. Her ruby lips curved in a smile.

"All right." The scholar heaved another long exhale, as though to summon his strength. "Since you've upheld your end of the bargain, there's no reason for me to hide anything any longer." He wet his lips. "We've established there are traces of magek imbued in certain materials and elements. So, theoretically, there might exist an element—a type of relic—that can manipulate the existence and manifestations of magek itself."

"Which you failed to mention in Bregon," Ramson said pleasantly, though his heart was pounding like a hammer in his chest. He shoved the misericord harder against the scholar's throat. "Go on."

"Kerlan . . . had naval forces scouting as his trading paths expanded across the world, collecting rare minerals and elements that he believed to contain traces of magek—alchemical power—in them. He studied ice and snow spirits, water spirits, sirens, ghostwhales, the Deities' Lights . . . which is how he got his hands in the searock trading business. Well . . . throughout his journeys, he came across rumors of an artifact of magek—one so powerful, it could indeed manipulate magek itself. A . . . core of magek, if you will."

A loud, unceremonious snort came from behind them. Ramson turned to see Olyusha covering her mouth with her hand. She shrugged. "That's ridiculous. I'm no devout worshipper, but I believe in the Deities . . . and all this sounds like old fishwives' gossip."

"Thought you were intent on finding out all about your husband's death," Ardonn retorted through half-lidded eyes. "You think it was old fishwives' gossip that created the tool to change him into a gold Affinite before it killed him, eh?"

Olyusha moved so fast that Ramson nearly missed her. The woman lunged at Ardonn, her face twisted in fury as Ramson caught her against his arms, restraining her and praying that none of those daggerlike nails would scratch him.

"Olyusha," he panted. "Olyusha, *control yourself.*"

Olyusha wiped her chin and spat on the floor at Ardonn's pallet, calling him a string of words that impressed even Ramson. She turned to Ramson, her lips pale and trembling, and raised a finger. "No. You control *him,* Quicktongue, or I'm out."

"It's all connected," Ardonn continued, apparently invigorated by Olyusha's outburst. "When Cyrilia discovered blackstone's properties of magek and used it to restrain and oppress their Affinites . . . that was the first time humanity began to twist the magek the gods had left us in this world into something wicked. And now, we have the same thing, do we not? A mad monarch on the throne willing to do anything to gain the magek that the Deities had." He gazed up at the ceiling, a faint smile on his face, eyes wide. "This is not a tale about gods and monsters, my friends. This is a story of the rapacious greed and boundless cruelty of humanity, and how far we are willing to go . . . for power."

"Cut the bullshit." Ramson turned his misericord back to the scholar's neck. "So, you believe there is some artifact imbued with magek, and that it has something to do with reversing the effects of the siphon. That it can . . . it can control magek itself."

"It is a common theory," continued Ardonn, "among scholars from many lands and kingdoms and empires who have dedicated themselves to the study of magek, or alchemy, or *magic* . . . that there is a core—a source—to the magek of this world. Like a beating heart, it pulses, emitting power that flows into our world. Whoever finds it . . . may be able to control all the magek in this world. To direct it as they please. To take it, to inhibit it. To create it . . . and to destroy it."

Ramson's knuckles whitened against the hilt of his misericord. "You mean it would be able to destroy a siphon?"

"Presumably so."

His breathing came shallow. "So what is this core? Where can I find it?"

Ardonn rasped a laugh. "You think if anyone's managed to find it, the world would still be as it is, boy?"

A cord drew taut inside Ramson. Did Morganya know of this? No one in the Blue Fort had known at the time of Ramson's departure, which meant Ana—wherever she was, on her way to overthrow Morganya's reign—was unaware.

But someone, somewhere, had to have knowledge of this source, this core.

Ramson simply had to find it first.

And then there was the matter of Sorsha Farrald and the lost siphons, he thought with a sudden pang. Alone, the siphons were already unimaginably powerful, with the ability to steal and store Affinities. Indestructible, as far as anyone knew thus far.

Unless Ramson used this core to destroy them . . . and to restore Ana's Affinity.

His heart began to race again as he paced the room, tapping his misericord against his thighs as his thoughts sped ahead. Morganya sought the siphons, yet it was Sorsha who had siphoned Ana's blood Affinity onto the one *she* bore on her own wrist. Ramson needed to find those siphons, wherever they were.

Sorsha had jumped off the edge of Godhallem to escape, yet so far, there had been no reports of a body. And Ramson knew better than to underestimate his half sister.

He had a plan.

He whirled, mind spinning to something else Ardonn had said, back in the Blue Fort's infirmary. "You said there were ways to alleviate a siphon's effects, and to prolong the life of a siphoned magen."

"Ah," Ardonn sighed. "Yes. We fed certain elixirs to the subjects of our experiments to test their limits. Some slowed the effects of a siphon on its bearer—it can be extremely overwhelming to have access to new magek, you see—and some prolonged the life of those whose magek was siphoned from them, though that was never our priority. Those, I can deliver with certainty. But . . . I am no alchemist myself. I will need help from those experienced in the makings of balms, salves, and potions."

Ramson tilted his head. "What about a poison magen?"

Ardonn shrugged. "I will work with what I have."

"Good." He kept his voice even against the tide of relief that crashed into him. Hope, there was hope—now he simply needed to find Ana. "Then I want these elixirs developed as we search for this core of magek."

The shadows on Ardonn's face cut deep. "I should warn you," the former scholar said in a tone that stirred caution in Ramson. "The elixirs will prolong life, yes . . . but there will be pain, and there may come madness. You see, when one wishes to take from magek, one must pay a price. Should you wish to claw back a life that belonged to the gods, that life will be a cursed one. One that drove many of our subjects to the brink of madness, to the depths of despair."

His words hung in the space between them for several moments, haunting, echoing.

A knock on the door rent the silence. Ramson stood abruptly, straightening as one of his men entered. The soldier saluted. "Captain Farrald. Our morning patrol came across tracks in the snow. A lot, sir; seemingly from several days ago."

The practical matter was jarring against the discussion he'd been having with Ardonn. Ramson pressed two fingers to his temples. "Is there a direct threat to our safety?"

"Well, no, sir, but—"

"Then explain to me why you think I care?" he demanded.

"Well, sir," the soldier said. "I thought you'd be interested, because . . . because the bootprints, Captain—they appear to be of Bregonian make. To be specific . . . Bregonian Navy make."

Ramson stopped breathing as all other thoughts fell away. He knew, instinctively, who would have left those footprints.

Specifically, whose army.

Ana.

*   *   *

The footprints were covered in a layer of snowfall a ways beyond the copse of conifers that shielded Ramson's hideout from view. It was snowing lightly, the sky still dark in the early hours of the morning.

Ramson knelt. His patrol had spoken true. These prints were not left behind by a lone traveler or even a squad of soldiers. This was a legion—at least over a hundred in numbers. Beneath the fresh layers of snow, the prints were packed hard as ice, ridges upon ridges etched in a familiar pattern that Ramson would recognize anywhere: the grooves of a Bregonian Navy boot, complete with the pointed metal tip that left a smooth mark at the front.

He steadied his breathing, his thoughts threatening to careen out of control.

"The tracks are leading southeast," his patrol added. "I followed them for a bit, but they're days old."

"Get Narron," Ramson said, "and five more of our men, with supplies. Leave Olyusha and the rest with the scholar and tell them to guard him with their lives." He straightened and turned in the direction of the tracks.

"Yes, Captain Farrald, sir." The patrol saluted, and hesitated. "Will you . . . not wait for us?"

Ramson was already striding away, hand on the hilt of his misericord. "Try and catch up," he called over his shoulder.

By the time Narron and his men caught up, Ramson's thoughts were clear, his gait as steady as the compass in his hands. This was, without a doubt, Ana's army. If he followed these tracks, he would find her. He'd tell her about the core, that there was a way to return her Affinity.

They'd find it, together.

His small team kept up a rapid pace, the boreal forest waking around them as gold rays of early-morning light began to filter in. Yet even the warmth of the sun felt different somehow, *wrong*, the cold deeper than he'd known it throughout the eight years he'd spent in this empire. It was the same feeling he'd had as they'd approached the coast just one day ago, when the ice had pierced his lungs with renewed ferocity, and the eerie song of ruselkya had accompanied the unsettled movement of the Deities' Lights in the night sky. Ardonn had spoken of the world's balance unraveling as humans found ways to manipulate magek to serve their own greed: With blackstone, the Cyrilian Empire had plunged Affinites into decades of oppression and servitude; with searock, Kerlan and his scholars had created siphons that would cause devastating effects if in the wrong hands.

The very existence of those siphons, Scholar Hestanna had said, *is a poison to this world.*

Ramson wondered whether the bone-chilling cold, the uneasy stirs of creatures in the forest, and the agitated paths of the Deities' Lights were a part of the consequences.

It was midday when they happened upon a deserted campsite in a clearing between trees. The snow here was flattened and trampled, and a stack of logs sat in the center, ash fallen around it. Ana and Daya must have rested here with their Navy.

"Do you smell that?" Ramson asked.

"Smoke, sir," Narron replied. "They can't be long gone."

Adrenaline coursed through Ramson as he stalked around the campsite, taking in every detail and hoping to find more. On the other end, the footprints continued—only this time, they were fresher.

"They must've stayed here a few days," Narron said, crouching by the logs and swiping a finger through the soot. He hurried over to the tracks leading away. "These are fresh, sir—I'd say from less than a day ago. And they're leading . . ." He looked up, to the long trail that wound steadily away through the pines.

"Southeast." Ramson gripped his compass tightly, the arrow pointing resolutely the same way. "They're going to Salskoff."

By his estimations, Salskoff was over three days' travel away—two, if they traveled overnight.

"Gird your loins, team," Ramson announced. "We're on a light sleep schedule until we catch up."

"Sir?" Narron said. "Can I ask . . . whose forces are they?"

Ramson looked to the sky, an indelible blue streaked with dusk-gold clouds. "We," he said steadily, "are tracking the Red Tigress's army."

They kept on at a rapid pace throughout the day, at times breaking into a jog. By sundown, when the watery light seeping through the canopy had almost drained away, Ramson noticed the footprints were growing fresher and fresher.

They were drawing closer.

"Not long now. We move throughout the night," he announced to his men. "Follow Narron's globefire. Weapons out. And stay alert."

The boreal forest seemed to change as the night crept on, an ominous wind rising and sifting through the branches. Several times, Ramson thought he heard voices, blending sounds of the flora all around him. There was a malevolence to the air, he thought, one that he hadn't felt before, when he had been traveling through forest with Ana.

It was several hours into the night that Ramson realized they were being followed. It started with a flicker of a shadow at the corner of his eye, one that he dismissed as a trick of the light. And then he heard it: the crunch of a boot, the snap of a branch.

Ramson made a gesture behind his back to Narron. Bending slightly to study the tracks, he noticed a few diverging to the side here and there, rounding through the trees and disappearing from sight.

He swore mentally. Fatigue had worn down his team's attention; they hadn't seen the signs.

Ramson spun around and drew his misericord just as the clinks of swords being drawn and the clacks of arrows being nocked sounded through the forest.

"Drop your weapons!" called a voice. A female voice.

A *familiar* voice.

Slowly, Ramson let his sword fall and raised his hands, turning to face the source of the voice. His men stood frozen, but when Ramson spoke, his voice was calm. "I would've thought you'd be happier to see an old friend again," he said, "Daya."

A pause. From the depths of the trees, something moved. "Ramson?"

He blinked as a figure stepped into the light, the tension in his stomach unraveling into disbelief. She was thinner than he'd last seen her, muddy and disheveled, but her face split into a grin.

"Thank Amara," Daya croaked.

He rushed over to her. She was limping, and there were cuts and scrapes on her face and neck that looked still fresh.

"We've been hiding in the forest," she said, and turned. "You all can come out now!"

Shadows emerged from the trees—Bregonian Navy soldiers, their uniforms worn and dirty. He scanned their faces, and his stomach tightened. "Where is she?" The words left him in a rush. "Where is Ana?"

Daya's face crumpled, and that alone nearly knocked the strength from his legs. "We were ambushed right before we landed. My ship was blown up, most of the others, too—they had trained fire Affinites—and we lost half our crew, Ramson. I couldn't find her in the chaos—"

He looked away abruptly, a terrible pain seizing his chest, the indelible thoughts of *what if* gripping him. What if he'd chosen to sail to Cyrilia with her on that bright blue day one moon ago? What if he'd been there? Would he have been able to save her?

For Ramson knew with a burning conviction deeper than his life that he would have held on to her this time, and never let her go.

". . . and then we received a letter from her." Daya's voice reached him as though from a distance, faint and muted. "Ramson, she's with the Redcloaks. She's going to Salskoff to find Sorsha Farrald."

He looked up sharply. There was a pressure in his ears; his heart slammed painfully against his rib cage as he reached for the parchment that Daya held before him. It fluttered between his fingers as he unfurled it, greedily drinking in every word on the page. He recognized her handwriting: eloquent, Palace-trained, with a flourish and ferocity that pressed itself too hard into the page sometimes.

Ramson might have laughed. Of course she would be alive, and of course she would be fighting. Ana was not the type of girl to let anything get in the way of what she wanted.

He should have known.

Ramson loosed a breath and steeled himself, his attention focusing. *Sorsha Farrald.* "You know, Daya, I'm searching for a half sister of mine," he said slowly, looking up to lock gazes with her. Those familiar umber eyes curved in mischief. "I really ought to teach her some manners."

Daya's eyebrows crooked a challenge. "You and your . . . army?" she said, sweeping a gaze over the handful of his men that stood behind him.

Ramson tilted his head. "Me, and my army equipped with *blackstone-infused* armor and swords," he clarified.

"Excellent," Daya said, and stuck her hand out. "Well, then, fellow Captain, I propose a Trade."

Ramson's grin stretched. "You do learn fast," he said with a wink, and grasped her gloved hand with his own. "By my calculations, we're due in Salskoff by dawn, overmorrow."

Daya hoisted her cutlass higher and turned. "Better keep up, then," she called over her shoulder, and then called to her army. "Swords sheathed, boots laced! We're moving out with Captain Farrald's forces!"

Ramson signaled to his own men. As they began the trek again, the night suddenly seemed less lonely, the sky a little clearer and the stars a little brighter. He'd never felt more certain of anything in his life, with the steady crunch of his boots on snow, the compass solid and warm in his hands, its arrow unyielding.

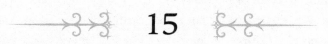

15

They arrived at Bei'kin on the cusp of the fourteenth day of their journey, as the sky began to turn from deep midnight to gentle periwinkle and the trees began to thin. Ahead, between weaving trunks and shifting leaves, were glimpses of the capital city.

Linn's pulse spiked. She'd only been to Bei'kin once, in her childhood with her Wind Masters. It had been to visit the Temple of the Skies, the greatest congregation of Temple Masters in Kemeira. Every wielder from all around the land came to be blessed by them: first as children before they began training, second as graduates initiating into Temple Masters.

But the hazy memories of a six-year-old were no match for the sensations of a young woman standing before the homeland she had been taken from. As though in a dream, the trees parted, jagged Kemeiran pines bowing out to the sight of the Northern Capital.

And what a sight that was. As far as the eye could see was a gleaming expanse of gray-shingled roofs, flowing from one to the next like the scales of a mystical dragon. Red lanterns lent bursts of color where they hung from rooftops, bobbing in the breeze. Golden larches were interspersed throughout jagged street corners.

The government palace stood at the very north like the head of the city, but rising at the city's center like its great, beating heart was the Temple of the Skies. The old legends said that the gods themselves had requested the first Kemeiran disciple to create it, before they ascended back to the skies. It pierced skyward in layers of gray roofing that spiraled upward in concentric circles.

Linn knew from memory, from reading about this temple for so long, that the grounds around it had been penned off in a square courtyard where the Temple Masters came out to pray and conduct their governing sessions with the people. And, adjoined to the structure, she knew, was the Bei'kin Bookhouse.

"It's beautiful," she heard Kaïs say, his voice pulling her mind back to the present. They stood at the edge of the forest, muddy and hungry and tired.

"It is more," Linn said. "It feels as though this land holds a thread to every Kemeiran's soul. And when I am far, it tugs at me insistently. It called me to return, for years."

Yet it was a peace that felt ephemeral. As Linn took in the sight of the capital city, she couldn't help but think of Gen, of the Temple Masters that had died at the hands of Cyrilian Imperial Patrols.

Her heart squeezed painfully as she watched the hustle and bustle of the familiar streets, the colorful tarps propped up and donkey-drawn carts squeaking down the roads. Bei'kin—and the entirety of Kemeira—was in danger, and nobody knew yet.

By her side, Kaïs tilted his head. The sun was just beginning to rise, threading the sky that had turned a tapestry of pinks and corals and violets.

Hope bloomed inside her as light washed over her face.

They had made it. Against all odds, they had arrived. And they were here to bring Gen's message to the Temple Masters.

"Is there someplace we can get food and drink?" Kaïs asked.

Linn licked her chapped lips. Her tongue felt like sandpaper. Kaïs was right—they needed sustenance.

And they had arrived just in time for that.

It was dawn, which meant the Sunrise Market was beginning to open. A dirt road appeared beneath their feet, turning into cobblestones, as though the city itself were rolling out a red carpet for them. Scattered clay cottages turned into neatly lined rows of houses across paved roads, and a passerby here and there turned into a steady stream of people filing out of their doors to begin their days. People, dressed in the same wheat-colored robes, swept their front steps with straw brooms, dusted off the heads of stone lion statues in front of their homes.

Several paused to stare at Kaïs, who stood a full head taller than the average Kemeiran. Most foreigners here were traders, and the Jade Trail connected Kemeira—and kingdoms of the Aseatic Isles—to many other lands across the seas: Bregon, the Crown of Nandji, the Crown of Kusutri, and many others beyond that.

All but Cyrilia, "the Other Empire," as it was known here. The one with which Kemeira had been in a state of inactive, cold war for decades, foreign relations frozen and trade embargoed.

Linn and Kaïs purchased food—meat buns and sweet bean soup—with the Bregonian gold that King Darias had given them. Linn sighed as she bit into her first pork bun.

Kaïs chuckled and handed her the waterskin they'd bought. "I have never seen such an animated reaction from you," he commented. Then he took a bite out of his own bun and made a deep, satisfied sound before popping the rest of it in his mouth. "Though I understand it. I could stay in Kemeira forever, for the food." There was a playful glint to his gaze that made Linn feel warm and golden as honey inside.

They finished their food in several bites, and then Linn asked for directions to the Temple of the Skies.

"The Temple of the Skies?" repeated the meat bun vendor, an old woman with gaps between her teeth that showed when she smiled. "Well, it's just down the Main Road, nine streets away. But it's closed to the public at this time."

"When will it open?" asked Linn.

"Not until noon," the vendor replied, flipping four sizzling dumplings over.

"Noon?" Linn echoed, distraught. She glanced at Kaïs, who was eyeing those dumplings. "That's . . ." *Too late.* Morganya's forces might be here long before then.

The meat bun seller grinned. "Not from this province, are you, girl? You're welcome to take a seat here and wait. My red bean soup's the best on this street and piping hot for a cold day such as this one."

Linn was about to respond when something caught her eye. In the midst of the crowd on the main road was a flash of pale skin, gold hair.

Linn grabbed Kaïs's arm. His expression darkened as he followed her gaze. "Cyrilians," he muttered. "Dressed in plain clothes." His jaw clenched. "Imperial Patrols—I recognize several. These are not the same ones we encountered. This is a full unit."

Linn's hands brushed her knives. A small wind tousled her hair, bringing with it the whispers of Gen's parting words. "We must get to the Temple of the Skies," she said quietly. "We must warn the Temple Masters." Quickly, she relayed the conversation between her and the meat bun seller.

Kaïs's brows stitched together. "Even if we reach it before they do, how will we get inside if it is closed to the public?"

Linn reached to her collar and drew out the small wooden token that had rested by her heart for the entirety of their journey. It swung slightly in the wind, but it might have borne the weight of empires. "This belonged to Gen shi'sen. I believe it will hold some sway with the other Temple Masters." She turned and pointed. "We are only nine streets away from the Temple of the Skies. But if we try to pass by the Imperial Patrols on the same road, they will see us. They will see *you*."

"Maybe that's exactly what we should do," Kaïs said slowly. "Have them recognize me."

Linn frowned at him.

"A distraction," he clarified. "We split. I go after them, hold them up for as long as I can, and you take a detour. Deliver the message."

She hesitated. "There are at least twenty Imperial Patrols to one unit."

Kaïs's eyes were calm, a sparkling blue of sunlight lancing off a stream. "I'll bet they won't put up half the fight you did."

She wanted to tell him no, it was dangerous, that twenty against one were no odds at all. But Linn thought instead of the quiet certainty he'd conveyed to her in his words since the very start of their relationship, back when he'd fought her tooth and nail on top of the Salskoff Palace walls. All along he'd acted with the instincts of a soldier. An unspoken respect, from one warrior to another.

And she would honor him by doing the same.

Linn stood, and he, too, rose to his feet. There was the hiss of metal as he unsheathed his swords, steel flashing in the Kemeiran sun.

He turned. For a moment, she thought of calling after him, of bidding him luck with a Kemeiran greeting, but that would not have been fitting. Neither would a Cyrilian one. And Linn knew no Nandjian sayings.

Besides, he had no need for one. His strength was enough.

Linn turned. She could not fail on her part.

The quickest way through Bei'kin, one of Linn's Wind Masters had once told her, was not by the main road, nor on the ground at all. It was over the roofs. They stretched, curving generously over streets so that the gap between each one was narrow enough to be bridged with a slight leap.

To Linn, the rooftops were freedom. She kicked off against a windowsill in the back alley, caught the low tapering end of the roof, and using the forward motion, swung herself up. Then she was off, sun warming her cheeks, wind streaming through her hair, the city opening before her like a patchwork quilt.

The Temple of the Skies loomed ahead, drawing closer with every step. She could make out the white clay walls of the courtyard, the gray stone and winding streams and trees bending to the wind. Looking farther, she saw the Ever-Burning Torch, flames streaming in the azure sky, and then the Cup of Gold. Kemeiran wielders believed in the unity of the Five Elements that gave root to life: earth, water, air, fire, and gold. Each was present in every single Temple across the kingdom.

Directly facing the road was a set of round courtyard doors, cinnabar red. They were currently sealed shut, gold lion knockers firmly locked in place. Wielder guards lined the outside, stationed every three paces along the stretch of wall as far as the eye could see.

She needed to get past the guards. Instinct told her to make a run for it and leap over the walls. Yet Linn's fingers brushed against Gen's wooden token, resting against her collarbone. She felt the grooves of the Kemeiran characters against her skin, written vertically like a waterfall or a bloom of flowers compared to the Cyrilian script. *Bei'kin Shiu'gon.*

She would not enter the Temple of the Skies, the most venerated location in the entire Kemeiran Empire, like some backdoor thief. She'd go in with a straight spine and honor in her steps.

Linn dropped from the roof, landing evenly on the street. Then, she walked up the steps that led to the gates of the Temple of the Skies.

The guards watched her as she approached. They wore loose silk shifts with silver sashes tied to their waist. There were no weapons visible on them, but that was simply the Kemeiran way: You felt the dagger before you saw it.

Linn touched her fist to her palm in a salute. "Respected wielders, I come to seek an audience with the esteemed Temple Masters. I bring urgent news."

The one closest spoke. His sash was gold, indicating that he held the highest rank among them. "The Temple of the Skies is not open to the public at this time."

Linn inclined her head. "My name is Ko Linnet, wind wielder." She reached into the folds of her shirt and drew out the lacquered token. It hung, spinning gently in the morning light. "I bring urgent news of a potential attack from Gen Fusann."

Recognition flickered in the guard's eyes as he studied the characters on the token, assessing its authenticity. Satisfied, he leaned back with a sharp nod. "You may relay the information to me, and I will take your message to the Temple Masters for consideration."

Linn swallowed. She'd been counting down the seconds since she had left Kaïs, reaching as far back with her winds as possible to feel any stirrings. There was no telling when the Imperial Patrols would arrive.

But this was perhaps the only way.

As quickly as she could, she relayed the events of the past two weeks. "They search for the Heart of the Gods and are on their way to the Temple of the Skies," she finished.

The guard had remained silent as she spoke, his face as still as the surface of a glass-smooth lake. Only his eyes glinted like black steel. "Very well. Wait here." From within the folds of his shift, he drew a set of golden keys. Then, he turned to the doors and called: "High Guard Innen Yunn requests to enter with an urgent message!"

There was a responding call from inside; the High Guard inserted his keys and twisted. Then, he pushed open the red courtyard doors.

That was when Linn felt it. Heard it. The whistle of a blade slicing through the wind at her back.

Linn reacted instinctively. She leapt, pulling on her Affinity, arcing her body. As she flipped in midair, she saw, as though time had slowed down, the arrow shoot past where she had been standing.

The High Guard's hand snapped up; there was a flash of metal, and the next moment the arrow bit into the wall, feathers quivering.

Linn landed and flipped round.

To her horror, a different group of Cyrilians emerged from a side alley. They were dressed in plain tunics and breeches, but as they drew their swords, Linn saw the glint of blackstone beneath their clothing.

Kaïs had delayed the unit they'd seen—but there had been another. *There should be five in total,* she thought, thinking back to the number of ships she'd counted.

Linn made a split-second decision. As one of the nearest Cyrilians raised his hand and a crack whipped across the cobblestones beneath him, she summoned her winds to shove aside the two Kemeirans nearest to the door. They gave way easily, caught off-guard as they defended against the Cyrilian stone Affinite's assault.

The gates were left wide open, with nothing in her path.

Linn hurtled up the steps and darted through the great courtyard doors. She slammed them shut, latching the lock in place—a pitiful attempt at holding back the Imperial Patrols, but anything would help in this moment.

Then, she turned, only to find an entire row of temple guards staring at her, daggers drawn.

They would soon have bigger things to worry about.

Across the clear blue sky, a bolt of lightning streaked downward.

The gates behind Linn exploded, debris showering the front section of the courtyard—burnt wood and chipped rocks and cobblestones.

Perfect. Linn threw up her arms and, in perhaps one of the most dramatic renderings of her entire life, cried: "Intruders! Cyrilian spies! They're attacking the Temple!"

This spurred the temple guards into action. As they leapt forward, weapons drawn and Affinities stirring at their fingertips, Linn slipped past them. At last, the path to the Temple of the Skies was clear. A little ways behind it stood the Bei'kin Bookhouse, paper windows sealed shut between stone pillars, wooden doors closed. A bronze bell hung above it, to be rung at noon each day, indicating the bookhouse was open to scholars and vagabonds alike.

Now, it looked so open, so vulnerable. In Kemeiran culture, bookhouses were revered, near-holy places that even the worst of criminals wouldn't think of ransacking. Such buildings had not been made with war in mind.

Linn turned and sprinted toward the Temple of the Skies, drawing on her winds to propel her forward, fast as her legs would go. Within heartbeats, she was through the vermilion pillars, bronze lions and serpents twisting on the beams overhead, watching her in silence.

The interior was dark, the hallway before her stretched long. For several moments, she blinked rapidly, trying to clear her eyes of the searing sunlight. It was utterly silent but for her own ragged breathing.

"Hello?" she called, and her voice echoed. The corridor before her appeared empty.

She had not long to wonder about it. Without warning, a

knife pressed to her neck, silent and cold. Linn froze as a voice spoke by her ear, so softly that she had the impression a ghost whispered to her. "This girl does not belong here."

She hadn't even heard the intruder behind her. Hadn't even *sensed* them through her winds. She swallowed against her panic, her tongue sticky in her mouth and her heart thumping in her ears. "Please," she whispered. "I bring urgent news. Cyrilian spies have invaded Bei'kin."

A chuckle somewhere in front of her. There was the smell of incense, and then a woman appeared, so suddenly that the darkness might have fallen apart to reveal her. Her hair was cropped short and fell like a sheet of moving snow. In her hands, she held three sticks of incense. "She means no harm, Ying shi'sen. Let the poor thing go."

The cold kiss of steel vanished from Linn's neck. This time, she paid attention, and sensed it: a figure slipping through the folds of her wind like a blade. A sallow-faced man appeared to her left with a single step that parted the shadows behind him like a veil. He scowled as he stashed his dagger. "Ruu'ma shi'sen, you spoil my play."

Shi'sen. A trickle of cold fear slipped down Linn's back as the realization came to her. These were the Masters of the Temple of the Skies—the most powerful wielders in all of Kemeira, the most feared assassins in the world. As a young windsailer, she'd heard rumors of the greatest Temple Masters who served to consult the Emperor of Kemeira. Legends that chilled her to the bone and had once sparked within her the distant dream to achieve great things.

The woman continued to smile gently at Linn. "Why does this child interrupt our morning prayers to the gods? Though . . ." She tilted her head to the entrance. "I have an inkling. Pray, speak."

Linn pried open her lips. "I . . . Apologies, esteemed shi'sen." She inclined her head, and then, as though remembering herself, sank to her knees. "I bring urgent news."

"Spies from Cyrilia," Ying said dismissively. "My shadows heard it all. Our wielders will not fail."

Linn's head snapped up. She lifted her hand and unfurled her fingers. Gen's lacquer token gleamed dark in the dimness. "They killed everyone at the village of Shan'hak." Her voice shook. "They seek information about the Heart of the Gods. Gen shi'sen asked that I relay this message to you."

"Gen? Fusann Gen?" A third voice came from the dark, fluid and amused. Its owner stepped forward, and as they did so, a beam of sunlight seemed to fall on them out of nowhere. Ying gave a hiss of displeasure, stepping back.

The newcomer surprised Linn. They were young, perhaps in their thirties or forties, tall and lithe, hair long and black as a cascade of ink.

Another explosion sounded from the courtyard and screams were cut short.

Ruu'ma tilted her head to the entrance. She hummed softly. "Ying shi'sen, your energy overflows. Would you give these guests our warmest welcome?"

Ying's grin was a thing of darkness. "*Warmth* is not a word in my repertoire, but I'll certainly give them a taste of our reputation, shi'sen." With a bow, he stepped back and was swallowed by the shadows.

Ruu'ma turned. "Rii shi'sen, will you summon the others?"

The shi'sen with the sunbeams inclined their head, hair sweeping like a ripple of silk. "As you wish," they said, and when the sunbeam disappeared, so, too, did they.

So this was the true power of the greatest Temple Masters in the land. The ability to weave darkness and light like gods, to effortlessly appear and vanish as though stepping through space and time.

Linn looked to the Temple Master before her—Ruu'ma shi'sen, as the shadow wielder had addressed her. Throughout their entire exchange, the woman had never lost her serene smile. "Ko Linnet, you must forgive me," the shi'sen said. "I must warn our Imperial Palace, and I have some divination to attend to. It seems the dream I feared most is on the precipice of becoming reality." The smallest crease appeared on her forehead. "And if so . . . the harmony of our world hangs in question."

"Wait," Linn began, but the woman had already turned and was gliding down the hallway. Between one breath and the next, she became a shadow, then nothing at all, as quickly as she had appeared.

Linn was alone.

She reached for her daggers, feeling utterly lost. This wasn't the way she'd imagined her meeting with the Temple Masters to go. Gen shi'sen had *died* to get this message to them, yet they had given her no more than two minutes of their time before turning away. And from what Ruu'ma shi'sen said, she seemed to have anticipated something like this happening. If so, why not galvanize the entirety of the Temple of the Skies to fight? Why not send word to the Emperor immediately, to warn him? She'd heard of the oft-indecipherable decisions of the Temple of the Skies, shrouded in secrecy and steeped in Kemeira's principles of harmony, peace, and balance. There was never counteraction without action.

But that is stupid, Linn found herself thinking. Did it take an invasion for the Temple Masters to act? She stood in the low-light, the hallway stretching long and empty to either side of her, the carvings of gods and monsters watching her from shadowy corners with gleaming gold eyes. The chill of Ruu'ma shi'sen's words twisted dread through her. *The harmony of our world hangs in question.*

Gen had died battling the Imperial Patrols, protecting the knowledge of the Heart of the Gods—whatever it was—from them. If there was one thing Linn prided herself on, it was her blades.

She would fight, even if she stood alone against an entire army of Cyrilian Imperial Patrols. She would fight, to her last breath.

Linn touched her hand to her heart and drew her daggers. The wooden token pressed against her collarbone, as though urging her, the smooth strokes of its characters etched into her mind, reminding her of the promise she had made Gen Fusann.

She knew what she needed to protect.

Bei'kin Shiu'gon.

The Bei'kin Bookhouse.

16

As Ana and the Redcloaks drew close to Salskoff, the amicable chatter and light atmosphere turned to silence. The gravity of their mission rested heavy on their shoulders. Yuri took to reminding them of the plan: Once they arrived at Salskoff, a little before dawn, they would lie in wait at the city borders and undercut Sorsha before she could even reach the Palace walls.

Ana noticed people grasping for their Affinities, hands twitching for snow or the soil beneath. Some had found ways to incorporate the elements of their Affinities into their outfits: A sand Affinite had padded his chest and back with bags of silt, while a copper Affinite had fashioned an entire suit of armor out of his element, allowing him to break off quantities of it to use as weapons.

In turn, Ana was acutely aware of the dull ache in her own bones, the hollowness in the pit of her belly where she had once felt full and whole with her power. Where she might have ridden confidently into battle with her blood Affinity before, she now only felt a sense of unease. The winter nights in Cyrilia were unbearably long, and somehow, in the span of the past two moons, the Syvern Taiga seemed to have changed, too. The air held an unnatural stillness that rendered every crack of a tree branch, every sound they made, too sharp and too unnatural. There was a feeling of malice to the way the wind shrieked, its distant echoes resembling wails in the night. Ana noticed Yuri raising his hand higher, the flame in his palm burning brighter.

The colors around them began to shift, the pitch-blackness lifting into a murky gray, and at last, a pale silver in the spaces between the trees to herald impending dawn. And when the hills began to slope downward, Ana knew, with a certainty in her gut, that they were close to home. The trees began to thin, trunks and branches giving way to slices of sky and ground, and then there it was, materializing before her eyes like a dream.

In the distance, between the rolling tundra and snow-covered pines, stretched an expanse of red-tiled roofs, gleaming wet beneath a blanket of morning mist. Rising above it all was the Salskoff Palace, white steeples plunging into the predawn sky, a palace of stone and snow come to life. Her ancestors had built this on the eve of unifying what was now known as the Cyrilian Empire, and there it had stood for centuries, unflinching and unyielding over the tides of time. Her empire's history was etched into the lines of its ancient marble walls.

Ana gripped her reins tighter, the sight stirring an unquiet thought in her mind.

What kind of a legacy would she, Anastacya Mikhailov, leave within those hallways?

She heard Yuri draw a sharp breath. They paused over the outcrop of cliffs, the weight of the moment hanging thick as smoke in the air between them. She knew from the look on his face that he remembered just as she did: the stolen mornings begun with hot tea and ptychy'moloko, evenings by the hearth with the warmth of his company. Days of sunlight, witnessed through her window with her hand pressed against cool glass; days of storm, her blood running in rivulets down her arm, her fear and fury lashing like wind and rain.

The edges around his eyes softened, and for a moment, Yuri looked as though he were about to reach out to her, put a hand over her shoulder as he had during her bad days, and tell her *it'll soon be all right.*

But then there rose a shout from up ahead.

The moment splintered. Yuri's eyes narrowed and he spurred his valkryf in the direction of the call.

Ana's valkryf followed.

And came to a sharp stop.

Skewered against a tree, like an ugly scar across the portrait of Salskoff, was a body, mangled beyond recognition. Blood dripped into the snow beneath it, steaming gently in the cold.

Yuri leapt off his valkryf, drew his sword, and hacked through the branches impaling the body. It fell to the ground, and only then did Ana notice its cloak, which was dark on the outside and a vibrant, cardinal color on the inside.

A Redcloak. One of their scouts.

"Sofiya," Yuri choked out, and the Redcloaks gathered around their fallen comrade.

But Ana had noticed something else. Something lying in the bloodied snow, glinting in the pale morning light. She slipped off her horse and bent to pick it up.

A chill spread through her as she beheld the iron spike: long as her forearm, the tips tapering off to a ruthless sharpness. She recognized it.

"Sorsha," she said, and the Redcloaks turned to her as she

held up the iron spike. "She's taunting us." Ana swallowed as she voiced her worst fear aloud. "She must know we're after her."

Back in the Blue Fort, during the battle against Sorsha and Kerlan's forces, Ramson had closed a blackstone collar around Sorsha's neck, inhibiting her ability to channel the Affinities in her siphons. Ana thumbed the iron spike in her hand, its tip crimson with blood. It was safe to say that Sorsha had found a way to take off the collar.

A fiery glow emanated from Yuri's fists; his knuckles were white. "Deities be damned, who would do such a thing? Sofiya—" His voice broke.

"It's a game," Ana said. "Everything is a game to her. And we're already behind."

Yuri's jaw clenched. "Redcloaks, this is it. Rescue team, follow Seyin and head for the Salskoff Palace. Remain undercover at all costs." There was a slight commotion as the rescue team set off, led by Seyin. Ana loosed a breath as she watched his head of dark hair duck out of sight behind a copse of conifers. "The rest of you . . . we'll need to partner up and split—"

"Yuri," Ana interrupted, "she's dangerous—"

"And she will be even more so if we let her reach Morganya," he snapped.

"Yuri, listen to me . . . ," she tried again.

But his eyes held a challenge, daring her to defy him. Ana understood that this wasn't about Sorsha; this was between them. He needed to prove that he was the more capable leader of the Redcloaks, that his strategy was the winning one.

He wasn't going to listen to her no matter what she said.

And perhaps he was right. It would be difficult to find Sorsha in the sprawl of a city that was Salskoff. Splitting up might be the quickest way.

Ana turned to the group of Redcloak soldiers, who had already divided themselves. "I've briefed you on this, but I must repeat myself," she said, her voice ringing loud and clear. "Sorsha is the most dangerous Affinite in existence. She wields at least ten different Affinities through her siphon. Not to mention, she is a sadist who delights in torturing her victims."

Yuri stepped to her side. For a moment, she thought he would admonish her, but he only gave a firm nod. "Leave your steeds here; we go on foot, remain hidden. Spread out through the city and close in toward the Palace. We marshal her in like a fish in a net. First unit to find her, send a signal with your Affinities." He flared a flame on the tip of his index finger and pointed it at the sky. "If you find her, slow her down, but *do not* engage in direct combat. Not until the entire team has arrived. Remember: Our goal is to rescue the prisoners, and take the siphons."

There were nods between the Redcloak soldiers.

Yuri reached to the weapons pack on his valkryf and withdrew a dagger and a shield—forged by one of his metal Affinites. He thrust both at her. "Ana, you're with me."

Ana hesitated as she accepted them. The Redcloaks had begun to disperse through the trees. They were armed and well-suited for battle; she looked to the shield and blade in her hands, weapons that she could barely lift. What use would these be against the likes of Sorsha Farrald?

"You should take someone else," she said. "Another Affinite. You know I—"

"I know," he said shortly. "I won't let anything happen to you."

She saw the tilt of his chin, the pride in his eyes, and knew he would not yield.

She strapped on the knife and shield and followed.

Salskoff had always been the most vibrant during winter, the season of their patron Deity. Ana recalled the rare occasions she'd been allowed out into town after her Affinity had manifested, the snow thick and soft beneath the hooves of horses and her carriage wheels, the air tinged with cold and the feeling of magic. Lights would be strung between lampposts, hung on doorways and windowsills, their gentle blue glow pulsing deep in the night and rendering Salskoff the image of a fairy-tale town from one of Ana's storybooks. The streets had rung with the sound of laughter, the smell of pirozhky pies and hot kashya drifting from open windows as shoppers, dressed in the celebratory colors of white and silver and blue, milled about.

This year, she might as well have been looking into an abandoned town. The dachas stood silent and still, lit only by the stark glow of streetlamps. Clouds roiled overhead, a bleak light washing over colorless streets. It was nearing dawn, when the town should have been rousing, stalls springing to life with colorful tarpaulins, shutters opening and children pouring into the streets for school. But wind whistled down empty roads, discarded cans rolling against alleyway walls.

Everywhere they looked, posters and banners had been hung up bearing portraits of Morganya in her illustrious beauty: white crown glittering over ink-black hair, elegant cheekbones, and those eyes, the color of midwinter lakes. *Celebrate the Winter of*

Our Divine Liberator, one declared, and another: *Freedom and Justice Will Be Delivered by Our Deities-Chosen Empress.*

"It makes me sick," Yuri said quietly. "To lie so blatantly to your people, to claim that you were chosen by the Deities . . ."

The people are no more than sheep, their thoughts malleable to misdirection, Morganya had said. *And I, as their divine shepherd, must guide them the right way.*

"It's calculated," Ana said. "She's controlling all the information, presenting herself as the Deities-chosen heroine of this story."

"Therein lies the danger of a monarchy. The people are powerless to resist, to find the truth, and to decide for themselves." His head tilted, his eyes on one of the pale banners fluttering in the wind, Yuri let out a breath. He turned to look at her. "A government exists to serve its people, Ana. The people should not fear their government; it is the government that should fear its people." Yuri's eyes blazed, and in them, Ana saw the fires of the Imperial Inquisition, torchlight in the dark, cries and pleas splitting the night. "A monarchy may work so long as we assume benevolence in the ruler's intentions. But should that not be the case"—he swept a hand at the ghost town around them—"this is the consequence."

Ana was silent, his words churning in her mind as the two wound through the snow-covered streets. Seyin had said the same thing to her, one moon past. Back then, the possibility that her resuming the throne was not the best way to save this empire had been such a shock, she hadn't given thought to those words.

But . . . as much as she despised the notion, the truth of it was that Papa had been an inadequate emperor, letting crimes against

Affinites run rampant under his regime. In his last years, his slow poisoning at Morganya's hands had taken his mind and rendered him incapable of making logical decisions.

Yet still, an entire palace, an entire empire, had continued to bow its head to a sickened monarch, incapable of changing the system to save itself.

In the steel-gray sky high above them came a bright beam of light, followed by what resembled an explosion. Sunbeams scattered, sparks drifting and fizzling out over the rooftops.

A signal.

Yuri cursed. "A signal," he said, his voice rising as he broke into a run. "Must be Kann's unit—it's coming from several streets down!"

Ana sprinted after him. A stitch bloomed in her side immediately, and her arms began to ache from the weight of the shield. She focused on her breathing, the *pat-pat-pat* of her boots on snow-covered streets. Overhead, more sunlight came, flashing and swirling in a way that mimicked explosions.

Abruptly, they cut off.

"It's coming from the direction of the Palace," she said, dread mixing with the adrenaline that rushed through her veins. "The Tiger's Tail."

Before them, the streets began to open, the narrow alleyways and residential dachas becoming wider and more spaced apart. Overhead, the spires and cupolas of the Salskoff Palace loomed ever closer from behind crenellated cream walls.

They turned onto the riverside promenade near the back of the Palace, separated from its high walls by the ferocious Tiger's Tail. Across the street by the edge of the water, two figures were engaged in combat, the blur of their elements obscuring their faces from view. On the sidewalk, draped across bloodied snow, was a third figure, unmoving.

It was too easy to pinpoint Sorsha Farrald—she moved with an erratic ferocity, a mad dance that somehow had its own rhythm. Ana watched as she leaned forward and thrust out both her palms.

Bursts of fire shot out, slamming into the stomach of the other fighter. Ana heard the splash as the second figure was flung over the balustrade into the Tiger's Tail.

Maniacal laughter rang out. Ana would recognize it any-where. "That's her," she said. "Sorsha Farrald." The last time she'd faced off against the girl, Ana had held one of the most powerful Affinities in existence.

This time, she had nothing.

Yuri stepped forward. As his hands balled into fists, flames erupted from his flesh, snaking up his forearms and licking over his skin.

"Two siphons," Ana reminded him. "One she carries for Mor-ganya, the other she bears."

"There won't be anything left of her once I'm through," Yuri gritted out, raising his fists before his chest in a combat stance. His hands shot out in two rapid-fire punches, fireballs launching from them. They smashed into the other side of the street on either side of Sorsha Farrald.

She looked up, a grin splitting her face as she turned to Yuri.

He launched himself at her, fists flaming, trails of fire blazing behind him.

Ana drew a dagger and made for the unconscious figure on the pavement of the promenade. It was a boy, barely breath-ing. She recognized him from their planning sessions in Yuri's quarters at camp—Kann, a sun Affinite who had sent the signal. His skin had paled, and she knew instantly from the amount of blood soaking his cloak that it was too late. His cloak was torn to ribbons, and she saw with sickening fury that Sorsha had shredded the flesh on his stomach.

Helplessness descended upon her as she looked at the dying boy, at the blood spilled all around them, knowing that there was nothing she could do. Her Affinity was gone.

Footsteps: Four more Redcloaks appeared, fists outstretched, the elements of their Affinity already spinning around them. Over the rush of the Tiger's Tail waters, Ana heard Sorsha's sharp, wild laughter.

"How *fun!*" Sorsha shrieked. Her iron spikes had shifted into flat discs; she manipulated them easily to block Yuri's and the Redcloaks' blows. "I'd been holding back until now, but . . . I've always wanted to try *this* one out!"

She whipped out her hand and turned to face three of the newly arrived Redcloaks. Time seemed to slow as Sorsha clenched her fist in their direction and twisted—and Ana, with nauseating horror, realized what was to happen.

Three of the Redcloaks fell. The air misted red, vapor coating the balustrade, like rain.

"Oops." Sorsha brought a hand to her mouth, her skin speckled crimson. "I didn't realize it would be *that* powerful!" She turned, her gaze pinning Ana like throwing knives as she licked the blood from her lips. "All that power, wasted on you until now. No matter. It's never too late to begin."

Rage splintered Ana's mind, wiping her thoughts blank save for the scene of Sorsha using *her* Affinity, her *blood* Affinity, against three Redcloaks. Murdering them before her eyes without batting an eyelash. And it was with the same overwhelming numbness that Ana watched Yuri bellow and charge toward Sorsha, flames shooting from his fists in such rapid succession that they might have been one long, continuous pillar of fire. Sorsha, laughing as she retreated, dodging and blocking each of his advances in an effortless dance.

They were headed toward the Kateryanna Bridge and the front gates of the Palace, Ana realized. Palace Guards would be standing sentry there.

They needed to stop Sorsha before she reached the bridge.

Ana drew her dagger and stood. An explosion of light stopped her in her tracks, so bright that she threw her arms up to cover her face. Squinting between the cracks of her fingers, she found its source: Yuri. The flames that had previously been spiraling over his arms now engulfed his entire body, burning so hot it was blinding.

He was burning, Ana realized with horror. The scene felt utterly familiar; just as she had lost control of her blood Affinity many times before she'd learned to harness it.

If she didn't stop him, Yuri was going to burn himself alive with his own Affinity.

Ana broke into a sprint toward him.

Yuri swept his arms in an arc and pushed. Flames shot out at Sorsha, pulsing higher than the dachas across the streets, engulfing Sorsha in searing white heat. When it faded, Ana saw two silhouettes outlined against a blood-colored dawn. Yuri swayed where he stood. His cloak had burned off. Parts of his clothes were singed, revealing painful red flesh beneath.

A dozen steps from him, Sorsha lowered her iron plates. She was giggling, her eyes bulging and her mouth parted with utter delight as she beheld Yuri. "Oh, that was *marvelous*! I could do this forever," she crowed. Then her lips stretched into a smile that sent a chill down Ana's spine. "Unfortunately, playtime has to come to an end. I have business to attend to." An iron plate she had been using as a shield began to morph, lengthening into a spike, stretching over her shoulder.

Yuri fell to his knees. Blood dripped from his lips, splashing the pavement.

"Fare thee well," Sorsha sang, angling the iron spike at Yuri.

Ana didn't think; she acted on instinct. She ran. Time seemed to slow as she closed in the last few steps, sliding in front of Yuri, shield raised, eyes closed.

Sorsha's spike smashed against her shield, ramming the breath from her lungs. Ana skidded backward, colliding painfully with Yuri.

It took her a moment to haul herself back to her feet. Her ribs ached. Her head spun as she swallowed lungfuls of cold, wintry air. She tasted copper in her mouth—a bittersweet reminder of everything that had once represented her.

Ana wiped the blood from her lips and raised her shield and dagger against the most powerful Affinite in existence. It was foolishness.

But it was get the siphons, or die trying.

She looked to the statues of the Deities lining the Kateryanna Bridge. She'd gazed at them from high up, behind the glass of her window, her entire life. The bridge had been named after her mother, and she'd once clung to the faintest hope that the spirit of her mama lingered there, watching over her. Faintly, she wondered whether Seyin and the rescue team had made it across, and into the tunnel that had saved her life not once, not twice, but thrice over.

Protect them, Mama, she thought now. *And give me the strength to protect the land our family has forsaken.*

There it was, the thought that had been growing at the back of her mind since she'd left the Palace and understood the truth to the corruption of her empire. It was a wound that continued to bleed with the death of May, the discovery of Kerlan's Affinite trafficking scheme, the knowledge that Papa and her predecessors had had the chance to do something about it all, but hadn't.

Mama had come from the South of Cyrilia, raised in the Salskoff Palace yet remaining a perpetual outsider due to her birth. Had she, too, seen the darkness of an empire that had, for so long, basked in its own light? The history of empires and kingdoms was of conquest and bloodshed, of oppression and silence masked in unity and grandeur.

Ana had always believed that to love her people was to protect her reign.

In this moment, she understood that, to serve her people, she had to *destroy* her family's legacy.

Across the cobblestone pavement, Sorsha's eyes widened in delight. "Oh, the Blood Witch wants to play, too!" she exclaimed. "What are you going to do with that dagger, my pretty, wave it at me? Here, let me wave back!"

Sorsha lifted her arms, and the water in the Tiger's Tail *moved* like a sentient thing, rearing its head. The water crested, then plunged, surging beneath Sorsha's feet and freezing into ice even as it propelled her forward. In the blink of an eye, Sorsha leapt off only paces before Ana.

Ana broke into a run. Lifted her blade. And swung.

It was a hopeless attempt, and they both knew it. Her blade clattered onto cobblestone; she stumbled, caught off-balance by her own momentum and unaccustomed to the weight of her shield.

Sorsha shrieked with laughter as she seized a fistful of Ana's hair. Cold, ruthless fingers closed around Ana's throat; she was lifted bodily into the air. An iron spike brushed against the skin of Ana's cheek, almost like a caress.

"How would you like to die?" Sorsha whispered, her breath in Ana's ear. "Shall I give you a taste of iron? Or would it be more poetic to kill you with your own Affinity?" She drew back, tilting her head. "It would be lovelier if I used my own magek. For *I* am the most powerful magen, and I'll have you remember that iron is harder than blood." She raised her iron spike. "And now, the Iron Maiden vanquishes the Red Tigress."

A far-off whistling, and then the sound of metal slicing through flesh.

Sorsha jerked, her eyes widening, this time in surprise. She stumbled and let go of Ana, her hand going to the spot on her abdomen where a streak of blood appeared. The arrow that had grazed her clattered on the cobblestones several steps away.

A voice called out from behind Sorsha, "You didn't think I'd miss all the fun, did you, Sister Dearest?"

From behind the statues of the Deities lining the Kateryanna Bridge stepped a familiar figure.

"Sorry, Ana, didn't mean to be tardy," Ramson said, his sharp hazel eyes trained on Sorsha. "I see my baby sister's made quite the mess. Here, Sister Dearest, I think you dropped this."

And he let loose another arrow.

17

Sorsha fended off Ramson's second arrow, swinging one of her iron plates to shield herself—but the arrow had achieved its intended purpose: to distract her from Ana.

A savage sort of spark had flared inside Ramson when he'd seen his half sister holding Ana. Every nerve in his body, every fiber of his being, had stretched taut, and he'd moved as though propelled by an invisible force, cutting through air like the gods willed him.

She was alive.

And she was *right in front of him.*

Ramson slammed his blackstone helmet back onto his head, the visor snapping down just as Sorsha swung out a hand to him. He'd needed to show his face to goad her and lead her away, to execute his plan.

His men hid in the nearby alleyways, beneath shop awnings and behind walls, their entire bodies covered in blackstone armor. Undetectable. Several streets down, Daya's forces lay in wait: a second line of defense should Ramson's unit fail.

For now, Ramson strolled down the streets toward Sorsha alone, knowing that the eye of every single soldier in his squad and in Daya's army was trained on him. He felt vulnerable—Sorsha could easily pierce his blackstone armor like paper with her iron spikes—but Ramson knew she wouldn't do that yet. His half sister watched his approach with the slanted eyes of a cat trailing a mouse.

Sorsha wouldn't kill him without playing a game first.

He raised his hand in a casual wave. "Salutations to you, Sister Dearest," he said cheerfully. "Is murder on your itinerary again? Shame, you really ought to diversify your interests. Have you tried reading?"

Sorsha straightened, her face alight with frenzied bloodlust as she surveyed him. She wiped spittle from her chin and bared her teeth in a snarl. "Brother Dearest," she simpered, and then her voice rose into a shriek. "Did you think you could chain me forever, with that little collar of yours?"

He looked to her neck, which was bare but for a strip of paler flesh where the blackstone collar that their father had used to control Sorsha's powers had once rested. It was long gone now, as evidenced by the trail of destruction she had left in the wake of her journey through Cyrilia.

Ramson raised his misericord, the blackstone-enforced metal glinting pale in the drained morning light. "Interested in playing another game with me?" he called. "You haven't won yet, as I recall."

"Oh, I'll win," Sorsha snarled, spreading her arms, the iron spike and disk she held at her sides transforming into two long, thick blades. "As soon as I skewer this bitch."

And then she turned and plunged an iron blade into Ana.

* * *

Ramson heard his own shout as though it had come from some-one else. He was running, misericord out, each step thundering against the cobblestones, and yet somehow still he couldn't move fast enough.

Through the pounding of his heart in his ears and the rush of blood to his head, he heard Sorsha's laughter. "Oh, how *precious!*" she screamed. "You love her, don't you? Just like Daddy Dearest loved your filthy mother!"

Ramson reached to his hip, drew out a blackstone throwing dagger, and flung it. Sorsha's face twisted into a snarl as she raised her hand to defend herself—but instead of iron soaring to her fingertips, flames exploded from her knuckles.

He heard her shriek as his blade cut into her flesh.

The fire subsided; she bent over, the blade of his dagger now protruding from her waist. When she looked up, her expression was ugly. "No more *games,* Brother Dearest," she snarled, and plucked out the dagger. She dropped it to the stone path of the bridge, its clink resonating even over the roar of the Tiger's Tail below. "I won't be fooled again."

But Ramson was staring at her hand, where she'd conjured flames instead of calling up her iron. *So she makes mistakes,* he thought. Back in the Blue Fort, Ardonn had explained that si-phons could only borrow the properties of that which they stole, and that siphon bearers had difficulty controlling their new Af-finities. Bogdan himself had died when his Affinity spun out of control. Would it not make sense that Sorsha wasn't familiar enough yet with all her Affinities to wield them effectively?

If so . . .

Ramson raised his hand. Crooked two fingers.

At his signal, his men poured out from every alleyway in the surrounding area, their arrows nocked. Ramson made another gesture: one that would communicate to Daya and her army to remain where she was. He'd seen Sorsha pulverize a Redcloak from far away; her possession of Ana's blood Affinity, coupled with her uninhibited penchant for violence, made her extremely dangerous to anyone without blackstone equipment.

Ramson turned to his half sister. She was bent over a balustrade between him and Ana, only twenty or so steps away. Still too far. And still too close to Ana.

He looked to her left wrist, where a sea-green band wound around her flesh.

"What's the matter?" he called. "Too weak to handle the siphon properly? I always knew you were no more than a sniveling little girl, crying for Daddy's approval."

Sorsha looked up. Her eyes were blazing. With a wild scream, she flung two blades of iron at him. Ramson dodged them both, heard them crack against lampposts and trees behind him.

"Even with a gods-given weapon, you can't best me," he continued loudly, backing away. He tapped his blackstone armor. "Can't get past these, can you? You think yourself superior with your birth status, but I've outsmarted and outmatched you time and time again, Sister Dearest."

She was practically spitting, bent over in agony, face pale with rage. Her lips curled white as her eyes snapped to him—a gaze swallowed by madness and hatred, a gaze from which there was no return.

With an animalistic yell, Sorsha broke into a run toward him.

He was aware of the soldiers in his unit poised just beyond the riverside promenade, in the shadows of dachas and back alleys. Bows drawn, arrows trained on Sorsha Farrald. Awaiting his signal.

Ramson held his hand high in the air for just a moment longer.

And then he brought it down.

Arrows whistled through the air.

He had to admire his half sister for her tenacity. Her hands wheeled and her iron gathered into a shield before her, forming to her arm as she ran. Arrows plinked off its surface and the ground cracked beneath her feet, slabs of concrete and earth rising to shroud her in a tunnel.

Ramson began to run toward her, misericord lifted.

Ten steps away, Sorsha's shield began to morph, tip sharpening into a blade.

Four, three, two—

Ramson dodged. Swung.

She pivoted.

His blade caught.

Pain bloomed.

Intertwined, they fell together on the steps of the Kateryanna Bridge.

The pain was lightning, searing white into his vision. Looking down, he saw her half-formed iron spike digging into his stomach; felt the cold of it through his skin. Hoped against hope that it would give him just enough time to finish this.

His misericord, though, had cut through her heart.

His half sister made a small, choking sound. Red ran down

her chin and neck, coursing down her arms, staining the turquoise siphon on her wrist.

She looked at him then, black gaze meeting his hazel one, the light rapidly fading from hers. Blood welled from her mouth as she scrabbled at his hands, her fingers weak as a newborn's. The siphon on her wrist was clouding, strands of black drifting across the surface, growing slower and slower every second.

In the moments before death, the cruelty on his half sister's face seemed to fade, leaving behind an expression resembling fear. She stared at him, eyes wide, still grappling with his hands, the hilt of his blade in her heart.

Ramson might have felt sorry for her, this girl raised to be a monster, who had embraced the worst and cruelest pieces of this world and turned them into a part of herself.

"Good-bye, Sorsha," he murmured. "May the next life treat you kinder than this one."

She drew a shuddering breath. And there, beneath the statues of the watching Deities, she grew still, her eyes turning glassy to reflect the emptiness of the skies.

Ramson's own thoughts were dimming, the familiar haze of blood loss and pain clouding his world. It was growing harder to breathe, to see, to feel . . . yet there was one thing he still had to do.

He stood and turned back to the riverside promenade.

It was agony to lift one foot in front of the other. Time blurred; it seemed like an eternity and no time at all before he was standing in front of her.

Ana.

She lay in front of him in a pool of blood, dark hair fanned out in the snow. His legs gave way and he fell to his knees by her side. The pain in his abdomen was excruciating, reaching into the dark of his mind and drawing out stars, but Ramson gathered the last of his consciousness and focused on her.

Gently, he touched a hand to her face, tracing the sharp curve of her cheeks with his bloodstained fingers. Her eyes were closed, lashes dark and thick as the stroke of a brush on an oil painting. He pushed her hair back, his vision fading in and out, his head growing light. His fingers trailed down the edge of her jaw to her neck.

And *there,* faint as the flutter of a butterfly's wing.

A pulse.

Relief spread warm across his chest—or perhaps it was his own blood. He couldn't tell anymore, and it no longer mattered.

Ramson tipped her face to his. In his imagination, her eyelids flitted open, deep brown eyes meeting his.

He smiled. "Hello, Witch," he mumbled. "Must we always meet in the direst of situations?"

He exhaled; the world grew black.

18

Linn flung open the doors to the Temple of the Skies to piercing sunlight and winds that screamed of chaos. Most of the courtyard bore traces of battle, clay-brick rubble strewn everywhere. There were bodies, too—the guards, their pale shifts now stained red. Of the dozen or so Linn had seen, there were only a few left, trading blows with the Cyrilians.

In the midst of it all, strolling unhurriedly toward the battle as though it were a morning walk, was Ying shi'sen, the Shadow Master. In the daylight, his hair was dark, streaks of it hanging in his face. He kept his black cloak wrapped tightly around him like armor.

Several Cyrilians looked up as he approached. Their faces twisted in snarls. One of them stepped forward, a man with hair almost as pale as his skin.

There was only a flick in his eyes, and the earth before them shifted to sand, twisting into columns that lengthened into sharpened, hardened spears.

They flew at Ying shi'sen.

The Temple Master spread his arms, opening his cloak. Darkness exploded from him—it was the only way to describe it as his cloak seemed to *expand,* shadows enveloping the sky. For a moment, Linn's vision went black. When it cleared, Ying shi'sen stood exactly where he had been, utterly still but for the smallest ripple across his cloak as it fell back into place. The sand swords were gone.

For once, Linn's place was not in this battle. She touched a finger to the token that rested against her collarbone. She knew what she had to do. Her gods, the threads of fate, whatever it was, had set her on this path, and she'd made a promise to an old man who had saved her life.

Action, counteraction.

By the time Linn arrived at the Bei'kin Bookhouse, its doors had been smashed through, ancient wooden frames and delicate carvings that had withstood the tides of dynasties destroyed with a single smash of a sword.

Rage simmered in her veins.

She palmed her blades and stepped into the dark.

The interior of the bookhouse was silent, the air heavy with centuries of knowledge perfumed in the scent of wood and scrolls and ink. Pathways wound into the heart of the building, the ceiling-high shelves forming a maze of walls. In the dimness, Linn could make out books, scrolls, and even the most ancient of stone tablets stacked neatly on shelves throughout the hallway, like the scales of a long, winding dragon. Here was where, to preserve the sacred relics, light did not reach.

The jade tablet that Gen had told her about lay in here.

And it must not fall into the Cyrilians' hands.

Linn flared her Affinity, stretching her consciousness into winds that wove a map of the bookhouse in her mind, and stepped into the darkness.

A few turns later, she felt it: a tremor in the air down the next right. Several bodies, their breaths stirring ever so slightly against her Affinity.

Linn flattened herself against a shelf, inching toward the end of the corridor. Lifting her dagger, she peered out.

There was nothing there. Shelves looming out of the near pitch-black, ridged edges of books lining them. Yet . . . her winds traced to her an outline of someone standing there.

Linn crept forward, squinting.

And then drew a sharp breath.

In front of her, the narrow maze of shelves opened into the center of the bookhouse. Even in the dim lighting, Linn could make out a marble pedestal; on it rested a slab of rock that pulsed with a green hue.

The jade tablet. She closed the distance to it, reaching a hand out—

Her fingers swept right through it, as though there was nothing there.

She blinked. Yet there it was, in front of her, a slab of jade etched with Kemeiran characters that spilled down it like a waterfall.

The moment of confusion cost her. Something whistled behind her, and before she could react, pain sliced across her left shoulder.

Linn spun round, raising her knives. There was nothing there. Yet the air to her right shifted again: She felt, through her winds, a figure hurtling toward her, parting the air with edges of pointed metal. Linn turned to the nothingness, lifting her knives to where her Affinity told her the opponent's knives would be—

They shifted in the last moment, and she felt their sharp bite across her abdomen. Linn stumbled back, alarm bells pealing in her mind, confusion scattering her response. She had *seen* nothing, but she had *sensed* it with her winds. . . .

When the air behind her parted a third time, Linn turned. This time, she caught a blur of movement through the dark.

Linn closed her eyes and tuned in to her Affinity.

She met the attacker's sword with both her daggers, grunting as her wound screamed. Blood warmed her clothing. Her opponent moved again and Linn reacted—but not fast enough.

Pain exploded on her temple. She staggered back, spat blood, and looked up just as her opponent materialized seemingly from thin air, his arm retracting from the blow.

He raised his sword. Metal arced, splitting the curtain of her winds—

And then the man's sword was flying through the air in the opposite direction. The Imperial Patrol stared at his hand, stupefied, and looked back to Linn.

Ruu'ma stood between them. The woman held a pair of curved scythes in her hands. Her stance was low, defensive, her robes rippling around her as they settled.

"The Cyrilian is a sight wielder" was all she said to Linn, and everything clicked into place.

Sight wielder. An Affinite who manipulated vision and specialized in illusions. She thought of how she'd *seen* the jade tablet but her hands had felt nothing.

Linn spun round to the marble pedestal just as the illusion collapsed. The jade tablet flickered into nothingness, revealing an empty plinth.

In front of the shelves a few steps away, where Linn had sensed the tremors in the air, two more men materialized: two more Cyrilians materialized, holding a blackstone chest between them. Their first attacker stood in front of his squad, hands raised in a defensive position. She recognized him from his lean build, the curve of his outline, and the edges to his armor that her winds had carved out. It was the sight Affinite. An Inquisitor.

Linn's gaze snapped to the blackstone chest. "The tablet," she said.

"Run," the Inquisitor barked at the other Imperial Patrols. He turned back to Ruu'ma, unsheathing a second sword from his back as the footsteps of his fellow patrols faded down the aisles, the blackstone chest—and the jade tablet—disappearing with them.

"Ko Linnet. Leave this fight to me." Ruu'ma's countenance had been patient and fair thus far, but in this moment she spoke rapid-fire words to Linn: *"Retrieve the tablet, windsailer."*

Linn didn't have time to ponder this order, so abrupt was the delivery. She gritted her teeth and pushed herself from the ground, daggers in hand, hilts slick with blood.

Face twisted with rage, the Inquisitor charged.

Linn didn't have time to send a blessing to the Temple Master. It was the Inquisitor who would need it, after all.

She turned and ran. With every step, the gash in her abdomen seared.

Linn reached the entrance of the bookhouse to find chaos in the courtyard. Bodies were strewn across the clay-brick floor, along with remnants of whatever elements the Cyrilian Affinites and the Temple Masters had used to fight with. The ground shook with the sound of battle.

There were ten Temple Masters still fighting—and now, the

other unit of Cyrilian Imperial Patrols had arrived. Her stomach tightened as she took in the scene.

A Water Master, standing in the middle of the man-made lake in the courtyard. He appeared to be meditating, *floating*, on the surface, water roaring around him.

A Metal Master, forming a blade that twisted and thrashed like a snake.

Rii, the sun wielder, lighting up the courtyard with bright flashes from the sky that struck where the Cyrilian Imperial Patrols stood. They moved gracefully, leaving a trail of burnt corpses in their wake.

At last, Linn spotted her quarry: two Cyrilian Imperial Patrols running through the battle, a snarl in the weft and warp of the tapestry of war.

Linn took off after them. Fatigue was beginning to wear into her muscles now, the loss of blood making her head light. She stumbled once or twice on patches of ground that had been torn away. Sweat poured down her forehead, stinging her eyes.

The two Imperial Patrols were too far ahead, sprinting through the now-empty main roads of Bei'kin. Linn swiped a hand across her face and called on her winds. They came from the front this time, sweeping in shrieking gusts that stirred up the dust on the roads. Trees rattled, tarpaulins fluttered, and discarded pieces of food were tossed into the air.

Up ahead, the Cyrilians slowed, pushing against the gale. One turned around, pulling a dagger from his hips. He flung it at her, forcing her to duck and roll.

The move broke off her focus; her winds died as the weapon clattered to the ground, passing a hand's breadth from where her neck had been. The men took off again, hefting the large black-stone chest between them.

Linn swept her hands against the sheaths at her hips. Her daggers leapt into her palms, sharp, smooth, and cool, shifting to every subtle move of her body like an extension of her arms. Her sheaths were now empty; these were her last two knives.

Her last chance.

Linn's grip tightened against them as she parted her cracked lips to whisper a prayer to her gods.

The answer came: Her blades struck straight and true. In front of her, the two Cyrilians sagged and collapsed onto the road.

Linn limped over to the men and their bounty. With trembling hands, she pried at the lock on the chest. It clicked open. Not even locked.

The inside of the chest was empty.

Linn pushed it back, nausea roiling in her stomach as she turned to the two dead Cyrilian soldiers. It was only when she flipped them over that she realized their faces were different from those of the men she'd seen in the bookhouse.

She'd been duped by the multiple units of Imperial Patrols. They'd known the value of the jade tablet, known she and the Temple Masters would chase after them.

Linn reached for her Affinity but found the winds to be faint as an echo, slipping between her fingers where they would have once leapt at her command. The world was swaying around her, shapes morphing and shifting before her eyes. Any further overuse of her winds and the hallucinations would utterly incapacitate her. Her tell with her Affinity had never been external—it was her mind that it warped.

She closed her eyes, the gravity of her failure hitting her. She'd spent all this time pursuing the wrong people—the true tablet could have been taken anywhere in Bei'kin now. They could have reached the harbor, taken it onto the ships. She'd exhausted her Affinity and her body; the entire front of her shirt was warm and wet with her blood.

But she could not stop. Ruu'ma had given her this command; she'd addressed Linn as a windsailer. In Kemeira, disobeying a Master was as good as a sin. Even if her chances of finding the Cyrilians and the jade tablet were slimmer than the stir of winds around her, even if she bled out and died en route, Linn needed to try. For this was the Kemeiran way.

Linn pushed herself to her feet and began to limp forward, one step at a time.

She'd gone half a street when something caught her eye. A figure, lying crumpled to the side of the street beneath the awning of a shop. From here, all she could make out was a flash of brown skin and black hair. He could have been Kemeiran—but she had come to know Kaïs's build as well as the shape of her own fingers.

Linn took one, two steps, and then she was running, her exhaustion forgotten as hope roared through her veins. She knelt by the figure's side, turned his face up.

Kaïs's eyes were closed, his lips parted. A large gash on his cheek still bled; his body was covered in slashes. A long, thick wound gaped on his abdomen.

No. No. No. . . .

Linn placed a trembling finger beneath the straight edge of his jaw.

At first, there was nothing.

Then, in that eerie stillness, there came the faintest flutter. A pulse, tapping against the pads of her fingers, whispering to her. *Alive.*

She looked up. If she took Kaïs back to the Temple of the Skies right now, he might live. If she continued her fruitless pursuit of the Cyrilians and the jade tablet, there was no guarantee that she would even find them, let alone catch up to them before their ships sailed, in her current state.

Linn thought of Fusann Gen, of how he and the other Temple Masters had died to protect the information about the jade tablet. Of how choosing to save one individual over the greater good was selfish, of how it was against the Kemeiran way—no matter how ridiculous the odds. Vows were forged of iron, unbendable and unbreakable even as the circumstances and the world shifted around them. Tradition and deference were carved of unyielding stone, unchanged throughout time.

But Linn looked down at her friend, at her ally, at the man who had fought by her side for so many nights and saved her life more than once. She owed him, and she had promised herself that she would repay her debts. Action, counteraction.

Perhaps the years in Cyrilia had changed her; perhaps, as much as she'd hated herself for it, a small part of her heart now belonged to the icy Northern Empire, which had undeniably, irrevocably, and indelibly carved itself into her skin and bones. She was Kemeiran, yet fate would have it that she was also something else now—someone completely new.

The choice lay in none other than her own hands.

* * *

Linn had no idea how she made it back to the Temple of the Skies. All she knew was that she did.

The battle had quieted. The courtyard, once a peaceful harmonization of the elements, had been cleaved apart down the middle, a tumultuous mix of rock and water and molten metal and trees strewn about chaotically. The Temple Masters stood in a line before the entrance of their temple, deep in conversation. Around them, the wielder guards and apprentices worked to remove the bodies of the Cyrilian spies.

With the last of her strength, Linn staggered up to the Temple Masters. Fell to her knees. Looked up, and found Ruu'ma.

"My friend." Her voice was a rattling breath. "He is gravely injured . . . near the meat market." Blood welled into her mouth; she fell forward onto her hands, black spots in her vision closing in. "Please . . . I beg you . . . help him."

The gods might frown upon her, yet as Linn lay on the cold stone floor of the Temple of the Skies, she thought that she could live with the choice she had made today.

She was, after all, only human.

 **19**

Her body was on fire, the pain was excruciating, but Ana forced her eyes to open. Sorsha had driven an iron blade into Ana's side; she could see the hilt from where she lay, looming over her beneath the brilliant dawn sky in the shape of a cross.

Ana turned her head. If there was a small miracle, it was this: the boy she had been waiting for, lying on the ground next to her, his chest rising and falling in shallow breaths. She studied the length of his face, that hawk nose broken and slightly crooked at the bridge, those full lips normally quirked in a smile.

Ramson, she wanted to say, but then her thoughts were drowned out by the sound of footsteps all around them.

Shapes moved into sight, men in blackstone armor surrounding them. These, though, weren't the blackstone uniforms that the Cyrilian Imperial Patrols wore, Ana thought hazily.

One of them spoke frantically, issuing orders in a foreign language. Somehow, she understood the words.

Bregonian, she thought. The slur of her thoughts drifted to the snowhawk she'd sent Daya. Was it possible that they'd actually made it?

Two of the soldiers knelt by Ramson's side. With a grunt, one pulled out the iron spike impaled in his stomach. Another rushed forward, pressing her hands to the wound.

Before Ana's eyes, the gush of blood slowed. Flesh and skin began to expand, weaving themselves together.

Healer, she thought. *Magen.*

Ramson's men were here.

She craned her neck, looking up and down the sidewalk. Yuri, where was Yuri? In a split moment, memories of their last private conversation flashed through her mind: a fire burning low, the sticky taste of stolen cake on her lips. The dance of flames in his ash-gray eyes that told her not everything of the friendship they'd once had was gone.

When she found him, her heart stopped.

A half dozen paces from her, Yuri lay crumpled and unmoving on the pavement, his torn clothing showing patches of angry red skin.

Someone nearby called her name. Before she could place the voice, a face appeared in her vision.

Daya broke into a half sob, half laugh as she looked Ana over. "Amara bless," she croaked, and then, as her eyes fell on Ana's wound, *"Healer! Someone! Help!"*

Ana felt herself slipping; in the jumbled stream of her consciousness, she thought she saw a hooded figure striding down the Kateryanna Bridge toward them. She blinked, and the sword impaled in her side was gone, Daya's face swimming into the edge of her vision. By her side, the slim-faced Bregonian healer who had been working on Ramson drew back, surveying Ana's torso. The pain had dulled, Ana realized with faint surprise, and it wasn't until the healing magen lifted her hands from Ana's stomach that she understood why.

Her head swam. She drifted, like the river roaring by her side.

Blink. Metal-gray skies overhead, dawn bleeding in, Daya and the healer gone. Now, a different shadow loomed over her, cool hands at her side, applying a soothing cream to her wound.

Ana's breath hitched. *"Tetsyev."*

The alchemist's face drew into focus: large, bulbous eyes, a bald head covered by his white prayer robes. "We haven't much time, Kolst Pryntsessa," he whispered. "Your Redcloak team triggered the alarm of some Palace Guards on their way out."

Relief warmed her, and for a brief moment, it felt as though everything would turn out all right.

Then Tetsyev said quietly: "She is coming."

The slur of her thoughts pulled together, sharpened, crystal clear. There was no doubt as to whom he was referring.

Gritting her teeth, Ana pushed herself into a sitting position. Her abdomen protested with searing flashes of heat, but her flesh was now smooth, if only slightly puckered with a scar. The healer's work.

Ana's blood ran cold as she swept a gaze around her. By her side, Ramson was still unconscious, his soldiers bent over him, his healer working on his wound. Daya and several others were crouched over Yuri; Ana could just make out the bright flame of his hair. Strewn along the riverside promenade all around them were casualties of war.

"The siphons," Ana croaked. "Sorsha—"

"She is dead," Tetsyev said dully. "We must leave immediately."

"We?"

Tetsyev reached to a bag on the ground, pulled out strips

of gauze, and began to wrap her midriff. "Listen carefully. The siphons are only a part of it all. There is a bigger picture to this— a much, much greater plan she has chartered for our world."

His words tugged on a memory just beyond her grasp at the moment. Before she could make out the meaning, there came movement from the Salskoff Palace. A sharp gale gusted past them, rippling over the rooftops of dachas and stirring the surface of the Tiger's Tail. The waters roared, churning with a viciousness, a hunger.

The Palace gates were opening, stone grinding on snow. From within, pouring out in immutable waves of white and gray livery, came an army of Imperial Patrols. In their midst, a rock in a wending river, was their Empress astride a valkryf white as bone.

She turned her gaze, and those cold, still eyes came to a rest on the Kateryanna Bridge.

To where Sorsha lay.

Ana thrust herself to her feet. She could feel the newly knitted flesh on her wound tearing from the movement, pain splicing through Tetsyev's healing salves as she began to walk. Warmth leaked down her side, but she didn't stop.

She staggered up the steps of the bridge and dropped down next to Sorsha's body. Sorsha's left arm hung limp, bent at an odd angle, and there, against her wrist, was the ocean-colored band Ana had searched for. Whereas previously, it had clung tight to Sorsha's flesh as though it had been welded into her skin, it now hung loose like a regular bracelet.

Ana's fingers closed around it just as Morganya's Affinity found her. The Empress's power twined around Ana, squeezing and twisting and burrowing its way into her flesh with poison wrath. Ana barely had time to draw breath, to clutch the siphon as tightly as she could, before she was flung back through the air.

Her body cracked across the stones of the bridge, skidding back to the steps, trailing snow in its wake. Pain exploded in her shoulder and across her back so that, for several moments, she could only lie there, stunned and attempting to draw breath.

Dimly, she heard Daya shout her name.

But all that mattered, in this moment, was the band Ana held in her grasp. The morning light reflected on it, but its surface swirled as though it held rivers, lakes, entire oceans within its turquoise patterns.

Ears ringing, head singing, she looked up to see Morganya lift Sorsha's body. The girl's head tipped back, exposing the bare flesh of her neck; her arms and legs flayed out like a rag doll's. And, at her waist, looped into the leather of her belt, came a glimmer of green.

The second siphon.

Horror washed over Ana.

"Ana!" Daya yelled again. Her voice sounded very distant; the world slowed as Ana watched Morganya's hands close around the second siphon. Her own fingers still tightly gripped the first, the one Sorsha had worn and used.

Somewhere deep inside, she knew how this would unfold.

The *only* way it could unfold.

Morganya and Ana raised their siphons, and at the same time plunged their hands through.

The world fractured. The colors leaked, rendering her sight in monochrome: gray sky, pale palace, white river, black bridge, all faint as though she were seeing them through a frosted-glass window.

Amid it all, there came sensations. They churned into the empty pit of her belly where her blood Affinity had once rested, and she tasted them deep inside. They warmed her mind, and she found that each tug of a thought rang a different note. Crimson blood, bright fire; steady earth and sharp iron, clear water and cold stone, blending in her head in a blur of consciousness, a chaotic harmony.

Affinities.

They spun faster and faster, growing louder and brighter, each demanding her control, each needing a piece of her. Her mind—it was splitting into too many fragments—any more, and—

She screamed then, expunging them from her head in the only way she knew how. By instinct, as though she were using her Affinity again, she pushed.

The world coalesced, sharp sounds and garish light. Her mind seemed to have cracked like a pane of glass, splitting into fragments, each reflecting a different view. The grind of stone and marble, the deluge of river water, the trembling of the earth, the burning of blood. A colossal rift had split the Kateryanna Bridge in two: she on one side, Morganya on the other. They were both bent over the ground, hands clutched to their heads.

An echo of Ana's name from somewhere behind her; she turned to see Daya waving at her from the riverside promenade. The ground had cracked, giant crevices running jagged along the streets. There were bodies, tucked away behind dachas and alleyways; she could sense them all, she could sense their—

Blood.

Her throat closed; she looked down at her wrist, where the

siphon nested against her flesh like a part of her skin. It glowed. She could see shimmering threads of light weaving like veins just below the surface of her skin.

She turned again to the Salskoff Palace. Beneath the great walls, an entire garrison of Palace Guards and Imperial Patrols had gathered, their livery a sea of silver-blue and gray-white. They stood at the other end of the Kateryanna Bridge behind Morganya.

For a moment, the roiling power in Ana's belly surged as the siphon seemed to brighten, and she thought of finishing this battle right here, right now.

But she looked to the streets, painted in blood: the dead and the injured, lying in the silent snow along the riverside promenade. This was not a battle they would win. Not today. Not as they were.

Ana turned. One step, then another, and she was half running, half limping, calling out to Daya as she did. "We must retreat. Make sure Ramson's men go with you safely."

Daya tipped her head. "One step ahead of you, my friend. We came together."

"Thank you." Ana paused, her eyes roving to the spot farther down the promenade, where a crumpled figure lay like a burnt-out match. "Will you help me get Yuri out of here?" She lifted her eyes to the Palace across the waters, the army of Imperial Patrols and guards shimmering like a layer of ice. "I'll hold them off."

Daya called out orders; the armies sprang into motion. Out of the corner of her eye, Ana saw Ramson's Navy unit begin to retreat, led by several of Daya's soldiers. One of the men hoisted Ramson onto his back while the healer followed closely behind.

At least, she thought, her Affinity reaching out to him, sweeping phantom fingers over his body, the bleeding had stopped.

He was alive.

Ana looked across the Kateryanna Bridge. Morganya was moving, clinging to the balustrades as she rose to her feet unevenly. And there . . . in the midst of the snow-white cloaks and glittering armor . . . Ana's attention snagged on a single figure.

She froze as the figure looked up, her gaze lancing true as a silver arrow, right across the river, the Kateryanna Bridge, the gaggle of soldiers and Redcloaks and bodies. Right to Ana.

Shamaïra was restrained by no fewer than four Whitecloaks, yet for all their hard armor and polished steel, they stood like rocks to her diamond. She held her head high and proud, unmoving and unyielding, her face blazing brighter than fire. Her hair, once done in a beautiful long braid, had been cut short, the strands falling ragged to her chin.

Shock froze Ana momentarily. Had the Redcloaks failed in their rescue mission? Tetsyev had said they'd triggered the alarm of some Palace Guards. Then, the single thought that it didn't matter—none of it mattered, other than the fact that her friend stood across the bridge from her, just steps away. Within reach.

Ana would not lose Shamaïra again.

She moved forward, Affinity rising to her call.

This time, though, it was a different one.

Fire surged from her palms, aimed not at the Imperial Patrols across the bridge—but at the waters of the Tiger's Tail. The bright streaks of flame met the roar of water—

And exploded.

Mist swirled in the air. Through the fog, she heard confused shouts, the sound of someone screaming. She thought she could make out Morganya's voice, shrieking at her forces to guard Shamaïra.

Ana was already one step ahead.

This time, she thrust out her hands, and it felt like coming home.

Her blood Affinity blazed to life. There was a roaring in her ears, immutable and unstoppable as the waters of the Tiger's Tail, swallowing her whole in a surge of power and strength. It soared past the soldiers, galloping through their different blood signatures, rushing and spilling until—

There. Incense and rosewater, the fire of an unbreakable spirit. The Imperial Patrols hadn't even taken the time to put Shamaïra in blackstone cuffs, perhaps because her Affinity could do no physical harm.

Ana limped forward, sweeping her Affinity. All around her, soldiers fell like grass to a scythe. The blackstone fused into the Imperial Patrols' armor dulled her senses, but unlike Ramson's men, the Whitecloaks had no helmets and no visors. Ana's Affinity easily wrapped around the exposed parts of their bodies, tearing past flesh into blood.

The world was beginning to fade around the edges of Ana's vision, black spots erupting everywhere. Warmth trickled down her nose, copper in her mouth. She recognized the danger signs, the warnings of burnout—but she was so, so close.

In the midst of it all, in the swirling fog, she finally found the person she had been searching for.

"...Ana..."

She reached out and Shamaïra was in front of her, real and alive and solid. Hands, closing over cold, papery skin grown so fragile; fingers, wrapping protectively over a head of oil-black hair.

In that fog, though, cut another silhouette, fast approaching. Ana looked up into the murderous gaze of her aunt.

Morganya's teeth were clenched, her eyes so wide that the whites ringed her pupils. She reached forward with a hand, twisted. Shamaïra cried out, her legs buckling beneath her as Morganya seized control of her body.

Ana whipped her Affinity toward Morganya, pushing with all the strength she had left. With a shriek, Morganya tumbled back, releasing her control over Shamaïra.

Ana slung Shamaïra's arms over her shoulders, wrapped her own hands over the Unseer's too-thin waist, then turned and staggered away from the Salskoff Palace. Step by agonizing step across the bridge, to where she knew her forces waited. Overhead, the shadows of the angels and Deities on the Kateryanna Bridge loomed, silent and cold as stone.

The last that Ana remembered was the fog clearing and shapes moving ahead, voices calling her name. Her vision slicked and slipped as she lurched forward.

To the other end of the bridge.

20

Ramson remembered little until he woke up slumped on the back of a valkryf, dizzy and dehydrated and—*gods be damned, what in the hells was that pain in his midriff?* It was dark, too; he blinked, and shapes swam into view, fuzzy and flickering with the light of torches and snowglobes.

"Captain Farrald?" A voice in his ear.

He groaned. He'd been leaning against Narron this whole time, the soldier holding him before his breast like some gods-damned princess.

Not, Ramson amended to his own trail of thought, that it was an apt comparison at all. The only (former) princess he knew was tougher than his entire unit of Navy soldiers combined.

He made an attempt to straighten himself, but a searing pain tore through his abdomen again.

"Stay put, Captain. Looks like the wounds cut deeper than we thought. The healer will patch you up again once we make camp—we're almost there."

He tried to steady his breathing. They were somewhere in the thick of the Syvern Taiga, trees clustering tight around them, firelight lancing off their frozen trunks. They appeared to be climbing uphill, his valkryf straining against the steep slope, its clawed hooves digging into the rock beneath the snow, lending them a sharp grip.

Between the conifers, he glimpsed other silhouettes, traveling in the same direction. Ramson made out the gleaming gray armor of his unit, and then the regular Bregonian livery of Ana and Daya's forces.

"Where is 'there'?" he slurred.

"Camp," Narron replied, "with the Red Tigress's forces. I'm told it's located at an abandoned village north of Salskoff, deep in the Syvern Taiga. We should be arriving shortly." A pause. "Unless you'd prefer we leave—"

"No," Ramson said. "No."

Craning his neck, he caught a glimpse of another valkryf. A man slumped over the saddle, secured by ropes. Ramson would have recognized that bright red hair anywhere.

A girl followed dutifully in the wake of Yuri's horse, the insides of her cloak flashing red. She moved her hand in long, sweeping motions. Behind her, snow gusted, sweeping the ground clean of their footprints.

"How long have I . . ." He winced as he looked down at his wound. His doublet had been slashed open, the bandages across his stomach turned dark red. The stain had crept to other parts of his clothes.

"You've been out the entire day, sir," Narron reported. "Iversha made a quick fix of your injury, but she has to look at it more extensively once we arrive. And worry not, Captain, I sent word this morning to the rest of our squad standing watch over Ardonn and Dama Olyusha that we are safe. They should be on their way already."

Ramson exhaled. "Narron, you're a blessing. Did your mam ever tell you that?"

"No, sir."

"Well, don't let it get to your head."

Their procession slowed, the ground flattening beneath their valkryfs' hooves. They passed through a set of gates and stopped in front of what appeared to be a small village plaza. Dachas were scattered around the space, roofs jutting into the night. It was utterly dark, the windows shuttered, the buildings abandoned.

At the front of the line, he caught a glimpse of Daya, armor glinting and captain's cloak sweeping as she dismounted. And there, cradled in her arms—

"Stop," Ramson choked. *"Stop."*

At his tone of voice, Narron yanked on the reins; the valkryf had barely drawn still before Ramson slid off. He hit the ground with a jolt, his knees buckling beneath him, stomach nearly splitting with pain.

Ramson pushed himself to his feet and shoved past the ranks of soldiers, until—

"What in the hells do you think you're doing?" Daya turned her glare on him, but behind the sharpness to her voice, there was palpable relief. "You're still *bleeding*—"

"Is she all right?" His voice was barely a croak. "She—let me see—"

Daya's eyes softened, and she shifted slightly. Behind her, two soldiers had brought out a makeshift stretcher; Ramson caught a glimpse of chestnut hair, a curved neck, head lolling like a doll's.

Something in him seized, and for a moment, he couldn't breathe. His head spun.

"She's alive." Daya's voice was gentle. "She'll be all right."

No, whispered a voice in his head. *She won't be.*

They all die.

The dizziness was overwhelming. Pain slicked up his body, and nausea churned in his stomach. Gods be damned, his stomach . . .

"She needs rest," Daya continued, authority returning to her tone. "And so do you. Look, you're swaying—agh!" She rushed forward and caught him under his armpits as he toppled forward and threw up.

Blood and vomit splashed on the ground, complementing the mouthful of colorful curses Daya spewed.

"I've always admired people who swore like sailors," Ramson muttered woozily, attempting a grin as his men surrounded him, lowering him into a cloth gurney.

"I *am* a sailor, you arse," came the reply. "And a captain, don't you forget. You there, let's get him into the dacha with Ana before he ruins another part of my uniform, Amara curse him and his breakfast."

He drifted in and out of consciousness, dimly aware of his men shifting him to a bed, of the air growing warm. He woke several times to find Iversha and another medic bending over him, their hands weaving over the flesh of Ramson's abdomen. The pain grew fainter each time he came around, until, at one point, it faded to no more than a dull memory.

Ramson opened his eyes. The room was silent. Somebody had lit a fire in the hearth; the flames cast a warm light over a tray of food on the floor, a tub of water by the hearth. Checking his wound, he saw that someone had removed his bandages. The flesh over his stomach was taut, a jagged white line cleaving neatly between his ribs. It fit beneath the puckered, marred flesh of his chest, where the brand of the Order of the Lily gleamed in the firelight. Spatters of blood and mud clung to his skin.

Ramson wolfed down the dinner of salted fish and hard bread and cheese, suddenly voracious now that his wound was mostly healed. Then he bathed himself with the water by the fire and a bar of soap, pulled on a clean shirt and his breeches and boots. He strapped his misericord to his waist and left through the door.

He was on a second-floor landing. A set of wooden stairs led down to the first floor, illuminated by a fire from somewhere below. Voices drifted up, and he froze halfway down the staircase.

There, sitting up on a bed, draped with furs by a low fire, was the girl he had crossed oceans for.

21

Ana awoke to the crackle of flames across a hearth. Light stirred, orange chasing shadows across her eyelids, and something smelled pleasant, like pine needles, lavender, and rosewater.

She opened her eyes. The ceiling overhead was low and sloping, wooden beams supporting a clay roof. She was in a dacha, barren but for the pallet she lay on, curled in a bundle of blankets and furs. A set of stairs led to a second-floor landing; beyond that, darkness. The world had stilled from earlier, the ground solid beneath her, the cracked walls steady.

Memories tumbled back to her. A bridge, someone's weight slung across her shoulders, a familiar face—*Daya*—emerging from the fog, catching her just as her legs had given way.

"Daya?" she croaked.

"She'll be by in a moment," came a familiar reedy voice. "She asked me to stay by your side."

Tetsyev came into view, clutching a globefire. The light painted over the harsh ridges in his face, the thinness of his skin that stretched like vellum over bone. For a moment, fear seized her, stalling her breath—and then she remembered that he had saved her life.

"You came with us," she intoned. A question.

He bowed his head. "I . . . only wished I'd had the courage to sooner."

Ana studied him, old memories resurfacing. She shoved them down. If Tetsyev had wanted her dead, he'd had many, many chances to ensure that happened. Instead, at each turn, he'd saved her life. The things he had done to her family—poisoning her father and her brother—he'd done under Morganya's mind control. It didn't make up for any of it, nor did it excuse him from his cowardice and denial afterward—but looking back, he'd helped her at several crucial points throughout her journey. He'd saved her at the Salskoff Palace, when Morganya had ordered him to kill her. Then he'd found her and warned her of the siphon scheme.

The siphons.

She twisted to look down. Someone had taken her black gloves off. Her wound appeared to have mostly healed. There was a faint pain deep in her bone, but she could move.

On her left wrist, a sea-green band twined tightly over her skin. Ana now felt something cold across her neck as well, something that weighed heavy against her collarbone. She touched a finger to it—

"Blackstone," Tetsyev said. "Please accept my apologies. It was the only way to stabilize you, after . . ." He gestured to her wrist.

It was a horrible reminder of what Sorsha Farrald had gone through: used as an experiment for siphons and restrained her entire life with a similar blackstone collar.

"It was only a theory of mine, yet wearing blackstone should provide you refuge from the power of the siphon," Tetsyev said quietly. "An Affinity is like an added sense, in the way that an Affinite learns to navigate the world with awareness to one's element. I can only imagine how it must feel with the siphons suddenly enabling access to a dozen more Affinities." He leaned forward and unfurled his palm. In the center was a small black key. "It's for the blackstone. Whatever you choose to do with it."

Ana took it. It weighed heavy in her palm, a temporary refuge from the fate that awaited her.

"The second siphon," Ana whispered. "What happened?"

Tetsyev bowed his head. "It is with Morganya."

She put her head in her hands, squeezing her eyes shut. Rehashing the scene from the bridge, the moment Sorsha's body had dangled in the air, the siphon visible for all to see. "We failed," she said quietly.

"Not all is lost," Tetsyev said. "You did a very brave thing, Kolst Pryntsessa—"

"Don't call me that." She winced and softened her voice. "Call me Ana."

The alchemist watched her for a long moment, then dipped his head. "Ana," he said quietly, as though tasting the word on his tongue. "As I was saying, with the siphon, *you* have the power to fight Morganya. The siphons cannot be used to steal power from each other, you see; by bearing the second siphon, you have evened the battlefield. You have given your side a chance to stand against her." He paused. "Yet it does not appear she is finished in her quest for power."

She blinked, the memory of the bridge and the words he'd spoken to her swirling back. "What do you mean?"

"Morganya searches for another artifact imbued with alchemical power," Tetsyev said, and Ana suddenly remembered the dark room, the woman with eyes that burned with mad fervor, whispering that the Deities had left behind remnants of themselves for humans to use. "As to what this artifact does, I do not know exactly, but it seems related to the flow of alchemical power. I believe she intends to use the siphon to plug in to that endless flow of power . . . and take it all for herself."

Alchemical power was the magic behind Affinities, behind ice and snow spirits and the Deities' Lights and everything the gods were rumored to have left behind in the human world. Ana looked down at her wrist, the siphon gleaming against her skin. Even now, she could see tiny threads of darkness snaking across its surface.

It was bad enough that Morganya had a siphon—but that there was something else even more powerful . . . the thought made Ana feel hollow.

"Then, we either stop her, or we find this artifact before she does," she said.

"Morganya has had a head start already," the alchemist said quietly. "It seems information with this artifact lies in the Kemeiran Empire. About a moon ago, she sent scout teams there to retrieve the information."

Horror seeped into Ana's veins. "The Kemeiran Empire," she whispered. *Linn.*

"I am sure they are more than capable of defending themselves. They have, after all, protected this secret for thousands of years." Tetsyev gave her a piercing look. "The decision lies in how *we* are to act."

"Strategically, it makes no sense for us to attempt to go after it," Ana mused. "We have fewer resources compared to Morganya and it seems we're already far behind." She bit her lip, her mind racing. "With my Bregonian Navy, I have the start of a formidable army." A flash of a night with darkness absolute, broken only by the flare of torches, the chants of a distant protest she'd seen through barred windows. "And I believe the people will rally to my name, should I declare war."

"The sentiment churns," Tetsyev supplied. "All they need is a spark to set the tinder ablaze."

Ana looked up, certainty gripping her. "I need to gather an army large enough to destroy Morganya before she can find this artifact."

Tetsyev inclined his head. "I would agree."

They fell silent, each absorbed in their thoughts, until Ana sucked in a sharp breath. "Shamaïra." She strained to get up, but a sharp pain lanced across her midriff. "Is she all right? Where—"

Tetsyev raised his hands in a placating gesture. "She is being tended to and resting for the night—as should you," he added, looking at her in a way that suddenly reminded her of a stern schoolteacher. "The healers have seen to your body, but you need rest. Drink this." He handed her a vial of clear liquid that had been sitting on the makeshift table next to her pallet.

Ana drained the medicine—it tasted like syrup, sticky and sweet. A warmth spread in her stomach.

Tetsyev took the vial and set it on the floor. "The siphon you wear is dangerous, particularly for someone in your state of health," he said, and she had the impression he was choosing all of his words delicately. "The blackstone is counterbalancing its effects—for now."

For now.

She turned away, lifting her wrist to study the band melded into her skin. A question formed on her lips before she had time to think about it. "What's going to happen to me?"

The Bregonian scholars had said that most of those subjected to testing siphons had died; all but Sorsha Farrald. And for the Affinites who had lost their powers, none seemed to have lived to tell the tale.

Sorsha's siphon held Ana's blood Affinity, and Ana had wielded it once again back at the Kateryanna Bridge. But she'd felt a subtle difference—a dullness to the once-bright tang in the Affinity she'd once wielded like an extension of herself. Now, her power rested in the siphon instead of inside her, separated by only a thin turquoise band.

The silence was what made her look up.

And there, in the helplessness in Tetsyev's eyes, she saw a shadow of the answer even before he spoke. "The Affinites whose abilities were siphoned . . . none ever made it past three moons."

Three moons. Her mind flipped through the past weeks like the chapters of a book, counting down each day: the journey through Cyrilia, the time spent at the Redcloak camp, the fortnight it had taken her to sail back . . . and the battle at Godhallem, when Sorsha had slit her neck and drained her Affinity.

Memories poured through an hourglass, sifting into an inevitable conclusion.

She had less than two moons to live.

Somehow, her mind was calm, her heart beating ever so strong against her chest, as though insistent that, in this moment, she was alive, alive, alive. And perhaps it was the knowledge of the fact that she had an entire empire to fight for, that she had a war to win and a monarch to overthrow before it was all over, that kept her world from falling apart.

Her head cleared, and Ana's resolve sharpened. "Well, then," she said, her voice smooth as steel. "I need to raise an army strong enough to defeat Morganya before she finds this artifact, and before my time is up."

Tetsyev's expression was heavy. "There is not yet enough research and evidence to establish certainty," he said, but she held a hand up.

"I will consider it a fact until proven otherwise," Ana said. "I cannot stake the future of this empire on possibilities."

Slowly, the alchemist nodded. "You may."

Before either of them could say anything else, the door to the dacha swung open, and in a gust of bone-chilling wind, Daya swept in. Snowflakes coated her hair and clung to her captain's coat. She slammed the door shut behind her. "Amara's armpits, it's cold up here," she gasped, and held up a bundle in her arms. "Dinner and clothes."

Ana sat herself up, gingerly shifting her healing arm. "Daya," she said, relief seeping through her at the sight of her friend.

Daya dropped off the bundle and gestured to the back of the dacha. "There's a tub behind those curtains; I've heated water so you can take a bath, because by Amara's hair, you smell."

Ana looked to the back of the dacha, where a set of coarse brocade curtains hung from the second-floor landing. Steam rose from behind them. "Daya," she said. "Thank you."

She started on her dinner as Daya perched on her bed, recounting the rest of the day, how they'd fled into the Syvern Taiga, covering their tracks. Her friend's presence and chatter seemed to chase away her previous conversation with Tetsyev like a bad dream, grounding Ana in the present: the crackle of flames, the musty scent of wood, the wind raging beyond their doors. That, until Ana bit into the cornbread Daya had brought her and found it tasteless.

She kept eating mechanically, nodding and asking questions where Daya paused, but her mind was far away. She'd felt the deterioration in her body all along, from the nausea to the loss of appetite and the loss of ability to taste, back in the Northern Crimson camp with Yuri's ptychy'moloko.

At the thought, Ana set down her spoon. "And Yuri," she said, "is he all right?"

Daya nodded. "The rest of the Redcloaks—those who survived—split from us when Morganya's forces took over, but we saved Yuri. He's healing in another dacha. I'll take you to him in the morning. It's getting late, and I plan to sleep like there's no tomorrow." She frowned and raised an eyebrow. "Not too unrealistic of a metaphor in these times, eh?"

Ana smiled. Daya was here, Yuri was safe, Shamaïra was being tended to . . . it felt as though an immense weight had lifted from her shoulders.

And suddenly, in the haze of her memories, she recalled something she'd thought had been a dream. A familiar figure stepping out from behind the statues of Deities like the answer to a prayer. Quick hazel eyes, defiant curve of his lips even as he bled.

Hello, Witch, he'd said, a greeting that had become something intimate between the two of them.

"Ramson," she whispered.

The stairs creaked; a figure descended, stepping out from the shadows, moving toward her like a ghost.

"Hello, Witch."

Time seemed to slow as Ramson stopped at the foot of the stairs. In the fading firelight, his eyes flickered. They did not leave her.

Daya shot Ramson a look that Ana couldn't catch. "Well," she said, standing and stretching in a suspiciously exaggerated manner. "It's late, and I should return to the headquarters, ensure shifts are set for the night before I sleep. C'mon, Baldie."

It seemed to sink into Tetsyev several seconds later that she was addressing him. With a startled look, he rose to his feet, inclined his head to Ana. "We'll speak more tomorrow. I recommend keeping the collar on, until you are strong enough to control the siphon."

Daya turned to Ana on her way out. "Don't wake me unless the world's ending," she called.

The door closed behind them. Silence fell in the dacha, thick and heavy, as Ana finally, finally turned to Ramson.

The firelight painted him in shadows and light, a perfect contrast of sharp edges and soft gaze that she might have captured in a portrait once in a lifetime ago. There was something different in the way he looked at her, something that sparked a flame in her and sent it roaring through her veins.

They looked at each other and she could swear her heartbeat pounded out the moments passing by, the seconds that had suddenly become irrelevant.

Her lips parted. "I didn't think I would see you again."

His laugh came in a sharp release of breath, filling her with its familiarity. "Well, I told you I made no promises." Ramson lifted his arms halfway in a semblance of a shrug, a crooked smile on his face. "I hope you're not tired of me yet."

She matched his smile. "Don't get on my nerves, and we'll see." A pause, glancing around her for something, anything, to break the tension in the air. Her search stopped at her half-finished cornbread and salted sardines. "Please," she said, sweeping a hand over the meal. "Join me for dinner."

His lips quirked and he approached, footsteps sounding loudly in the silence. The bed creaked as he sat himself tentatively at the foot of it. The entire time, his eyes never left her face. "I suppose it's true what they say about royalty. In the presence of a princess, a common dacha can feel like a palace and a peasant's meal like a king's feast."

Ana lowered her gaze, staring at her meal without really seeing it. The shape of his outline in front of her seemed to take up the entire room, the entire world. With her blood Affinity gone and the powers in her siphon muted by the blackstone collar she wore, she realized this was the first time she'd taken in the sight of him as he was without the churning warmth beneath his skin. He'd bathed, his hair still wet and clinging to the ridges of his face, and he smelled of soap and salt and swordmetal all in one. It was a scent she remembered, that she'd tasted beneath a rain-soaked night an ocean away.

She was suddenly aware of her own disheveled hair, mud and blood and sweat clinging to her. Even so, as she summoned the courage to look into his face again, she found his eyes fixed on her as though he were drinking in the sight of her.

"Are you . . . all right?" he said. The hesitation in his voice was new; she couldn't recall many times Ramson Quicktongue had run out of words.

She licked her lips and glanced down at the siphon on her wrist. The patterns on it continued to shift and swirl, black and gray and red blending into a sea of blue-green.

Three moons, of which two remained.

The dark rings beneath her eyes, the coughing fits, the blood on her hands and sleeves. The ache in her body as she ran, the bright flame of Yuri's hair dimming as she fell behind; propelled by a fighter's spirit that could no longer overcome the weakness in her legs.

"I . . ." *I'm fine.* But the words faded as she looked into those familiar hazel eyes, and realized that she might not have many more chances to tell him the truth.

That she owed it to him. Before any of this—whatever this was, whatever had happened between them that night in the storm—went any further.

Before it became too late.

Ana swallowed, and finished her sentence. "I'm dying, Ramson."

His face shifted like waters beneath an ice-covered lake, emotions passing through his eyes, beneath the mask of his frozen smile. And then the façade began to crumble slowly, terrifyingly, like a mountain into dust, and it was then that Ana realized the time for playing pretend was over between them.

Ramson leaned forward and caught her hand in his. She shivered at the way his fingers felt on the bare skin of her gloveless hand. "There is a way, Ana." His voice was rough. "I *know* there is, because I—"

"Stop. Please." Her head hurt, her heart was pounding too hard; fatigue, adrenaline, the ache of something so sweet and so sad that she could burst, all rushed to her, and she found herself squeezing her eyes shut. Hope. It was hope that she heard in his voice, and it was hope that cut deeper than anything else. Because after that day in the Blue Fort, after that kiss in the rain, she'd allowed herself to hope that there was some semblance of a future left for her and the man she'd grown to care for. That, possibly and impossibly, he'd come to care for her, too.

To have it all snatched away in the span of a breath was too cruel a punishment to bear. She couldn't let herself think there was anything left for Anastacya Mikhailov, the girl who once was, who'd hoped for a family and a future and love.

She needed to be the Red Tigress, leader of the rebellion, the one to overthrow a mad monarch and give her people the life they deserved.

Pain bloomed deep in her chest, so painful that, for a moment, she couldn't breathe.

Amid it all, there was the sound of water hissing as it turned to steam.

Ana drew a shaky breath and opened her eyes, focusing on the room before her. Above the curtain to the back of the room, the water Daya had heated for her was boiling over. Steam rose in coils overhead.

"I'd like to take a bath," she heard herself saying, her voice hollow. "I—can we speak tomorrow? After we've rested?"

Ramson was still looking at her, his expression giving way to surprise and then something hinging on embarrassment. "Oh," he said, and quickly withdrew his hand, running it through his hair. "I—sorry. Yes, of course."

Ana slid from the bed. She winced as her body twanged in pain—and a new realization occurred to her. She saw it spread over Ramson's face at the same time as he looked to her stomach, the raw flesh of her still-healing wound peeking out beneath her shirt.

A spot of color crept up his neck. "You . . . Do you . . ." He gestured helplessly at her midriff, and then her tunic and pants.

Her face heated. "I think I can manage," she said. "Perhaps if you could help me put out the fire—"

Ramson looked both mortified and relieved at the same time. He nodded and stood quickly, almost tripping on his way over to the sequestered bath. He drew aside the curtain revealing a wooden stove and a tub.

Ramson extinguished the flames in the stove, dipped his hand in the bathwater. "It's hot," he said. "Gods be damned, if I'd known there was a stove . . . The water Daya gave me was practically ice."

Ana laughed, relieved that they were jesting again. "It's no secret that Daya likes me better," she teased as she stepped through the brocade curtains, thick and patterned with stitchings of deer.

"Oh, she'll succumb to my charm soon enough," Ramson replied, and then he stepped back and cleared his throat. "I . . . I could wait out here in case you . . . you need anything," he managed.

"Oh." She realized that, for the first time in their relationship, she had no Affinity to defend herself with. That in her current state, injured from battle and weak from what the siphon had done to her body, she was vulnerable.

Ana curled her hand before her chest. "Thank you, Ramson." She drew the curtains, the light dimming slightly. It took her several minutes to wriggle out of her tunic, and then to kick off her boots and pants. The water was bliss, the heat seeping into her bones and warming her to the core. She sighed as she tipped her head back and closed her eyes, lathering soap onto her skin.

There was a sliver of light that fell evenly in the center of her tub. The two sides of the curtains bore a gap in the middle, and through it, Ana saw Ramson's silhouette as he stood outside, straight-backed and stiff-shouldered.

She couldn't see him now without remembering that night, the way he'd drawn her against him as though he'd planned to never let her go. One kiss, hasty and clumsy and fumbled in the dark, didn't mean he still wanted the same.

Even if she did.

Somewhere along this journey, one that neither of them would ever have expected, she had fallen for him. For the way he filled her stubborn silence with jokes, for how his laughs came so easily and so naturally when she kept hers sealed tightly inside. For the times he'd challenged her, utterly unafraid that she held one of the deadliest Affinities in the world. For the jests and banter between them, the way he treated her no differently whereas others would bow at her feet.

Yet . . .

In the lowlight, through the haze of steam, she caught the glimmer of the siphon on her wrist—a reminder of what had happened to her and what *would* happen to her. Ana knew, too deeply, the pain of losing those you loved in your life. Mama, Papa, May, Luka, Markov . . . she carried their names with her like scars on her heart. The worst phantoms were in one's mind, and for now, she couldn't imagine a day when their losses would no longer ache.

If Ramson felt even a hint of anything for her . . . the thought of him going through what she had with her family, with those she'd loved, filled her with dread.

He had an entire life ahead of him. She was dying.

It wasn't fair of her to want him.

Ana inhaled deeply. Steam rushed down her throat, and the heat was making her dizzy. She should sleep.

Ana reached for the towel draped over the edge of the tub— and it was then that she realized she'd forgotten to bring a pair of clothes in her haste earlier.

She swallowed, darting a gaze at the curtains that billowed gently in the waves of steam. Then, steeling herself, she grasped her towel and cleared her throat. "Ramson," she said, wishing her heart would stop pounding in her ears. "Could you bring me the clothes in Daya's bundle?"

"Yes, meya dama," came the response, and she heard the scuff of his boots as he crossed the small distance to the pallet.

"Thank you," Ana said, and rose, wrapping the towel around herself.

She stepped out from the tub the precise moment he stepped through the curtains. They collided in the tight space, she clutching her towel, he with his mouth open as though he'd been about to say something, arm outstretched with the clothes she'd requested.

Shock flooded his face as he regarded her, towel clasped to her chest, water dripping down her hair, and steam rising from her shoulders. She saw his throat bob, heard the sharp intake of his breath.

Instantly, he turned away. "Gods, Ana, I didn't mean—"

Almost instinctively, she caught his hand. He froze as she

pulled him back toward her and closed the gap between them. In the dim light, the tight space behind the curtains, she saw his pupils dilate.

Ana tilted her head to him in the curve of a question.

And he pressed his lips to hers in answer.

He let out a sharp breath as she twined her hands into his shirt. She heard her clothes fall to the floor as his arms came to rest around the small of her back, holding her as though she were made of glass, as though he were afraid that touching her would break her.

Between them, she let her towel fall to the floor. No more questions. No more hesitation.

He thawed quickly, a moan escaping his throat as he buried his hands in her hair, kissing her as though he'd been waiting his entire life. He tasted of salt and sea and a hint of mint, she thought as she let her hands trace the familiar edges of his jaw, the curve of his cheeks, and the crook of his chin, his skin rough in the way she'd always wondered.

The kiss turned hungrier, and in a single motion he lifted her, holding her over him, head tilted to her as though in worship. She wrapped her legs around his waist, the fabric of his breeches coarse and warm against her bare skin.

He carried her to the bed. The fire was dying, the room warmed from the steam of her bath. Gently, he lowered her, the sheets growing wet beneath the water slicking from her body.

She pulled him to her, fingers quick and nimble as she undid the buttons on his shirt. He yielded to her, hands spread out on the bed beside her to shield the weight of his body. She trailed her thumb over the smooth plane of his stomach, fingers making patterns over his skin as she explored.

He paused, catching her hand as it latched on to the leather of his belt. Ramson broke the kiss, panting heavily, sweat dripping down his brow as he looked at her. "Ana." His voice was husky, low, his mouth parting, his eyes darting frantically over her cheeks, her lips, her eyes. "I . . ."

She looked up at him, at the curls of hair sticking to his forehead and temples. Waiting.

"I . . ." His breaths were coming fast, panic blooming in his eyes. They hovered, her hands at his waist, her eyes on his.

Ana touched a finger to his cheek. "Say it."

He swallowed, his throat bobbing, fear freezing his features. He opened his mouth, and words tumbled out. "I'm sorry."

For what? she wanted to ask. Ana trailed a touch down his neck, remembering the last time they'd kissed. *I'm sorry,* he'd said, over and over and over again, *I'm sorry, all right?* In the nights she'd spent away from him, she'd turned those words in her mind. And it had occurred to her that perhaps, all this time, he'd been meaning to say something else.

Who was this boy who had learned to say *I'm sorry* in the place of three other words? What piece of his past drove such fear into those clever eyes at the thought of giving himself so utterly and completely to another?

Ana cupped a hand to his face, pulling him in for a soft, long kiss. He yielded to her touch, his lips melding perfectly against hers, and she found that she . . . she wanted this. That, in spite of everything she'd tried to tell herself, there was a part of her that was selfish, too. A part of her that desired, as well.

If there was one moment in which she would allow herself to be selfish, Ana thought, looking into those familiar hazel eyes, pupils dilated and utterly vulnerable as they drank her in, this was it. The single person in her life for whom she'd let herself go. For whom she'd allow her heart to speak over her mind.

Just for this one night.

"I know," Ana whispered, her voice breaking. "I'm sorry, too."

Afterward, she only remembered the tender way his lips brushed kisses against her, the hiss of his leather belt as it slipped over the edge of the bed, the warmth of his touch as the fire in the hearth flickered low, moonlight draping a hundred moments left to the dark.

22

Linn was both light and heavy, floating and falling at the same time. She was adrift in a warm coil of winds, held in their arms like a mother's embrace. She could smell the scent of citrus, chrysanthemums, and incense all in one.

Her awareness began to surface from a deep, deep sleep, swimming up toward the light.

She opened her eyes. The darkness flickered with the glow of candles, illuminating a ceiling arced with wooden rafters that crisscrossed over the rough roof of a cave. Slowly, she became aware of the lapping sensation of water over her skin.

She was afloat in a spring of sorts, carved into the stone ground of the cave itself. Linn righted herself and stood, her toes touching the rocky bottom. Steam curled around her as droplets traced gentle paths down her skin. Someone had stripped her of her clothes and bandages.

Looking at her right arm, she realized that the wound had healed.

"We call this the Spring of Miracles," came a voice. It was low, soothing. Linn turned to see a woman sitting at the edge of the pool. She was dressed in the same silk shifts as the Temple Masters, and she had no hair, no eyebrows. There was a calming loveliness to her face, an effortless grace to the way she made stirring motions with her fingers, causing little ripples in the waters of the spring. Behind her, the cave itself seemed imbued with a soft glow, glinting against the steam and the edges of plants and vines twined against the walls. The woman might have been an immortal from the storybooks, ensconced amid the plants and rocks like this. "When this temple was built, thousands of years ago, the first Temple Masters brought a ladle of the waters from the Northern Sea of Whispers to this room." She smiled. "You are reborn, child of the winds."

Linn examined her body. Her skin was soft, the wounds from the last few days reduced to pale white scars.

Wounds.

Blood, oil-black hair and chiseled features, red spilled upon the ground.

Linn looked up sharply. "My friend," she breathed. "Is he—?"

"You should be thankful for Ruu'ma shi'sen's generosity. It is not every day that a foreigner may enter the sacred Temple of the Skies." The face had not moved. "Your friend was brought to the Spring of Miracles before you. Would you like to see him?"

Relief spiraled up her throat. Linn breathed in the warmth of the steam. "Yes," she whispered.

The Temple Master stood, handing Linn a thin cotton shift. The girl shrugged it on and followed.

The Temple Master held a paper lantern, shedding light onto the room around them. They looked to be in a sanctuary of sorts, the ground made of uneven, natural stone. Patches of moss tickled Linn's bare feet as she padded across, passing trees she had never before seen. The flora looked like they had grown from another time, another place. Ancient relics of the past.

On the ground, on a ring of soft grass, was a sleeping boy. His hair curled at his temples, his eyelashes sweeping dark crescents beneath his eyes. His cheeks were full, the gash from earlier already healed into a scar. And the skin on his abdomen was smooth, corded through with muscle, the gaping wound she had seen earlier gone. The sight of his bare chest somehow made her feel guilty, as though she were intruding on something private.

Linn turned her eyes away, heat blooming in her neck and cheeks. Examining her own scars, she suddenly thought of something. "Excuse me, shi'sen," she said. "This Spring of Miracles . . . can it heal *anyone*? My friend—she is a wielder whose power was taken away from her." She remembered the dark circles beneath Ana's eyes, the hollow grooves to her cheeks. "Her health was declining."

"Ah," the woman said. "That is a question for Ruu'ma." She spread her hands. "The Temple Masters await you. Once you are ready, follow the lights."

With a sweet smile, the woman turned and walked farther until all that Linn could see was the ghost of her shadow.

Behind her came a stir of breath against her winds. Kaïs's voice, rough. "Linn?"

She peeked over her shoulder, saw him sit up. "You are awake."

"I . . . what happened?" Kaïs sat up, fighting against the sleep that fogged his eyes. She watched them clear like clouds from a silver-bright moon. "Where are we?"

Linn went as close to him as she dared and sat. She drew her knees close to her chest. "We are in the Temple of the Skies," she said. "The Temple Masters fought against the Cyrilian spies."

The sharpness returned to his gaze. "And?"

She parted her lips. Hesitated. "It is . . . complicated."

He scanned her face and pressed his lips together, allowing the silence between them to sit. He did not prod her for more, as others might have. No—it almost frightened her how much he had grown to know her throughout their time together. How easy it was to be around him, to not need to fill silences with meaningless chatter, but instead, to find the meaning *in* the silences.

Linn loosed a breath, hanging her head in shame. "I let the Whitecloaks slip through my fingers. They . . . they took the jade tablet of the Bei'kin Bookhouse." She continued, drawing a deep breath and looking up again, "Now they have information on the Heart of the Gods."

Kaïs's brows creased. "It seems our journey is not yet over."

She nodded.

He traced a hand over his stomach, where the long red wound had gaped earlier. "You saved me." A small smile twisted his mouth. He gestured around them. "Perhaps this is the spiritual dominion of the Sister, and you are still with me."

She knew vaguely of the Nandjian faith, of how the world was split into a duality of physical and metaphysical with two forces named the Brother and the Sister. Linn curled her lips into a smile. "In Kemeira, we have the belief of yuan," she said. "It translates to . . ." She paused to think of the word. "*Destiny.* We believe some people's souls are connected by threads of fate." She looked down, suddenly feeling bashful in this confession.

But Kaïs leaned forward, holding his weight by his elbows. He reached out and touched the tip of her finger with his. "I know," he said. "I feel it, too."

Linn tensed. He was so close, she could see the cave's soft glow gilding the slick black of his hair, feel the heat and power rippling from his body. The instinct of touch had become foreign to her, beaten from her by the hands of traffickers throughout the long, enduring years. Her breath quickened, her muscles tightening to anticipate the nauseating revulsion she'd grown used to at any prolonged or intimate contact. Her eyes flicked up, her senses flared, her body reacting as it would to a threat.

Gently, Kaïs slid his hand along hers, the tips of his fingers warm and roughly calloused. Inch by inch, he unfurled her palm, splaying his own against hers. His gaze never wavered from hers, silver discs of moon against her ink-black night. His touch was a question, his eyes searching hers for permission.

Linn looked at his face, open and steady, and within, she found the answer. Once her rival who'd matched her in sword-fighting, then her ally who'd trusted her to fly; now her friend through a thousand trials and dangers. They were warrior souls, connected, against all odds, across time and space and culture. Somewhere, somehow, sometime, their gods—or whatever forces above existed—had woven their fates together.

Her breath steadied, and she found the tension seeping from her shoulders. Linn looked down and slipped her fingers through his, his large palm fitting perfectly against hers, all the scars he held pressing against her own. His touch grounded her like the unmoving earth to her shifting winds; his pale eyes brightened, and meeting them again was like coming home, darkness finding light, yin joining yang.

Kaïs's black lashes flickered, but otherwise, he held very still. Only the corners of his mouth lifted.

Linn let herself match that smile. Still holding his hand, she said: "We must return to Cyrilia. We must find Ana. And we must take back that jade tablet."

He nodded. It was that wordless gesture that locked the feeling into place: that he'd been carved from the same stars as she in this life, stolen and trapped by their enemies, forged into weapons and tools, forced against their will to serve. Now, they were, at last, making a choice of their own, a stance for what they believed in.

Action, and counteraction.

They had come full circle.

"We fight," Kaïs said. "Together."

Linn and Kaïs followed the light of the paper lanterns as the woman from earlier had instructed Linn to do. The ground shifted to smooth flooring, and then they were met with a set of stone steps that wound up to a long hallway. Sunlight streamed through open-air windows carved with intricate wooden patterns. Wooden beams soared upward into ceilings covered with bright paintings of the Kemeiran gods resting on clouds, watching over the beings on earth. Wielders and givers, fire and water, earth and wind, twined around one another in perfect harmony.

In the center of the hall were a redwood table and chairs, made intricate with fretwork that ran along all of their surfaces. The Temple Masters stood gathered around, conversing in low voices, silken shifts billowing softly in an invisible breeze. Linn noticed that there were several people with partially shaved heads and long braids, dressed in gold-threaded doublets.

In Kemeira, gold was the color of the Emperor and his envoys.

A cold shock trickled through her as she averted her gaze. There was no doubt as to who they were: Imperial Messengers.

The Emperor's men were here.

Ruu'ma shi'sen looked up as Linn and Kaïs approached, and the rest of the gathering fell silent. There were twenty or so people congregated and Linn recognized Ying shi'sen and Rii shi'sen, along with several others who had fought outside.

Linn knelt before the group, inclining her head. By her side, Kaïs did the same.

Ruu'ma spoke. "Wind wielder, your warning helped us save the Temple of the Skies. What is your story? Tell it before the witnesses to the Skies and the eyes of the Emperor."

Linn looked up. When she spoke, her voice was soft. "Revered Temple Masters, my name is Ko Linnet, a wind wielder of the village of Hu'kian. I met Gen shi'sen at the village of Shan'hak, and together, we tracked down the Cyrilian spies."

"And where is old Gen now?" Rii asked.

Linn lowered her eyes. "Gen shi'sen did not survive."

"And the jade tablet is stolen," Ruu'ma murmured.

Her words were met by a heavy silence.

Linn had to summon all of her courage before she forced the next question through her lips. "Pray tell, shi'sen, what is on that jade tablet?"

"It holds information on the Heart of the Gods," Ruu'ma answered.

"Ruu'ma!" Ying's admonishment was sharp. "That is sacred knowledge, protected within these walls."

"Knowledge that we have failed to protect; knowledge that has been taken *out* of these walls," Ruu'ma shot back. "In fact, these *walls* we stand in now might have been burned or looted had this girl not warned us in time. If the current Empress of Cyrilia has the tablet and is, indeed, on the hunt for the Heart, the world as we know it is at the cusp of unraveling. Our empire is one of tradition and custom, but we must move with the changing times, Ying shi'sen. Action, counteraction."

The Shadow Master pursed his lips with an air of sullen deference; even the Imperial Messengers remained quiet.

Linn recognized her chance. "What is the function of the Heart of the Gods, shi'sen?" She was careful to keep her head bowed in respect. She could sense Ying's glare on her, an uneasy tension in the air between the Temple Masters.

Ruu'ma watched her for several moments longer. And then the Diviner Master yielded. "Ko Linnet," she said. "Let me tell you a story.

"Long ago, according to legend, the gods left the earthly world for ascension to the Heavenly Palace. Before they did, they scattered remnants of themselves around the world—traces of energy that we still strive to understand. In the snow daemons of our winters, the spring tree nymphs and summer ocean spirits, the searock of Bregon, the Deities' Lights of Cyrilia . . . and in us, the wielders."

Linn had heard this story before and had been surprised to find it echoed in other nations' folklore as well. Ana had told her of Cyrilian myths, and Ramson of Bregonian legends . . . all mentioned the remnants of the gods—whichever ones those happened to be—left in this world.

"Over time, their energies flowed into certain elements, imbuing them with unusual powers. Stones of the Dark, able to stifle magic of this world. Reins of the Sea, to steal and control the gods' powers . . ."

Her words sank slowly into Linn. *Blackstone,* her mind whispered in Cyrilian. *Searock—or siphons.*

Ruu'ma continued, "But the most coveted of all is a living, breathing source that pulses with the gods' powers, filling ours with echoes of their magic."

"The Heart," Linn whispered.

Ruu'ma turned heavy eyes on her. "It is said that our first Temple Masters watched the gods carve out a piece of their hearts and sink it into the Northern Sea of Whispers. Since then, the Heart has continued to beat, with all the magic of this world originating from it. Truth faded to lore, facts to myth, with some claiming the heart will grant a mortal the powers of a god." A wry smile. "Power, power, always *power.*

"But what the Heart truly does is connect to all the energy—alchemical power, or magek, as the Cyrilian and Bregonian scholars would call it—in this world . . . and whoever holds it can control it at will. Everything related to the flow of energy—of magic—in our world will be in their hands. Imagine, then, what one can do with that kind of power. Destroy our world . . . or re-create it at will."

A shiver ran up Linn's spine. "So . . ." She spoke slowly, the path between dots slowly winking into existence. Why Morganya had been so adamant on seeking out the siphons. Why, now, she had sent forces halfway across the world, to find the map to the Heart. "If one had the Heart and the Reins of the Sea . . ."

". . . then, one would hold the ability to take all the power of this world," Ruu'ma finished for her. She nodded gravely at Linn's look of horror. "The world has slowly been tipping, Ko Linnet. With the discovery of the Stones of the Dark came a means to oppress magic wielders of our world, as we have seen in Cyrilia.

With the Reins of the Sea, one may borrow as much power as they so desire." Her voice rang, steady and powerful as the currents of a river through the temple. "I have long studied the lore of gods through my divination, just as the alchemists in Cyrilia study their Affinites and scholars in Bregon study magen. And I, for one, fear for the path that humanity has set itself upon."

"Enough." A voice rang out, piercing their conversation. There was movement from the back of the assembled crowd, and among the Imperial Messengers, one stepped out. The sash around his waist, red as opposed to the black of the others around him, marked him as the authority here. His gaze was steel as he set his eyes upon her. "This is a matter for the Emperor and the Temple Masters—His Imperial Majesty has not even received the full report of what transpired today. You—and that *foreigner*—"

"His name," Linn interrupted, straightening, "is Kaïs. And we are emissaries of the Red Tigress of Cyrilia. We came here to warn—"

There were murmurs around the hall between the Temple Masters. It was unheard of, taboo, even, to speak of fighting for an enemy nation. The red-sashed Imperial Messenger narrowed his eyes.

"A traitor, then," snapped Ying. His shadows twisted around him. "Ruu'ma, my tolerance has run out. Already, we have said too much. Look at her; listen to her speak. She is as good as a foreigner to us. And she fights on behalf of an enemy empire."

Linn grasped for words, but it felt as though her voice had died. The enmity between Cyrilia and Kemeira was long known, and it had seeped into the minds of their people.

Ana had sent her here to try to change that.

"Please, listen to me," she said, but the dissenting voices grew louder as the Temple Masters and Imperial Messengers began to speak among themselves. Next to her, Kaïs found her gaze. He hadn't understood the exchange between her and the Temple Masters, but he'd read the desperation on her face and heard enough of their tones to guess.

He gave her a single nod. *You can do this.*

You must do this.

"Temple Masters!"

They froze. Linn's voice reverberated around the hall, startling even herself. Swallowing, she continued: "The Cyrilian spies you encountered today—those were sent by the current Empress of Cyrilia, Morganya, who took over in a coup. Since then, she has been killing innocent people, and working to change the order of the world. I have seen her regime with my own eyes; I know that she will not bring good to this world." Linn drew a breath. "I fought her forces in Bregon, to protect the siphons made from the Reins of the Sea, designed to take the powers of wielders."

"And you lost," said the Imperial Messenger. "The Cyrilian Empress's allies are to take the Reins of the Sea. Our Diviner Master warned us herself. Oh, no need to look so surprised. Kemeira has long refined its arts of Divination. Our Diviner Masters catch glimpses of Time, past and future; our emperor relies on this to make decisions." The Imperial Messenger spoke flatly. "If Kemeira were to act at every possible threat, at every potential war, we would be fighting into eternity. Our people would suffer, and, unlike the Cyrilian Empire, we will not impose our way of life upon other kingdoms in this world. At every turn, we have made the conscious choice to watch and to protect only our own." He spread his arms. "Besides, such decisions are to be made by the Emperor after he receives full counsel. We are not to simply

sail off on the word of a"—he looked at her from head to toe—
"little girl."

Linn's voice sounded very small as she spoke. "But if we do
not act immediately . . . Cyrilia will fall."

"The Emperor will determine that," the Imperial Messenger
replied coldly. "Our principle is action, and counteraction. We
will not defy the laws our gods have laid."

Linn looked between the Imperial Messengers and the Temple Masters. Harmony and balance were core Kemeiran values.
Without action, there could not be counteraction. To march into
war against Morganya meant provoking an attack, meant launching a counteraction without action.

And yet . . . Linn thought of the vow she had sworn to herself.
That no other person—Affinite or non-Affinite—in this world
would go through what she had gone through. What Kaïs had
gone through.

What her brother, *Enn*, had gone through.

The thought was the spark that kindled a trail of fire inside
her, leading to a memory: she and Kaïs, freeing those trafficked
Affinites from the Blue Fort's dungeons in Bregon. She recalled
how powerful she'd felt, daggers in hand and feet rooted to the
earth, how she'd understood then that she, the smallest wisp of
life in this grand universe, could make a difference with her own
two hands and feet and knives.

And that trail of fire leapt into a roaring flame.

"You are *wrong*." The words spilled from her mouth before
she could even stop herself to think of the consequences. Shock
rippled through the congregation, but she felt Ruu'ma's eyes
keenly watching her. Linn lifted her chin, looking directly at the
Imperial Messenger. "Cyrilia has acted against Kemeira—has

been acting against us—for *years*. They have been coming to our land and committing crimes against our people in secret." She raked her gaze over the Masters and Messengers, sparing none of the anger that finally welled out like molten lava. "Where was your counteraction when the Cyrilian traffickers came and took my brother from me? Where was your counteraction all those long years I toiled in a foreign land, praying to our gods for someone, *anyone*, to help me?" Tears stung her eyes, but she was too angry, and she could not stop. "It is not the gods who live in this world; it is *us, humans.* And the good thing about humans is that we are mortal, that we can hurt and bleed and bear scars. That we can always make the choice to continue to live, and continue to fight for good. I am but one human girl, but I will *never* stop fighting so long as I am alive."

The most powerful people of her homeland were silent, their faces shuttered as they watched her outburst. Only their eyes flickered, midnight black like her own.

Linn brushed a hand over her face. She knew exactly what they thought. Knew her own people, in all their shades of good and bad, their rigid set of values and morals that they held so tightly.

Knew it all, because it had shaped half her heart, half her life.

It felt like betrayal for her to stand. To look to Kaïs and say, in near-perfect Cyrilic, "We go. We have overstayed our welcome."

Linn bent at her waist in a swift, deep bow. "Esteemed Temple Masters, Imperial Messengers," she said curtly, and, stiff-shouldered and straight-backed, she turned and marched from the revered Temple of the Skies.

Through the destroyed courtyard, past the wide, familiar roads of Bei'kin. With every step, the thread at her heart tugged, whispering to her that this was betrayal. Her every nerve and instinct fought against her, pushing her to return, to prostrate herself at her Temple Masters' feet, and to beg them to take her back.

Linn continued forward. She had made a choice, and that choice was to keep fighting.

To ensure that no other Affinite went through what she had.

That night, Linn and Kaïs waited by the docks of Bei'kin's Port of White Clouds for passage out. They'd found a trade ship scheduled to leave that would take them as far as Bregon, from where they would need to seek passage to Cyrilia. It was a clear night, the stars bright overhead, the moon pouring down all her silver light.

Linn had never thought that she would choose to turn her back on these stars again.

Kaïs stood by her side, his face tilted to the wind as he kept his eyes trained on the sea, scanning for their ship. The breeze tossed his hair as he turned to look at her, those eyes speaking the words in the silence between them. "You are sad," he observed.

"I never thought I would leave this land again." The words hurt for her to say. "I have dreamt of returning here every night for the past ten years." She shut her eyes, lest the tears threaten to spill.

"Ko Linnet."

She jolted from her maelstrom of thoughts as footsteps sounded in the empty quay behind her. Kaïs spun, hands flying to his swords—but Linn's winds told her otherwise.

Ruu'ma strode toward them, robes billowing, hair impossibly white like a fall of snow in the night. Only when she drew closer did Linn make out the fine lines around her eyes, the shadow of exhaustion on her face. The Diviner Master drew to a stop several steps away.

Then she inclined her head and stooped into a bow.

Shock coursed through Linn's veins. It was unheard of, in Kemeira, for an elder—a Temple Master of their land, no less—to bow to someone junior to them. "Shi'sen, what—"

"On behalf of the Temple Masters, I want to thank you for what you have done for us today, Ko Linnet," the Diviner Master said. "You have given us much to consider in preparation for our meeting with the Emperor."

Linn lowered her gaze. "I am sorry if I overstepped earlier, shi'sen. I merely—"

Ruu'ma cut her off. "Listen to me carefully, Ko Linnet," she said, and clasped her hands together, in a familiar gesture. "Action, and counteraction—this is the principle we in Kemeira live by. Do you know how it came to be?"

Linn shook her head.

"From the very first Temple Masters, who communed with the gods and spirits and all that is magic in this world. You see, this principle was derived from them. The Heart has the ability to create the flow of magic . . . to control it, as well as to destroy it."

Linn frowned, mulling the words over. "'The ability to create the flow of magic . . . as well as to *destroy* it,'" she whispered, and suddenly, it felt as though someone had lit a lantern in her head.

"Do you understand?" Ruu'ma raised an eyebrow and gave her a significant look. "Healer Wennin spoke to me about your query—about your wielder friend whose power was stolen by the Reins of the Sea. To save her, you must destroy the vessel that holds it. The wielder must be present. Otherwise, the power trapped in the siphon may simply dissolve into the grand flow of energy." Ruu'ma paused, eyes heavy. "You must hurry—she is not long for this world."

Linn's chest was suddenly tight. "Ana is dying?" she whispered.

Ruu'ma inclined her head. "A wielder is not meant to live without their power."

The monumental task finally settled around Linn's shoulders. It took her a moment to remember to breathe.

"Shi'sen," she whispered, her knees suddenly weak. In spite of everything she'd gone through, in spite of all that she had fought for, the whispers of her Wind Masters came back to her in this moment. *A wingless bird,* they'd called her, after Enn had been taken and she'd stopped flying. The old fears welled in her chest, spilling from her lips. "I cannot . . . I am nobody important—"

The Temple Master took her hands, and Linn fell silent with surprise. "A sparrow's wingbeat may cause the biggest of storms," Ruu'ma said, and slipped something cool and hard into Linn's hands. Gently, she wrapped Linn's fingers around it and stepped back. "Be the sparrow, Ko Linnet."

Then, the Temple Master stepped back and strode into the darkness.

Linn uncurled her fingers. Nestled in her palm was a small wooden tablet with the Kemeiran insignia of a dragon on the front . . . and a series of strange symbols and jagged lines on the back. In the very center was the Kemeiran character *shin*—heart.

She stared at it blankly for a moment, her conversation with Ruu'ma swirling in her mind, before holding it out to Kaïs. He examined it, then drew a soft breath. "It's a map," he said. "A map of Northern Cyrilia—I recognize the port of Leydvolnya. And that . . . that must be the ocean. The Silent Sea."

It clicked for Linn, then. "Shin," she whispered, tracing a finger over the engraving. "Heart." She looked up at Kaïs, a shiver running down her spine. "Kaïs, this is a map to the Heart of the Gods."

Understanding bloomed in his face; he clasped both hands around hers, cradling the small wooden tablet. "She wants us to find it," he said quietly.

"Ruu'ma shi'sen says it is the way to control magic. She wants us to *prevent* Morganya from finding it. We have seen what using the gods' magic—alchemical power, whatever it is you wish to call it—has done to this world. Blackstone, siphons . . . it must all be destroyed and kept out of human grasp." Her throat tightened as she pieced together another part of the puzzle. "The Heart must be used to destroy the siphon that holds Ana's Affinity. But Ana must be with us, or her Affinity will be gone—forever."

"Ana is hunting down Sorsha and the siphons. So we must bring Ana to the Heart as quickly as possible," Kaïs said simply. "Save Ana and save the world."

It sounded so foreign to her, so grand, like something she would never have thought herself to be a part of back when she'd first set out on this journey. Saving the world was usually left to princesses and heroines, not a girl trafficked from her homeland, robbed of her freedom and her voice.

The edges of the map dug insistently into her palms; Kaïs's voice was steady as he spoke. "Then let us go," he said quietly, "and put an end to it all."

Linn looked into Kaïs's face and met his quicksilver gaze. Nor, she realized suddenly, were the tales of heroism ever reserved for people like him: a boy stolen from his kingdom and coerced into fighting for an empire that oppressed him and his kind.

But perhaps that was exactly why they needed to do this.

Linn nodded and this time, she reached for his hand. He twined his fingers around hers, his gentle steadiness warm in a way that filled her with a golden glow in this hour of night. "Together," she whispered.

Several hours later, Linn stood at the railing of the trade ship, watching the shores of her home draw farther and farther away, the ocean lapping in to fill the space in between. She remembered taking this exact journey eight years ago, when she'd chosen to leave behind her homeland in search of her brother. The path she'd chosen had not been kind, and it had irrevocably changed her as a person. But it wasn't the gods, Linn thought, who had gotten her through each grueling, hopeless day of being indentured in a foreign, frozen land. It wasn't the gods who had helped her survive.

All along, it had been her.

She had no idea what they might return to, what might have happened with Ana or Daya or Shamaïra. But for the moment, in the quiet, shared space between her and Kaïs, they would have strength enough.

Be the sparrow, Ko Linnet.

23

Ramson held Ana in the morning light, a soft golden glow spilling like honey over the curls of her hair, the curves of her shoulders. He watched her almost greedily, his eyes raking in the contours of her face, from the sharp edges of her jaw to the crook of her nose to the bold slash of her eyebrows. Even in sleep, her mouth was a stern line and her brows creased.

He could spend forever like this, and forever would be too short. Here, stretched out by her side beneath the twisted bundle of furs and blankets, the world silent and still all around them, it almost felt as though they could have it all.

She sighed, her eyes fluttering, opening. It was simply enough, to watch her lie peacefully with her head tilted to the window, the dark stroke of her lashes shifting as she took in the world beyond the glass.

Her gaze drifted, and the sleep vanished from her eyes as they landed on him, a clear, pure brown. Ramson trailed a finger over her cheek and she crooked her face to study him. He somehow had the impression she was searching for something. For answers.

Summoning the courage and steadying his breath, he pushed back a strand of her hair. Then, with a flick of his wrist, he produced a coin, pinching it between his thumb and forefinger as he held it to her. "Cop'stone for your thoughts?"

She blinked, took the coin, holding it up to the light, brows furrowed as though examining it. Turned to the window, dark hair sweeping over her bare back. "Now that I have a clear action plan, I've been thinking about it all," she said. "The next steps for this empire, after all this is over." She drew the furs over her like armor, a cloak to hide in. "My entire life, I've been indoctrinated with the idea that I am an heir to the throne, and that I must rule to the best of my capability. But . . ." She drew a long breath, let out a shuddery exhale. "What if this legacy in itself is a broken one?"

From the tentative way she spoke, the heaviness to the words, he could tell she had been pondering this for a while, now. Ramson set his hand in the space between them, wishing he could close their distance. "You mean to say, the Cyrilian monarchy?"

She swallowed. Nodded. "When Morganya captured me . . ." Another gulp. "She seems to believe she is doing the right thing, Ramson. And that's what scares me the most." Ana turned to him, and her face was colder than he had ever seen it. "My father thought he was doing the right thing. And my brother was incapable of even trying. I am afraid that one day, I will not know what the right thing is. That, even in this moment, I do not know what the people need."

Ramson thought to his own birth kingdom, to a conversation he'd had with a boy king not long ago. "King Darias is taking steps to make the Bregonian government fairer and more representative of the voices of the people."

She watched him carefully. "How?"

"I once said the Bregonian government is made of checks and balances—the King has no absolute authority, and all decisions are ratified by the Three Courts."

She quirked an eyebrow at him. "You once said it was all a lie."

He cleared his throat. "Historically, our Courts have only been open to the nobility—to those with the power and resources to get into the system. King Darias is reforming this, with his new general elections. He's filling the seats with magen, with civilians from unprivileged backgrounds. From *all* different backgrounds."

"Yet there is danger in that, too," she said. "For years, the Bregonian monarchy remained under your father's control. The King was merely a puppet, and whoever controlled the King pulled the strings. The same happened with my father, when Morganya was controlling him. No one in the government stepped forward—they were all too afraid to contradict him." She worried her lips. "I . . . no longer trust in a system that relies on a single point of authority."

They had never broached this kind of a subject, and he marveled at the logic to her words, the knowledge churning in those eyes. "I think that's wise," Ramson said softly.

She looked at him, but he could tell she wasn't really seeing him. It was a long while before she spoke again. "You are correct about the need for equal representation in government. My father took my mother as Empress in order to strengthen the union between Northern and Southern Cyrilia. The people of Southern Cyrilia are different—culturally and ethnically—and the Salskoff Palace needed to integrate the two peoples more. And so . . ." She twisted a lock of hair around her finger absently, and Ramson suddenly hated himself for never having asked her about this; for never having even tried. "Luka and I looked different from everyone at the Salskoff Palace. We *were* different." She turned her gaze to him and he looked at her anew. Taking in the fawn color of her skin, the deep chestnut of her hair and eyes, the way her features curved in a blend of Northern and Southern Cyrilian. "Southern Cyrilia does not have representation in our government. And neither do Affinites." She swallowed. "My father failed to see me, and he failed to represent people like me in our system. Me, and so many others."

Ramson reached for her hand. Pressed her palm to his lips. "You can change it," he murmured against her skin. "You can change it all."

She shuddered, her fingers curling against his cheeks as she looked away. "I know, and I will. But . . . I'm afraid."

The confession pried something open within him: an age-old chest of memories he'd kept firmly locked and tucked away in the recesses of his mind, yielding in her presence.

"When I was twelve years old, my best friend was murdered by the Bregonian government." The words cut like shards of glass in his mouth, but he pushed forward. "Nobody cared. A poor, orphan boy like him with no power and no gold to his name was disposable; he would never have moved too far up in the system, anyway." Memories, now bleeding from his heart, pouring out in torrents. "It's why I left Bregon. Instead of fixing the system, I ran from it." His voice came tight, hoarse, the locks in his heart fighting to open. "But not you, Ana. You see the injustices of your empire, and you are not afraid to stand against them. You *care*. You're braver than anyone I know. It's why I . . ."

Say it, a small voice inside him urged.

He couldn't.

"It's why I look up to you," he finished, turning away.

He could feel her gaze on him, burning brighter than he'd ever seen it, as though she'd known what he'd meant to say, heard the words on the precipice of his mind. Seconds, heartbeats, tumbled between them, trickling away into eternity.

And then something like recognition clicked on her face. She drew a sharp breath, eyes growing wide. Abruptly, she sat up, untangling herself from his arms and staring at him. He recognized the look on her face. It was one of calculation, of defense. "I can't do this, Ramson," she said suddenly.

Ramson blinked. "Do what?" he asked, but she was already turning, the furs closing over the skin of her bare shoulders, her gaze shuttering. "Ana—"

She flinched away from his grasp and slipped on her shift, then picked up her crimson cloak from the floor and fastened it around herself. When she was dressed, she finally faced him again, and it was as though he was looking at a completely different person. Gone was the girl who'd lain in his arms, who'd kissed him as though there were no tomorrow, who'd murmured his name in the dark.

Ana lifted her chin. "Last night was a mistake, Ramson, and I apologize."

"What?" The change was so jarring that his mind struggled to keep up. Ramson propped himself up, suddenly feeling cold. "Ana—"

"Did you come back to fight by my side?" she demanded, and there it was: that flash of the icy princess he'd met back at Ghost Falls, the stone exterior of a girl who carried too many scars.

He traced his gaze to her left wrist. The siphon gleamed a pale green in the morning light. And, on her neck, that wretched band of blackstone.

They all die.

Ramson decided to tell the truth for once. "No. I came back because I think I've found a way to save your life, Ana."

"Who ever told you I needed saving?" she snapped.

"Your Affinity has been siphoned," Ramson retorted. "And if we don't find a way to reverse it, you're going to die. But—there is a way, Ana."

She gave him a cold, flat look, and it was then that Ramson understood two things. First: that she knew. And second: that she didn't plan on doing anything about it.

He stood abruptly, wrapping a set of furs around his midriff as he strode across the room to her. She blinked. Confusion broke through the ice on her face as she backed away, stopping only when she ran into the wall.

Ramson reached for her. She flinched, and he let his hand fall to his side. Something stretched taut inside him. They were so close now that he could feel the warmth of her breaths against his face, hear the rustle of her cloak against the wall. "Ana," he said, very clearly. "I'm not leaving you, and I'm not going to let you die."

Her jaw clenched; she stared back at him, unyielding. "I never said I needed you," she said, the words cutting like glass. "My only goal now, Ramson, is to raise an army to defeat Morganya before she destroys this empire once and for all."

He wrested his voice into patience. "Ana, please hear me out. There is an artifact imbued with alchemical power that can destroy the siphons and reverse your condition—one with more power than any other known artifact. It's believed to be the core of alchemical power—of magic—in this world."

"A core of magic," she repeated quietly, and recognition slitted into her eyes. "I know about it."

He loosed a breath; a laugh of relief slipped from him. "So we should be searching for it."

Ana was silent for several moments. Her next words came under a veil of caution. "I've spoken about this with Tetsyev already. I believe it's the same one Morganya is after. We don't know enough about this artifact—what it is, where it is—to be able to find it before Morganya does. She's been searching for the past moon and studying it for even longer." She drew herself tall. "The move that makes the most strategic sense right now, Ramson, is for me to focus on raising an army so that I can march upon Salskoff Palace before Morganya siphons more Affinities, and intercept her before she finds this artifact."

"*Strategically,*" Ramson said, "going after this artifact is the best choice. It's three fish with one hook, Ana: Stop Morganya, reverse the effect of the siphons, and save your life."

"It is the risky choice, and you know that," she retorted.

"A risk I'd be willing to take," he replied without missing a beat.

Her gaze was flat. "Then it's a good thing I'm the one making the decision, Ramson, because I'm not willing to stake the fate of this entire empire on a chance when there's already a certain path to victory." Ana drew her cloak tight around herself and lifted her chin in a gesture that he knew all too well. "If there's nothing else, Ramson, I have a campaign to plan."

He didn't try to stop her as she pushed past him, the cold rushing in to fill the space where she had been. His hands fell to his sides.

"So that's it?" he said. The silver moonlight and soft whispers of the night before faded; in their place were cold, black waters, and he felt as though he were drowning again, just as he had when Jonah had died. "Last night—"

"Was a mistake," Ana replied, her face unmoving as ice. "I've told you before, and I'll say it again: I'll never care for anything other than this empire, and its people. Even if it's no longer mine."

He had no idea what to say.

She was breaking his heart.

Ana looked away. She was breathing harder now, her lips pale and her face wan, as though their conversation had drawn what little strength remained in her. One hand clasped over her ribs— a subtle move, but one that he caught, nevertheless. A trickle of blood threaded down to the curve of her lips; she reached up to swipe it away, as though it had become a habit. "If you want to stay here and work with me, I could use your help in my campaign, in training the new recruits."

There was a roaring sound in his ears, the swell of an icy river, engulfing him. The water was too high; there was no going back and, Ramson could see from the jut of her chin, the glare in her eyes, no changing her mind.

"I know there's not much in it for you," Ana continued, "and I'd understand if you chose to leave. It's what you're best at, isn't it, Ramson Quicktongue?"

The flood in his mind rose to a scream, a deluge—and suddenly, fell silent.

"It's Farrald now." His voice was strangely smooth, devoid of emotion.

Her gaze flickered; the hardness of her face disappeared, and he was suddenly reminded of the moment he'd realized that he'd begun to fall for her. Fyrva'snezh, the First Snows, beneath the slow twirl of flakes from a night sky, when she'd asked him to choose to be good.

"I'm glad we cleared that up," Ana said. Her voice was quiet, the fire within extinguished, given way to hollow darkness. "I apologize if you assumed anything of last night."

She pushed the door open. A whirl of cold wind blasted into the dacha, sweeping gusts of snow between them. He felt trapped beneath a thick layer of ice, watching as the woman he'd searched for his entire life turned and walked away from him. It was in this moment that Ramson was hit with a crushing realization: that all along, Roran Farrald had spoken true. Love was a weakness.

Ana stepped outside, and the door slammed shut behind her.

Ramson stood there, the space where they'd spent the night together suddenly closing in on him, suddenly suffocating.

I'd understand if you chose to leave. It's what you're best at, isn't it, Ramson Quicktongue?

No . . . he was no longer simply Ramson "Quicktongue," crime lord and Deputy to Alaric Kerlan. He was Ramson Farrald, now, too—captain of his own Navy squad and the son of an admiral fallen from grace. Perhaps there would always be a little bit of both in him, just as the two halves of his life had been carved out from under the shadows of Alaric Kerlan and Roran Farrald. He had sworn to undo their legacy, but more importantly, he needed to unravel the paths they'd set him on—and to forge his own.

And this time, he was no longer going to run.

Ramson dressed and fastened his cloak over his shoulders. The day was a bitingly cold one, the sun a colorless haze on the horizon beyond the stretch of the Syvern Taiga. He made for the stables, where he swung himself onto a valkryf and urged it into a canter away from camp.

He didn't look back.

24

"**B**y the Goddess Amara, you want to *what?*"

Ana held up her hands as Daya spat out a mouthful of kashya. The two of them were sitting around a makeshift table in Daya's dacha, taking their breakfast and discussing the plans and strategy of their campaign. Globefires hung from the ceilings, and lamps had been lit along the walls, lending the place warmth.

After what had happened earlier, Ana needed the company of a friend and some semblance of normalcy to pull herself together again. She'd known loss, known to shut the memories and feelings into a chest in the back of her mind and to bury herself in the motions of the day-to-day.

She had an army to raise, and a war to win.

Daya had, Ana learned, organized the camp so that the soldiers took various shifts to keep everyone fed and safe. Today's breakfast, apparently, had been brought to them by a young soldier named Parren whose family ran a restaurant in Bregon.

"I'm considering a government reform," Ana replied evenly, "and wanted to learn from you." She drew a breath, digging through her brain into the meat of all the tomes she had consumed, the textbooks she had studied throughout her time at the Palace. "I understand the Crown of Kusutri was a chiefdom before the Kusutrian Revolution."

Daya chewed on a pancake—a Bregonian bliny, Ana had learned. "We're a republic now," she said. "When we were a chiefdom, my people were segregated into social classes chosen by the stars, I suppose. If you were born into the elite class, you ruled. If you were born a peasant, you served. People were hungry, and tired, and so . . ." She shrugged. "They revolted."

Ana took a sip of tea, Daya's words roiling in her mind. *If you were born into the elite class, you ruled.*

"A republic," she said softly. "A government by the people, for the people."

Yuri had first raised this idea to her over two moons ago, beneath the dark stretch of the night sky in the midst of the Syvern Taiga. *The future lies here, with us. In the hands of the people.*

The concept had seemed so foreign to her back when she had studied it, briefly, with her tutors at the Salskoff Palace. With a good and just emperor to uphold the rule of law, surely there was more peace and affairs were processed more efficiently?

She listened to Daya speak of the Kusutrian government structure, nodding and assessing her own knowledge. *Checks and balances,* she thought. Bregon had the Three Courts, and every decision the King made had a vetting process. The Salskoff Courts had their Imperial Councilmembers, yet they were merely advisors to discuss policies with the ruler, never to contradict the ruler's wishes. This was how, Ana reflected with a twinge of nausea at the pit of her stomach, her father had been sick and under Morganya's influence for so long without anyone daring to defy him. This was how Affinite trafficking had spun out of control: with emperors—her ancestors—turning away, caring only about the prosperity of an empire and seeing only the light.

This was the danger of appointing a single person to be in charge.

The era for the monarchy has come to an end, Yuri had said.

Perhaps it had, Ana thought, tracing the curve of the siphon over her flesh. Her skin looked pale, almost translucent, the veins in her left arm running dark as though they held poison.

"Daya," she said, and looked into her friend's steady brown gaze. "If I am to reform an entire government, I'd like to appoint ambassadors, advisors from all walks of life and backgrounds. Do you have thoughts as to what you'd like to do, after all this is over?"

If, said a small voice in her head.

Daya set down her spoon with a clink. Through the frosted window of their dacha came movement in flashes of navy-blue livery and gray steel. Laughter drifted past the panes; soldiers stood in clusters, running errands or on patrol.

"This," Daya said quietly. "I want this. I've had more opportunity with your campaign than I've had in a long time in this empire, Ana. Captain of my own ship . . . and now, commander of an army. I'm an immigrant, and I know how most stories of people like me go—Affinite immigrants end up indentured, and the rest of us, we're left working from the bottom up in a system that's stacked against us."

Ana let her gaze drift outside, to the soldiers clamoring, the entire movement they had built. Together. "You've commanded an entire army by yourself while I was gone," she said. "Don't ever believe you are worth less than that."

Daya wet her lips, fiddling with her spoon. "I'm mostly good at sailing, but . . . if there is the chance, I'd love to be able to do that while making a difference." She gave a light laugh. "Of course, I don't expect you to just create a job for me, but—"

"You are a leader of this movement," Ana said, cutting her gaze to her friend. "When this is all over, one would be a fool to not recognize that this empire owes its future to you. And . . ." She smiled. "I am certain we'll need to rebuild a navy to rival Bregon's."

Daya beamed, her eyes brightening like the sun. "Good thing we already have the son of their former admiral on our side, eh?"

The words struck Ana like a bolt of lightning. She hadn't let herself think of what had happened with Ramson earlier, but now the conversation came back with a sharp, piercing pain in her chest that had nothing to do with her sickness. Last night had been a glimpse of a sliver of the boy Ramson had once been, the man he might have become. Happy and whole, with none of the scars or shadows the past eight years of his life had carved in him. She needed him to stay in the light, long after she was gone.

She needed to break him away from her before it was too late. Slowly, systematically, over the course of the next moon, Ana would need to remove the casualties that she might leave behind in this life.

Daya must have heard her sharp intake of breath. "Did something happen?" she asked, her smile slipping.

"No." Ana slammed those thoughts shut in the back of her mind, homing her focus to the present. A new day had begun.

She had work to do. There was no use for her to dwell on what might have been. "Daya," she said, "would you summon a meeting with our soldiers? I'd like to begin the plan for our campaign."

Ana took time to walk around camp, greeting the Bregonian soldiers and thanking them for their service. The camp was over a day's travel north of Salskoff, near the Krazyast Triangle. This, Daya had said, was close to where the blackstone mines were. Cyrilians traditionally kept away, believing the region to bring bad luck. Most of the villages around this area had emptied out, leaving them rich pickings as to which one they wished to occupy.

Ana spent the afternoon strategizing with Daya and the Bregonian captains, organizing scouts to take watch on all roads leading from the Salskoff Palace. Then, with Daya and the military advice of the Bregonian Navy captains, Ana began planning the roots of her campaign.

Night had fallen by the time they agreed on a strategy and a route across Northern Cyrilia; they would not have time for her to personally visit the south, and so emissaries would be sent to gather forces who wished to fight with the Red Tigress.

Ana took the walk back to her temporary dacha alone, letting the cold night air cool her head. After the flurry of work throughout the day, she found her thoughts straying back to what Ramson had said about the core of alchemical power, about reversing the effects of the siphons. On her way back, she passed by the dacha Daya had assigned to Tetsyev; the soft auric glow of candlelight spilled out from the mullioned windows. Ana hesitated, her conversation with Ramson rushing back to her in the silence.

It's three fish with one hook, Ana: Stop Morganya, reverse the effect of the siphons, and save your life.

On a whim, she turned and walked across the path to Tetsyev's dacha.

The Bregonian sentries on duty saluted her as she entered. In the sitting room, several pallets had been laid out on the floor, stacked neatly with the soldiers' belongings.

Ana found Tetsyev in a back room, hunched over a wooden table against the wall. He was reading. The tome he held was thick, the leather practically falling apart. The title had been stamped in gold: *The Theory of Alchemy and Magic.*

He looked up as she approached, then straightened and shut his book quietly.

Ana drew out the stool across from him and sat. The dacha was empty, the soldiers presumably out on whatever duties Daya had assigned them. "I'd like to speak with you," she said. "We didn't have the chance to finish our conversation last night."

He watched her carefully. "Of course," he said.

"It seems you've been studying siphons." She touched the blackstone across her neck. "You knew how to stabilize me."

He waited, his expression inscrutable.

"The artifact Morganya is after," she continued. "Tell me more."

Tetsyev began: "I first caught wind of the siphons back when I was working for Alaric Kerlan. Back when . . . we met, you'll recall."

She did. It felt like a lifetime ago that she'd tracked down the conspiracy to kill her family to the man sitting before her. The man who'd exposed a much larger scheme.

"Back then, I discovered some of his ties to Bregon, which is how I learned of the siphons. But there was more. Alaric Kerlan was a trader, and a *collector.* He'd collected relics from all over the world, placed them like prized trophies in that estate of his."

Ana nodded, remembering, with a sick feeling, how he'd kept anything, from rare animals to artifacts, from as far as the Aseatic Isles and the Southern Crowns in his mansion.

"In his travels, he'd heard rumors of a long-lost relic from traders of the Aseatic Isles, and I learned that he'd begun research on this. He'd begun whispering in Morganya's ear long before any of us were involved." Tetsyev raised the book he'd put down and handed it to her. "This book mentions a point where the Deities' Lights gather closest to our mortal world, which has me believe that the artifact may lie very close to Cyrilia. Unfortunately, we know nothing for certain, and I am more inclined to rely on evidence and science than on old legends. But if Morganya's search for this item tells us anything, it is that this artifact would hold far more power than the siphons did. In Morganya's hands, I have no doubt she will use it to change our world forever."

Ana considered him for a moment. "Why did you finally decide to leave Morganya?" she asked instead. "You have had the chance previously, but you chose to stay by her side. Why now?"

Tetsyev blinked, slowly. When he spoke again, it was in the manner of one choosing each word carefully. "I have lived my entire life as a series of mistakes. This all began when Morganya and I were no more than children, living a life in hiding, in fear of those who might find out that we were Affinites. Mine was subtler—an Affinity to the merging and morphing of elements, to alchemy—but Morganya, with the ability to manipulate flesh and mind, held so much power. I should have seen it from the start."

She'd heard this story before—parts of it, at least.

"We wanted change, and we were so bitter, so tired. Anger makes fools of the best people." He paused. "As does love."

Ana had never heard him speak of this.

"I loved Morganya." Tetsyev bowed his head, his voice hoarse. "Even when her ideas became more and more radical, even when she spoke of murder, I loved her. And I couldn't see past that . . . for a long, long time." The alchemist shut his eyes and pinched the bridge of his nose. "A part of me still does." He looked up, his features twisted into sorrow. "What do you do when the ones you love cause harm?"

Ana thought of Papa, his coldness, his unwillingness to acknowledge her Affinity. How much that had broken her, and how much of her was still seeking to heal from it. More importantly, how his views had ravaged an entire empire.

She loved him—still.

But she needed to stand for what was right.

"I suppose that is the most difficult of all," she said quietly. "It takes courage to admit that someone you love is wrong. And it takes courage to stand against them."

Tetsyev gave her a watery smile. "Courage, I do not possess in any comparison to you," he said. "I know I cannot repent for the sins I have committed in this life, but I must keep trying. I have no clear reason to give you as to why I left her side . . . perhaps I felt that time was coming to an end, that her choices were hurtling toward an inevitable conclusion, one from which humankind will not recover. I suppose the most difficult thing to understand in this world might be our own minds." He paused. "And I may never stop loving her. But I must choose to do what is right."

Ana nodded. In this world, the line between good and bad, right and wrong, was nonexistent; it all blended together in a murky in-between of gray.

And yet, they all continued forward, moving—hopefully— toward that light.

She stood, her long crimson cloak falling to the ground. It trailed behind her like blood as she walked. "My only priority right now is raising my army and intercepting Morganya before she can find this third relic." She paused, turning to look at Tetsyev. "But if you think there is a chance of finding out what this relic is . . . then I want you to continue your research, on the side."

The alchemist's eyes were heavy. "If there is a chance, it is a slim one."

"Fortunately for you, I don't like to sit around staking my bets on slim chances," came a familiar voice.

Ana spun. Outlined in the doorframe, hair tousled and clothes windswept and covered in a dusting of snow, was Ramson.

Her mind blanked. She had taken care to direct her thoughts away from him all day, and she'd presumed the same of him after she'd stormed out on him in the morning. Seeing him was like opening a fresh wound.

Ramson's smile cut. There was something different about him, as though he'd reverted back to the old version of himself, the one she'd met moons ago in the graylight of a prison cell. "I like to keep expectations low so the people around me can be pleasantly surprised once in a while," he said casually, strolling in. His gaze flicked up. Held Ana's. "Certainly beats the other way around."

Ana's face hardened. "What do you want?"

Ramson turned to the door and gestured. The next moment, a squad of his guards came in, carrying a wheelchair between them. A man sat in it, face gaunt, skin sallow; he had the markings of a Bregonian tan that had long faded.

"Ardonn, meet the Red Tigress," Ramson said, motioning. "Ana, meet Ardonn, former scholar of the Blue Fort and part of Kerlan's siphon team."

Ana's breath caught. She looked to Ramson. "What are you doing?"

"Ardonn and I have a Trade," Ramson replied. "As a former member of Kerlan's inner circle of siphon researchers, he knows all that we do not about them . . . including how to destroy them." He stuck a finger in the air. "And that's how this artifact—this *core* of alchemical power that we spoke of—comes into play. Ardonn is to help us find that artifact before Morganya does. My squad will remain on his guard. And . . . he is developing elixirs that can mend your health in the meantime." He splayed his hands. "No resources taken from your end. You go ahead and plan your campaign, raise your army; nothing for you to do here."

There was a glint of a challenge in his gaze, and the corners of his mouth curled in mirth. She knew that look—it was the face he had shown her back when they'd first met. That trouble-making old smirk.

Something shifted in her heart, but she stilled her expression as she turned to Tetsyev. "If he gives you any trouble, report to me," she said, and then swept out of the room.

She was aware of someone following behind her, footsteps sounding against the wooden floorboards. Ana didn't stop until she'd stepped outside. Out here, it was dark, empty. Between the silhouettes of trees, she could see the flickering torchlight of guards on patrol at the perimeters of their camp.

Ana turned around. "All right," she said. "You've proven your point."

From beneath the shadow of a large conifer, a figure stepped out. They were far enough from the dacha that the firelight spilling from the windows was but a dusting of gold against Ramson's hair and cheekbones. "Not even a word of thanks?"

"Don't push your luck, con man." She hesitated, and her voice was soft when she spoke again. "Thank you, Ramson."

He watched her with his hands tucked in his pockets; from here, she caught the glint of torchlight reflected in his eyes. "I'm not the one who chose to run this time, Ana," he said quietly.

She had the desire to weep, to yell at him. That if things had turned out differently, she would *never* have run from what she wanted most selfishly for herself. That she had no choice. That she couldn't stand the thought of his heart breaking two moons down the road, if this sliver of a chance didn't work in their favor.

That every single part of her ached from wanting to be with him.

"I'm tired, Ramson." Her breath unfurled in a cloud of vapor. "And I have enough to think about without wasting my energy on chances and possibilities." She began to walk away.

He called after her. "I told you when we first met that I'm a businessman, Ana. I never take a gamble that I don't think I can win."

His words rang in her head the entire way back. Her dacha was dark, deserted. It was hard to imagine that just this morning, she'd woken up in Ramson's arms, feeling safe and whole, a peaceful kind of contentment she hadn't known since her days with May.

Ana curled up on the bed, gathering her knees to her chest. It was blacker and colder in this part of Cyrilia, the wind seeping into her bones in a more insidious way that made her wonder if the stories were true. The Deities' Lights danced overhead, closer than she'd ever seen them. Their colors changed erratically, almost angrily.

She stared up at the night sky, watching the lights shift and churn. The day's events came back to her, and she focused her thoughts on the tasks she still had to accomplish.

Raise her army.

Defeat Morganya.

Establish equality.

Reform her legacy.

She felt detached from the thought of her own ending. It was a concept she'd seen foreshadowed since the very start, since she'd watched her entire family pass through death's maws. Mama, Papa, Luka, and now her. Perhaps, she found herself thinking, this was the Deities' will. With each regime, it was the blood of the rulers that had paved the way for a new dynasty.

It was clear, then, what she would have to do. Before her death, she needed to transition the government of Cyrilia.

Her dynasty had fallen. She was the last heir of the Mikhailov regime. The era of Cyrilian monarchy had come to its end.

The future lies here, with us. In the hands of the people.

That night, Ana was sleepless as she lay on her bed, gazing

up into the sky through her window at the stars above, as she had her entire life. She wondered how the history books would write her tale, what kinds of stories the people would spin of her . . . and what kind of a legacy she would leave in this world, long after she was gone.

25

Ana was grateful for the hot koffee that the young Bregonian soldier and restaurant owner, Parren, brought her the
next morning. She sipped it as she made her morning rounds,
thanking the soldiers for their hard work. But there was a specific
dacha she was headed to.

Daya had set up Yuri and the one remaining Redcloak not
far from where Ana's dacha was. Bregonian soldiers stood sentry
outside; they saluted her as she approached, and she inclined her
head.

The dacha was a single room, with two makeshift beds. The
snow Affinite, Yesenya, was curled up on one bed against the
wall; she looked up as Ana entered. They'd met, once, a moon
ago, back at the Redcloak base in Goldwater Port. She looked
to be Southern Cyrilian, her tan skin and brown hair holding
echoes of Ana's own. She watched Ana with large golden eyes,
silent.

Ana moved toward the occupied bed. As she approached, she
could make out Yuri's bright red hair, singed so that it now only
reached his ears. His pale skin still showed signs of the burns
he'd sustained from the Kateryanna Bridge, but it seemed the

healers had worked hard. The marks were faintly red, glistening with salve.

He stirred, opening two puffy eyes to look at her. There was no emotion in them, only dull recognition. "Have you come to kill me?" His voice was a rasp.

The question was jarring. "What are you talking about?" she asked. There was a strange expression on Yuri's face, almost like guilt.

He blinked, and it vanished; his face cleared. "I—nothing," he mumbled. "Bad dream." Slowly, he shifted himself into a sitting position on his pallet, wincing in pain as he moved.

Ana drew up a chair. Sat. There was something off about him and the way he shuttered his gaze. Their partnership had never been easy, but she'd thought their battle against Sorsha and Morganya would have brought them closer together.

Or, Ana thought suddenly, taking in the movement of Bregonian patrols through the frosted-glass windows, it would have confirmed Yuri's fears. That she'd raised her own army away from him; that she'd been holding on to her own plans all along, secretly communicating with her own forces behind his back—just as Seyin had accused her.

And now, she realized with a pang, Yuri knew that Seyin had spoken true.

She wrestled her emotions into place, steadying her voice. "How are you feeling?" she asked.

He massaged his abdomen. "Alive," he said, a wry smile twisting his cracked lips. She poured him a cup of water from the pitcher on the table next to her. He hesitated only slightly before taking a long gulp.

She returned his smile, but it felt forced. "The Bregonian

healers are something," she said. "They've trained their Affinites efficiently, and their military is stronger for that."

A shadow swept across Yuri's face, and for a moment, Ana saw a flash of cold fury in his eyes. "I should have believed Seyin," he said, dropping any semblance of friendliness as bitterness clouded his tone. "You lied to me. You went behind my back. And now you're holding me hostage."

"Wouldn't you have done the same?" Ana asked. "If you were in my place, Yuri, and the leaders of the rebel group you're trying to work with refuse to believe your intentions—wouldn't you look after yourself as well?"

"You're damn right I would," he snapped.

She wanted to shake him, to tell him to forget Seyin's voice in his ear; to stop blaming her for the Imperial Inquisition raid in Goldwater Port—the one that had killed his mother. That he'd never truly listened to her all along and—for what? Because she was the heir to the Cyrilian throne? Because she'd been born into the bloodline of a system that he despised?

But Ana only drew a deep breath and said evenly, "I want to work with you, Yuri."

"And I told you," he replied just as evenly, "we are not allies. We might have worked to take back the siphons from Morganya, but anything more than that, we won't accept any alliance without—"

"I want to work with you to reform our government," Ana interrupted. "I want to step back and transition to a government run by the people, and for the people."

Yuri blinked. Opened his mouth. Closed it, then sat back and stared at her. "What?" he blurted.

The reaction was so pure, so reminiscent of the stubborn,

quick-tempered, and straightforward Yuri she'd known in her childhood that she felt the atmosphere instantly loosen. Ana let out a sharp breath, holding back the ridiculous urge to laugh. "You were right all along." The confession came easier now. "I've always thought you doubted my ability to rule, Yuri, but now I know that is not so. Perhaps I would be a benevolent ruler—and perhaps not—but I see that we cannot trust in the monarch to be just, to be good, and to do right by the people." She inhaled deeply. "We must break this system to make a new one."

He was looking at her as though he didn't quite believe what she was saying. "Truly?" he asked.

"Truly," she replied, and pulled out what she had been working on: a scroll of parchment on which she was drafting her transition plan.

Yuri took it, eyes roving over the page, growing wider and wider.

"I'm thinking bodies of representation," Ana continued, "for Affinites and non-Affinites, to start with. No policy is passed without a vote."

"We'd need checks and balances," Yuri added. "Different courts to hold different functions, just like they do in Bregon. Representation from the bottom up, so the voice of the people can be heard." He looked up. There was suddenly a light in his eyes that warmed his entire face, and Ana felt as though they were back in the Salskoff Palace together, he conspiring to steal treats from the kitchens for her.

"But first, we must win this war," she said. "I plan to begin a campaign to gather forces across Cyrilia."

"Once Morganya's regime is overthrown," Yuri said, "then our parties can work together to reform the Cyrilian government."

He was gazing at her as though seeing her in a completely new way, those coal-gray eyes flickering. His voice was quiet when he said: "And after that, you'll yield the crown?"

Ana parted her lips to speak.

An explosion tore through the air outside, the force of it rattling the walls of their dacha and throwing her off-balance. She caught herself against the table, crying out as the water pitcher and various plates and furniture smashed to the ground.

A second explosion shattered the wall of their dacha.

The ground tilted beneath her, and the next moment she found herself on her hands and knees. Her palms were scraped and bleeding; there was a ringing in her ears that she couldn't shake off. The floor was covered in debris, clouds of dust stirring in the air all around her. The acrid scent of smoke choked her lungs.

She heard someone shouting her name; felt a pair of firm hands on her shoulders. Dazed, she looked up, her vision doubling and tripling before it focused. Flame-red hair and coal-gray eyes, brows creased in concern.

She saw Yuri's lips move. Everything was muted, as though she were underwater.

And then the light of the fire in the hearth dimmed. The paltry sunlight filtering through the windows turned to black. From the writhing darkness stepped a figure dressed in pure white.

Seyin's expression was tight, but there was murder in his eyes. He looked from Yuri to Ana and raised his hand in a gesture. Several more hooded figures materialized from the billowing dust. Their hoods nipped red at their heels.

Redcloaks, Ana thought dully, her mind still struggling to shake off the aftermath of the explosion, the high-pitched whine in her ears. Seyin had found their camp—and he was attacking.

As one of the Redcloaks ran past her to Yesenya, another raised his hand.

The air in the room shifted. Suddenly, Ana couldn't breathe. She clasped her hands to her throat, bending over on the floor, opening and closing her mouth to draw in the breath that wouldn't come.

The Redcloak's gaze was merciless; he tightened his fist. An air Affinite, Ana realized, like her friend Linn. Only she had never seen Linn use her Affinity in such a cruel manner.

Her lungs burned as she reached to her blackstone collar. Her siphon was blocked—she couldn't use any of her Affinities. The key, where was the key that Tetsyev had given her? She felt through the pockets of her shirt, but they were empty. It must have fallen out during the explosion. Coughing, eyes watering, she swept her hands across the floor, sifting through debris.

By her side, Yuri stood. In a single step, he positioned himself between Seyin and Ana. The world spun around her as she watched Yuri approach Seyin. He was yelling something, making motions with his arms. Through the ringing in her ears, Ana heard only muffled sounds.

As Seyin began to speak, Yuri pressed his lips together. The former Second-in-Command looked to her and pointed, his jaw clenched.

Black spots dotted Ana's vision; her limbs were growing weak. She was going to die, right here, in the middle of her own camp—

And then, without warning, the pressure on her chest lifted. Ana gasped, swallowing lungfuls of sweet, cold air. The world shifted beneath her as though she were being lifted; dimly, fragments of conversation filtered through her consciousness.

". . . dare disobey your Second-in-Command?" Seyin's voice was twisted in a snarl, directed somewhere toward the doorway. There was a mumbled reply—perhaps from the air Affinite who'd released Ana.

"Might I remind you that *I* am the commander." Yuri's words were icy, and they came from nearby. Her eyelids were heavy, yet sensation began to return to Ana: bitter smoke, strong, warm arms encircling her. Yuri held her, she realized. He pressed her head against his chest, the rumble of his voice in her ear as he spoke. "What in the hells do you think you're doing?"

A hint of uncertainty to Seyin's voice. "Rescuing you."

"I was never a prisoner," Yuri said heatedly. "I was in the middle of negotiating with Ana. We need her, Seyin—we have no sizable army of our own with which to fight Morganya, and the enemy of our enemy is our friend."

"Not if she's also a monarch, next in line to take the throne."

"She isn't," Yuri replied. "She's going to give up her crown—transition the government and hand over power to the people."

Seyin's tone was derisive. "And you're going to take her at her word?"

Before Yuri could reply, shouts came from outside, followed by thundering footsteps. Ana's eyes fluttered open as Seyin and the other Redcloaks pivoted, arms raised to defend themselves from the impending attackers.

"Ana." Yuri shifted her in his arms, and she found his coal-gray gaze, burning into hers through the dust and smoke. "Forgive me. This was all a mistake."

Ana reached for Yuri's hand; his fingers were there, solid and warm, just as they'd always been when they were children.

"Can you stand?" he asked. When she nodded, he set her down. Gently, he wrapped his arm around her waist to steady her as the world spun.

Outside, someone called her name: someone whose voice was utterly familiar. Through the plumes of smoke, Ramson emerged, decked out in his full Bregonian naval uniform and blackstone-infused armor. His misericord glinted in his hands as he strode toward them. Behind him followed his squad of soldiers, weapons drawn, several coated in soot and dust.

Seyin and the Redcloaks had drawn their own daggers, but even as Affinites, they were outnumbered. The Second-in-Command's face was furious, his eyes cold with the intent to kill.

A battle here would end badly for both sides.

Yuri's gaze never left Ana's face. "Give me the chance to make it right. We started this together, with May; now, let's finish it together."

Ana studied his face, searching for a trace of the childhood friend she'd known and loved. The one who had stood up against injustices in his own ways, back at the Palace. The one who'd never been afraid of the consequences for his own life if he'd been caught talking to her or sneaking her treats or even sitting outside her door for all the lonely nights. That Yuri had held the spark of what had begun his revolution: a quest to make things right.

"Let her go," Ramson called from near the opening in the wall. "If anything happens to her, I'll make it so you'll wish you were dead."

At last, Ana squeezed Yuri's hand. Drew a breath. Her voice came out as a rasp. "Ramson," she said. "Stand down."

She would never forget the look of fury that flashed across Ramson's face as he beheld her. His lips tightened; his gaze pinned Yuri like daggers. "Let her go first," he snarled. "And tell your men to stand down."

Yuri's hand tightened around Ana's waist, but he stood his ground. "Redcloaks, fall back," he said.

Seyin was the last to lower his daggers.

Ana straightened, testing her weight. There was a pain in her chest that she'd have the healers examine later—but for now, she could stand. From all around came the sound of more footsteps as soldiers from her army congregated, weapons drawn. She needed to de-escalate the tension, before a full-on fight broke out.

Ana straightened and, wrapping her cloak tightly around her, pushed past Ramson and his men. Her soldiers were emerging from all corners of the camp, weapons drawn.

Ana held up her hand. "This is a misunderstanding," she called, and was grateful for the utter silence, the way her soldiers watched her with rapt attention. "We are in alliance with the Redcloaks. I am safe, and I am repeating this order for my forces to *stand down.*"

She caught Daya's face among the group. Ana gave her a nod; her friend nodded back, then held up her hand in a motion to her troops. "Stand down!" she shouted. "The Red Tigress is safe!"

As the command was passed through the soldiers, Ana turned back to Yuri. The commotion outside fell away as she spoke again. "You once said we would come full circle again." Ana held out her hand. "Let us make it right, together. And let us finish it, just as it was meant to be."

Yuri broke into a smile as he wrapped his fingers around hers. "Together," he said. "We'll come full circle again, Ana."

"Ana."

She kept walking, trying to ignore the stir of emotions in her stomach at the sound of that voice.

"*Anastacya*, stop."

Ana whirled round. The name cracked like a whip; she'd never heard Ramson use it. He strode behind her through the jagged silhouettes of conifers, the sky breaking silver over them. A few dozen steps away, she could see the shapes of the dacha where her soldiers gathered, listening to Daya's orders on repairing the camp.

"Ramson," she said, unable to keep the weariness from her voice.

He came to a stop before her, navy-blue cloak billowing about him, cutting him in a crisp, sharp outline. His eyes were cold as he spoke. "I want to know what you were thinking, allying with them after they've betrayed you round after round after round."

"Yuri and I have reached an understanding," Ana replied. "We'll campaign together to gather an army and overthrow Morganya's regime. Then I'll transition the government and step back." She lifted her chin, daring him to challenge her. "The Redcloaks are our allies now, so you'd do well to remember that."

"Oh, some *allies* they are, going around blowing up our camp," he bit back. "Did you see that shadow Affinite's face? He was about to kill—"

"Ramson." Her anger sparked white-hot in her. "Stand down. This is an *order*."

His eyes narrowed a fraction. "Since when were you under the impression that I took orders from you, Ana?"

She swallowed her anger. When she replied, her tone was even. "You're right, I'm sorry. You are my ally, Ramson; I overstepped."

Without another word, she swept past him. She needed some peace and quiet. . . . She'd intended to visit someone she'd come to think of as a mother.

She was relieved to find Shamaïra's dacha untouched, guarded by four soldiers who stepped back to let her in. The interior smelled of medicinal balms; a fire burned in the hearth, lending the room warmth.

She'd visited several times each day; sometimes, she'd entered to see healers tending to Shamaïra, dribbling kashya down her throat, applying salves and medicines to her in hopes that she would wake.

She hadn't.

Ana knelt by her friend's pallet, the tension inside her uncoiling into something tender as she looked into the Unseer's lined face. Within nearly two moons, Shamaïra seemed to have aged ten years. Her skin was waxen, a stitching of cuts and bruises overlaid atop one another, some fresh and some fading. The sight brought a deep ache to Ana's chest.

She took Shamaïra's hand and laid her head next to it.

"I'm sorry," she whispered. "I'm sorry it took me so long."

The Unseer lay unresponsive, her chest rising and falling with quiet breaths. The silence was almost too much for Ana to bear. Shamaïra had been a woman with a crackling spirit and a sharp tongue and a presence larger than life.

"Your son, Shamaïra," Ana tried again. "Kaïs. He is alive. He is well. He is coming home to you."

No response.

A clean towel and tub of water rested at the foot of the bed. Ana wet the towel and, tenderly, dabbed at Shamaïra's sweat-slicked face, smoothing out the wrinkles in the Unseer's forehead.

"You told me once," Ana said softly, "that there would come a day when I would have to sacrifice that which I hold dearest for the good of my empire. I did not truly understand the meaning behind your words until now.

"And I am ready to make the sacrifice."

She might have sat like this forever, with nothing but the crackling of flames in the hearth and the gentle breathing of her friend filling the air around them. But there was so much left to do.

She rinsed the towel off and rested it at the edge of the tub, then stood. She pressed a kiss to her friend's forehead, brushing back a few stray hairs, taking in the faint scent of rosewater that clung to Shamaïra's skin. "We miss you," Ana murmured. "But you've done more than enough for this revolution. You can rest, now."

Shamaïra continued to slumber as Ana left. She made for the center of her camp, where a group of people had gathered: Bregonian Navy captains and Redcloaks alike. She sensed their gazes on her as she strode over, cloak whipping behind her. In the distance, columns of black smoke drifted from several different locations around her camp.

Daya straightened at her approach. "No casualties," she said. "We've assessed the damages. It shouldn't take too long to repair."

"Don't bother," Ana said, waving a hand. "Have them put out the smoke—it's giving away our location. After that, call a meeting. I want all the commanders and captains involved."

Daya tapped her forehead in a salute. "What will the meeting cover?"

Ana looked to her army, to the few Redcloaks clustered to the side. To Ramson's squad, with their blackstone-infused armor.

It was time.

"We march at dusk," Ana replied. "Tonight, I begin my campaign as the Red Tigress. I declare war on Morganya's regime and all who support her."

The rest of that day, Ana wrote. Letters upon letters upon letters, signed and sealed with an image of a roaring red tiger. She watched the wax dry, dripping down the scrolls like blood. The letters were distributed among riders—emissary units dispatched to towns in Southern Cyrilia, where Ana and the main body of her troops would not have time to reach.

She would take her forces farther north, to cities where Morganya's Imperial Inquisition had passed through and ravaged. To towns Morganya thought had been subdued.

And she would ask them to fight with her, for a different future.

A better future.

The night was cold and starless as they began their journey in silence, the snow muffling the steps of soldiers and the hoofbeats of steeds. Flags were raised, rippling silver in a cutting wind and bearing the sigil of a red tiger.

Red Tigress.

It was time for her to bring her people together.

Together, they would make the revolution.

Together, they would break the system.

At last, Anastacya Mikhailov decided, she knew what kind of a legacy she wished to leave behind.

PART II

26

The winter had plunged into its coldest weeks yet as Ana and her soldiers made their way across Northern Cyrilia, the world blanketed by the gray silence of snow.

Ana woke to a fit of coughing. It was a feeling that had grown familiar over the course of the past few weeks: a gut-wrenching hacking that made her entire body lurch. She leaned over the side of her bed to retch into the bucket she kept there at all times.

The deserted dacha was cold; she drew her furs over her shoulders and went to the hearth to light a fire and draw a bath. Even in the warmth of the water, her shivers would not stop.

Her body was beginning to fail her. It was something she felt in the strength it took for her to do tasks as simple as scrub her hair, towel off, and lift her fur cloak around her shoulders. The way her hands shook when she held a brush to her face for too long so that she had to powder her face in sections, then apply salves to the dark circles beneath her eyes, rouge to her cracked, colorless lips.

Ana leaned back and examined herself in the looking glass: fawn skin powdered back to fullness, blush swept across her jutting cheekbones, dark hair toweled off and twisted in a bun. None but those closest to her knew of her deteriorating condition; she needed to present a strong front to her allies and her soldiers.

She'd unlocked the blackstone band at her throat since the Redcloak attack, spending her spare time in training with her siphon, testing out the Affinities it held and learning to control them. Tetsyev had asked to observe on several occasions, recording her thoughts and experiences in wielding the siphon for his research. Ardonn, a bespectacled man with sunken cheeks and a rattling voice, had left his dacha to watch her from the shadows on several occasions. Ramson had mentioned that the former scholar had supervised the siphon experiments on Affinites while he worked for Kerlan.

Each Affinity, Ana had learned, bore its own characteristics. Her blood Affinity fit her like a well-used glove, but the others— fire, ice, wood, earth, and a few others—were difficult to wrangle.

And shifting between them was the hardest of all—a technique she'd only practiced with the most powerful Affinities her siphon possessed.

It hadn't escaped her that each of these Affinities had come from somewhere, from some*one*—a fact she was acutely aware of during every second of her training. Using them had felt like intruding on a private part of someone else's soul; none but her own blood Affinity felt right to her, and even so, it felt distant. The Affinities in her siphon gave no tells, no distorted bulging of veins on her hands, no reddening of her irises. Ardonn had called the siphons unnatural, an unbalancing of the world, and it certainly felt that way.

Leaning forward to the looking glass in her dacha, Ana

touched her fingers to her reflection's eyes, and thought of the days when they would bleed crimson as she wielded her Affinity.

But this girl staring back at her from the looking glass was no longer Anastacya Mikhailov. She was the Red Tigress, leader of the rebellion, whose only purpose was to find the third relic and defeat Morganya. Whatever happened to the girl she had once been no longer mattered.

She simply had to live long enough to win the war.

Not long, now.

The chill of a true Cyrilian winter wrapped itself around her as she stepped outside, boots plunging into the thick snow. The sunrises up north were bleaker, and she found herself thinking of the picturesque ones in the Kingdom of Bregon that had seemed to set sky and sea on fire. Here, the sky held a monochrome duality of gray and white, watery light sludging across the horizon.

It was the fourth week of her campaign as the Red Tigress, and they were drawing close to the end of the journey. They had arrived just last night at Osengrad, a town close to the western border of Salskoff. It was the last planned stop on their campaign.

The camp was awake already, borscht and kashya bubbling over a fire. Soldiers clustered around: those from the Bregonian Navy, as well as new recruits without uniform. The sound of conversation and laughter lent Ana a sliver of warmth as she took her own bowl of rations. They were to march through town by dawn, knocking on doors and handing out posters for the Red Tigress, persuading people to gather in the town square. There, Ana would give her rallying speech.

Her soldiers were ready and waiting in formation, and as Ana surveyed their ranks, she couldn't help but feel a surge of hope coursing through her tired body. Their efforts over the past moon hadn't been for nothing: Their army had tripled in size. Between journeying, Daya and Ramson and the other Bregonian captains spent time teaching the new recruits, most of whom were civilians with no previous swordfighting skills.

For the Affinites who joined them, Ana supervised their training, along with Yuri and his team of Redcloak Affinites. Between writing speeches and making copies of posters and organizing the movement, however, they were all stretched thin—and though their army was growing in numbers, they would be woefully unprepared to face trained soldiers of Morganya's Imperial Inquisition.

"Morning." Daya drew up by her side, leading two valkryfs. "Sleep well?"

Ana took the reins of her steed. "As well as I can," she replied, studying her friend's face. "You?" There were dark circles under Daya's eyes, and she held a canteen of hot koffee. Daya was responsible for the units they had sent out to the rest of Cyrilia; she'd remained in contact with them, frequently penning letters deep into the night.

Daya's grin was laced with fatigue. "As well as I can," she echoed, and swung herself onto her steed. "Last run of the show. Let's do this."

Ana followed, ignoring the cramp in her side and the way her arms and legs shook with the effort. She steadied herself on the saddle and, drawing a deep breath, lifted a hand in signal to her army.

As they began to make their way through Osengrad, the town began to wake. Faces peered at them through dacha windows, eyes roving over Ana, then to her soldiers and the flag bearing the crest of the Red Tigress they held. Her men knocked on doors and slipped posters where they could.

Word of their recruitment seemed to have spread through the entire town; children playing in the streets paused at their procession and pointed to Ana, whispering excitedly.

"That's her, that's her!"

"The Red Tigress is here!"

At their sight, Ana broke into a smile. She thought of the girl she had been, of the children she'd known—May, Yuri, Liliya, the Redcloaks—who'd lost their innocence too early.

The future belonged to them, and she would fight for it until her dying breath.

By the time they reached the town square, a sizable crowd had gathered. Mothers held their children close to them as fathers and young people held drafting scrolls in their hands. A wooden scaffold stood erected in the center of the square, built earlier that morning by a wood Affinite in their ranks. Torches had been erected at the corners.

Ana stopped her valkryf and dismounted. The movement was jarring; her knees nearly buckled under her weight, and for a moment, she held on to the saddle of her steed, steadying herself.

In the ranks of her soldiers, she somehow caught sight of Ramson and his Navy squad. His face was blank, but his eyes found her through the crowd.

Ana straightened. Walked to the center of the platform. Raised her hands, dug into the slumbering Affinities held in her siphons, called on one. Fire sparked to life in her palm, sweeping in an arc around her so that she was alight in its glow. The torches burst into flame, lighting the square.

She took time to catch her breath. This was an essential part of the performance: a show of her power to build confidence in her movement. It was also one that cost a lot of strength—strength that was ebbing away from her day by day.

Drawing a long breath, Ana lifted her chin and addressed the crowd gathered. "My fellow Cyrilians." Her voice rang out clear and loud. "My name is Anastacya Mikhailov, and I am the Red Tigress of Cyrilia. Today, I come before you with a vow.

"The Empress Morganya promised us equality. She promised to protect Affinites. Yet three moons into her regime, and our empire burns at her hands. Our people are slaughtered by her forces." She paused, sweeping her gaze around the square. "Morganya lied."

She caught sight of Yuri in the midst of her troops and he gave her a small nod.

Ana continued. "Today, I ask you to fight with me. And my vow to you is this." She raised a finger. "One: abolishment of persecution of both Affinites and non-Affinites. My government will, instead, lawfully investigate Affinite trafficking in this empire, and bring these practices to a stop—by fair means.

"Two: equality between Affinites and non-Affinites. My government will focus on policies put in place to promote a world where we can coexist. And we *can.* How many of us have mothers and fathers, brothers and sisters, sons and daughters, people in our lives who are Affinites, or not? How many have lived under fear of persecution? I know I have." Her tone shifted, power yielding to emotion. "I was the only Affinite in my family. My only wish was to be allowed to live, regardless of my Affinity."

Silence stretched across the square.

Ana raised a third finger. "Three: a government made by the people and for the people."

A collective intake of breath; murmurs all around.

She had come to expect this—it had happened many times before when she reached this point. Ana looked around and nodded solemnly. "You know me as the blood heir to the Mikhailov regime, the supposed rightful Empress to the throne. But . . ." She drew a breath. "The monarchy itself is an imperfect system with which to govern and is the reason our empire has had these pervading issues for so long. I want to put power in the hands of the people. In *your* hands."

Ana paused. The torches flickered. She stepped forward, to the very edge of the scaffold. "Fight with me. Together, let us rebuild this empire. Together, let us rebuild this world. For the better."

The town square was silent.

And then, out of nowhere, a cheer rose, growing louder and louder until the square thundered with applause. Threading down the streets, spilling over from the alleyways that led to the town square, the Red Tigress's army, too, began to make noise, clanging swords on shields and walls in unison.

Yet in the midst of the celebration, something caught Ana's eye. Ramson, standing stock-still in the crowd, his previously inscrutable expression morphing into one of alarm. His lips parted; he was mouthing something at her. He lifted his hand and tapped his fingers to his nose.

Ana mirrored his motion; it was then that she felt something hot and sticky trickling down her lips. She already knew what she would see before she drew her thumb and index finger back. They glistened crimson in the firelight.

She had a moment before her body convulsed with a cough—and liquid seeped into her mouth, tasting of copper. Black spots erupted in her vision; the last that she saw of the world was Ramson, shoving through the ranks of her army.

Ana was barely aware of her head hitting the wooden floor of the scaffold.

Darkness closed in.

27

L inn had forgotten how cold this land could be.

It felt as though she still had half a foot in a dream. The time at sea had gone by so fast and so painfully slowly at the same time. She'd woken up gasping in the middle of the night, dreaming of Kemeira yet feeling the dreaded lull of a ship, just as she had so many years ago.

They'd landed on the shores of Northern Cyrilia, at a small fishing port where immigration checks were not stringent. Linn and Kaïs slipped through the Portmaster's cursory glance. No yaegers around to sniff out the scent of their Affinities. She wondered whether that had changed, with Morganya on the throne. Would the yaegers now go after those *without* Affinities?

Tonight was the second night of their journey east to Salskoff in search of Ana and her army. They kept their eyes and ears out for any clues of the Red Tigress's whereabouts; until they found her, though, Kaïs suggested Salskoff was the best destination. In the sprawling capital city, they would be sure to find information.

Throughout the past moon of their travels, whenever she wasn't eating or training with Kaïs, Linn would look at the little wooden token Ruu'ma had given her. It seemed to hold all the secrets of their world. She'd memorized every groove and etching as well as she knew the lines of her own palms. She'd turned over every word the Temple Masters had spoken, wringing meaning from them until they'd run dry.

The Heart of the Gods lay at the northernmost point in this world, where the Silent Sea met the shores of the Cyrilian Empire. And, as Ruu'ma had said, it was the source of all alchemical power that, combined with siphons, could harness all the magic in the world—to restore balance to the world . . . or to destroy it.

They *had* to get this information to Ana, and bring her to where the Heart was supposedly located, before the Imperial Patrols brought the jade tablet to Morganya.

Linn and Kaïs slept huddled in an abandoned dacha the first night. They ate rations they'd purchased at the fishing port's market, and melted snow to add to their waterskins to drink. On the second day, they came across a destroyed village.

It was near dusk, the Syvern Taiga drawing a jagged outline against a gray winter sky. Linn smelled the smoke in the air, its acrid stench woven into her winds. It wasn't long before they found the source.

Several dachas near the outermost edge of the village had been burned black. It was only when Linn touched her cheeks and her fingers came away smudged with streaks of gray that she realized it was ash twirling down from the sky and not snow.

They walked down empty streets, a gale rising like the moans of phantoms all around them. The village square was empty, yet Linn couldn't help but feel as though they were being watched. She could sense Kaïs's tension by her side; he flexed his fingers every once in a while, as though yearning to grasp the hilts of his swords.

And then, in the landscape rendered monochrome, she glimpsed a flash of color. Linn bent, sweeping aside the blanket of soot and snow, and let out a soft gasp.

It was a frozen piece of parchment, painted in bold themes of crimson and gold, but what drew Linn's gaze was the portrait on the page: a face she knew all too well.

ANASTACYA MIKHAILOV, THE RED TIGRESS OF CYRILIA, the poster announced, *DECLARES WAR AGAINST THE BLOODY REIGN OF EMPRESS MORGANYA.*

"Kaïs," she exclaimed, turning around, but the next thing she saw took her breath away.

Kaïs crouched on the ground several steps away, bent over what resembled a bundle of furs. Upon closer look, Linn realized: It was a person.

She stumbled across the snow and fell to her knees. It was a woman the same age as Linn's or Kaïs's parents. Her pale blond hair peeked out from the shawls she'd wrapped around her face—but blood was splattered across her chin and lips. Linn shivered.

"Her lips are blue," Kaïs observed. "Linn, pass me a globefire."

Wordlessly, Linn reached into their pack and took out a fresh globefire. With a few rattles, the alchemical powders within were ablaze. Gently, Kaïs took the woman's hands and wrapped them around the orb.

"Meya dama," he said. "We are here to help. Can you tell us what happened?"

The woman's lips moved faintly, and Linn caught a whisper. "Red Tigress . . ."

Kaïs unlatched the waterskin from his pack and tipped it to her mouth. The water mingled with blood as it dribbled down her chin. The woman's eyes fluttered open, focusing on Linn with sudden urgency.

"My son," she rasped. "He pledged himself to the Red Tigress's army . . . then the Empress's forces came and . . ."

"The Red Tigress's army," Linn repeated sharply. "They were here not long ago?"

"Just yesterday morning," the woman whispered. Her lips trembled. "The Empress's forces passed through . . . just hours ago . . ." Tears leaked down her cheeks. "We should never have resisted. Fighting is fruitless. All that it has brought us . . . is this. . . ."

Looking around the scorched dachas, Linn thought of another city that had fallen not long ago. Novo Mynsk had suffered the same fate, under Morganya's Imperial Inquisition.

Was this what awaited the world if Morganya found the Heart of the Gods and siphoned its full power?

She gripped the woman's shoulder, and it was then that she noticed the large gash on the woman's abdomen. "Meya dama," Linn said quietly. "Can you tell us where the Red Tigress's army went?"

"East," came the reply. "To . . . Osengrad."

"And the Imperial Inquisition," Kaïs cut in. "Where did they go?"

The woman shook her head. "Not . . . Inquisition," she whispered. "They were too few in number. . . ."

Linn looked up sharply, meeting Kaïs's eyes.

"They were going . . ." The woman's eyes were fluttering shut, her voice growing faint. ". . . to Salskoff . . ."

Linn saw the spark of realization in Kaïs's eyes as he reached the same conclusion she had: that there was a high possibility the Imperial Patrols who had passed through this village were the very ones who had stolen the jade tablet from Kemeira—and they were now delivering it to Morganya.

Kaïs drew a small glass vial from his pack. Linn recognized it as the same sedative he'd given her back in Kemeira, when the pain from her wounds had been too much to bear. "Here, meya dama, drink this," he said, tipping it to her lips. "It'll ease the pain."

The woman gulped it down, then leaned back with a sigh. "Sacha," she whispered. "My son . . . Sacha Zykov. Will you . . . tell him . . . I'm waiting. . . ." Her eyes fluttered shut; the tightness to her face bled out, giving way to peace.

"Osengrad," Kaïs muttered to Linn once they were sure Dama Zykov had fallen unconscious. "That is one day's travel east of us. We must reach Ana's army before Morganya's forces deliver the tablet."

Linn was already scrambling to her feet, her heart pumping, all else forgotten. Judging by the still-smoking ruins, Morganya's army could not be too far ahead of them. "We go, now." She hesitated, her gaze drifting to Dama Zykov.

"Her injuries are far too grave," Kaïs said softly. "She is beyond our help. A swift death would be a kindness at this point." He drew a dagger from his hip. Hesitated. His eyes glinted as he turned to Linn: the cut-glass look of a trained soldier, expressionless, emotionless. "Scout ahead, see if you can find Ana's army's tracks."

Linn swallowed, looking from his blade to Dama Zykov's chest, which rose and fell gently in the injured woman's sleep.

Kaïs's face betrayed nothing but calm as he gave Linn another nod. His voice, however, was bladed. "Go, now."

She took off without looking back. There was warmth in her eyes that blurred the world, spilling over onto her cheeks. She swiped her tears away with a hand; the pain in her chest gave way to anger.

Dama Zykov had been a person, with a family and a life. Morganya had razed over her entire world without so much as a blink, wiping her from existence like a star blinking out in the night sky.

And she would do the same to tens of thousands of innocent lives, should she prevail.

By the time Linn reached the path leading out of the village, her hands were shaking. The snow here was flattened by what looked like hundreds of pairs of boots; she knelt down to examine them, her head sharp with a new emotion.

Hatred.

There were footprints she recognized as the steel-tipped boots of Bregonian Navy soldiers; fresher, though, were prints with rounded toes, and rows upon rows of sharp grooves specialized for traveling in snow. Cyrilian Imperial Patrols' boots.

Morganya.

Night had fallen; the skies above her flared with sudden light. Linn tipped her head up. Through the sheen of her tears, the glow of the Deities' Lights was magnified. Yet there was something different about them: a violence to the way they twisted and writhed, colors flashing and bleeding into one another with urgency—as though they were running out of time.

"Even the weather looks agitated, does it not?"

She turned at Kaïs's low voice. He gave her a half smile; his dagger was nowhere to be seen.

Linn shook her head. "The spirits are angry," she said quietly. "Ruu'ma shi'sen was right. The balance of the world . . . has not been right for a very long time. We have simply accepted it as our reality—yet this is not how it was meant to be. How it *could* be."

Affinites, toiling under blackstone chains, the first element imbued with the gods' powers to be discovered and exploited by humanity. Searock, twisted and remade to be used against humans, prompting another cycle of Affinite trafficking to the Kingdom of Bregon. Linn would never forget the haunted gazes of the Affinites she had rescued from the dungeons of the Blue Fort.

And now, Morganya was on the brink of harnessing the source of magic that, combined with siphons, would allow her to control anything that held alchemical power. Linn could only hope that Ana would find the siphons before Morganya did. That they would not be too late.

So much of this world rested on hope—on their shoulders.

A cold wind suddenly gusted their way, scattering stray pine leaves in a susurrus. Snow whirled into the air, twirling silver in the moon's fluorescence. When it settled, though, Linn realized there was something crouched in front of them, a dozen paces away.

Out of a pool of moonlight rose a shape, twisting like smoke. It glowed a soft blue sheen as it stretched, two nubs forming claws and another two forming wings, then a head.

"Syvint'sya," Linn whispered. "Snow spirit."

She'd encountered some of these with Ana before, and certainly many a time she'd woken outside a trafficker's wagon to see these spirits dancing beneath an open sky. Eagles, soaring with wingspans longer than her own body; deer loping through trees;

rabbits bounding in the underbrush, all shimmering a gentle blue. Back then, with so little to look forward to in her life, she'd thought of them as friends.

The syvint'sya turned to her. Surprise bloomed in her stomach: It had taken the shape of a small bird. It cocked its head at her, and she thought those blank white eyes stared directly at her. And then it hopped two paces forward and took off, its silhouette shrinking until it was swallowed by the night sky.

Somehow, Linn felt lighter. Surer. *Hopeful.*

She straightened, glancing at Kaïs. "We go," she said. "And we do not stop until we have reached Osengrad and found Ana."

28

Night had fallen outside, and the windows reflected the soft glow of the globefires and the fire crackling in the hearth. Ramson sat at the makeshift table, book splayed across his lap. He couldn't help but glance up every so often at the figure sleeping on the pallet so close to him.

Yuri and Daya had reached Ana first, on the scaffold earlier that day; he'd only watched as a team of soldiers lifted her onto a stretcher and carried her away to be examined by healers.

Ramson had followed at a distance. He'd gone about his daily duties, training new recruits and taking reports from the scouts Daya had sent to Southern Cyrilia to help them recruit in regions where they could not reach.

It had been dusk when he'd finally returned to this dacha, where Tetsyev and Ardonn had settled to continue their research. Ramson had assigned his squad to monitor the two scholars full-time, and to help carry the books they collected from libraries in the towns they passed. Ramson could hear the rumble of his men's conversation outside; he imagined Tetsyev and Ardonn would be hunched over their desk, a single candle lit between them as they browsed through tome after tome of lore, legend, and alchemical theory. He'd spent many a night sitting by their sides, attempting to make sense of the theories they'd posited.

Daya had been grateful when he'd offered to relieve her of her duty of watching over Ana in the late afternoon. He'd spent the evening attempting to get through the book Ardonn had assigned him, but he'd found himself distracted, glancing outside the cracked glass window every so often, hoping against hope to see the outline of a Bregonian seadove appear in the cloud-ridden skies. He'd yet to receive a response from King Darias since his last letter. It was one he hadn't consulted Ana on, and he hadn't needed to: It concerned a private Trade that King Darias had offered him.

Finally, as his thoughts were anywhere but on the pages before him, Ramson slammed his book shut and turned to Ana. Even in her sleep, she looked tense, her brows creased in a permanent frown.

He nearly smiled. Almost against his own volition, he reached his hand out. Ramson hesitated only a moment before he pressed his thumb to her brow. Gently, he traced out her frown line, remembering that the last time he'd done this, she'd leaned into his touch, smiled up at him. It had been dawn, her face had been streaked in sunlight, and everything had seemed dusted in a layer of tentative hope. "I know what Ardonn told me about the core, about reversing the siphon's effects," he said. "I'm going to find it, Ana. I'm just as stubborn as you, and I don't like to lose."

She shifted, and her lips moved in a murmur so faint, he might have missed it.

Ramson.

He sat there, numbness seeping into him, every inch of his skin buzzing with what he'd just heard.

Ana's eyes fluttered open, her gaze landing straight on him. It was soft, open, without a trace of hostility—the way she'd looked at him that night, lying in his arms. "Ramson?"

He leapt to his feet and stumbled back as though burned.

Someone knocked on the door, several sharp raps. "Captain," came Narron's voice, "Alchemist Tetsyev and Scholar Ardonn request your immediate presence."

"Coming," Ramson called. He thought he heard Ana mumble something, but he was already pushing through the door.

Tetsyev and Ardonn had stacked piles of books around their worktable, along with scrolls of notes they'd accumulated over their visits to any available library in the towns they'd passed. He was surprised to see Olyusha leaning over Ardonn's desk, tinkering with several glass vials. In the back of the room, three others from Ramson's squad were in the midst of a game of Crib the King. They straightened and saluted as he entered behind Narron.

Ramson pulled out a chair and sat. Ardonn's complexion had improved drastically over the past moon under Olyusha's care; his cheeks had filled out, his skin was back to its healthy tan, and the effects of his poisoning were but a shadow across his face.

"Ah, Captain Farrald," he said slowly, mockingly, leaning back in his chair and regarding him with that sly smile. "An honor, it is."

The several times Ardonn had been wont to give Ramson attitude, Ramson had been all too happy to help him understand what exactly happened if the scholar did not uphold his end of the bargain. All it had required was an isolated basement and some of their former master Alaric Kerlan's most persuasive techniques.

Ramson ignored him and turned to Tetsyev. The Cyrilian alchemist's face was lined, rings under his eyes from the little sleep they had all been getting. Ramson had never thought there would be a situation where Pyetr Tetsyev was his preferred choice, but here they were.

"Captain Farrald," Tetsyev said, jotting down a last note on a piece of parchment before setting down his pen. The way he spoke Ramson's title held none of the mockery that Ardonn used.

Ramson pulled a piece of parchment toward himself, casting a cursory glance at the notes. There were diagrams, too, and formulas he could only imagine would take years of studies in the field of alchemy to understand. "Well?" He spread his arms in a shrug. "You called."

"First things first," Olyusha interjected. She lifted a hand; between her fingers, a small glass vial shimmered. She shook it, and the liquid inside sloshed. "It's been a hells of a pain working with *him*, but . . . I've done it." She threw a glare at Ardonn. "Well, Bregonian arse? Won't you explain?"

"The woman is a gods-damned demon from the fieriest pits," Ardonn muttered in Bregonian. At Ramson's look, however, he straightened and flicked a finger at the vial Olyusha held. "One aspect of our Trade, fulfilled. This is the elixir you asked for, Ramson Farrald."

The room suddenly narrowed to the small glass vial, its reflections lancing light crystals on the ceiling. Ramson stepped forward; Olyusha handed it to him. It felt so small, so frail between his fingers.

"She is exhibiting the same symptoms as our magen near the end," Ardonn said quietly. "Should she choose to take the elixir, it is now or never."

The room pulsed, and from the swirls of innocuously clear liquid in the vial, a memory found Ramson. *Should you wish to claw back a life that belonged to the gods, that life will be a cursed one. One that drove many of our subjects to the brink of madness, to the depths of despair.*

He thought of Ana, the blaze in her eyes and the fierce yearning for life she had always held.

Madness. Despair. He wanted to hurl the concoction across the room.

Ramson looked up. "And the core?" he asked in Cyrilian this time, gaze pinning Ardonn and Tetsyev in turn. "Have you results yet?"

Tetsyev drew a long breath, pinched the bridge of his nose, and let it out again. Slowly, he nodded. "Scholar Ardonn and I have combined his existing knowledge with new research over the past moon," he began. "The records are few and far between, often steeped in mythology and folklore, but . . . they exist. Some were even taken from foreign lands; the Aseatic kingdoms possess a much deeper and fuller knowledge of our origins and the magic in this world than we do."

"I honestly couldn't care less about the process of your research. No offense," Ramson added. "Not the scholarly type. Your findings?"

"Our findings," Ardonn cut in, "are that this core allows access to all magek in the world. And with the siphons, Morganya can steal the powers of whichever magen she wishes, whenever she wishes. And"—he paused for a self-satisfied smirk—"we believe we know what it is."

At this, Ramson stilled. "Go on."

"It is a gem of pure magek that, according to legend, was cut off from a god's heart—as a scholar, I believe it was formed by an ancient source of power hidden in the core of our world. Its power manifests in the Deities' Lights, in our ghostwhales and water spirits and all other things of magek in this world."

Hope burned through Ramson's veins. "And this," he said, looking between the two scholars, "is the relic that can destroy siphons?"

Tetsyev's eyes flickered. "Create, harness, destroy . . . whoever holds this holds the world's alchemical power—magek—in their hands. A mortal with a Deity's power."

It was no wonder Morganya was after it, Ramson thought. Throughout the past moon, journeying through Cyrilia and speaking to the civilians that still remained in its towns, he'd seen the impacts of her reign of terror. Their initial fear had turned to resentment, and resentment to anger, as more and more of their family and friends had been unjustly slaughtered at the hands of the Imperial Inquisition.

There was nothing more dangerous than people with nothing to lose and everything to gain. It was part of the reason why the Red Tigress campaign had gone so well.

"Well," he said, folding his arms. "Let's get it before Morganya does."

Tetsyev and Ardonn shared a glance, and that was when Ramson had a sinking feeling in the pit of his stomach. "We have presently been unable to find any records of its location," Tetsyev said quietly. "We do believe, however, that it would be somewhere north, where the Deities' Lights are strongest . . . perhaps in the region of the Krazyast Triangle. . . ."

"So this is what you wished to inform me today?" An irrational anger was coiling its way up Ramson's chest, heat spreading through his throat and cheeks. "That you've confirmed that this relic can unleash the power of the gods upon this world, but you have no idea where to find it? And that my best option is an elixir that can prolong her life at the cost of pain and madness?"

Tetsyev lowered his gaze. Ardonn looked away. Even Olyusha's expression was sympathetic.

Ramson exhaled sharply through his nose. His chest was tight. Time was running out; their campaign had reached the end of their trail, and any day now, the Southern Cyrilian recruits would be arriving.

"Well, that settles it, then, doesn't it?" came a soft voice from behind them.

Ramson spun. Ana leaned against the doorframe, wrapped in furs, her hair draped loose over her shoulders. The candlelight flickered on her face and Ramson had never seen her look more tired—and yet there was a stubborn gleam in her eyes that he recognized all too well.

Ramson cooled his tone. "Settles what?"

She flicked a gaze at him. "We march on Morganya first," Ana replied, "and defeat her before she finds this relic." She threw a pointed look at the vial he still clutched in his fingers. "And I'd thank you not to go about making decisions involving my life, Ramson."

He lifted the elixir, but his heart wasn't in the motion. "Ana, this helped prolong the lives of magen whose magek were siphoned."

"'At the cost of pain and madness,'" she quoted, arching a brow. "How am I to lead a battle in such a state?" Seeing his silence, she moved across the room, put a hand over his, and plucked the vial from his fingers. Her touch was electric—heat and pain and shock all in one. He might have imagined the way it lingered, a moment more, before she pulled away. "Is that how you would wish to see me in my last moments, Ramson?"

His lips parted, his throat closed. She might as well have gently slid a knife through his heart.

Harried footsteps pounded down the hallway, summoning their attention. Daya burst into the room moments later, panting, a look of wide-eyed triumph on her face. Ana stepped quickly away from Ramson, turning to the door.

"They're here, Ana," Daya said. "The Southern Cyrilian re-cruits. They've arrived."

Everyone in the room turned their gazes to the window. In the deep Cyrilian night, pinpricks of torchlight flared, outlining a line of silhouettes stretching all the way to the town walls and beyond.

"Over five thousand recruits," Daya said quietly. "A small group are Affinites that have managed to escape Morganya's draft and have been hiding out in remote southern cities."

There was conflict on Ana's face as she turned from the window: muted pride, mingled with exhaustion, and something that resembled grief. "It's time," she said. "Our army is ten thousand strong. We've planned battle strategy with the most experienced commanders for the past moon. If the Deities are ever to send us a signal or let the stars align, it is now. Morganya's forces are strong and highly trained—but we have a chance if we launch a surprise attack at night." Her hands fisted, and she lifted her chin. "If we march tonight, we will be at Salskoff by early morning, before dawn."

Looking at the army lined up outside, every argument that had been at the tip of Ramson's tongue faded to ash. The strategy made perfect sense—even he could not convince himself to speak against it.

As he walked from the room, he heard footsteps behind him; a familiar head of chestnut hair came into view.

"So this is it," Ana said. She tracked a sidelong glance to him, and for a moment there, he thought he saw a spark of a challenge in her eyes. "Any objections?"

Once, it might have set him ablaze, like flint striking stone.

Now, there was only the frozen stretch of reality unfurling before him—one he was powerless to stop.

It was simple, really.

He'd lost his bet on finding the relic first. They had entered the game too late, with the odds stacked against them, and Morganya was too far ahead for them to have even a chance at winning the game. It was either act now or lose everything.

He looked at her. In all the endless, empty nights of the past moon, he'd closed his eyes many a time and thought of what the future held for him. Equality, peace, yes . . . but selfishly, he'd always imagined sailing between strange lands from horizon to horizon, sunrise to sunset, wind in his hair and water at his back.

And a part of him had always imagined her to be a part of it.

"No, Ana," Ramson said quietly, turning away. "No objections. However this ends, know that I'll be by your side."

Love was a weakness, and dreams were for fools—and the end to both had finally come.

29

There was a feeling of finality in the air as Ana sat astride her valkryf. The cold came a bit sharper, the light of the stars a bit brighter. In front of her, Daya was silent as she steered her valkryf, back straight, expression stony. They'd left those who could not fight in the town in a secure dacha. While Tetsyev had asked to ride out with Ana, Ardonn was being watched by some of Ramson's squad, including Olyusha, the poison Affinite who had once worked for Alaric Kerlan.

And Shamaïra . . . Ana had left her in the care of her most trusted soldiers, as well as Liliya and two of Yuri's Redcloaks. The Unseer had woken several days after they'd arrived at the camp, yet her eyes had been blank, the once-bright sheen to them dulled. She'd been silent, seeming only able to eat, drink, and perform basic functions before falling back into her slumber. It had pained Ana to see her in such frail condition, skin papery-thin, eyelids fluttering in what appeared to be restless dreams. The time she'd spent imprisoned by Morganya seemed to have taken its toll on her, both mentally and physically, and the harm Morganya inflicted was taking its time to heal.

Before leaving, Ana had pressed a kiss to Shamaïra's forehead, comforted by the fact that if they lost the battle and their plan failed, Shamaïra would at least be at the Redcloak camp, where she would be safe.

As Ana passed through Osengrad, her army's footsteps muffled by snow, window shutters were thrown open, the soft golden glow of candles and globefires spilling into the night. Silhouettes were carved against the light: families with children's heads barely peeking above the sills, mothers cradling babes, lovers leaning against each other. Watching. Waving.

And, gently, they began to sing.

It was a melody Ana had heard in the Palace: a lullaby for children, about the stars that watched over snowy mountains, the spirits that frolicked beneath ice-tinted conifers, the lights that wove in the skies. A song of hope.

A song of Cyrilia.

Ana tipped her head, taking it all in. This was why she fought: for an equal world, a peaceful world, one in which none of her people had to suffer or flee persecution no matter whether they were Affinite or non-Affinite, no matter how they were born. And as the Red Tigress's procession drew farther from Osengrad, the warmth and the light and the song remained with Ana even as darkness shrouded them.

They made haste through the night, scouts spread out among trees while the majority of their army marched behind their respective commanders. When the time came, they would split into squads and surround the Salskoff Palace; a first wave of soldiers would break through the gates, and the battle would begin there.

And when the time came, Ana knew, she would be the only one who could beat Morganya—siphon against siphon.

It felt like forever and no time at all that the Syvern Taiga began to thin out. Ana pulled a silver pocketwatch from around her neck; the light of her globefire told her that it was the early hours of the morning. From up ahead came the whistle of a scout; the captains in the lead held up their hands in the signal for their troops to split into formation. As though in a dream, Ana watched her troops split into battalions, fan out, and melt away between the snow-covered trees like ghosts, led by their respective commanders to their positions all around the periphery of the capital city.

And there, almost like the curtains of a play parting, the Syvern Taiga came to a sudden and sharp end, yielding to the sight of a city that never ceased to take Ana's breath away.

Salskoff stretched all the way to the distant horizon. The red-roofed dachas were monochrome in the night, still and silent in their slumber. From here Ana could make out the spires and cupolas of the Palace, veiled in shadows at this hour.

Ana's squad, led by Daya and flanked by Yuri's squad of Redcloak Affinites, entered the city in utter silence, their footsteps muffled by the fallen snow. Salskoff was shrouded in darkness, and as they passed by the dachas half-buried in snow, Ana thought of how once, even in the night, her home city had been bathed in the lambent light of snowglobes, of lanterns and lamps that draped the streets in a gentle blue. Winter had been the season of their patron Deity, a time for joy and celebration and worship.

Dirt roads yielded to paved streets, the buildings straightening and falling into uniform architecture as they neared the city center. Ana spread her blood Affinity, combing for Imperial Patrols. Even among the population of Salskoff, there were dachas that lay deserted, windows shuttered or broken through and looted. Her army would be creeping through the streets, too, closing in on the Palace from all directions.

As they drew near a corner that led to a market square, she sensed it: Ahead, faint as the flicker of a candle, were five blood signatures standing in formation, too still and too neatly aligned to be regular civilians. There was a shadow over them that her Affinity could not breach: blackstone infused into their armor.

Still, as long as their faces were in the open, it wouldn't be a problem for Ana.

She held her hand up in the signal to stop, then gestured at Daya and Yuri to remain where they were. They fell back, passing the command along to their troops.

Alone, Ana spurred her steed forward.

She sensed one of the blood signatures turning to face her as she approached, felt a familiar pressure on her Affinities. *A yaeger,* she thought. She'd be a fool to think the yaegers and Whitecloaks no longer hunted Affinites under Morganya's rule. They still did, only for a different purpose, now: to force them to fight under Morganya's army.

Ana slashed her blood Affinity down the soldier's throat and pulled. She heard his choke cut off, heard the beginnings of alarm as the other four Imperial Patrols stirred into action.

She seized them all, and four bodies crumpled to the ground, blood blooming around them like poppies in a field. A wave of exhaustion hit her, so strong that she doubled over in her saddle, clinging to the ice-frosted mane of her valkryf as she focused on breathing in and out.

Slowly, her strength returned. Ana lifted a hand, and Daya's and Yuri's squads slipped through the alleyways to her side. It was eerie, Ana thought, how empty the square was, without a trace of the regular Vyntr'makt stalls or food carts. Beyond, the Salskoff Palace loomed, a shadow cut of a darker piece of the night.

Monster, came a half-forgotten whisper from her past.

Once, this square, this city, this empire had been filled with glittering light and riches and opulence, so much so that no one had wanted to see the cracks in its shadows and those who toiled in the darkness. Now, Morganya's reign had brought fire and destruction to the entirety of this land.

"Almost there." Yuri's voice was barely a murmur as he drew up next to her. His Redcloaks followed, Seyin riding close behind to lend them the cover of shadows where they might need it.

Daya slowed her steed on Ana's other side. "Just four streets away, if I remember correctly."

Behind them, Tetsyev's face was drawn, fear showing plainly through his gaze. He caught Ana's eyes, however, and gave her a pinched nod.

Ana's breaths misted in the air as she tipped her head up, gazing at the Palace that had been her home and her prison. From here, its walls were in sight; from here, they would lay siege to it and break through its gates.

From here, there was no going back.

She was aware of her soldiers watching her. By now, the rest of her army would be in position.

Ana raised her arm. "For equality."

Linn, performing on a stage with shackles on her hands and feet.

"For justice."

May, lifeless ocean-eyes staring up at the stars that she would never see again.

"For the people."

Yuri's restaurant ravaged to ruins; the Imperial Inquisition, marching through the streets of Goldwater Port, burning down dachas and breaking apart families.

Ana summoned the spark of fire inside her, channeling it to her fingertips. Flame burst from her hand, spiraling high and triumphant into the sky.

From all around her arose a battle cry as her army charged from all directions. Fire, rock, marble, and ice rained down on the Palace gates, and the night lit up in shades of crimson as the Red Tigress's army laid siege on the Salskoff Palace.

To create a future, one first had to destroy the past.

30

The Syvern Taiga stretched in an endless blur of shadows. Linn's heartbeat thundered in her ears as she and Kaïs rode, their harried breaths misting white vapor before them. Even in the depths of a Cyrilian winter night, sweat seeped into her clothes, freezing into ice.

At midnight, they'd arrived at the Red Tigress's camp at Osengrad—only it had been empty. Tracks had led away from the city gates to the east, the snow flattened by thousands, even tens of thousands, of boots. It wasn't difficult to figure out where Ana and her army were headed.

Salskoff.

The streets had been completely deserted when she and Kaïs passed through, yet they'd found a single pub with its globefires lit and doors open for the weary traveler. They'd found a thick-hooved horse tied in the stables, its sturdy and large build used for lugging wagons and supply carts. Kaïs hadn't hesitated to cut through its bindings; they'd left all that remained of their coins on the ground.

In the patches of sky that filtered through the canopy, Linn saw stars. She'd learned to read the night sky throughout her years indentured in this cold, harsh land; the constant, slow turn of constellations over her head had comforted her back then, knowing that no matter how long the night, there was always a dawn to come.

By the stars, it was the early hours of the morning—the ghost hours.

And Salskoff was still nowhere in sight.

Linn held on tightly to Kaïs as they crashed forward through brush and branches. Through it all, she could feel the press of the small wooden token against her collarbone.

They had to reach Ana before Morganya's Imperial Patrols reached the Palace.

They had to find the Heart before Morganya did.

Their horse gave a sudden, shrill bray. A moment later— a moment too late—Linn spotted it. With no warning, the conifers of the Syvern Taiga parted, revealing the precipice of a cliff buried beneath snow.

Kaïs let out a grunt as he pulled sharply on the reins, but it was too late. With an abrupt twist, the world spun over them as they plunged sharply down.

Snow, air, and trees; between it all, Linn held on tightly to Kaïs. She sensed his Affinity reaching out to hers, a warm, steady hand bridging their minds, lending his strength to hers. Heard the echo of his voice in her head from what seemed like forever ago.

Now, fly.

Linn flipped over in midair and called on her winds.

They came, roaring and whistling all around, and Linn wove

them around her and Kaïs, cocooning them in a spiral of currents. Their fall slowed; the ground rushed up to meet them, and within moments, they landed in a giant drift of snow.

Linn sat up, gasping and brushing powder from her face. "Kaïs!" she cried, pulling herself to her feet.

She heard his answering call from behind her; she found him sitting several steps away. He winced as he stood, shaking snow from his shoulders. Beyond lay the motionless body of their horse, half-buried beneath a pile of snow. Dead.

But Kaïs's eyes lit up and he straightened, pointing. "Linn."

She turned, and her lips parted.

They'd tumbled off a cliff into an open part of the Syvern Taiga, the trees spread thin. Above them, a shadow looming in the midnight sky, was a silhouette Linn would recognize anywhere, spires and cupolas carving out an absence of light, its edges outlined in faint silver.

"The Salskoff Palace," she whispered. "We are there! Kaïs—"

But, spinning back to him, she realized he was leaning to his left, the edges of his eyes tight with pain.

"My ankle," Kaïs said quietly, looking down. "It's twisted."

Linn hurried over to support him, drawing his arm over her shoulder. "I have strength enough for the two of us," she said, though she could feel the ache of fatigue seeping into her bones. They'd traveled without stopping, stealing no more than a few hours of sleep each night, and since they'd found the tracks of Ana's army, they'd ridden throughout the night.

Before Kaïs could reply, a huge explosion cracked across the night, echoing in the silence of the boreal forest. Light flared from directly ahead so that, for a brief moment, the Salskoff

Palace was alight in the corals and crimsons of a fire, as though it were drenched in blood.

A chill ran down Linn's back. "Do you think . . . ?" she whispered.

Kaïs's hand tightened around her shoulder as several more bright flashes lit the sky. "That is an attack on the Salskoff Palace." A pause. "I believe it to be launched by Ana's army."

Cold crept through Linn's veins, a shadow of dread twining around her heart so tightly that she could barely breathe. Possibility after possibility flitted through her mind, each worse than the last.

That the Imperial Patrols had handed the jade tablet to Morganya.

That Morganya had already found the Heart of the Gods.

That the mad Empress was going to destroy Ana's resistance.

"We are too late," Linn said. She could not stop her teeth from chattering.

"No," Kaïs said calmly. He shifted his weight, hobbling so that he turned to look at Linn. His eyes were as peaceful as moonlight. He took her hands in his. "You must bring the map to her. You must tell her about the Heart."

"But you—"

"—will slow you down," he continued in that placid tone.

There was an ache deep in her throat. The shadow of the battle at Bei'kin had not yet faded from her memory, when she'd found him afterward on the cusp of death. "N-no," Linn said. Her fingers tightened involuntarily against his.

Kaïs pried his hands from hers. His expression was open,

tender, as he touched a finger to her chin. "Remember what the Temple Master said."

A sparrow's wingbeat may cause the biggest of storms.

Kaïs pressed his forehead to hers. "Action, and counteraction," he said, and she closed her eyes, remembering the first time they had met on the highest tower of the Salskoff Palace. "I am glad to have found you and your warrior soul, Ko Linnet. And I swear to you, no matter where you are, I will find you again. Now, go."

Linn cupped her hands around his face. In a future split wide open by ten thousand possibilities, she closed her eyes and whispered a prayer for the one where she would find him again.

Then, she turned away. Tapped a finger to her breast where the wooden token rested. Brushed her hands against the hilts of her daggers and broke into a run.

Be the sparrow, Ko Linnet.

She didn't look back.

31

Blinding flashes lit up the sky as the Red Tigress's army began to lay siege to the Palace. Ramson watched as they surged across the Kateryanna Bridge, Ana's and Yuri's flames shooting into the night and painting the entire scene—the statues of the Deities, the Tiger's Tail roaring beneath—in a haze of crimson.

It was easy to differentiate the Imperial Patrols across the bridge, caught off-guard, their pale cloaks flashing like the underbellies of fish as they fought back. Yet the Red Tigress's army was relentless. Lines of non-Affinite soldiers surged forward, razing down the guards with their numbers and clearing the bridge.

Ana's unit of Affinites charged, pummeling the gates with stone, flames, ice, earth, wood. Ramson combed the crowd for Ana and Daya, wishing once again that he were there with them.

But he was needed elsewhere, and the calling came soon enough.

On the pale, crenellated walls of the Palace, between the parapets, Ramson caught flashes of movement. A glint of silver here, a glimmer of white there.

Archers. His and Ana's first Palace break-in attempt had been crucial in planning for the siege; they'd been able to point out all defenses that the Salskoff Palace employed. Security had tightened since Morganya had ascended the throne—they'd run into several Patrols in the streets of Salskoff alone—and there was no telling what tricks the mad monarch had up her sleeves . . . but this was a start.

Ramson raised his hand; he knew the captains of the other archery sectors would be doing the same, defending their quadrant and taking out any threats that could stop the Affinite squad from getting through the Palace gates. Behind him, there was a surge of movement as the archers in his squad nocked their arrows.

Ramson swung his arm down. Hundreds of arrows took flight with a uniform hiss, arcing through the air for the Palace walls. Most crashed against the crenellations—a weakness in their strategy that Ramson and the other Bregonian commanders had foreseen, for the Salskoff guards held the high ground.

Sure enough, the counterattack came: a volley of arrows hurtling across the night sky, glowing as red as embers, straight toward them.

Ramson flung his shield over his head. "The arrows are on fire!" he bellowed. "Take cover!"

The arrows whistled between them in streaks of light—only, there was a second trick to them that Ramson hadn't expected. As they hit the ground, they seemed to burst, liquid splattering from pouches attached to their sheaths. The smell was familiar—and it took Ramson a half second to understand what it was.

Flames roared to life across the pools of oil drenching the snow, rearing bright and hot and encircling his army. Ramson barely had time to scramble away from a growing fire when he heard another uniform *whoosh* behind him.

He turned to see the next barrage descending upon them.

He raised his shield—but this time, the impact knocked him completely off his feet.

When he blinked again, he was shaking snow and mud from his face; his shield was completely torn apart and strewn in pieces next to him, his hand bleeding from the splinters of blackstone and metal. All around him, the ground shook, and his line was in utter chaos. The air was filled with the screams of his men as they were hit, as the flames clung to their armor and began to burn them alive.

There was a faint ringing in his ears as he climbed to his feet unsteadily, the world weaving in and out of focus. Someone familiar stood in front of him; Narron was shouting orders at his men for them to retreat behind the burning riverside promenade.

Ramson's deputy caught sight of him and yelled, "Explosive powder!"

"I know!" Ramson roared. "Take cov—"

The ground where Narron stood ruptured in a cloud of vaporized snow and silt.

"*NARRON!*" Ramson lurched forward, keeping an eye on the battlements from the Palace and another on the maze of fire that his sector had turned into. Between the mist and smoke, he found his young deputy: unmoving, face unrecognizable beneath a layer of blood and mud.

Ramson hoisted the boy into his arms and began to drag him away from the bombardment. Across the bridge, the assault on the front gates had not stopped—only, now, the archers on the walls were beginning to turn their attention to the army on the bridge. There were more, now, Ramson realized; he'd seen signal fires lit between the parapets, and as he watched, there came additional movement between the crenellations.

To get into the Palace, Ana and the Affinites were relying on his squad and the other battalions to engage the guards on the walls.

Barely five minutes into the battle, and Ramson was already failing.

Another deafening explosion struck so close that his teeth rattled. Ramson set Narron against the stone balustrade of the riverside promenade.

The boy wasn't breathing.

Ramson had no time for grief. He chanced a look over the railing and, seeing no movement on the other side, stood and raised his arm. *"FIRE!"*

His men—those that were still standing—let loose a volley of arrows, yet the ones that found their marks were few and far between. Smoke and heat pressed in on their battalion from all sides, and in the momentary break between attack and counterattack, Ramson took in the scene. The careful formation of his battalion was gone; here and there, he saw bodies of his fellow Bregonian commanders, their badges streaked with blood. Soldiers crouched over their fallen and injured comrades, some of whom were barely out of boyhood, their soft weeping intertwined with the crackle and spit of flames all around.

Half their battalion was wiped out.

And as there came uniform movement on the other side of the walls, Ramson turned to face the Palace with a sense of dread.

That was when it happened.

As another volley of flaming arrows shot toward them, someone darted past the battlefield of fallen soldiers. It was a girl Ramson had never seen before, barely out of her childhood. She skipped and skidded over the flaming puddles of fire, and where her fingers pointed, ice bloomed from the ground, meeting and extinguishing flames.

She stopped several feet in front of him. Her lips were blue, and frost cracked across her cheeks as she shoved both hands in the air.

There came a thunderous roar, as though the earth itself were awakening from a slumber. And then as Ramson watched, a wall of ice rose from the Tiger's Tail itself, lunging at the walls of Salskoff. It groaned as it continued to lengthen, until most of the embankment was shielded beneath its shadow. Cracks sounded as the incoming arrows exploded along its surface, sending fragments of ice raining down upon them.

Below, frost covered the girl's face, tracing beautiful, swirling patterns. The firelight, muted through her wall of ice, reflected in her eyes.

Behind her came movement. From the streets of Salskoff itself emerged groups of people dressed in the furs and boots of ordinary civilians. They carried with them large pieces of wood: doors and cupboards from their kitchens and bedrooms; some knelt next to the fallen soldiers and began pulling out medical supplies from bags slung over their backs.

A middle-aged woman stepped up and placed a hand over the ice Affinite's shoulder. She looked directly at Ramson. "You are with the Red Tigress's army?"

He nodded.

The woman's eyes were fierce, her hair the same gold curls as the ice Affinite's. "The people of Salskoff have arrived," she said. "Those who have suffered in silence as Affinites . . . and those who have suffered under the current Empress's regime. We are here to fight for the new world the Red Tigress promises."

All along the river promenade, the civilians of Salskoff were setting up their furniture as shields for the wounded soldiers, some even having brought wagons and carts. Archers clustered behind makeshift shelters, some dousing the flames with nearby snow.

Ana might have been overwhelmed at the poetry of this moment—the uprising of regular civilians as they joined her in the fight for equality and justice—but Ramson's mind was already spinning, weaving out new ideas, new tactics.

He knelt before the young ice Affinite, who watched him with pale eyes. The memory of another child who'd looked at him with an intelligent, ocean-colored gaze softened his tone as he spoke. "What's your name, darling?"

"Marya," the ice Affinite said softly.

"Marya," Ramson said. "Can you take down the wall of ice on my command?"

She nodded.

Ramson turned back to the Palace walls, thinking hard. Once the ice shield came down, the barrage on him and his troops would continue. He needed to somehow penetrate the Palace walls; he needed to take down the Imperial Patrols from within the battlements.

Yet there was only so much an Affinite could expend of their Affinity; he'd seen Ana on the verge of collapse when she'd over-exerted herself.

"Are there any other Affinites here?" he asked Marya and the older woman.

"Yes. They are all going to the Kateryanna Bridge," Marya replied. "I came here with my mamika to help."

If there was a way to infiltrate the Salskoff walls with only one use of her Affinity . . .

And then, thinking back to the flames that Marya had extinguished on her way here, he suddenly had an idea—one that could turn the tides of this battle. It was a slim chance . . . but it was all he could think of. And that meant it was worth a shot.

"Can you turn the water from the Tiger's Tail into ice and lift me up to the walls?" Ramson said. He'd seen another ice Affinite at work before, back at Kerlan's Affinite trafficking ring; she'd created a bridge of ice from water and propelled herself into the air.

Getting up and over those Salskoff Palace walls would be significantly more difficult, but . . . he had to at least try.

Catching the aunt's look of apprehension, he added: "Just get me up there; you can come back down to safety as soon as we reach the parapets."

"Marya," her aunt began, but Marya cut her off.

"Please, let me do it, mamika," Marya replied. "I have had to hide my Affinity my entire life. Just let me do this one thing, to help."

Her aunt hesitated, then sighed and nodded. Marya looked up at Ramson, her face set. "I will take you up."

Ramson turned to the comrade closest to him, a Bregonian captain that he recognized. "I'm going to try something," he called. "I need you to hold down the fort for me."

Then he stepped next to Marya, who wrapped a hand around his waist to secure him. "When I say 'now,' you're going to take down the wall of ice," he told her. "Can you do that for me?"

She nodded.

Ramson lifted an arm. "Archers," he bellowed. "On my mark—"

A flurry of movement and noise as arrows were nocked.

Ramson nodded at Marya. "Now."

Her irises whitened and frost spread over her cheeks. With a colossal crack, the wall of ice splintered and plunged back into the Tiger's Tail. Water exploded into the air.

Ramson swung his arm down. "FIRE!"

As the next bombardment of arrows whistled past them, Ramson drew his misericord and turned to Marya. "Take me up there."

Ice crackled beneath their feet, forming a plate for them to stand on; the river water and snow all around them shifted, pushing them higher and higher. Mist from the Tiger's Tail sprayed across Ramson's face; he trained his focus on the crenellated walls of the Salskoff Palace as the ground beneath them fell away. By his side, Marya was a solid, steady figure, the platform of ice beneath their feet evenly balanced as it continued to lengthen, forming a bridge that lifted them into the air. Up, up . . . the Kateryanna Bridge could fit on the palm of his hand, and the people there were no larger than the nails on his pinky fingers . . . Ramson couldn't help but sweep a searching glance for Ana, but then they were eye level with the crenellations, the shadows of guards flickering as they readied more flaming arrows.

Ramson leapt into a cluster of Imperial Patrols. He barely had the chance to catch their startled looks before his misericord slashed and their throats bled red. Behind him, Marya had

clambered over and had erected a wall of ice against the Imperial
Patrols incoming from the other side.

"Get back!" Ramson shouted, lunging in front of her to parry
an Imperial Patrol. Marya huddled against the ice she'd erected,
squeezing her eyes shut in concentration. On the other side of the
ice wall she had made, the trapped Imperial Patrols had begun to
swing at the ice barrier with their swords.

Turning to face the Imperial Patrols before him, Ramson
had the distinct feeling that he'd landed right in the center of a
wasp's nest. He cut, slashed, ducked, and wove; bodies fell before
him, yet there was an endless line of Whitecloaks surging toward
him . . . his arm was growing tired, his reflexes thrown off in his
growing panic—

A flash of a sword and his misericord went flying. Ramson
stumbled.

The Imperial Patrol who'd knocked the blade from Ramson's
hand approached, weapon swinging.

Ramson ducked.

He felt the cold metal of the sword slice a hairsbreadth from
his cheek; in an extension of the same movement, Ramson pivoted and struck out, as hard as he could, with his steel-tipped
Navy boots.

He heard the crunch of bones and hiss of breath as the guard
stumbled back. Ramson dove for his misericord and, with a flourish, pierced it through the Imperial Patrol's neck. The salty tang
of blood coated his lips; his opponent doubled over.

"I happen to value my face," Ramson panted, "and I very much
dislike those who seek to mar it."

He plucked his blade from the dead man, who collapsed with
a thump.

Yet it was with increasing desperation that Ramson found a group of Whitecloaks charging toward him. He backed away until he stood in front of Marya, squeezing her between him and her wall of ice.

A sudden burst of fire lit up the night from behind him. He heard Marya screaming; turning around, he saw a silhouette outlined behind the rapidly melting ice wall. The man's armor was pale, with none of the blackstone reinforcements that regular Imperial Patrols held. Flames shot from his bare hands.

Inquisitor.

Within seconds, the ice was gone, and Ramson was surrounded.

Ramson's heart pounded in his ears as he thrust Marya behind him and raised his single misericord against the incoming army. And as the fire Affinite Inquisitor raised his palms toward him, Ramson Farrald realized that he'd never thought he would die fighting on his own two feet. That this wasn't the life he'd wanted for himself, yet it was the one he'd *needed*—to change, to atone for all the crimes he'd served and the evil he'd turned away from.

He thought of Ana, fighting down at the gates, of the life he'd briefly hoped for. With her.

Fire exploded from the Inquisitor's hands. Blades flashed as the Imperial Patrols charged.

And a howling wind rose all around.

From the night tumbled a blur of a shadow. Four flashes of metal, and the Imperial Patrols crashed onto the ground, the hilts of daggers protruding from their necks. The gale slammed into the Inquisitor's fire, pushing it back; a blade cut through the flames and struck true.

With a choked gasp, the Inquisitor stumbled, clutching his throat. As blood poured from his mouth, his head rolled back, and he collapsed onto the battlement.

The slim figure straightened, a breeze stirring her short, midnight hair. Dark eyes turned to Ramson.

"It seems I must save you every single time we attack this palace, Ramson Farrald," said Linn, her daggers gleaming a wicked scarlet. "Have you not learned your lesson from last time?"

32

The night was awash in blood and crimson as Ana's battalion continued to lay siege to the gates of the Salskoff Palace. She sat astride her valkryf, alone across the Kateryanna Bridge, watching from a distance as Yuri's Redcloaks and the Affinites in her army pummeled the entrance with all that they had. The ground shook with explosions as the other battalions continued to engage the archers and defenders along the Salskoff walls, drawing firepower away from Ana's unit. Already, Tetsyev was tending to the wounded, his pale alchemist's robes ghostly from here.

The strategy—the one all battalions and commanders of her army had agreed upon—was for her to remain behind and conserve her energy in order to face Morganya once they got through the gates. Yet sitting in the background, watching her army and friends put their lives at danger for a revolution in *her* name, was unbearable.

Ana's knuckles were white as she maintained her grasp on her reins. The statues of the Deities loomed against the darkness on either side of her, their melancholy gazes reflecting the red glows of fire.

A blood signature flickered to life behind her just as the sound of hooves drummed along the pavement. Ana turned to see a Bregonian commander riding toward her. Half his face was drenched in blood. Beyond him, the riverside promenade to the left of the Kateryanna Bridge was afire, and as Ana watched, flaming arrows—visible as tiny flickers of light—launched from the Palace walls.

"Red Tigress," the commander panted, drawing to a stop before her. "We're losing ground. The Palace is retaliating with fire-tipped arrows that explode—half my battalion is down—"

Ana looked to the front gates, hesitating. The key to a battle was for every unit, down to each individual soldier, to fulfill their duties and carry out their orders. Improvisation, her commanders had advised her, was the downfall of strategy.

The moment cost her.

The ground shook as an explosion thundered behind them, from the sector where the commander had come from. She was barely aware of her valkryf shrieking, dust and debris fogging the air; all that she could sense was blood pooling across an entire field, countless bodies lying in the snow, cooling.

Red unfurled across her vision; she could sense the power in her siphon writhing, begging to be unleashed.

Ana wrenched on the reins of her valkryf, turning it toward the riverside promenade, and dug her heels in its sides. Ramson had always called her impulsive, quick-tempered, and stubborn. Morganya had pointed out that Ana's inability to let people suffer was also her greatest weakness.

Yet standing behind and watching as people fighting under *her* name died was not the way of Anastacya Mikhailov.

She drew her valkryf to a sharp stop. One sweep of her blood Affinity told her that the entire riverside promenade was choked in blood, its scent at once intoxicating and nauseating. There were bodies buried in the snow, some half moving as she passed by, their moans haunting.

Ana called on the fire Affinity in her siphon, and the world roared to life in a burning haze of smoke, heat, and light. She flung her focus far beyond the burning promenade, up the walls of her Palace, and beyond the crenellations. There, she felt the faint flicker of flames.

As the next barrage of arrows was launched over the walls, Ana flung her hands up and grasped at each individual flame.

It felt as though her mind were splintering. The flares of fire were small, yet numerous, and she had the impression she was trying to stop an entire shower of comets across the sky. They sped forward, some yielding to her call, others slipping from her grasp.

Ana held her arm out and in a commanding motion sliced it down. Half the arrows dropped, plunging directly into the Tiger's Tail, where their flames sputtered out.

Exhaustion flooded her. She clutched the reins of her steed, trying to steady the shaking in her hands as she watched the remainder of the arrows—those that had slipped from her grasp—slam into the promenade. The ground shook with explosions; the air was laced with the scent of smoke and oil, yet all that Ana could think of was the familiar, warm taste of copper on her tongue. She brought shaking fingers to her lips and swiped.

They came away red.

"First Battalion!" roared the commander. "Nock!"

Lifting her gaze, Ana found that most of the soldiers seemed to have found cover; that the new flames burning on the ground were fewer.

"Draw!"

As the archers' grasps tightened on their bowstrings, Ana's attention was diverted by motion from across the bridge. The assault on the gates seemed to have slowed, and it took her a moment to realize why.

The gates were opening.

Even from this distance, she heard her battalion cheering—yet for some inexplicable reason, Ana only felt a sense of dread tightening her chest. She spurred her valkryf and raced toward the bridge in a canter.

Above the pounding of hooves, she heard the cheers of her battalion fading, dying, changing . . . and turning into cries of panic. And as Ana urged her steed on, she glimpsed, above the motley outfits of her soldiers, something that turned her stomach to lead.

An ocean of pale armor, glinting like bones in the moonlight. *Imperial Inquisitors.*

Morganya's army fanned out into formation, and the Salskoff gates clanged shut again.

The Inquisitors lifted their hands, Affinities erupting in streaks of blinding light. Screams rent the air as cracks split across the ground; water rose from the river and transformed to daggers of ice. Even from where she watched, she could tell that the skill with which the Inquisitors wielded their Affinities far exceeded that of her Affinite soldiers and Yuri's Redcloaks.

Ana heeled her steed forward across the Kateryanna Bridge, and out of an old habit, she sent a prayer to her mother.

Protect me, Mama. Let me finish this. For our land. For our people.

And then Ana plunged into the battle.

As she drove her horse forward, she reached deep inside herself and unleashed her blood Affinity. It felt as though she were burrowing through layers of herself, pushing past the bone-deep fatigue that seemed to have become a part of her in the past few moons, digging into her very flesh and blood and sinew, to draw the vestiges of power from her siphon and channel it. Ana flung out her blood Affinity, casting it like a net over the lines of Inquisitors. They were easy to grasp, their armor free of blackstone that would impede their Affinities.

She ripped.

Blood salted the air and sprayed the flattened snow and the stones of the Kateryanna Bridge.

An overwhelming sense of nausea and fatigue washed over Ana. She leaned over her saddle, cold and suddenly aching all over. The screams had quieted. From halfway across the bridge, she could make out a new line of bodies lying beneath the Salskoff Palace gates, covered in their own blood.

Monster. Blood Witch. Murderer.

If this was her legacy, then she would carry it through until the very end.

Movement in her line of sight. Ana looked up. There, beyond the first line of Inquisitors, came more—pouring out of the Salskoff Palace gates, marching in formation, Affinities already sparking at their fingertips.

"No." The word fell from her cracked lips, her voice hoarse, her breath misting in the air before her. It felt as though the ground were slipping out from beneath her, the inevitability of an end drawing closer with each beat of the enemy's footsteps.

Ana looked to the battalions fighting on the Salskoff riverside embankments behind her, half-decimated. She looked ahead to the gleam of the Inquisitors' armor at the gates, glowing red in the light of the fires all around. To the Affinites in her own army before her, outnumbered and outmatched.

Affinities exploded from the line of Inquisitors before the gates: ice and fire and lightning and air, lashing out and raining down upon Ana's army. There came screams and yells as people dove for cover; Ana's valkryf shrieked, bucking as a rock smashed before them into the cobblestones of the bridge. Clinging on tightly to regain control of her steed, Ana searched the scene before her for Daya's familiar figure. She found Yuri's bright red hair among the tides of the crowd, his frantic gestures at them to *retreat, retreat.*

They would not have enough time to make it back to the safety of the riverside promenade and the Salskoff city streets.

As the Inquisitors lifted their arms once again, Ana reached for the power of the siphon and realized that her blood Affinity would not come. She had overexerted it.

Then, stone and soil exploded beneath the first line of Inquisitors' feet, throwing them back. There came water, roaring from the Tiger's Tail to curl over the Inquisitors. Wind, rising into a screaming gale; wood, splintering from the nearby trees.

By Ana's side came several dozen figures, hands outstretched, dressed in plain furs and clothing. The man closest to her turned to her and she saw that his eyes were aglow in white light, streaks blazing across his irises like flashes of lightning.

"Red Tigress," he said. "The Affinites of Salskoff have arrived to fight on your side."

Ana looked beyond the lightning Affinite. There were at least thirty, forty others marching steadily toward the Salskoff Palace gates, Affinities writhing from their hands. Several were clad in rags too thin for the deep Cyrilian winter, their faces gaunt, bearing the shadows of a hard life. Others were draped in opulence, furs rippling and gems glinting on their hands as they pushed forward. Affinites, her *people*, from all walks of life, gathered and fighting under one purpose.

She glanced across the bridge, to where Yuri's and Daya's forces continued to retreat, under fire from the Inquisitors.

Ana turned to the lightning Affinite. "Are you the leader?" she asked. He nodded. "I'm going to open the way across the bridge to the front lines, where they need reinforcement. Can you follow?" Ana said.

He drew a circle over his chest—the sign of the Deys'krug, a confirmation.

Ana spurred her valkryf toward the Palace, plowing through the stream of Affinites in her army that were now retreating across the bridge, under assault and outnumbered by the Inquisitors. As the civilian Affinites joined the ranks of Ana's Affinite army, the tides of the battle shifted. The Inquisitors' relentless forward march began to slow.

Still, Ana's army was losing ground. Whereas before they had been at the Palace gates, they were now halfway across the Kateryanna Bridge, a trail of wounded and dead left behind them. The other quadrants of the Palace, defended by Ana's battalions, faced uneven challenges. To her left, the previous sector she had helped defend was struggling to hold their ground, her soldiers falling back to volleys of arrows—some of which were beginning to find their way to the Kateryanna Bridge, to Ana's battalion.

Yet the battalion to her right—the sector under Ramson's command—seemed to press forward. Someone had frozen a section of the Tiger's Tail stretching from one bank to another, and even as Ana watched, her troops pushed across the river. On the battlements between the crenellations of the wall, someone had lit a torch and was waving it back and forth.

Ana frowned, momentarily distracted. She recognized that signal. It was the signal for her army, an indication that a quadrant had been captured.

This early in the battle, it was impossible that anyone had breached the Salskoff walls already.

An explosion thundered to her right, pulling her attention back to the battle. She was near the front lines now, the bridge shaking with the ruthless pummeling from Morganya's Inquisitors. Ana's battalion was still being forced back; if they yielded the bridge, they would allow the Inquisitors to reach the other sectors.

Someone shouted her name; looking up, she found Daya and Yuri racing toward her astride their steeds. Through the chaos and sound of battle all around, a sharp, lucid relief pierced Ana: Her friends were safe.

"We're losing ground!" Daya yelled, drawing to a stop by Ana's side. Her face was covered in sweat and dirt and she had a cut that was bleeding on her left cheek. Behind her, Yuri turned to fire two more blasts at the Inquisitors, so close that Ana could make out the crests on their breastplates, the shimmer of a crown at the center of a Deys'krug. "They're too strong—we underestimated their numbers—"

It felt like the final straw. Ana looked to the burning Palace—the place she had once called home—shrouded in crimson smoke. To the ranks of her army, people shouting and crying out in pain. To the Inquisitors, barely twenty or so paces away, their armor gleaming fresh in the night. To her own hand, coated in blood that continued to drip from her nose down her mouth and chin. The command—to *fall back*—was lodged behind her lips, an ache building in the back of her throat.

"Ana!" Yuri shouted. He was panting, and even as he punched his fists into the air, his flames sputtered weakly in the wind. His knuckles and the back of his hands were burnt red and raw, the skin peeling. "I can't hold them back—we need more forces—the other battalions, can they—" He faltered at the look on her face.

Ana's lips parted to give the signal.

And a flash lit up the ground where Yuri stood.

33

Linn could recall clearly the last time she had been on these walls. It had been her first taste of freedom after having been held in forced servitude throughout her many years in this empire. She'd lost hope until the boy behind her right now had found her in the dungeons of Kerlan's Playpen and handed her the keys to her chains.

She plucked her dagger from an Imperial Patrol's neck and flung it, hearing a satisfying thud as it found its next mark. The parapets behind her had been cleared; Ramson had snatched a torch from the guard tower and was signaling his troops. The ice Affinite leaned over the crenellations, her eyes squeezed shut and face creased in concentration as she held up the bridge of ice she'd frozen across the Tiger's Tail. From up here, Linn could make out the figures of Ramson's battalion making their way across, ready to scale the walls.

The next Imperial Patrol fell beneath the slice of her blade, and Linn suddenly found herself face to face with an Inquisitor. She paused, startled by how young he was, his face barely past boyhood, the armor fitting too large on his shoulders. He stared at her, throat bobbing, the tip of his sword unsteady as he fought to stop the trembling of his hands.

Yet it was his eyes that she focused on: eyes that held a shadow of familiarity. Eyes resembling those of a trapped animal.

Linn recalled what Ana had told her of Morganya's mass capture of Affinites and the mandatory draft into her newly created Inquisitor ranks. Many must have been forced into their positions against their will.

Her bloodlust suddenly faded. When Linn blinked, time seemed to fracture and she was looking back at herself, cornered and vulnerable.

I am not your enemy, Kaïs had told her once. And it had been true, she realized; it was *still* true. That she and this Inquisitor—this *boy*—were simply two sides of the same coin, Affinites with nowhere to hide, forced to live and fight and die for a conflict that wasn't theirs.

Except, now, Linn was fighting for this all to end.

She lowered her blade. "I am not your enemy," she said quietly.

Surprise flashed across the Inquisitor's face.

"I do not wish to hurt you," Linn continued, and she heard Kaïs's voice in her head, speaking the same words; words that she had thought over time and time again. Knowing now that he had recognized the same thing she did now: that it was not each other they were meant to be fighting.

The Inquisitor's lips trembled. "I don't have a choice."

"I know," Linn said. "I was once where you were. Forced to serve a cause in which I had no say. But this war that the Red Tigress is waging—it is for equality. When I could control my own path again, I chose to fight with her because she is one of us, and because her side is one in which I have a say, in which I have a choice." Her knife was steady in her hands, but her heart thumped against her chest.

Tears trickled down the Inquisitor's cheeks. "I don't want to fight anymore," he whispered. The tip of his sword wavered. "I just want to be with my mama."

Slowly, Linn lowered her own weapon. "Then help us end it," she said.

A clatter of metal as the boy dropped the sword, falling to his knees.

Linn grasped his shoulders. "You did a brave thing," she said, before turning to Ramson. She cried: "This section of the wall is clear!"

"Help me with these rope ladders!" he shouted. "Once my unit gets up here, we can open the gates from the inside, and we'll have the Palace!"

Several ladders already hung from the wall, secured; below, Linn caught sight of soldiers beginning to scale them—Bregonian soldiers, their armor glinting, their hands and feet steady from years of training.

Linn rushed over and began to help Ramson fasten the rest of the ladders. "Ramson," she said, her fingers fumbling and clumsy in the cold. "Where is Ana?"

"At the gates," he panted, breath fogging before him. "Her army's trying to get through the entrance—"

"I need to find her," Linn said. "Ramson, in my journey to Kemeira, I have learned of an artifact—one that Morganya is seeking. One so powerful that it can grant a mortal the powers of a god."

He froze, looking up at her. The coil of rope in his hands slid from his grasp, falling to the ground with a thud. "The core," he said quietly. "Is that what you're talking about? A source of all the alchemical power in this world?"

She was so astonished that she nearly dropped the rope ladder she was holding. "How do you—?"

Ramson's expression tightened, and in the instant before he looked away, Linn caught a flash of helplessness. "Ana caught wind of Morganya's search for it. We've been trying to locate it, but Ana decided to march on Salskoff before we could puzzle out where it could be."

Linn's mouth fell open; she touched her fingers to the wooden token pressed to her collarbone beneath the folds of her clothes. "I have the map to it," she said. "Ramson, we must destroy the siphon that holds her Affinity. If we do, it will return to her." The words tumbled from her lips in her rush to speak. "And this core—the Deities' Heart—can do it."

In three strides, Ramson was at her side. He took her shoulders in his hands. Linn had never seen such urgency in his gaze. "Linn," he said. "Sorsha's dead. Morganya took the siphon stolen from Bregon. Ana took the one Sorsha was wearing—but it's killing her." The open desperation in his tone unmoored her, his expression wild as he glanced to the soldiers mounting the walls, the smallest slice of enemy territory they'd fought to take. Within the span of a breath, a war waged in his eyes. "I can't leave—I can't abandon my battalion, my soldiers. You need to go to her. Go to her—and find the Heart."

Before Linn could respond, there came an enormous explosion and a crack that whipped like thunder. Linn leaned over the crenellations to see that a giant crevice was torn across the Kateryanna Bridge. On one side was the Red Tigress's army, a mixture of Bregonian Navy uniforms and civilian dress; on the other, like an immutable white wall, was a regiment of Inquisitors, bearing down upon Ana's battalion.

Ramson swore. His face seemed to have drained of color, and his knuckles shone white as he gripped his misericord.

Linn hesitated. She had not anticipated that this might be the last time she would see Ramson. Had she even thanked him yet for releasing her from her contract at the Playpen at the very start of this journey so that she could make her own choices?

From the distance, a shift in her winds caught her attention.

She froze, her gaze sifting over the parapets to the city beyond. Beneath the ink-black sky, weaving through the darkened streets of Salskoff, were small flares of flickering light, approaching at a uniform pace. And as they began to spill out onto the riverside promenade, she saw, with a rush through her veins, what they were.

"Wait, Ramson," she gasped. "Wait—look!"

From all around came glints of navy-blue armor reflected in torchlight. And as Linn watched, they filed in perfect formation to the riverside walkway, behind the battered ranks of the Red Tigress. There were squads flanking entire carts, carrying what appeared to be firepowder and launchers; commanders on sleek, tall horses followed, holding flags that rippled like an ocean, bearing the sigil of a roaring seadragon, a soaring hawk, and a rearing stallion intertwined.

The Bregonian army had arrived.

By her side, Ramson let out a string of swear words. "By the gods," he said, sounding, for the first time since Linn had met him, reverent. He leaned over the wall, lips parted in amazement. "I don't believe it. That bastard actually did it."

"King Darias?" Linn asked.

Ramson nodded. "I've been writing to him over the course of Ana's campaign. He never responded—I didn't think—"

But Linn had sensed something else, something that came to her like a whisper through the booms and explosions below. Something that touched her Affinity like a steadying hand and twined around her heart.

Kaïs.

34

"*YURI!*"

The scream tore from her throat as Ana lurched forward in her saddle. Her valkryf shrieked, stumbling away from the cloud of dust, snow, and debris settling at the site of the explosion. A giant hole had been torn in the center of the Kateryanna Bridge. On the other side, there was only silence and stillness.

Ana dropped the reins and slid out of the saddle. She stumbled forward through the smoke, her vision blurred, her hand cupped to her mouth. "*YURI!*" she yelled through the chaos.

In the tide of her grief, her blood Affinity answered.

The world flared to life, silhouettes of blood signatures approaching. The bridge was littered with bodies in pools of blood—but as she combed her Affinity through it all, she latched on to a familiar signature: one that smelled of coal and warmth, of hot chokolad and ptychy'moloko, of strong arms that held her in an embrace.

Ana dropped to her knees. Yuri lay crumpled atop rubble, his flame-colored hair coated gray with ash. There was blood everywhere, and as she pulled him into her arms, she could tell he was too pale.

Ana pressed her fingers to his neck. There, a pulse flitted, faint, but present.

He moaned; his eyes fluttered open, and his gaze came to rest on her. His lips formed her name.

"Hush," Ana whispered. She pressed her hand to his stomach. Her Affinity latched on, blood gushing like water from an uncorked bottle. Tetsyev, where was Tetsyev, her battalion's healer? Ana was weak, her Affinity sputtering out like a candle against a roaring gale. As blood leaked between her fingers, Yuri's hand came to rest on hers. His eyes were gentle, fading.

In the sudden silence all around, there came the sharp *click, click, click* of footsteps. A flash of darkness; a looming shadow.

Seyin stepped out of the smoke, daggers gleaming in his hands. His eyes flicked from Yuri to land on Ana. Fury flashed across his face, followed by fear. "What have you done?" he whispered.

"Seyin." Her voice came out in a rasp. "It wasn't me—"

"I always knew it was a matter of time," Seyin continued. His eyes burned, reflecting the red of the fire before them. "You used us, and now, you plan to eliminate us."

Something behind him drew Ana's attention; something moving through the swirling gray smoke. Wisps of a signature of blood, and a dark opaqueness deflecting her Affinity where she tried to probe. Instinctively, Ana flung up a hand—just as an Imperial Patrol leapt out of the smoke, sword raised.

"Seyin, watch out," she gasped.

The soldier swung his sword down as Ana shoved with her Affinity. In her weak state, she only managed to draw his balance off; his blade bit into the cobblestones by Seyin's boots.

Darkness spread across the bridge; for a moment, Ana's vision flickered. When she could see again, Seyin was gone.

The Imperial Patrol plucked his sword from the ground. Time seemed to slow as he approached them, each footfall pounding a heartbeat. Ana's connection to his blood slid and slipped in her focus; sweat beaded on her temples and upper lip as she struggled to call on her power from her siphon again and again. A dark green tinge had spread through her veins like poison leaking from the siphon. All around, her flesh had become mottled.

Ana looked up as the Imperial Patrol raised his sword over their heads.

Another flicker, a shimmer of shadows across her vision, then a dagger across the Imperial Patrol's neck drew a line of red. The soldier staggered and fell to his knees.

Seyin wiped his blade on his cloak. His gaze snapped to Ana.

There was war in his eyes; conflict of a buried story, of grief and suffering and wrath. In that moment, Ana might have understood the fury Seyin had directed her way all along. It wasn't *she* whom he loathed. It was the kind of a world her ancestry had enabled, the violence they had watched in silence, the voices unheard from a broken system.

Seyin lowered his dagger and opened his mouth, and in the days to come, Ana would wonder what he might have said.

A second Imperial Patrol burst from the smog on the bridge, sword flashing across where Seyin stood. This time, there were no shadows, no tricks of light.

Seyin's lips parted in an O of surprise as he fell, the shadows in his eyes growing blank.

The Imperial Patrol turned to Ana.

The air whistled; a pair of swords slashed out of nowhere, one parrying the soldier's blade and the other finding its mark true to his heart. Red bloomed across Ana's senses, and through a film of blood, a silhouette appeared by her side.

Kaïs kept his swords raised as he stepped toward her. "Ana, King Darias's army is here, and they have fired explosives at the gates. The bridge is secure."

There was a wall in her mind; a numbness, spreading. Somehow, Ana pushed past that. "A healer," she choked out. "Kaïs, I-I need a healer—"

His eyes glinted as he nodded. "Stay here, don't move." He straightened and limped forward, swords gleaming from both hands.

Ears ringing, Ana looked to the figure lying before her, a shock of black hair against an outfit white as snow. Seyin's face was cleared of anger and fear so that he looked younger: a boy, innocent and unmarred by years of hardship.

In her arms: another boy, bleeding out. Yuri leaned against her shoulder, face buried in the crook of her neck. His ash-covered hair draped across his face, covering the blood that bubbled from his lips and nose. She could feel warmth seeping across her lap, flowing out of his body.

Ana reached out a shaking hand and pressed it to his chest. Her vision blurred. "Yuri," she whispered. "A healer is coming—hold on—"

His breathing came shallow as he took her hand in both of his. They were cold, charred and blackened from the flames that had eaten away at his own flesh and skin. His face was etched with pain—yet in his coal-gray eyes, she found the warmth of the boy she had known her entire life.

The one who had *saved* her life.

"I . . . can't." His voice was fainter than the whistle of wind. "It . . . hurts . . . too much."

Warmth trailed down her cheeks. "Yuri—"

"I'm sorry I didn't trust you for so long. That I . . . I wasted our time together." He inhaled deeply, his eyes suddenly growing bright and clear. "Finish what we started, Ana. The revolution. The transition." A faint smile curled his lips and he exhaled. "We have come . . . full circle."

His hand fell. The fire in his eyes flickered out.

Dimly, she was aware of her army surging forward from behind her; could hear Kaïs calling orders, passing word that the bridge was secured. She knew she should be standing at the very front, watching as they closed in on the Salskoff gates.

Ana brushed her thumb over Yuri's cheeks. She was merely steps from the Salskoff Palace gates. Moments from victory.

It felt infinitely unfair.

But she had a battle to lead, and a war to win.

Gently, she closed his eyes, and with that, she locked her emotions in the very back of her mind as she had done so many times before. Then, Ana stood and turned to Kaïs.

His hair had grown longer, curling to the nape of his neck; he walked with a slight limp. He met Ana's gaze and inclined his head. "I am sorry for your loss."

She couldn't think of that right now.

Ana looked away, toward the distant banks on the other side of the Kateryanna Bridge. Beyond the burning riverside promenade, lined up on the streets surrounding the Palace and standing in perfect formation, were rows upon rows of soldiers wearing fresh, gleaming armor. Commanders sat astride valkryfs—

commanders she didn't recognize—bearing a flag that rippled in the wind.

"King Darias sent reinforcements," Kaïs said steadily, following her gaze. "It is my understanding that Ramson wrote him, pleading for support."

Her mind blanched. All along, he'd appeared to disagree with her strategy—only to quietly support her from behind the scenes.

Ana's fists clenched. She lifted them into the air, thinking of Yuri. Fire bloomed from her knuckles, shooting into the sky. "Let's finish this."

As Kaïs turned away and began signaling behind them, Ana suddenly remembered something else. A promise she was going to keep to an old friend.

"Kaïs," she called after him. "Shamaïra, we have her. She's safe at our camp." It felt good to remember a spark of light in the seemingly endless darkness. "She's waiting for you."

His eyes shimmered with the vastness of oceans, of time, of loss and longing that she might never understand. Before Kaïs could reply, someone leapt onto the balustrade of the Kateryanna Bridge between them, holding on to a statue of a Deity for balance.

"Affinite Battalion!" Daya roared, lifting an arm. "Bregonian reinforcements have arrived! Wait for their archers, and we take the gates!"

With a sudden whistle, a thousand arrows plunged through the smoke and fire, raining down upon the other side of the bridge, before the gates. Ana wrapped an arm around Kaïs's waist, steadying him and keeping her other hand on the balustrade of the Kateryanna Bridge. The Tiger's Tail roared into eternity beneath them as Daya's shout rang out with the final command.

A shout rose into the night sky from the Bregonian reinforcements and the Affinite battalion as they charged toward the entrance of the Salskoff Palace.

With an earth-shattering boom, the gates of Salskoff cracked.

And, slowly, they opened.

Inside were silhouettes, blurred with smoke and vapor from the siege. Yet in the darkness, a spark flared; a torch was raised, and began waving a signal.

Their signal.

Wind pulsed through the entrance, and suddenly, Ana saw who stood inside.

Linn, her daggers glinting in the torchlight.

And, by her side, Ramson, one hand on his hip, the other waving the torch.

They had done it. They had broken through the Salskoff gates.

Daya let out a shout of triumph; everywhere, their troops were cheering, clapping their hands. Through the crowd, Linn was making her way toward Ana.

Ana untangled herself from Kaïs and stepped forward, wrapping her arms around Linn's familiar, lean build. Her friend let out a small choked sound as she hugged Ana tightly.

When Linn drew back, however, her expression was grave. "Ana, I bring urgent news." She touched a hand to her chest. "I know where the Deities' Heart is—the artifact Morganya seeks. I found out through my Temple Masters. It has the ability to destroy the siphon, return your Affinity . . . and save your life."

It took Ana several moments to process Linn's words. As she took in the earnest, anxious expression on her friend's face, the realization finally cleaved through the maelstrom in her mind: Linn told the truth.

There was a way to the Deities' Heart.

There was a way for her to live.

She squeezed her friend's hand. "I must first settle the battle and secure the Palace," Ana said, "and ensure that Morganya and her troops are being held. That they properly surrender."

Linn's lips curved in the ghost of a smile. "Then, we go."

For some reason, Ana looked across the bridge, past all the people gathered before it, celebrating, and met Ramson's eyes.

His lips were curling, that old, cunning gleam returning to his eyes as he tipped his head and raised an eyebrow. And suddenly, in the fog of her loss, a ray of light as clear and as bright as the sun. An image of a quiet dacha, the silence of a predawn morning, a sunrise that breathed life and fire into the world.

Between one heartbeat and the next, in the space between her and Ramson, Ana saw a world of possibilities unfurl.

Take the Palace.

Defeat Morganya.

Find the Heart.

Transition the government.

They were so, so close. Between the smoke and the snow and the swirling mist, the tantalizing promise of a life after—of a forever—hung in the air.

Ramson's eyes crinkled. *I always win,* he mouthed.

Through the stinging in her eyes, Ana smiled back at him. Then she turned back to Linn, Kaïs, and Daya. "Ready?" she said, looking to the gates, yawning wide.

"Ready," they chorused.

"Together, then," Ana said.

With Kaïs's and Daya's help, they hoisted Yuri's body onto her valkryf, and Ana cradled her friend's head in her arms as she took the reins. Daya, Linn, and Kaïs followed close behind. Ana never looked away from the familiar walls of the Salskoff Palace. Cracks ran along the once-smooth marble; soot licked up the walls, turning them black; the flicker of still-burning fires rendered it all crimson. Here it was, the truth of what her empire had become, exposed for all to see.

Ana laced her fingers between Yuri's. Like this, he might have been asleep, his pale lashes curving against his freckled cheeks, and she remembered opening her bedroom doors a crack to find him curled against the wall next to her chambers, head tucked against his knees, a tray of hot chokolad and ptychy'moloko grown cold by his side throughout the night.

She squeezed his hands and pressed them to her lips. "We're home," she whispered, and turned to the army behind her. Torchlight stained their armor crimson, winding all the way to the streets of Salskoff and beyond.

Ana pumped a fist into the air. "Citizens of Cyrilia," she shouted, as loudly as her voice would carry. "Today, we destroy the past to pave the way for a better future!"

Cheers and cries of triumph spread down the lines of her army like wildfire, like a song of hope. Ana threw back her shoulders, lifted her chin, and entered the gates of her childhood home.

This time, for the last time.

Whereas the mood only moments earlier had been one of jubilation and triumph, there was only silence as Ana rode through the gates of the Palace. She was aware of all eyes on her: Affinites and non-Affinites, soldiers and civilians alike, gazes following her as she passed.

Ramson's battalion had infiltrated the walls, a crucial step to their victory—yet the courtyard was strangely empty as Ana and her army entered the Palace gardens. The snow hadn't been cleared from the paths, as was custom when Ana had lived here; instead, it had been trampled and flattened by hundreds of footprints. Everything was coated in a layer of ice, from the evergreens to the garden sculptures to the lampposts. It was beginning to snow, the flakes twirling silently from the skies like ashes.

It all felt off. The silence was too loud. The spaces hollow where Morganya's Imperial Patrols and guards should have been.

Ana turned to Kaïs, Daya, Ramson, and the other commanders within her vicinity. "Search the entire Palace. I want our men stationed in every hallway and every chamber, from the living quarters to the dungeons. I want every single Imperial Patrol brought to the Grand Throneroom and accounted for." She paused. "And if you happen to run into Morganya, do not engage—send for me. All Affinites, follow me. Morganya has a siphon; she has the ability to take away anyone's Affinity."

Orders and commands were passed along, and Ana tugged her valkryf forward as her Affinite squad, the Redcloaks, and the Affinites from Salskoff fell in behind her. As she fastened the reins of her steed to a pillar near the front steps of the Palace, she couldn't help but glance up, searching past the cupolas and twisting spires until she found the window that used to belong to her. Now it was mullioned and sealed shut, but how many days had she sat at the seat by the sill, looking out into the rose gardens and walkways, to the carriages and horses and people that passed by?

Ana pressed her bare hands against the heavy silver knockers, carved in the shape of white, roaring tigers, and pushed the front doors open. She stepped into old hallways that materialized from her memories. She kept her blood Affinity flared, searching for signs of movement as her army fanned out, moving deeper into different sections of the Palace. Ana made for the Grand Throne-room. The floors rang with the echoes of their footsteps, marble balustrades sweeping toward gilded ceilings engraved with symbols of the Deities. Chandeliers twirled gently, scattering golden light from above as the group moved through the corridors.

They progressed at a slow pace, Linn supporting a limping Kaïs by Ana's side. Linn's grip shifted on her daggers and Kaïs kept his double swords out.

"It's empty," Kaïs said quietly.

Ana pressed her lips together. With each step, a string seemed to tighten inside her. The Palace had once been filled with guards patrolling up and down. And as the group turned the last corridor to the Grand Throneroom, she felt her heart drop like a stone. Up ahead were the grand mahogany doors with the white-gold tiger handles. The entrance was completely deserted, without a single guard stationed in front.

Beyond was the faintest flicker of blood: several signatures that felt vaguely familiar to Ana. One that she knew—indelibly.

She began to walk faster and faster until she broke into a run, ignoring the calls of Linn and Daya and Kaïs. She didn't stop until she was at the doors, her hands ice-cold against the handles. Again, Ana pushed.

The doors slid open, and Ana looked into the site of a massacre.

On the floor of the Throneroom were the bodies of the Imperial Councilmembers, blood blooming out from underneath them. They had been dead for hours, perhaps even longer—their blood had frozen to the marble floors. Ana walked into the room, her heart lurching each time she passed someone she recognized from her childhood. Here, lying faceup, was Councilman Dagyslav Taras, once Papa's closest friend and councilor, with his gray-flecked hair and those eyes that had always held infinite wisdom. And there, the ex–military commander, Councilman Maksym Zolotov, the scar on his nose covered in blood. He'd stood up for her the last time they'd met; it felt like a physical blow to see his expression vacant of the fierceness it had always held.

Morganya had killed them all.

In the center of the Throneroom, a single heartbeat pulsed through Ana's Affinity. Faint, flickering, the composition of the blood utterly familiar to her.

Ana was barely aware of herself stumbling forward, dropping to her knees. Lieutenant Henryk lay at the foot of the dais. She cupped her hands to his face. Someone—Ana had a very good idea who—had sliced his skin with ribbons of iron, the strips of metal red with blood.

But he was alive.

A roaring sound, like the rush of water, filled her ears as people rushed to help her free the lieutenant, several metal Affinites unwinding the sickening ribbons of iron. Tetsyev was already by Henryk's side, salves and vials out.

The lieutenant's breathing was shallow; his lashes fluttered as he looked at her, bleeding from hundreds of razor-thin cuts all over his body. His lips moved, but over the din and chaos, Ana couldn't catch his words.

"I need the premises secured," she called out. "Someone get the healers here, fast."

Lieutenant Henryk's mouth opened and closed. "G-gone," he rasped. "Morganya . . . took her regiment of Inquisitors . . ."

Ice bloomed in Ana's veins. She recalled her surprise at the empty gardens, the way the Inquisitors had fallen so quickly. "Where?" she asked, grasping Lieutenant Henryk's bloodied hand. "Where did she go?"

She knew the answer even before he replied.

"The Silent Sea," Henryk whispered, his eyes fluttering shut. "To find . . . the Deities' Heart."

And there, beneath the paintings of Deities and angels, on the marble floors of the Palace he had served for his entire life, he drew his last breath, and fell still.

35

The Throneroom was filled with the quiet murmur of soldiers and civilians as Ana leaned over the body of the young lieutenant. This time, she had no tears. She took in the hundreds of wounds covering his body, blood still seeping from them.

No—this time, she felt only a surge of fury.

Her hands fisted, and she pulled on the bone-pale cloak he'd worn, etched with the crown-and-Deys'krug sigil of Morganya.

Henryk had saved her life not once, but twice; he'd remained in Morganya's ranks to help *Ana,* and he had died for this reason. Morganya had known.

The Empress had left the Salskoff Palace because she no longer cared. She didn't need a palace—she only needed the Deities' Heart. And Ana knew that as soon as Morganya found it she would unleash her chaos upon the land.

A sense of calm washed over Ana as she straightened and turned. It was time to end this, once and for all.

"Ana!" Daya burst through the doors of the Throneroom. "The perimeter is secure; our troops are sweeping the Palace as we speak, and the Bregonian army has surrounded the Palace. We've—" Her jubilant expression vanished as she took in the scene around her, the somber faces of the living. Her steps fell still as she reached Linn's and Kaïs's side.

"Linn," Ana said quietly. "The Deities' Heart. Can you take me there?"

Linn nodded. "Ana, listen carefully. To restore your Affinity, you must destroy the siphon that holds it. You must remain close so that it may return to you, otherwise your Affinity will be lost to the greater alchemical currents of this world. Do you have Sorsha's siphon?"

Ana lifted her left arm. The searock band gleamed around her wrist. "I do."

Linn pressed a hand to her collarbone. From within the folds of her clothing, she withdrew a wooden token no larger than the size of her thumb, fastened to a piece of red string. "This is the map," she explained, and Ana saw jagged etchings on its surface resembling a coastline, dividing the token into half: land and sea. Out in the center of the space representing ocean was the shape of a heart. "I believe it is north of the very northern tip of Cyrilia, where the Silent Sea rages closest to the Deities' Lights."

"Leydvolnya," Daya said suddenly. She looked up, her expression troubled. "The Ice Port."

"You know it?" Linn intoned in surprise.

"All sailors know it," Daya said in a low voice. "It's said to be haunted. That the Deities' Lights are closest to our world there, and vicious spirits roam the land."

The Redcloak camp, Ana realized—the thought did not find her without a streak of pain through her heart—had been near Leydvolnya.

"The Heart seems to be out at sea," Linn said, tracing a thumb over her token. "I do not see a path to it."

"The Ice Port was once a port before it was abandoned," Daya said. She drew her shoulders back and looked to Ana. "Seems you'll be needing a captain once you get there."

Ana looked to her friends and hesitated. "I cannot ask you—"

Daya put her hand on Ana's arm. "You didn't ask," she said firmly. "What do you think will happen if Morganya gets that Heart? Everything we've fought for here"—a wave around them—"will be lost. What do you think will happen to us? To your troops here, to the Redcloak children, to the civilians of Salskoff who came to our aid? To everyone who fought for you knowing it was the only way to a better future?" Her earth-brown eyes blazed. "I'm your captain, Ana. Let me do my job."

Ana recalled the conversation they'd had aboard Daya's ship *Stormbringer* over a moon ago, before they'd landed in Cyrilia. *If the world falls, the last thing I want is to know I could have fought and made a difference and chose not to.*

Ana drew a deep breath and nodded. "There is no time to lose. We set out immediately." She hesitated, her gaze landing on Kaïs. "And . . . I need someone I can trust to monitor the situation here."

The soldier straightened and nodded, though she didn't miss the glance he gave Linn. "My sword is yours to command. I would gladly stay to monitor the situation. As a former Imperial Patrol, I know procedures and I am familiar with the workings of the Palace."

Ana reached into the folds of her shirt, where she'd tucked the piece of parchment she'd spent an entire moon refining with Daya's counsel and the wisdom of dozens of books. There was nothing more she wished than to see the plans writ within carried out to fruition herself, but . . .

She held it out to Kaïs. The parchment carried the weight of centuries, of all the lives lost and dreams stolen. "Inside the scroll you will find an outline of the new Cyrilia. One run by the people, for the people. Will you safeguard it for me?"

Kaïs's fingers wrapped around the piece of paper. "I will, until you return."

Their eyes met. "In the case that I do not return," Ana said steadily, "I want you to hand this to a Redcloak named Liliya Kostov."

She had no wish to see the shift in his eyes, the pity that was sure to come. But Kaïs only nodded, his expression solemn. A soldier, through and through. "Understood."

"Take a non-Affinite battalion, Ana," Daya said. "Morganya has a siphon, but surely non-Affinites can still be effective in a fight against her."

"I will." Ana lifted her left arm, pulling back her sleeve slightly. Light lanced off the siphon, which had grown darker and cloudier over the course of the past moons. "She can't siphon anything from me, which is why I must be the one to stop her from getting that Heart."

Linn stepped forward, taking her hand. "We will be with you, Ana," she said. "All the way."

At an earlier time in her life Ana would have hated the thought of putting a friend in danger; now, wearied and fatigued, she only felt a rush of gratitude. Ana smiled softly. "I would be glad to have a friend with me."

"Perhaps you will have use for an alchemist in navigating the most treacherous, magical lands of our world," came a quiet voice. Ana noticed Tetsyev for the first time, standing a little behind her friends. His robes were torn and bloodied, his face pale and drawn. There was fear in his eyes, but there was also resolve. "I have studied the ancient myths, the theories behind the forces that drive our world. Allow me to help."

Ana nodded. With Tetsyev's knowledge of alchemy and his research, he would be useful. She turned back to her friends. Daya's expression was graver than she'd ever seen it; Kaïs's face was locked, thoughts swirling behind the ice in his gaze.

"We leave now," Ana said. She took a last look around them. "Where is Ramson?"

"He's leading a sweep of the grounds with his soldiers," Daya answered. "I can go and get him—"

Ana held up a hand. "No. My troops must not be alerted that I am gone, or there may be panic." There was a wall in her mind, unyielding and unfeeling. So long as she focused on the tasks at hand, she need not think of all she was leaving behind.

Of the forever she had dared to imagine, standing on the bridge just a little while ago.

She turned to address Kaïs. "Please give those we have lost a proper burial. There is a prayer temple at the back of the Palace; I would like for each and every fallen soldier to be given the honors. And . . ." She met Kaïs's gaze. "Would you ask the commanders of my forces to send word to those in our camp we left behind? Tell them to bring Shamaïra here."

Kaïs's expression shifted, like ice melting to spring waters.

Ana managed a smile. "Give her my love when she wakes, won't you?"

"I will. And I await your return, Ana." Kaïs inclined his head, a lock of oil-black hair falling into his face. "It has been an honor fighting by your side."

*   *   *

Outside, the courtyard was packed with soldiers, some resting, some tending to the wounded, others standing guard. Standing in the shadows beneath the great double doors, Ana watched the movement outside, the entire battalions of soldiers and civilians that had fought for her cause. How she had dreamt of this day as a little girl: of donning Papa's crown and cape and standing before her very own army.

Now, she lifted the hood of her cloak, shrouding her face in darkness. "Linn, Daya," Ana said. "Would you both take Pyetr to gather my battalion and meet me outside the Palace gates? I'd like to have a moment."

She watched them go, finally letting exhaustion wash over her. The sounds of jubilation from the courtyard and beyond seemed strangely distant, the fires from torchlight haloing and fading as though she were already detached from them, already gone from this world.

Ana turned and walked into the shadows. The hubbub of conversation and song fell quiet as she drew farther away until there was only her, the Palace, and the silently falling snow.

Ana touched a hand to the Palace walls and inhaled deeply. She felt hollowed out, as though she had reached inside herself and dug out her heart and carved it into different pieces, scattered across her people, her army, and her land. A part of her wished to simply lie down and curl up on the snow beneath the walls of her home, closing her eyes right there and right then.

She'd given this revolution her all, and she was so, so tired.

Footsteps behind her, the crunch of boots through snow.

Ana spun round. The world fell away from her.

Ramson stepped out from behind a copse of conifers. He was gazing at her with such sharp intensity that she felt it crack her soul like glass, and as he strode toward her, she only beheld him with helpless resignation and unbridled joy. Her heart opened to him like a flower to sunlight.

"Ana," he said, and in that moment, there might have just existed this: the snow, the stone, the pines, and the two of them gazing at each other beneath a winter's night.

Looking at him, she saw in her memories a tender morning, their breaths fogged against the glass, the light of an early dawn serene against their skin. She remembered the moment on the Kateryanna Bridge, how she had imagined an entire life of possibilities unfolding between them—before the door had so quickly swung shut again.

Ramson held out a hand. "We could be together," he said softly. "If . . . if you'd still have me."

Something broke inside her. Perhaps it was the way that he watched her with a mixture of hesitation and hope in his eyes; perhaps it was that he still knew nothing of what they had discovered in the Throneroom. Of the victory that had been snatched so suddenly from them. Of what she still had to do.

She could not bear the thought of parting with him again. She did not know if she had the resolve.

Perhaps some good-byes were better left unsaid. Ana turned away, feeling the sting of tears in her throat, their warmth as they trickled down her cheeks. She held a hand up. "Ramson, I told you." Her voice threatened to crack. "I can't do this."

She began to walk away to the gates, to where Linn would be waiting for her.

"Ana," he said, following her. She heard the exact moment he stopped, the crunching of his boots in snow giving way to silence.

She strained to listen. Wished he would call her back, plead with her to stay.

She might just give in, if he did.

Instead, he said, "You've made your feelings clear. But I'm done lying. I don't want to have any more regrets of things left unsaid. I love you, Ana. I've only ever loved you."

The air around her fractured. She might have chosen death a hundred more times over what she was about to do.

No more casualties, whispered a voice in her head. *No more hurt, because of you.*

Ana turned around. Met his gaze. Held it. "I'm sorry, Ramson."

She saw his heartbreak written across his face. It took every ounce of strength to turn, to lift one foot before the other, and to walk in the direction of the gates. A numbness was spreading through her body, and it felt as though she were watching herself from above, no longer in control of what she did or what she desired.

Anastacya Mikhailov, the girl who had been the Blood Witch, no longer existed.

All that was left was the Red Tigress.

Ana left the boy she loved standing alone beneath a night of silently falling snow.

36

The Salskoff Palace was retaken. They had won the battle.

The victory felt hollow.

Ramson strode through the hallways, checking on their troops. The Palace was large enough to house their entire army, which meant it was packed, from corridor to corridor.

That was good. He could not take silence in this moment.

He'd instructed his men to go to the servants' quarters and the laundry rooms to retrieve all the blankets and pallets they could find. Parren had taken control of the kitchens and was already beginning to feed the army.

Ramson showed his squad the hidden servants' passageways in the walls that allowed them to move throughout the Palace without being seen—an old and outdated monarchic tradition. Still, as Ramson watched his men file out, sheets and laundry spilling from their arms, his thoughts drifted inevitably to Ana. He pressed a hand to the cold marble walls, dully taking in the engravings of Deities and angels and snow spirits and remembering how he'd run down these halls barely half a year ago with Ana. Gods, was there even a time when she hadn't been in his life and set his world on fire?

Shame pricked at him as the age-old lesson echoed in his mind. *Love is a weakness,* his father had insisted, but no one had ever prepared Ramson for the way his heart ached, the way his every breath felt empty. There was still work to be done; Ana still hadn't sent him word of where she'd captured Morganya and rounded up the rest of the Whitecloaks, nor had she brought up Linn or the Deities' Heart and her plans there. Ramson would straighten it all out with her—but right now, in this moment, he needed to be alone. Away from her.

"Captain Farrald, sir." A voice cut through his thoughts. A soldier from his squad stood before him, and for a moment, Ramson imagined Narron's face, the gentle grin of his former lieutenant.

He blinked the image away, but the pain in his heart remained. "Yes."

The young man—the fire magen named Torron—brought his hands against his chest in a quick salute. "Ardonn has arrived, along with the rest of our—and the Red Tigress's—squad. They have been taken to the healers' wing, as you instructed."

Ramson nodded. "Does Shamaïra—the lady—have everything she needs?"

"Yes, Captain. And . . . she is properly awake." Torron smiled. "Lady Olyusha had a helping hand, I believe."

A sliver of good news, at last. "Thank you. I will see her in the healer's wing." He paused. "Tell Kaïs to meet me there, please."

"Captain?" The young magen was staring at him. "Will we return to Bregon after this?"

He had not thought of this—not yet. There had been a moment when he'd first drawn open the gates of the Salskoff Palace and gazed across the bridge into Ana's familiar, bright eyes that

Ramson had actually dared imagine the possibility of a future with her in it.

He let out a sharp breath, cutting through that thought as well. She'd made her feelings to him clear all along. Ironically, it was he who had attached deeper meaning to their time together.

In the end, it was she who had conned him.

"Yes," he said. "Yes, once our forces are recovered. I will speak to the Red Tigress to understand her plans in dealing with Morganya and handling the Empire. Once we are no longer needed, we shall go." His tone softened at Torron's expression. "No need to look so worried. King Darias awaits your and our squad's return to your positions in the Navy."

"And you, Captain?"

The letter in his breast pocket—the one bearing the King's seal, delivered by one of the reinforcement commanders—suddenly weighed heavy. *Punishment,* stated the words inked in King Darias's handwriting, *by expulsion from the Three Courts and revocation of your role. Trial for treason should you wish to return to the Blue Fort. As monarch, my power is constrained and checked by the vote of the Three Courts. I can promise nothing.*

"Me?" Ramson let out a low chuckle. "Don't you worry about me, Torron."

He had nothing left—no men, no resources, no coin—and yet somehow, it felt liberating. Somehow, it fueled a spark inside him as he walked away.

He'd done this once before: started all over with nothing to his name, and it had carved him into a different man, led him in a direction that had made him stronger and tougher than he'd ever been. He'd gone down a path of darkness, but when he closed his eyes, he would remember Ana, and how she had shown him light.

He could do it again. Start over, but this time, not because he was running from his father or from Alaric Kerlan.

This time, he would build his life from scratch, and it would be for himself.

His steps were heavy as he traced the path up the marble staircase to the healer's wing. The smell of antiseptics and bottled salves reached him as he entered a vast hall lined with beds.

They were all filled. The air was rent with moans and sobbing from the wounded.

He entered a section that had been quartered off, where those not needing urgent care had been brought and were resting. Ardonn nodded at him from a pallet as he passed, but Ramson made for a different bed.

Olyusha looked up at him as he approached. She was holding the patient's—*her* patient's—hand with a fierce sort of protectiveness.

Shamaïra leaned against the headboard of the bed. Her cheeks were gaunt, hollowed, and at this point she might have been no more than skin and bones. A bowl of hot kashya sat at her bedside table, untouched.

The sight of her filled Ramson with equal parts relief and guilt. The last he'd seen of Shamaïra fully conscious and awake had been moons ago, when the Imperial Inquisition had burned down her dacha and dragged her away. Outnumbered, Ramson had only been able to watch.

The next time he'd seen her back at Ana's camp, she'd been unconscious, gravely injured from the battle against Morganya and Sorsha. Later on, even during the brief periods she'd woken to eat and drink, she'd been feverish and exhausted, falling back into her prolonged sleep afterward.

Now, her eyes turned to him with a piercing clarity as he eased himself onto a stool by her side. Ramson nodded to Olyusha. "Go get some rest," he said. "You've been up for long enough."

She pursed her lips and stood. "You'll be all right, mamika?" Shamaïra nodded. Olyusha turned to Ramson, and he saw exhaustion lining her eyes. "She's just woken. No strenuous activity, got it?"

He smiled as he watched the poison Affinite leave, but the smile faded as he turned back to Shamaïra. "You're awake."

Her cracked lips parted a sliver, and her voice was no more than a whisper. "That I am, and I've never felt better."

He'd forgotten how much fire was in her spirit, how her words crackled with power.

Ramson paused. What was he to say? *How are you?* Anything that came to mind sounded disingenuous, especially considering his remorse.

No more lies, he thought. *No more regrets.*

He gently touched her hands. They were like claws, brittle and curled. Ramson lifted his gaze to hers. "I am sorry." He had the urge to look away, to stand and walk out. But he pushed on: "I was there, the day the Imperial Inquisition took you. I'm sure you knew. I should have tried to save you."

Her eyes crinkled; she made a sort of noise in her throat that sounded like a rasping laugh. "And what, foolish boy? Be killed in the process? Who else would have gone to the Red Tigress, who else would have been able to raise an army and rescue not just me, but the other Affinites Morganya had imprisoned?" She gave him a devious grin. "I am an Unseer, Ramson Farrald, never forget."

Footsteps sounded in the hall behind them. "But some things," came a deep, steady voice, "you do not see."

Ramson turned to see Kaïs stepping forward. He had shed his armor and rinsed the blood and grime from his face; he stood in a simple and pale Cyrilian shift, mirroring that of his mother.

His mother.

It was impossible to deny it and unimaginable that Ramson had not spotted it before, the resemblance of their features: their straight noses and chiseled jawlines, strong brows and hair that gleamed like black ink in the candlelight. And those eyes—like the purest of spring waters rushing down a snowy mountain.

"Kaïs?" Shamaïra whispered.

The yaeger's voice was thick with emotion. "I am here," he said, and closed the gap between them. He knelt by her bed and she folded him into her arms, pressing her forehead to his. The years that had lined Kaïs's face and worn down his shoulders seemed to melt away.

Ramson stood and crossed the room to the door. He paused, throwing one last glance back.

"Sweet, isn't it?" came a bright, clear voice.

A girl had appeared in the doorway, several years his junior. Her shock of bright red hair framed her freckled face, which looked prone to smiling. Right now, however, she looked at Kaïs and Shamaïra with a quiet wistfulness. Her eyes were rimmed red.

"I'm Liliya," she said, holding her hand out. "Liliya Kostov."

He knew who she was—he'd seen her before around camp, and perhaps they had been in the same strategy meetings before, though they'd never had the chance to properly meet. She'd mostly hung around Yuri and the Redcloaks, a radiant flame of a presence.

Yuri. He'd seen Ana leading the valkryf with the Redcloak commander's body draped over its saddle.

Ramson clasped the girl's hand. "Ramson Farrald."

"I know," she said, and fell silent.

Ramson looked back to Shamaïra. Kaïs had taken a seat on the edge of her bed, their hands clasped together. Mother and son murmured words that Ramson had no wish to intrude upon.

"The waiting's the hardest part, isn't it?" Liliya said quietly. "When Kaïs told me, my first instinct was to prepare our troops for battle again. But . . ." She gestured to the ward around them, the beds filled with their injured. "I just couldn't take this moment of safety away from them. We've all lost so much."

Ramson frowned, the words stirring a whisper of wrongness into the serenity of the scene before them. "Prepare our troops for what?"

Liliya gave him a blank stare. "Did she not tell you?"

His chest tightened. "Tell me what?" Across the chamber, Kaïs had tipped his face to them. A frown began to crease his brows.

"Morganya left hours before our siege," Liliya said. "She took half her forces with her to search for that artifact."

The final piece of the puzzle clicked into place, the meaning of her words cutting like a dagger to his chest. The moment in the snow, the way Ana looked at him, tears limning her dark lashes silver.

He did not need to hear the rest of what Liliya had to say.

"Ana went after Morganya. She's gone to the Silent Sea."

37

The temperature seemed to plummet with every day of Ana's journey north. Overhead, the skies became eternally shrouded in gray snow clouds, and each morning they woke to frost clinging to their clothes, fog threading through the frozen conifers. At night, the Deities' Lights flared in the sky, jagged and erratic, the colors shifting sharply.

Each step of the valkryfs, each squeak of her carriage wheels, carved a path from which there was no going back. She looked to her wrist every so often, the siphon nested tighter than ever against her skin. Dark substances writhed across its surface, and around it, her flesh seemed leached of color.

When the time came, she would not hold back. She would fight to her last breath—for her empire and for her people, but also for those she had left behind and those who had left her behind.

Ramson's face came to her, hazel eyes open and earnest as he held her. Ana closed her eyes, trying to recall that exact moment: the roar of a burning fire surging through her veins, the rush of water in her ears, the touch of Ramson's skin to hers as his arms closed around her, the feeling of being made whole again. *I love you* were the last words he'd said to her, to which she had only been able to reply, *I'm sorry.*

Ana thought of Luka, of Papa and Mama, the wreckage of her family too soon gone.

She thought of all those who had given their lives for the revolution—Yuri, Kapitan Markov, Lieutenant Henryk, and all the fallen soldiers, on both sides.

Finally, she thought of a small friend she'd held close to her heart since the start of it all. The girl with the ocean eyes and soft black hair, who'd breathed hope into Ana the way she'd coaxed life into a dying flower in the midst of winter. Ana's lips curled in a smile, and as though in response, a soft wind stirred the fragrance of winterbells against her cheeks.

May, she thought. *I promised you.*

On the fourth night of their travel, Ana woke to Linn gently shaking her. Her friend parted the curtains on the windows of their carriage, and with Daya, they peered out. The landscape outside had shifted. The trees of the Syvern Taiga had given out to a frozen tundra, stretching vast and empty beneath a sky of weaving lights.

"This is it," Daya said quietly. "The Ice Port should be right up ahead."

They drew to a stop and stepped outside. The cold immediately invaded their bones with a biting vengeance. They were in the ghost hours before dawn, the moon low in the sky, half-hidden behind clouds that filtered an eerie, colorless light unto the land. Somehow, Ana thought, tipping her head up, the sky here seemed closer, the stars gleaming as though she could stretch out a hand and touch them. Behind her was the battalion of soldiers, trailing in a long, winding line. Ahead, Ana thought she heard the rush of the ocean, smelled the briny tang of sea carried by a breeze.

This was the northernmost point of Cyrilia, where the vicious waters of the Whitewaves gave way to the still deep of the Silent Sea.

A rider approached, drawing his valkryf to a stop. It was one of their scouts. He saluted Ana. "There are forces gathered ahead," he said. "Imperial Patrols."

Ana flared her blood Affinity. The toll it took on her was immediate, fatigue descending upon her like a cloud. She focused, spreading her awareness out to the distance. There out on the shores before them, faint but sparking like distant fires, came flares of blood and movement, blurred by blackstone-infused armor, standing still. She searched for a familiar signature—and she found it. Ahead of the army, Morganya stood on the precipice of the shores of Cyrilia.

Ana sized up her battalion. Morganya's army outnumbered theirs, but all that Ana needed was for her soldiers to buy her some time.

She turned to the battalion following her carriage, the commanders silently astride valkryfs, awaiting her command. Unexpectedly, she met Tetsyev's eyes. The alchemist rode on a horse, ice clinging to his cheeks and lashes. His expression was set as he nodded at her. "Allow me to accompany you, Red Tigress."

Ana nodded. "Ride with me, then," she said, and turned to her two friends. Against the night, Daya's face reflected the lights that shimmered up above. Linn's eyes held stars. "When the time comes, I need you to stay away from Morganya, Linn. You still have an Affinity that she could siphon."

They unstrapped the valkryfs attached to their carriage and mounted.

"We should stay behind our army, Ana," Daya said. "Strategically, let them carve an opening through the battlefield first."

"I agree." Linn brought her steed forward. A dagger flashed silver in her palm. "It has been an honor fighting by your side, friends."

"Aye," Daya said, tapping two fingers to her forehead in a salute.

"The honor has been mine," Ana replied.

She lifted her fists to the night sky and found the fire Affinity within her siphon. Steeling herself, she summoned the Affinity up her forearms and through her fingertips, feeling the heat as flames caught and shot up in a clear signal.

Shouts rang out among the commanders, and her army took off in a flurry of hooves. Ana followed, urging her valkryf into a canter. The beach came into view; snow turned to a glittering icy sand, a stretch of bone-white waves unfurling against pale shores. There, outlined against the expanse of vicious sea, was the silhouette of the army of Imperial Patrols. It fanned out along the coastline, a swarming mass of pale cloaks and gray armor.

A commander's sharp cry pierced the night.

Morganya's forces charged.

The two armies met in a clash of steel and blades, fire and water, air and earth.

Ana clung tight to her valkryf and rode low, her Affinity flared and thrusting against any bodies of blood that charged her way. Within moments, the sands around her had turned into a raging battlefield. Daya rode by her side and Linn in front of her. The Kemeiran warrior cut a path through the fighting toward the distant shores, which loomed past the Imperial Patrols. Un-spoken between them, Linn understood the need for Ana to con-serve her Affinity. She flung out her wind Affinity with abandon, blasting aside Imperial Patrols who charged them. The others met a quick death at the flash of her blades.

"Ana!" Daya's shout reached her. "Ahead—Leydvolnya!"

The sound of crashing waves wended through the clash of swords and cries of battle. And there—in the smoke-screen of snow and sand and mist, the outline of the ocean was broken by the silhouette of a port, of jetties and boats cast in darkness.

Linn turned to look back at Ana. Even in the cold, sweat and mud slicked her face in a sheen. "Almost there!" she cried.

Flames exploded before them. Their valkryfs let out screams, and as Ana's reared up and bucked away from the flames, the world tilted off-balance.

Ana slammed into sand, narrowly avoiding being trampled beneath her steed. She could hear Linn and Daya calling her name. Looking up, she caught a flash of silver armor and a ripple of a pale cloak as an Inquisitor stepped into her path.

He raised his hands. Fire shot out again. Ana barely had the time to roll away, the flames scorching the sand and ice just a hand's breadth from where she'd lain. Heat rolled over her in a suffocating tide.

And then the fire was pushed back by a squall of wind.

Linn stepped in front of Ana, hands thrust out, daggers re-flecting red. The Inquisitor staggered back, momentarily thrown off by the wind.

"Go!" Linn shouted, and she flung something to Ana. It landed in the sand between them: an object that could fit into the center of her palms. "I will hold them back!"

Arms wrapped around her own, and Ana found herself hauled to her feet. Daya's face was streaked with soot and dirt; Tetsyev's robes were singed, and red welts covered his face. "C'mon, Ana," Daya gasped, wiping tears from her eyes as she blinked against the smoke pluming from the fire. "The port's right up ahead— I see boats already—"

Ana snatched up Linn's wooden token and ran. Wind whistled against her face, the cold plunging into her like daggers. Ahead, the waves pounded, frothing white, dragging the corpses of Imperial Patrols and her soldiers alike into the sea; further, she could see the outline of the pier, dotted with small barges that bobbed in the waves.

There was no sign of Morganya. As they drew closer, Ana began to make out wooden docks stretching into the water like long, spindly fingers toward a horizon limned with the silver light of a distant sun, extending in the direction where the Heart was meant to be.

In front of the docks, standing guard, was a black-cloaked figure.

Ana slowed as sand turned to wet wood beneath her feet, damp and creaky from years of abandonment. Fear crawled up her veins at the sight of the man before her.

Sadov's teeth glinted white as she approached. "Hello, Little Tigress," he crooned. "I knew you wouldn't be able to stay away for long."

By Ana's side, Daya drew her weapon. Tetsyev had gone very, very still.

"Morganya's faithful lap dog until the very end, Sadov?" Ana said. And then with the strength and fury of all she had suffered beneath his cruelty, she flung her blood Affinity at him.

Their Affinities hit each other at the same time. The world bled black, familiar nightmares flipping through her mind.

Suddenly, it all vanished. She heard Sadov give a gurgling gasp. When Ana blinked again, the Imperial Advisor was on his knees. Tetsyev was drawing back, blood on his hands glistening red. Glass glinted between his fingers. He'd broken one of his tonic vials and jammed the shards into Sadov's neck.

Sadov turned, a flash of metal in his hands. When Ana cried out a warning, it was too late.

Tetsyev stumbled back. Red spilled from his throat, and even as he closed his hands over the wound, it ran down his chest, soaking his alchemist's robes.

Ana seized the blood in Sadov's body and tore. And just like that, the man who had tormented her for half her life crumpled to the frozen sand. The last expression he bore was one of fear, carved on his face even after the light had faded from his eyes.

Ana knelt by Tetsyev's side. Blood, there was blood everywhere—too much of it. She pressed a hand over his throat. Liquid warmth leaked between her fingers.

The alchemist's eyes were bulging, his lips opening and closing as he looked at her. She bent her ear to his face and caught the last of his words, no more than the whistle of wind between his cracked lips. ". . . atone for . . . my mistakes . . ."

Then, without another sound, the man exhaled, the muscles in his body loosening. His eyes closed for the last time.

Ana lowered him to the ground. She understood the meaning of the alchemist's words. Since her first meeting with him, moons back when she'd been on the hunt for her father's murderer, he'd told her of his wish to atone for his sins—for his complicity in the murders of her parents and her brother.

It was this that had driven all of his decisions: to save her life more than once, and finally, to leave Morganya's side and fight with her.

She traced the symbol of a Deys'krug on his chest. "May you find peace at last, Pyetr Tetsyev," she said softly, and rose.

Daya was out on the jetties already, circling one of the posts with a cutter tied to it. She looked up, her face drawn. "This one'll do," she said. "It's small, but it'll be fast."

The sky had shifted to a nebulous, colorless gray, halfway between light and dark. The waters of the sea broke against the docks, turbulent and vicious. Far off, she could make out the faintest flicker of a familiar blood signature, one that conjured the whisper of a prayer, the kiss of a dagger pressed to crimson lips, cold eyes the color of pale tea.

Morganya.

There was no more delaying it; every obstacle in her way had been met by sacrifice from the people around her—from Yuri and Henryk and the fallen soldiers on her battlefield to Tetsyev and Linn, and those still fighting nearby to buy her time.

Now, she looked to Daya, standing in the cutter with one hand on the mast and the other on the wheel to steady herself against the relentless churn of waves. Daya had always carried herself with assurance and staunch honesty; it was only in this moment that Ana saw fear color her friend's expression.

Daya gripped the sails tighter and nodded. She gave a thumbs-up, crooking her mouth into a grin. Her lips moved, forming soundless words. *I'm your captain, Ana.*

Standing on the precipice of her empire and gazing out into the infinite white waves, Ana had the urge to glance back, to catch a glimpse of her army, the sight of a familiar land she was not sure she would see again.

She swallowed. If she did not step forward now, she might never have the strength to.

Head held high, chin lifted, shoulders back, Ana stepped onto the boat.

She did not look back.

38

There was nothing in the silence but shadow and silhouettes, and the steady *pat-pat-pat* of his valkryf's hooves. They drummed out a rhythm of time trickling to an inevitable end.

The conifers farther south were beautiful, ice clinging to their branches like diamonds. This far up north, Ramson ventured into a world with all the color leached from it. The cold dug into his bones with a vengeance.

The nights were so long that time had begun to blur, broken only by an intermittent, watery dawn. He rode until he was exhausted, and slept huddled beneath his valkryf, a fire roaring before him and a globefire cradled between his hands. Several times, he dozed off on his saddle, only to wake up and find that his steed had strayed slightly.

His compass was steady in his hands, and the arrow pointed north.

On the fourth day, the air shifted. It was more by sense than anything else that he knew he drew close to the ocean. He could taste it in the wind that whipped ruthlessly against his furs: the briny tang of salt, the smell of the sea.

As the trees began to thin, Ramson had the strangest impression that the land itself was attempting to pull him back. Branches whipped at his face and clawed at his clothes; the air itself seemed to thicken, and once or twice, Ramson thought he saw the stir of phantom creatures out of the corners of his eyes, gone as soon as he blinked.

He gripped the reins of his steed tightly, one hand brushing against the hilt of his misericord for comfort. He'd spoken to Kaïs, who had explained everything before giving him an approximate location. Besides, it hadn't been difficult to follow the trail left by Ana's battalion.

He'd left instructions for his squad and appointed Torron to be in charge, letting them know that should he not return within a fortnight, they were to return to Bregon without him. He'd penned a letter to King Darias and the Three Courts telling of his treason, again cementing all blame and punishment on his head.

All was taken care of, for he had no idea what he would find up ahead, and for once, no plan—and yet, he felt no fear.

The shores of the Silent Sea opened up before him, pale and glittering like diamonds, the waves lunging at the land with a viciousness he'd never seen before.

In the distance, a battle raged.

Ramson's fingers tightened around his reins. He dug his heels into the belly of his horse and rode forward.

 **39**

They were outmatched in every way possible.

Linn spun, daggers flashing as they found their mark in another soldier's throat.

This was the problem: They had vastly underestimated the number of Inquisitors in Morganya's ranks. Ana had made the strategic decision to leave their Affinite battalion to guard the Palace, as well as to keep them out of Morganya's siphon's grasp. This decision had been a double-edged sword, for they were now faced with the onslaught of Morganya's army of Affinites with no Affinites of their own to match them.

Linn ducked as another Inquisitor came charging at her, diamond blades gleaming in his fists. She leapt and thrust—and Linn parried.

Just barely.

The second blow sent one of Linn's daggers spinning from her hands. She heard a *thwick* as it buried itself in the sand.

The next moment, a diamond blade cut across her cheek.

Linn staggered back, the rhythm of her steps interrupted. She barely had a moment to look up as the diamond Affinite leapt.

As the Inquisitor's diamond blades plunged toward her, she summoned wind and slid beneath the Inquisitor. Twisted. Pirouetted.

And landed on the girl's back, her lone dagger kissing her opponent's neck, her other hand pressing the girl's face against the sand.

The Inquisitor's hand twisted.

Linn reacted instinctively, but not fast enough. She felt the blade pierce her side; the pain came a moment later. She rolled off, spitting blood onto the snow-sprinkled sand.

Linn reached for her knives as the Affinite's blades plunged down.

A second shadow appeared, sword driving down.

Blood splattered on Linn's face, wet and warm. The Inquisitor's body slumped onto the sand, and Linn's savior stepped forward.

"What was it that you said about saving me every time we fought?" Ramson said, wiping his misericord on his pants. His tone was light, yet his face was grave, as though his heart wasn't in the jest.

He bent down to her. His hand was gentle as he slid it around her waist, and she thought of the first moment they'd met in the dungeons of Alaric Kerlan's Playpen. How different he'd been then.

"Ramson," Linn whispered. "I have never thanked you." She was bleeding profusely from her midsection—she could feel it seeping into her clothes.

"Now, why would you need to thank me?" He kept his misericord out, eyes scanning their surroundings before looking back to her. "I've been keeping a tally—I'm a businessman, after all—and I believe I still owe you one." His hand steadied her as they retreated. "Where is she?"

There was no doubt whom he meant. A terrible sadness shadowed Linn's heart. "She followed Morganya, out into the Silent Sea. When we arrived, it seemed Morganya had already gone ahead . . . to seek the Heart."

His grip tightened. "She went alone?"

"With Daya. They took a boat from the Ice Port." Linn looked away. "She needed me to keep Morganya's army at bay."

Ramson continued to watch their surroundings on all sides; he suddenly went very still. "Well, I think you've succeeded," he replied. Something in his tone kept Linn silent as he turned them around to face the sea.

Across the ocean, lunging like daggers across the bone-pale waves, were hundreds of ships. Their sails spread out like fans, like wings, hulls rearing round as they plunged through the waves.

Airborne above them were small shapes that Linn at first mistook for a flock of birds. As they drew closer, the wind rose to a sharp shriek, and storm clouds began to form over clear air.

Linn's heart began to race as the squad of Kemeiran windsailers alighted on the sands of the beach. Even through the mist of her pain, she found her gaze catching on the leader as he stepped forward.

She knew him. Had heard his voice through countless dreams and nightmares.

Fly, Ko Linnet.

"Shi'sen," she whispered. *Master.*

As the Kemeiran ships pulled to shore, the windsailers drew their daggers and charged into the fray of the battle. Only the

Wind Master remained, looking at Linn as hundreds of Kemeiran wielders began to disembark from their ships.

In her eight years away from Kemeira, her first Wind Master
had aged. White now flecked his once-gray hair like the first
falls of snow upon a thatched rooftop. Wrinkles lined his face,
winding like rivers between jagged mountains. But his eyes were
obsidian steel. With every step he took, the wind seemed to part
before him, the waves shrinking behind his heels.

He approached, followed by another wielder. Their shifts
were thin, billowing in the wind, and unsuitable for the cold this
far north, but they both moved as though through a blossoming
garden in the spring.

"Child," Fong shi'sen said.

Linn had imagined this moment hundreds, perhaps even
thousands, of times. Now that it had arrived, she was at a loss for
what to do. The only thing she knew was fear; life had taught her
to expect little, and brace for disappointment. She clung tightly
to Ramson, her head spinning—whether from the blood loss, or
the sight before her, she didn't know.

The Wind Master gestured to Ramson. "Leave her to us."

Ramson gave him a blank look; this small, familiar moment
broke Linn from her reverie. He did not understand the Kemeiran language nor the Kemeiran ways. And she did not need him
here.

"Go," she said, patting his back. "Sail straight north. It leads
to the Heart. To her."

Ramson hesitated. His eyes lifted to the shores, to where the
faint silhouette of the abandoned port lay in the watery predawn
light. He squeezed her shoulder and drew back. "Be safe. I'll see
you on the other side."

Holding her abdomen, Linn watched him leave before she turned to her Wind Master. He regarded her impassively. "Yirenn," he said to the wielder behind him. "Heal her wound, please."

The wielder Yirenn only inclined his head, but Linn felt a warmth in her side. Through the gash in her shirt, she watched the bleeding slow to a trickle, then dull and harden as the flesh around it began to heal. Within breaths, the wound was gone, and all that was left was the memory of pain across her midriff.

Fong shi'sen turned his palms skyward. "Stand, child," he said, and she did as she was told. "The Temple Masters of Bei'kin sent word that valuable artifacts had been stolen from the great Bei'kin Bookhouse. They reached an agreement with our emperor. He called for a group of Temple Masters to investigate and retrieve the artifacts . . . and to defend our land, and our world, from evil."

Linn's heartbeat rushed in her ears. She remained silent, hardly daring to believe. Around them, ships were continuing to anchor, Kemeiran soldiers rushing to shore, their boots splashing in the roiling waves.

"In particular, the Diviner Master spoke to me," Fong shi'sen continued, giving her a piercing look, "about a little bird who had arrived to warn them of the Cyrilian attack, which was the only reason the damage to our sacred Temple and bookhouse was so limited. Originally, the Emperor had decided against our participation in this war. But it seems that one sparrow's wingbeat can cause a storm."

Of everything she had expected after she'd broken into the Temple of the Skies and faced such heavy rebuke for overstepping her role, it was not this. She'd waited for a reprimand for her foolishness in going after Enn, cold rejection from her people for what the traffickers had done to her and made her do in her years under their servitude. But then, Fong shi'sen's face broke into a rare smile, and hope spread its wings in her heart.

"Shi'sen . . ." Her voice cracked.

"We need every windsailer we have to fight this battle." As her Wind Master spoke, he reached into the folds of his robes. "Little Bird, I have brought back your wings."

The chi glimmered like it held stardust as he unfurled it. It was brand-new, fashioned in the exact same way as the one Linn had owned: translucent, the material a cross between water and silk yet surprisingly resilient and warm.

It felt like a dream to take it between her fingers, to slip it over her shoulders and fasten the straps to her wrists.

"Ko Linnet," said her teacher, and she was suddenly plunged back to the earliest days of her lessons, when she'd leapt off a cliff with nothing but her courage and the winds at her back. Fong shi'sen had unfurled his own chi and was facing her, his robes billowing around him. "Fly."

Linn's heart soared. The waves roared in triumph behind her back as she turned, calling on her winds.

Linn began to run. Her daggers appeared in her hands, glinting wickedly like teeth.

Two, three steps.

The winds around her rose from uneven gusts into screaming gales.

Six, seven steps.

She spread her arms, her chi rippling like a bird yearning to be free.

Nine, ten steps.

With a small leap, she was airborne, winds howling around her like a pack of invisible wolves, loping by her side, carrying her forward and upward. Beneath her was a stretch of sea, the pale cloaks of the Imperial Patrols jutting out like a memory.

Help me, she'd cried out to them the first time she'd seen them as she'd disembarked from the trafficker's ship.

Eight years she'd spent in captivity, her power and her freedom taken away from her. Made to feel helpless and weak.

Linn was a Kemeiran windsailer. A fierce warrior. A free bird.

She was the girl of wind and shadows.

And today, she fought back.

40

Ana had heard tales of the Silent Sea of the North in her childhood. That it was a forbidden location. That it was cursed. That it was a place even the Deities dared not touch. The Salskoff Library had held records of ships that had gone missing on expeditions to the northernmost ocean. To this day, no sailor had survived to tell the tale.

Out here, the silence was heavy, muted, broken only by the sound of waves lapping at the edges of their boat. The sky was the shade of ashes and endings, the water around her a granite gray. Even her siphon looked colorless, veins shifting across the surface like smoke. The only color came from her cloak: a piercing shade of crimson. The color of blood. The color of her.

Ana's breath crystallized in the air. Ice clung to her lashes, to strands of her hair exposed beyond her hood. Before her at the wheel, between sprays of mist, Daya wove in and out of sight like a ghost.

Yet in the midst of all this nothingness, something seemed to stir inside Ana. Something *was* stirring, on the surface of her siphon. The little tendrils of darkness writhed, seeping deeper into her veins. And, inside her, there was the strangest feeling: like an ancient fragment of a puzzle coming alive.

Frost flowered on the wooden token in her gloved hand. She wiped it clean, peering at the jagged patterns leading from the curve of Cyrilian shores to the dent of the heart-shaped relic in the center.

A flash of color caught her attention and she looked up. Ahead was a crop of white-blue glaciers knifing to the sky. Goose bumps rose along Ana's skin. A strong wind had picked up, seeming to pummel their sails and pull at her cloak, relentlessly tugging them forward. From all around her came the echo of an eerie song. Silhouettes darted in the water by her sides as she drew closer to the glaciers.

Daya cast Ana an uneasy look. The girl's lips were wan, her knuckles straining against the wheel. "Ruselkya," she whispered.

Ana stood and crossed over to Daya. She put a hand on her friend's shoulder and squeezed. They were approaching the glaciers, faster now; the wind and water seemed to move in harmony, with a mind of their own, sweeping their little boat along the currents. The world darkened as they entered the glaciers' tall shadows.

"Hang on to your hats," Daya gritted, and she swung the wheel as they entered the field of glaciers. Walls of ice rose on both sides of them, forming a vast tunnel, the sky a mere sliver far above. The rush of water reverberated all around them. Overhead, the Deities' Lights looked subdued; light seemed to lance out of the glaciers themselves, refracting in the walls of ice all around them to become ghostly apparitions. Shapes and shadows darted between the ribbons of light: silhouettes of snowhawks shifting to foxes, wolves swooping into great whales, deer bounding into flocks of sparrows.

She'd seen this with Linn once, back in the Syvern Taiga: the great Deities' Lights wending overhead like an otherworldly river, snow and ice spirits darting from beneath it.

Yet Ana realized it was not the sky that glowed, but the *sea*. Up above, the clouds in the sky undulated like waves; below, the waters swirled incandescent. The effect was unnerving, as though the world had flipped and they were sailing across the skies. Her breath misted before her as she took it all in, her bones aching with cold. The lights swirled around her, spinning faster and faster, shapes swallowing shapes, until all of a sudden, they flickered out.

Far ahead, between the narrow opening in the maze of glaciers, was a flat stretch of ice. It appeared like an oasis in the midst of a desert, soft blue and unnaturally smooth.

The waves were now lunging at their boat in a relentless beat, as though the Deities and elements themselves conspired to draw their boat forward. Wind dug into her bones. The disembodied singing grew louder, rising from the depths of the sea.

An explosion sounded across the ice, and a shock wave of force slammed into their boat. Ana lurched, catching herself against the mast; Daya hung on to the wheel. Below the translucent surface of the ice, the ruselkya scattered like startled fish, their song rising in pitch and volume, thrumming with urgency.

Ahead, the landmass of ice drew closer, and Ana saw something that made her blood freeze. Smashed against the glacial walls, drifting in the pounding waves, were the remnants of Morganya's ships and men.

"Daya." Ana's voice was low, urgent. "You must leave. Drop

me off, and sail back. Get reinforcements, a bigger, sturdier ship."

Daya began to protest. "Ana—"

"Listen to me," Ana said, gripping her friend's arm. "If you stay here, you will end up like those men. And both of us will be lost."

Daya's eyes glittered as she turned the wheel, hard. The cutter slowed as it turned, then, with a groan, it knocked against the mass of ice. She pressed her lips together and nodded. "I'll be back, Ana."

Ana crossed to the gangway. "Don't make me wait too long," she said, and with a brief smile, disembarked. Her boots scuffed against smooth ice. She stood back and watched Daya steer the cutter back through the tunnels until the shadows and the sea swallowed their silhouettes.

Ana turned. From ahead came a pulse of warmth, of blood, flickering like a candle in the awareness of her Affinity. Massive glaciers rose jagged before her, yet there was only one path through.

The path that would lead to Morganya.

Alone, Ana began to walk.

Ash fell from the sky. Not ash—*snow*, colored the same dirt-gray as the storm clouds. They swirled, gathering weakly in broken shapes around Ana. Syvint'sya, little spirits of snow, limping, ears drooping, shivering.

Dying.

Ana felt it, too: an unraveling in her bones. Above, the Deities' Lights shuddered to a slow stop, glimmering weakly. A terrible cracking noise reverberated across the sky. Something was so terribly wrong. The moaning wind all around seemed to carry Tetsyev's and Ardonn's whispers. *The unbalancing of the world.*

Ana looked across a stretch of pure blue ice and saw *her.*

Morganya glowed. The diamond-and-white-gold crown on her head appeared dull in comparison to the radiance emanating from her skin. Long black hair trailing down her back, she hunched over the surface of the ice. She'd taken off her cloak and her bare arms were covered in curling patterns of frost. When she looked up, ice clung to her eyelashes and hair, coating them white. A jagged hole gaped from the ice before her, the ocean water pooling inside it trembling. Lights flickered within with the same erratic desperation as those in the sky earlier.

Ana clenched the wooden map tightly in her hands to stop them from shaking.

Her aunt's bloodred lips curved in a smile. "Still following in my steps, Little Tigress?"

"You feel it, don't you?" Ana replied. Somehow, at the end of the world, she found it easier to speak, as though the knowledge that she was steps, breaths, away from death held her voice steady. "The energy here—no human is meant to survive this, mamika. The legends hold true."

Morganya straightened. The ice mirrored her perfectly, amplifying her cruel and terrible beauty. And Ana saw that it wasn't frost that splintered across her face; it was veins, blood running blue. Her aunt's face had paled, as though something here were drawing the very life from her. "We were never meant to be human, Little Tigress," Morganya said, her voice resonating across the stillness. "We are meant to be Deities."

"You have seen what happens when humans try to play at being gods," Ana said. "It began before any of us, when they discovered blackstone and tried to restrain Affinites. When the siphons were used against Affinites."

"And I am correcting course," Morganya continued calmly. "I will hold the Heart. I will have the power to reverse the balance of this world. Those undeserving will bow to us, as they were always meant to." She stretched out a hand, her face slipping so easily back into kindness, into the soft, demure aunt Ana had known her entire life. "My love, you of all people should understand how it feels to be wronged. You remember the names they called you, the way your own *father* treated you, the nights locked away in your chambers, the childhood taken from you. Do not forget who it was who did that to you. Do not forget why that happened to you." Eyes glowing an otherworldly green, suddenly welling with sadness. "The world reviled us, my love. It gave us nothing. Anything we want in this world, we must take it with our own hands."

Morganya's voice washed over Ana in soothing waves, a lullaby opening its arms to her. Ana felt herself sinking into the soft gray. Memories stirred sluggishly in her mind, called upon by a phantom voice: her father, turning away from her and shutting the doors to her chambers behind him; the screams at the Salskoff Vyntr'makt as she sat in a river of blood weeping for help; the long white fingers in the dark that held silver scalpels to her skin.

All because she was an Affinite. All because the Deities had chosen *her*.

Why is it wrong, then, for us to do unto them what they have done unto us? a voice whispered in her head.

In the back of her mind, a voice screamed at her—but for what, she could no longer remember. There was something she had to do, something very important . . . but soothing waves of her aunt's words continued to wash over her, pulling her away. She had the impression she was drowning, but the water here was warm, and she was comfortable.

Morganya's smile stretched. "Stay with me, Little Tigress," she crooned, and in a flash, she closed the gap between them, her fingers cold as they touched Ana's cheeks.

Ana felt herself smiling back.

"We were cut from the same cloth, my child," her aunt continued. "Be with me. Together, we can take back the world."

"Yes, mamika." The words tasted so strange yet so sweet on her tongue.

"My powerful princess. I will give you this empire. I will sit you on a throne by my side, dress you in a crown of jewels and a dress studded in diamonds." A pause. "Just wait here."

Morganya tapped Ana's temple with a thumb, sparking daydreams that swirled in Ana's head like showers of silver. Her, at the Salskoff Palace again, beneath the Hall of Deities, sitting in her throne. A white-gold crown nested in her hair, diamonds and jewels glittering at her collar. The world bowing at her feet with a sweep of her hands.

Just as she'd always wanted. Just as it was always meant to be.

But—*no,* came a faint, insistent voice in her mind. There was something so, so wrong. It might have been what she'd wanted, once, but now, the whorls of dreams that eddied like stardust only tasted repugnant, reviling. Shadows began to spread through them, cracks of crimson that crawled upward.

And suddenly, the Salskoff Palace flashed in her head, broken and burning.

To create a future, one first had to destroy the past.

The visions cleared. The cold rushed back in.

Ana blinked, just as Morganya plunged her hands into the hole in the ice.

A rumbling noise started, reverberating from somewhere deep, deep down, as though the entire ocean itself were groaning. The glaciers surrounding them seemed to tremble with an ominous energy; the air hummed a low, thrumming note. The surface of the sea churned like boiling water, moving to the stir of Morganya's fingers. Beneath the ice, a glow grew brighter and brighter, buoyed upward by the shifting waters.

Morganya leapt back as a column of light and wind surged into the sky, ripping open a hole in the clouds themselves.

A glistening, shifting core slowly rose from the depths of the water into the air. It was radiant, so bright, that it hurt to look at it, and it glowed as though it held the entirety of the night sky's Deities' Lights within it.

And it *did*, Ana realized, watching as the tendrils of light spread from its heart, weaving in patterns as it dispersed through air and ice and water.

This was it. The Deities' Heart. The long-lost core of all alchemical power and magic in this world, rumored to grant a mortal the powers of the gods.

Morganya raised her hands. In that moment, the light of the Heart shone on her face. Ana had always thought her aunt to hold the great and terrible beauty of a Deity, but in this moment, there was nothing left on her face that resembled humanity. Her features twisted in greed and wrath, lust for power made brighter by the searing light of the Heart.

Ana flung her Affinity forward just as Morganya reached for the Heart.

Ana's Affinity latched on to Morganya's blood, bright and hot and pulsing. She'd done this before, so many times: One pull, and she could finish it all.

Ana looked at the woman whom she had once considered her aunt, whom she had once loved, and hesitated.

From all around them came a chorus of terrifying screams, shrieks that crawled beneath Ana's skin, as though the sky and the sea were crying. The glacier walls around them began to tremble; water spilled over the edges of the ice in violent lunges.

An explosion of force tore through the air, ripping her Affinity from Morganya and flinging Ana back onto the ice. She tasted copper against her tongue. Felt a hollow burn deep inside her as her Affinity flickered out beneath the cold current of energy that radiated from Morganya.

Shadows darted beneath the ice in jagged patterns. Through a fissure in the ice, a ruselkya leapt up and slammed onto the ice at Ana's feet. The siren's face was contorted in a silent wail, eyes rolling into the back of its head as it writhed, arms and legs and fingers bent at wrong angles.

The same thing was happening all around. From far off, an icewolf rose from the top of a glacier, its mournful howl slicing through the cacophony. It ran a few paces before collapsing, blue flames of eyes sputtering out. A hawk syvint'sya spiraled from the sky, crashing into the waves.

A dozen steps away, Morganya was bent over, gasping for breath. A strong gale had risen, howling with the fury of ancient pain. Ice spirits, ruselkya, and the Deities' Lights flashed all around them as the clouds began to shift, faster and faster until—

Morganya grunted. Heaved.

And with a resounding crack, the nebulous surface of the Deities' Heart fissured in her hand. Light began to bleed from its crack, spiraling into Morganya's outstretched fingers.

The strength was sapped from Ana's bones. She sank to her knees, aware only that Morganya was doing the same, both covering their ears as a shrill screaming pierced the air. It felt like losing her Affinity all over again, only this time, the pain was white-hot, electric, as though death itself were twining its grasp around her throat.

A brilliant light beamed upward from the Heart itself. It shot skyward, twisting like a tornado with all the colors of the world. And Ana could *sense* pain emanating from that spot, reflecting inside her as though she were a part of it all: an ancient anger, churning deep in the vast hollowness of her chest where her Affinity had once been.

The magic that manifested in all Affinites, in ice spirits and ruselkya and wassengost and all legendary creatures in this world . . . it was hurting.

And it was furious.

This was the Deities' might, Ana thought as she squinted up at that light that seemed to tear open the heavens themselves. This was how it felt to incur the gods' wrath.

This was how the end of the world began.

41

The tides of the battle had turned. As Linn soared overhead with her windsailers, the other Kemeiran wielders poured in like a wrathful wave, surging through the Cyrilian Imperial Patrols. Linn watched as the windsailers plunged down in a flash of blades before soaring back into the sky, scythes stained red. She thought of the time she'd sat at the edge of a lake watching white herons dive for fish.

Steel lashed out; red misted the air.

The Kemeiran wielder armies fought in formation, their fighting styles calling to mind dancing as they moved through the battle, smooth as silk yet sharper than swords. A shiver ran up Linn's spine as she beheld the wielders.

The Imperial Patrols, even with their Inquisitors, were no match for the trained wielders and Temple Masters of Kemeira. The Kemeirans wielded the elements with a strategy and precision that the Cyrilians lacked, coming from centuries of training and study. Ana's army, encouraged by the sudden appearance of powerful allies, began pushing back.

That was when it happened.

A sudden shock wave blasted across the skies, rippling over

the ocean and tearing apart clouds. The entire world shuddered, and for a moment, time seemed to come to a standstill.

And then the pain started.

It felt as though her head were splitting apart—a white-hot, searing flame cleaving through her temple. Linn cried out as her control over her winds faltered. She spiraled, crashing into the sand, daggers slipping uselessly from her hands. Stars burst before her eyes, and deep down, she felt a burning sensation where her Affinity might rest.

Through the mist in her eyes, she looked up.

Across the battlefield, every single Affinite had fallen, hands clapped over their heads, writhing with pain. It didn't matter whether they were Imperial Patrols, Navy soldiers, or Temple Masters; it didn't matter whether they were Cyrilian, Bregonian, or Kemeiran, or anything else. Enemies and comrades alike fell to their knees, paralyzed and incapacitated.

Linn trembled, holding herself on her hands and knees. Instinctively, she knew that this was something bigger than them all. That *this* was what her Temple Masters had spoken of—the devastation of the Heart of the Gods.

This was what the end of the world felt like.

With a sigh, she closed her eyes and let the blackness consume her in a tidal wave.

42

The pain was excruciating. Hot tears streaked down Ana's cheeks; her skin was catching fire, and each breath was the cut of a thousand blades. She could feel it, in the empty space somewhere in her bones where her Affinity once rested; in her left wrist, where the siphon had suddenly become searing.

Clenching her teeth, Ana looked over to the spot where Morganya knelt. Darkness from Morganya's siphon was spreading up her arms like molten metal against her skin, which had drained from golden-dusk to an ashen gray. Her eyes rolled back, and her cheeks were beginning to hollow out.

"Stop." The word fell from Ana's tongue in a gasp. *"Please."*

Her aunt did not hear her. Her head was thrown back, mouth gaping open in a silent scream. Molten light continued to pour from the cracked relic, swirling into her skin. A giant fissure had broken the ice beneath their feet; within, the waters of the Silent Sea *churned.*

And, as quickly as it had come, the pain, the screams, the vortex of chaos vanished. When Ana looked at Morganya again, she was no longer looking at a person.

The woman who had been her aunt was aglow, light shimmering from within her golden skin as though the Deities' Lights ran through her blood. The place on her wrist where her siphon had rested was bare. She looked more vibrant, more beautiful, and more terrible.

Morganya stood, slowly turning her hands over to examine them. "I am made . . . anew." Her whisper cut through the silence, comprising a thousand different voices layered over one another. "I have absorbed the siphon. Nothing physical constrains me now—*I* am the siphon, *I* am all that the Deities have left us. I can feel it, all the threads of alchemical power, in every Affinite and spirit and fragment of a relic. All mine to command."

Ana pushed herself to her feet. The sky and sea seemed to rock as she stumbled forward. The siphon on *her* wrist had nearly turned obsidian, tendrils snaking into her veins on her wrist like lead.

Three moons, came Tetsyev's whisper in her mind.

Her time was almost over—she could sense it.

"Morganya." Her voice was small, weak, in the vast space surrounding them. "Stop. I am *begging* you."

Morganya turned to her. Her gaze filled with an ancient cruelty and a power so vast, it might have been a god staring from the soul of this woman.

Her lips split into a smile. "I am *limitless*," she said, her voice like a discordant song. Her eyes were feverish, and she spoke as though to herself and to the skies at once. "At last, I will fulfill the destiny I began fighting for so long ago. I will shape the world to become the one of my dreams. I have no one left to fear and nothing in my way."

"You're wrong," Ana said, and, reaching into herself, flung out her Affinity from her siphon. Fire streaked from her fingertips, racing toward Morganya.

Through the waves of heat and blinding light, Ana saw Morganya turn toward her. Saw the woman's face shift into something resembling delight. In a languid motion, she flicked her wrist—and Ana's jet of fire froze, becoming a curved arc of ice, the tip whittled down to lethal sharpness. It plunged down.

Ana moved—too slowly. She felt the jolt of the ice pierce her side, felt the impact as she was thrown against the ice, her skull rattling with the force.

The pain came moments later.

"Pesky little tigress," Morganya sang. "I do not think you are deserving of the power you hold in that siphon. I think I'll just . . . get rid of it."

Lazily, she raised an arm and pointed a finger to Ana.

Pain hit Ana's left wrist, blooming up her arm and shoulders like fire. Over her siphon, fissures were appearing, glimmering with the same swirl of lights that she'd seen in the skies and the sea and now writhing in Morganya's skin. It felt as though the siphon had imbued a powerful poison deep in her veins that was now being drained. She breathed in and tasted blood on her tongue; her lungs were filled with wetness from the wounds Morganya had inflicted.

And yet . . . strangely, Ana felt a surge of relief flowing through her. The fatigue that had weighed upon her seemed to melt away. The air tasted sharper, colder, more *alive*, and she found it easier to breathe again.

If this was death, it was not so bad, after all.

With a resounding crack, the siphon around her wrist splintered. Its shards turned golden, dissolving into the air, and swirled up in a reflection of the Deities' Lights. This must be pure alchemical magic—the magek that Tetsyev and Ardonn spoke of. The power that made Affinites, snow spirits, the Deities' Lights, everything in this world the Deities left behind.

Lying against the ice, Ana could only watch as the Affinities she'd once held in her siphon, rendered as wisps of light, drifted away.

All . . . except . . . one.

A sensation of warmth, of wholeness, rushed through her, filling the cracks between her brittle bones. Something swooped into her chest and surged through her veins, into the spaces that had been empty for too long. When Ana breathed in again, the world pulsed to life with the shades of crimson she'd known for most of her life.

She lay against the ice, gasping, blood pumping in her ears and with every beat of her heart. Recalling Linn's bright black eyes, solemn as she spoke the words that would save Ana's life.

To restore your Affinity, you must destroy the siphon that holds it. You must remain close so that it may return to you, otherwise your Affinity will be lost to the greater alchemical currents of this world.

In attempting to rid Ana of the powers in her siphon, Morganya had inadvertently returned the single Affinity that Ana needed.

Ana tipped her head. Across the ice, Morganya threw her head back and inhaled deeply. The glow beneath her skin writhed as the unclaimed Affinities from Ana's siphon were absorbed inside her. She straightened and faced Ana again, her face rapturous.

"I told you once," the woman who had once been her mamika said, her voice ringing like bells across the Silent Sea. "We were chosen by the Deities to fight the battles that they cannot in this world."

Between the madness clouding those eyes, Ana recalled flickers of memories. Herself, as a child, crouched over her mother's marbled coffin, weeping. Looking up to see those tea-green eyes watching her from the darkness. There had been something like sympathy, there.

The Deities have long sent me a message through their silence, Morganya had whispered. *It is not their duty to grant us goodness in this world, Kolst Pryntsessa. No, Little Tigress—it is up to us to fight our battles.*

"That might be." Ana's voice came out as a rasp. It hurt to speak—*Deities,* it hurt to even breathe, and she could feel blood pooling from the ice shard that pierced her body. Yet a surge of anger, a *knowing* more certain than anything she'd felt in her life, pushed her to press on. "But you commit crimes in the name of the gods, and you call it justice. Innocents from our empire lie dead from the so-called justice you serve. You may have once held good intentions, but those have been compromised by your hatred and your desire for power. We are only human, mamika. We were never meant to play at being Deities."

Morganya's laughter was like dissonant wind chimes. "After all this time, you would still preach to me?" she screamed, her voice sweeping up a gale around them, stirring up ocean waves and rumbling through the sky. "You and I are the same. We both seek to reshape this world. Yet you do not see that what I am doing is all a means to an end."

"We are not the same." The pain was excruciating, yet as Ana lay there dying on the ice, in half delirium, she found the words that had guided her through it all. The ones she had clung to since the very beginning of this journey. "Someone I loved very dearly once told me, 'Your Affinity does not define you. What defines you is how you choose to wield it.'"

Morganya's smile was lovely. A crimson rose in a world of ice. "Ah. Yes. I had the pleasure of sending the speaker of those very words to his death—where he belonged. And now, I will have the pleasure of doing the same to you. Good-bye, Anastacya."

She lifted a hand.

Ana struck out with her Affinity.

The world flared to life with shades of blood. This time it came easily, for her Affinity was once again a *part* of her—more so than any of the stolen Affinities Morganya wielded from her siphon were a part of her aunt.

Ana's Affinity wrapped around the blood coursing bright and hot in Morganya's veins.

With every last ounce of her strength, Ana tore.

Morganya's lips parted in surprise. The lights inside her flickered. Dimmed.

Having the Deities' Heart granted one limitless power to control and command all alchemical powers around, yet it did not make one a Deity.

It did not make one immortal.

Through Ana's Affinity, she felt every beat of Morganya's heart like her own, thudding across her consciousness like the beat of a drum.

Thud ... thud-thud ... thud ... thud-thud ...

Thud ...

... thud ...

By the time Morganya's body hit the ice she was dead.

The world grew still, and Ana's vision blurred. The only movement came from the blood seeping across the ice. Ribbons of iridescent light were rising from it, swirling away into the wind, into the ice, into the water around them.

Ana pushed herself onto her knees and began to crawl across the ice. She was not yet finished; there was one last thing she had to do.

The Heart lay several paces from the hole Morganya had cut into the ice, glowing gently. Wisps of light from Morganya's body settled over the nebulous core, shimmering softly as, bit by bit, they began to mend the crack rent by Morganya.

Ana picked up the Heart. It was strange to touch, like ice and fire enshrouded in light too bright to look at. Its glow flared, and for a moment, she heard ancient whispers, echoes of wind and water and song, cries of snow spirits and howls of icewolves, the hubbub of human voices rising and falling like ocean tides. A feeling of euphoria, of invincibility, bloomed within her. Here it was, the source of all alchemical power in this world, held between her palms.

Ana leaned over the opening in the ice and let go.

She lay down on the ice, watching the glow of the Heart fade until it was swallowed by the deep blue sea. With her Affinity back, she was aware of the blood around her, staining her own clothes and dripping warm from the wound in her side. She exhaled and let herself slip into a space between unconsciousness and wakefulness. As though in a dream, the snow around her began to swirl a phantom wind, coalescing into shapes that wove in and out of her focus.

When she blinked again, the ghost of a girl stood before her, ocean eyes and dark hair falling still.

"May?" she whispered.

The snow spirit knelt by Ana, brushing her cheek with a cold finger, and a warm feeling of peace spread through Ana's body. The fire in her bones calmed and from far off, the wind seemed to bring echoes of words with it.

A world, May's spirit whispered, *where a small earth Affinite can grow flowers from the sidewalk.*

Another silhouette appeared before Ana, glimmering pale. Her memory filled in the gold of his hair, the fawn of his skin, the spring green of his eyes.

It's all right, sistrika, Luka said softly. *I'm here. Bratika's here.*

Another boy whose eyes had always smoldered coal-gray, whose hair she'd always remembered as the shimmer of a flame.

We have finished what we have started, Ana, Yuri murmured. *We have come full circle.*

From the edges of her vision, other shapes were forming. Papa, Mama, Markov, Henryk . . . all those too soon gone.

A tear slid down her cheek, dripping into the curl of her lips. Lying there on the ice in the midst of the Silent Sea, and blood bruising in her battered body, she could do nothing but gaze up at the sky above.

The clouds had parted. A cold breeze brushed against her face, bringing with it the scents of her beloved empire—of snow and pines.

In the very end, she was a daughter of Cyrilia.

As Ana lay, the last of her strength seeping from her, she caught a glimmer of light in the predawn skies above. Slowly, she turned her head to face it.

The sun was rising at last, its rays crowning the gap between sky and sea, staining it a triumphant, bloody red. The world basked in the light of the early morning, beautiful and ancient. It was humans who had inflicted ugliness and hatred upon themselves.

And it was humans who would fix it. Humans, who had the propensity for so much good, for so much evil.

Whose choices defined them.

A new world would be born.

Ana turned her gaze back to the skies and closed her eyes.

Exhaled.

Slowly, the sun breathed life into the sky. Wind continued to stir over the gentle waves that glittered like glass in a stretch of perpetuity. An era of bloodshed and war, come to its end; the crimson reign of the Cyrilian monarchy laid to rest at last.

43

The wall of glaciers appeared suddenly, startlingly: a set of jagged structures yawning up like colossal teeth, breaking the monotony of the slate-gray waves and pale, watery sky. It felt as though he were approaching the fabled edge of the world, and as he urged his cutter forward, Ramson couldn't help but think of all the legends and lore surrounding the Silent Sea and all the lives lost to it.

He would have braved the ends of the world for Ana.

He kept a steady grip on his wheel as he entered the maze of glaciers. Sound echoed inside, throwing off his senses: the slosh of water reverberating over and under, mixed with the creaks and groans of his brig. Earlier, a vicious wind had thrashed at his boat and torn at his sails while the sea had clawed at his hull with vengeance—now, all had fallen eerily still.

At last, in the narrow opening before him, Ramson caught sight of something different. A stretch of pale, glittering blue, unfurling like land that wasn't land.

It was an expanse of ice.

Flotsam drifted before it: pieces of wood, splintered sails,

parts of smashed-up ships already being swallowed by the ruthless waters.

A terrible thought came to mind: that Ana and Daya had met
the same fate.

Ramson lurched to the stern of his cutter, heart threatening to
pound out of his chest as he searched the debris.

A sudden rumbling sounded from above, followed by a series
of cracks. When Ramson looked up, it was too late.

He jumped, just as a massive slab of ice smashed into his
cutter.

Water engulfed him—freezing, black ocean waters, squeezing
the air from him and dragging him under before he could even
draw breath. Within barely moments his limbs began to slow, his
muscles tightened, and the daylight above him drew farther and
farther away.

He kicked out, but the currents were too strong, dragging him
beneath blocks of ice drifting at the surface. Stars burst before his
eyes, giving way to ghostly apparitions.

Then, the tides around him shifted, and threads of light began
to coalesce, darting around him like fish. From the depths of the
ocean came whispers, the sound of song.

Ruselkya, Ramson thought as a chorus of song drifted to him.
Swim, they sang to him. *Swim, Ramson.*

This far up north, it was too cold. His limbs were frozen, his
chest threatening to burst from lack of oxygen. It grew dark.

Then, something plunged into the water and pressure twined
around his chest. Again, the waters shifted—but, no, this time *he*
was the one moving, cutting upward through the depths.

Ramson burst through the surface, coughing, spluttering. He

was dimly aware of someone hauling him up, and the miraculous feel of dry wood warming his back. A face hovered over him.

"Amara bless, it's really you," Daya panted, water droplets falling from her hair, her lashes, her face. "Someone out there's really looking out for you, con man."

"It's Captain now," Ramson rasped.

"I saw your boat from a distance," Daya said. "I didn't know who you were—if you posed a threat to Ana—so I followed you."

He looked around her cutter, then back to her. "Ana. Where's Ana?"

Daya's eyes flitted to the expanse of ice stretching before them. Her face shadowed. "We got here and saw all the smashed-up ships. She told me to leave and get help."

"Well, you got help," Ramson said, and, gritting his teeth, pushed himself to his feet and stumbled to the gangplank. They were at the edge of the ice now. There—something *was* there across the expanse, something he hadn't seen before: a slip of crimson lying still against the backdrop of white like blood upon snow.

Everything inside him seemed to freeze.

"Go," he heard Daya say. "I'll hold the ship. But hurry."

He was barely aware of descending to the ice, of his knees nearly giving way as he stumbled forward. In the distance, the sun's first rays stained the horizon red, spilling over onto the colorless sea and ice.

Onto her.

She was laid out on the ice, her crimson cloak spread behind her like wings, red puddled around her head like a crown. Ramson knelt by her. Her eyes were shut, frost limning them white; her skin was ice-cold to touch. He gathered her in his arms, burying his face in the crook of her neck. There, against the curve of her throat, a pulse: faint, and slowing.

It felt like a dream—a worst kind of dream, a *nightmare*—for him to carry her to Daya's ship. The journey back was a new kind of agony as he sat with Ana's hand in his, finger on her wrist. Sensing her heartbeat die out, second by second. The clothes on his back had frozen over, but the kind of cold in his heart hurt far more than anything physical.

At last: the shores of Cyrilia, waves rocking their boat as they drew up. Linn, rushing over with a group of Kemeiran soldiers, then calling for a *healer, healer*.

They laid Ana out on the sands of Cyrilia, the healer's hands deft as he began work.

Ramson bent over the girl he loved. Closed his eyes.

And in that moment, the boy who had never believed in the gods whispered a prayer.

44

In the darkness, there was light. It shifted into the faces of those she'd loved: May, Luka, Yuri, Mama, Papa, Markov, and Henryk. She was cold, but growing warm. Her heavy heart began to lighten.

Ana could feel herself smiling. *I'm coming home,* she wanted to say to them.

But the glow began to fade, and the shadows around her began to bloom. They morphed into silhouettes, faces she'd known a lifetime ago from what seemed like a distant dream.

Ana hesitated, looking to the brightness. She found May's ocean eyes.

Go back, Ana, her friend whispered. *They need you.*

Our empire needs you, Luka murmured, his words falling like sunlight.

There is yet work to be done, said Yuri, his hair bright as flame.

And then, from what seemed like a world away, Ana heard her name.

She turned, and the shadows grew clearer. More solid. More real. A girl with hair like ink, her gaze rimmed silver like the edge of daggers. A second, a friend, with a face as open and steady as the earth and strong hands made for sailing.

And a boy—a boy with bright hazel eyes that pierced her heart.

The warmth began to fade; it grew cold, the air around her frosted, winds kissing her skin with the tinge of ice and sharpness. Her body, which had seemed to drift like smoke earlier, turned heavy.

Ana's eyes flew open, and she drew in breath.

45

FOUR WEEKS LATER

The Salskoff Palace materialized from the fog of her memory. Ana had known the Palace intimately, from the plush, silver-carpeted hallways to the secret passageways reserved for servants and caretakers.

Not that there would be any of those, any longer.

Ana walked down the halls, marveling at how quickly change took place. Gone were the marble statues of the Deities, the gilded paintings and opulent gems that had glittered on furniture. Only the ceiling engravings and the marble floors remained. The dungeons, Ana knew, were being destroyed, their prisoners sent to a holding house for their cases to be examined and presented before a jury of the people. Most, she had an inkling as she'd pored through the scant notes on their cases, would be acquitted and set free.

But those were far from the most important changes that would take place here.

Ana stopped at the door to the chamber once known as the Grand Throneroom. Now, a carved marble sign hung above it: *Great Lecture Hall, Salskoff Collegium.*

Voices rang out from within, and as she leaned against the

familiar cherrywood doors, she swept the long hall with a gaze. Chairs had been laid out, and people were clustered inside, dressed in regular Cyrilian furs and leathers. They were all Affinites— and some she recognized as former Redcloaks, others as former Inquisitors. Their attention was directed to the man who stood in the front of the room, speaking.

Kaïs paused as he caught Ana's gaze. He cleared his throat and said to the room, "This will be all for today. You're welcome to attend the Transition Ceremony—it will be open to the public."

Ana smiled as he approached her, steps ringing clear. He was dressed in a casual shirt and tunic; the absence of his armor seemed to take several years off him so that when he stopped before her, she had the impression she was gazing upon a tall, bright-eyed boy.

"Hello, instructor," she said. She was dimly aware of murmurs around the room as people spotted her.

Kaïs returned her smile. "I believe the correct term is 'First Guide,' or 'Fyrva Provyod.'"

The Salskoff Palace had been renamed as the Salskoff Collegium: a school for Affinites to learn to control and harness their abilities, funded by a portion of the coin from what had once been the Cyrilian Imperial coffers. Former yaegers—now known as "provyods," or "guides"—from Morganya's Imperial Patrols had been offered jobs as instructors, and today was the Collegium's opening.

"Any word from Linn?" Ana asked as she and Kaïs began to walk toward the front of the Collegium together. "Has she arrived safely?"

Linn had elected to stand in as the Ambassador to Kemeira for one last time; she had set sail for Kemeira with the rest of the windsailers a little over three weeks ago with a letter from Ana to declare the end of the Cyrilian Empire—and its transition to the Republic of Cyrilia. She had written asking to rekindle relations between Kemeira and Cyrilia . . . and to propose a partnership to eliminate the channels of Affinite trafficking that had once pervaded their lands.

"Not yet," Kaïs replied. "But I suspect it won't be long now."

"Are you sure you wish to remain?" Ana asked. "You don't wish to join Shamaïra on her journey?"

Of all reunions, it was perhaps seeing Kaïs and Shamaïra together that had warmed Ana's heart the most. The Unseer was making a long-overdue trip to her homeland; she was leaving today, after the Transition Ceremony.

Kaïs's brow creased slightly. "I have thought this over," he replied in that steady, careful way of his, "and I do wish to see Nandji again. But, whether willingly or unwillingly, I came to Cyrilia at a young age, and it is now my home as well. I will not step away when there is so much of a chance to make it better right now." His pale blue eyes flicked to her, and his lips curled a bit. "Besides, there is so much to do."

"That's right, and we'll need all the help we can get," came a familiar voice.

Daya strode down the corridor to them, a giant roll of parchment clasped in her hands. She waved it at Ana. "I've drawn up the full list of applicants for the General Elections."

Ana accepted the list, her heart soaring as she skimmed the names. She recognized quite a few as Cyrilians who had enlisted in her army and fought with her. There were a number of former Redcloaks running for office as well, including Liliya, who had been helping to rally the Redcloaks to the cause of the transition.

Most important, though, were the many, many names she did not recognize—ordinary civilians hailing from all regions and corners of the former Empire.

Ana ran a thumb over the parchment. Here was the future of Cyrilia, writ into parchment and ink. She smiled at the memory of a boy with sparks in his coal-gray eyes, long ponytail like the shimmer of flame. *The future lies here, with us. In the hands of the people.*

"Thank you, Daya," she said.

They had reached the Hall of Deities. At the other end, the great doors were still closed, but through the mullioned windows, Ana could see the stage that had been set up in the courtyard. It was a clear day, the skies an unbroken stretch of pure halcyon blue.

The world had settled. The Deities' Lights had danced in the night skies every night since Ana had woken, healed by the Kemeiran wielder, on the shores of the Silent Sea.

Word was out that both siphons had been destroyed, and envoys were bringing the news across the world to Bregon and Kemeira. But as to what had happened to the Deities' Heart, only Ana and a handful of people—including the Kemeiran Temple Masters that had fought with them in this war—knew. Ana had ordered an immediate ban on blackstone mining in the Krazyast Triangle, receiving word from King Darias that the same would happen in Bregon, with searock.

The knowledge of the Heart and the other elements of alchemical power, then, would die with Ana and the handful of people close to her who had known of them.

The past was behind them, and it was a time for change. At noon, Ana would announce her own abdication.

At the thought, she ran a hand over her outfit: a simple silver gown, sleek and smooth, spilling to her feet like a fall of snow. On top of that, she wore her old crimson cloak, mended and made to look new by tailors. With their nation healing from the effects of Morganya's regime and a civil war, extravagance was a thing of the past.

"How do I look?" she asked.

"Beautiful," Daya said, giving Ana a once-over. "But not like a princess. Like . . . a *revolutionary*."

Ana grinned back. She'd woken with each day to find color returning to her skin, the hollows to her cheeks filling out, and the dark circles disappearing from her eyes. She'd discarded the powders and blushes she'd carried with her for her former campaigns—she didn't need them anymore.

Kaïs checked his pocketwatch. "A half hour left," he said.

Ana had a sudden thought. "Would you wait here for me?" she asked. "I'll be back before the ceremony begins."

The grounds leading to the prayer temple at the back of the former Palace sat in silence, shrouded in a fresh blanket of white. The snow here lay undisturbed, just like the souls resting beneath.

They had buried the fallen soldiers of the war out here. Ana walked past their graves, her lips moving in silent prayer, pausing every so often to look at a gravestone and a name she recognized. Soon, this place would be open to the public—but in this moment, Ana wished to pay a last visit.

Lieutenant Henryk had been buried near the front; by his side, an empty grave with a headstone had been erected for Kapitan Markov. Ana knelt by each, inclining her head to pay them respect.

Next, she found Yuri's tomb at the very front, near the steps of the prayer temple. Ana stopped before it and touched a hand to the cold stone surface, tracing the etchings of his name. *YURI KOSTOV,* said the headstone. *COMMANDER OF REDCLOAKS, KILLED IN BATTLE.*

Ana drew the shape of a circle over her chest before continuing on. Snow crunched beneath her boots as she ascended the stairs to the prayer temple. She felt as though she had stepped back in time, into a distant dream. Inside, the marble-and-stone casings had rendered her family in a timeless eternity, their expressions tranquil and unmoving as the world outside spun forward.

Ana recalled a time when she had frequented her mother's tomb, tracing the carving and wishing that, if she just closed her eyes, she could return to a life where Mama was still alive and her family still whole.

There was a part of her that would never stop longing for this—but, Ana thought as she moved to her father's tomb, taking in the sternness to his features, her yearning for the past was born only out of a romantic notion for nostalgia. The dead and their deeds remained in the past; the future was out there, in the city, across the republic, with her people.

Lastly, there was Luka.

Ana turned to her brother's tomb. A knot formed in her chest as she stared down at the stone face that at once was and wasn't his. The stonemason had rendered Luka's face almost perfectly, down to the bow of his lips and the curls of his hair.

But they would never capture the way his eyes lit up when he smiled, the expression he'd worn when they'd conspired together. The way his words had shaped her entire world.

Your Affinity does not define you, he'd said to her once. *What defines you is how you choose to wield it.*

Ana turned to leave, the marble where her brother's soul rested newly damp.

Someone waited for her outside.

Ramson watched her with an inscrutable expression as she approached him. He was dressed in a fresh shirt and tunic, the hilt of his misericord strapped to his hips and glinting beneath his navy-blue cloak. His eyes never left hers as she stopped in front of him.

They looked at each other for a moment, and then Ramson reached up. His fingers were warm and rough and gentle as he brushed away the tears on her cheeks. Ana closed her eyes as he drew her to him, his hand falling against the small of her back, the other cradling the back of her head. She leaned against him, breathing in his familiar scent, and felt him rest his chin against the top of her head.

"Did you finish the reports I asked for?" she murmured.

She felt him nod. "I went through all of Kerlan's files, but I've been doing my own research as well." His voice was pleasant, a deep thrum in his chest, and she smiled against it. "Most traffickers have fled Cyrilia and seem to be intent on creating new networks across other kingdoms, just like Kerlan. I sent the funding request to King Darias—" He stopped himself, then drew back and tilted his head, his eyes narrowing a fraction. "But I didn't come here to tell you this." He took her hand. "I have something to show you."

She followed him as he led her toward the back of the prayer temple. When they rounded a corner near the high walls, Ana's breath caught.

There, bright and shining in the sunlight, was a trellis of winterbells. They shifted in the breezes that stirred every so often, their heads nodding as Ana approached. She touched a hand to the pale wood—an exact replica of the one in Shamaïra's back garden—and pressed her forehead against it.

"Hello, May," Ana murmured.

The wind picked up, and for a moment, Ana could swear she heard a soft chime of laughter.

"I've kept my promise," she said. "I only wish you were here to see it."

She stayed there until Ramson said gently, "Ten minutes to the ceremony. We'd better get back."

Ana patted the trellis. Among the white winterbells, color bloomed: New flowers were beginning to bud, their purples and pinks and reds and yellows like gems in the sun.

"Thank you, Ramson," she said, turning to face him.

Her heart was at peace as she walked, Ramson's fingers warm and steady between hers. They entered the Collegium through the back doors and, together, found Kaïs and Daya in discussion with several other members of the government transition process at the Hall of Deities. Down the corridor, the great doors of the Collegium had been thrown open, and from here, Ana could hear the crowd gathered in the courtyard, waiting for her. Their conversation drifted to her, faint and steady.

A figure appeared through the doors. Liliya was slightly breathless as she half jogged down the Hall of Deities. "We're all set up," she said. "They've opened the main gates and people are lined up to watch. You won't believe the crowd!" She flung her arms around Ana, her bright red hair obscuring Ana's vision for a moment. "You're going to be *great*."

A hush had fallen all around them; the courtyard outside seemed to have gone silent.

Ana drew a deep breath. "It's time," she said.

Every step she took seemed to echo with finality. The Hall of Deities was bathed in golden light, from its great marble floors to its high arched ceilings. Above, the intricate carvings of Deities and humans and history intertwined in one grand mosaic, painting the sweeping tale of the former Empire and all that had come before.

She recalled walking through this very hall, wondering what kind of a story they would write of her after she was long gone.

Sunlight warmed her face, and the cheers of the crowd grew louder as they drew near.

Ana lifted her head high and threw her shoulders back, the smile on her face true and bright as the blazing sun.

Today, she had the answer to that question. She knew what stories the poets would tell of her, what songs the bards would sing of Anastacya Kateryanna Mikhailov, last heir of Cyrilia.

She knew what kind of a legacy she would leave.

Ana tilted her chin up and stepped out of the shadows.

Into the light of the new world.

46

It was nearing dawn when the shores of Kemeira appeared, a stretch of black along a horizon rimmed silver. The stars had receded overhead, and a watery blue had seeped into the ink-black of night.

Linn leaned against the wooden railing of her ship, letting the wind run through her hair. After a sleepless night, she'd risen early; the deck was still empty. Behind loomed the jagged shapes of the rest of the Kemeiran fleet.

Ana's letter to the Emperor of Kemeira was tucked into the folds of her shirt, the weight of her task draped peacefully over her shoulders. *Ambassador to Kemeira.* It was only a temporary title, and if Linn so wished, she could apply for reelection.

She hadn't. She had found a better use for her blades, a new direction that opened before her like the call of destiny.

"Ko Linnet."

She turned, the familiar voice sending shivers up her spine. Fong shi'sen approached her from the lower decks, his pale shift billowing in the wind.

Linn pressed her palms together. "Shi'sen."

"I have received word from the Temple Masters," her Wind

Master continued. Linn looked at him in surprise. She had not known that he had written to them. "The Temple Masters and the Emperor have unanimously acknowledged your courage and bravery as a Daughter of the Kemeiran Empire." Fong shi'sen's face crinkled in a shadow of a smile, fleet as a passing breeze. "They wish to express their gratitude by awarding you the highest accolade of our land."

Suddenly, Linn couldn't breathe.

"We would be honored for you to join us, Wind Warrior."

The title was only given to the highest-ranking wind wielders in her land, once they had completed their training. It was one of the greatest honors that could be bestowed upon a windsailer.

It was what she would have given her life for.

Once.

Linn turned to watch the ocean. She had spent countless nights in the past eight years fervently wishing, praying, that she could erase the course of events, the turn that her life had taken when she'd set foot on that trafficker's ship. She would have cut off a part of her heart to have had things go back to the way they were.

But the past moons . . . fighting by Ana's side and teasing Ramson and laughing at Daya's jokes and getting to know Kaïs . . . day by day, with the spin of stars over her head, everything had changed.

She'd survived, and she'd learned to fight back. She'd understood so much more of the sinister network that sought to exploit her people and other vulnerable groups around the world, condemning them to servitude in a foreign land under terms they could not understand. There were so many in this world trying to merely survive, living without the privilege of choices.

Linn had a choice now.

And she knew, in her heart of hearts, that she was making the right one.

"Fong shi'sen," she said, and she found her tone steady, her heart calm and sure as she spoke. "Please accept my gratitude— the offer is more than I deserve." A spray of waves splashed against the hull of the ship, and when the mist settled, a port appeared in the distance, sampans and junk ships dotting the bay. "For the past eight years, I have been searching for my purpose, my path. I cannot erase what happened to me, and I no longer wish to. The people who took me—who took my brother—continue to exist in this world, between the shadows of the laws, in the darkness of when society turns away from them.

"I will not." Linn touched the daggers at her hips. "I know my purpose now, shi'sen. It is to hunt the traffickers and traders to the ends of the world, until the day no child must go through what I have gone through. I will fight for those who cannot."

They spoke so often of the gods, of the powers they had left behind. Yet it was humans, Linn thought, touching a hand to the daggers that hung from her hips, who would need to continue to fight for the slivers of goodness in this world.

Her master was silent for several moments. When she dared to turn to face him, she found that he was looking at her with a strange expression.

Then he pressed his palms together and inclined his head to her in a salute. Linn's lips parted in shock. "Ko Linnet," her master said. "You continue to surprise me at every turn. I once taught you to recognize your place in this world . . . but now, I think that I have much to learn from you." He turned back to the railing. "We will need to let the Temple Masters know of your decision . . . and I do wonder if they would be inclined to offer support. Our land has long been in a state of dormancy. Perhaps it is time we, too, fought back."

The crew and soldiers had awoken; they lined the deck of the ship, watching their approach to the harbor. The docks were in sight now, wooden jetties stretching into the sea. A procession of people had gathered, all liveried in pale shifts and colored sashes to indicate their wielder status.

Linn glanced at Fong shi'sen. "You did not mention a welcome party."

His eyes sparkled. "Look closer."

Dawn was imminent, the sky streaked through with corals and reds and fuchsias that set the clouds and mountains and oceans afire. Light swept over the people gathered at the docks, illuminating their faces. Linn found her mouth curving in a smile as she found several Temple Masters, Ruu'ma shi'sen at the very front.

And then her eyes landed on a face—one that had been a ghost, a memory, a slip of her dreams for so, so long. Her heart stopped.

On the shores of her home, her mother was waving at her.

"Ama-ka," Linn whispered.

At long, long last, the sun had risen.

The sky stretched beautiful and bright and blue—a perfect day to set sail.

Ramson leaned against the railing of the bridge, watching the supply wagons roll to the small ship bobbing gently in the Tiger's Tail. It was a cutter, large enough to fit only the several people aboard. The late-afternoon sun lanced across the river like broken glass, warming the pale stone walls of the new Salskoff Collegium.

The crowd from the ceremony had dispersed, but the streets were filled with people walking by to take a look, peering into the now-open gates and even wandering inside. The entire afternoon had seen a steady flow of visitors on foot or arriving in carriages—parents with children, older and younger siblings, and spouses—all registering for enrollment at the Collegium.

A world, Ana had told him once, *where Affinites and non-Affinites can exist in peace.*

"I'll be damned, Witch," Ramson muttered, sweeping his hair from his face. "You've done it."

He checked his silver pocketwatch. He was to sail down the Tiger's Tail all the way to port, where the barge he'd commissioned awaited him. His squad had left earlier in the day, along with the rest of the Bregonian battalion. Ramson had carefully detailed a list of those killed in battle—including First Officer Narron. He'd asked for their families to receive the highest honors in Bregon and enough compensation so that they would have no uncertainty as to their livelihoods again. His squad had also taken Ardonn back with them, along with a letter from Ramson detailing the role the former scholar had played in helping with the research of the Heart. As to Ardonn's fate, the Three Courts would have to decide.

Ramson's fate, though, had arrived in the form of a gray Bregonian seadove.

He'd come up with the idea late one night, upon reviewing the crates of records left over from Kerlan's network: an independent task force created in partnership with multiple kingdoms, dedicated to hunting down traffickers and traders across the world. The Republic of Cyrilia would sponsor them; he'd sent funding requests to Bregon and Kemeira and the Southern Crowns, including Nandji.

King Darias had responded.

The letter rested in Ramson's pocket now, stamped with the official sigil of the Three Courts of Bregon: five thousand Bregonian coronnes and a Navy squad on loan from the Kingdom of Bregon.

"You know once we get to my ship, I'll be captain?" came a gruff voice from behind him.

He turned to see Daya dropping a sack onto the barge. She looked resplendent in her royal-blue Bregonian cloak, which she'd asked to keep as memorabilia. The bronze shoulder pads shone in complement to her eyes, boots sturdy over her long legs.

Ramson grinned at her. "Well, look at you. You were naught but a scrawny pirate when I met you."

Daya snorted. "The correct term is *businesswoman.* And now I'm *captain.*"

"Surely you haven't forgotten who introduced you to this opportunity in the first place," Ramson reminded her.

"Surely you haven't forgotten that you'll be sailing on *my* ship."

Ramson pretended to sigh. "I swear, all the women in my life—"

"—put you in the place you deserve?" Daya winked. She came to stand next to him, and for a few moments, they gazed out at the waters in silent companionship. "You know, Ramson," she continued, "if I were you, I would never have given up what I had waiting for me in Bregon. I might have given you too little credit."

"People tend to do that," Ramson replied with a shrug. "I like to set expectations low and surprise people once in a while."

Through the Salskoff Collegium gates, a figure had appeared, cloaked and hooded, walking briskly through the crowds. From this distance, she might have been unrecognizable to anyone— but Ramson could feel the pull of her presence as steady as the needle of a compass.

"I'll be getting the boat ready," Daya said. "Come down as soon as Ana arrives, won't you? I'd like to stay on schedule."

"I will." His eyes never left the figure approaching. Ramson straightened and began to walk toward her.

They met by the riverside promenade, and as he took in the sight of her, the roar of the water beneath them and the rush of carriages and pedestrians all around them seemed to fall away. She'd shed her crimson cloak for a dark one, the hood casting shadows over her face—and Ramson suddenly had a fleeting memory: a prison cell, torchlight flickering against rough-hewn walls, the silhouette of a girl carved against the doorframe.

Ramson let his arms fall against the small of her back as she leaned into him, her breath warm against his cheeks. She lowered her hood and he reached up, tracing a finger against her jawline.

He kissed her, sighing as she thawed into him, her lips tasting sharp and sweet. She made a little noise of surprise as he drew her against him, holding her as he'd always wanted and letting his hands tangle in her hair. He felt her smile against him, felt her fingers roam over his chest, brushing down the length of his side. When she drew back to gaze up at him from beneath her dark lashes, her eyes brimmed with joy, and the smile she gave him bore the feeling of coming home. As he reached out to pull back a strand of hair and trail his fingers down her face, Ramson thought that this single moment might have been worth everything they'd been through.

"You have the map all prepared, as I asked?" she asked him.

"Have I ever disappointed you?" he replied.

A quirk of her eyebrow. "Do you really want me to answer that?"

"No." He smiled. "Kiss me again."

She did, and when she drew back, she looked to the Salskoff Collegium. A flash of pride crossed her expression; her smile was rueful. "This isn't how I imagined my life would go," she said.

Ramson looked up, his arm around her waist. "No, me neither."

"It's better," she said, grinning up at him. "I never thought I would be anything more than a monster, Ramson—I never thought I would use my Affinity for *good*."

He held her close to him, tilting his head so that his lips

brushed against her temple as he spoke. "And I thought it was an eternity of sailing the seas with *me* that you were excited about."

"Don't get ahead of yourself, con man."

"Don't lie to yourself, Witch." He took her hand, twining their fingers together. "Come, Daya would have my life if we were to delay any longer."

They made their way to the cutter. The sun hung low in the sky; beneath them, the river stretched all the way to the open sea. The sails bloomed like wings as they caught the wind; they hauled anchor and the cutter began to move, gliding forward with the current.

From the wheel, Daya tapped two fingers to her forehead in mock salute. Ramson grinned and turned to lean against the railing, a map and a compass in hand. Ana had spoken true, he realized, for there could be no life better than this: the wind at his back and the water out in front, sailing toward that open horizon with the girl he loved by his side.

He held out the map to her; on it, he'd marked the locations of the Affinite trafficking networks across the world, the ones that they would begin to hunt down. One by one.

Ana tilted her head as she studied it, then flicked a glance at him. He thought he saw a familiar flash of crimson in those eyes. "Where to first?" she asked.

Ramson took her hand and slipped his old, rusty compass into her palm. "Wherever your heart desires."

GLOSSARY

CYRILIA

Affinite: person with a special ability or a connection to physical or metaphysical elements; ranges from a heightened sense of the element to ability to manipulate or generate the element

blackstone: stone mined from the Krazyast Triangle; the single element immune to Affinite manipulation and known to diminish or block Affinities

bliny: a type of pancake made of buckwheat flour and best served with caviar

bratika: brother

chokolad: cocoa-based sweet

contessya: countess

copperstone: lowest-value coin

dacha: house

dama: lady

deimhov: demon

Deys: Deity

Deys'voshk: green poison that affects Affinites and is used to subdue them; also known as Deities' Water

Fyrva'snezh: First Snows
goldleaf: highest-value coin
guzhkyn gerbil: pet rodent from the Guzhkyn region in
    southern Cyrilia
Imperator: Emperor
Imperatorya: Empress
Imperya: Empire
kapitan: captain
kechyan: traditional Cyrilian robe typically made of
    patterned silk
kologne: scented perfume
kolst: glorious
kommertsya: commerce
konsultant: consultant
mamika: "little mother"; term of endearment for "aunt"
mesyr: mister
pelmeny: dumplings with fillings of minced meat, onions,
    and herbs
pirozhky: fried pie with sweet or savory fillings
pryntsessa: princess
ptychy'moloko: bird's milk cake
Redcloak: rebels; a play on the colloquialism "Whitecloak"
silverleaf: medium-value coin
sistrika: sister
sunwine: mulled wine made in the summer with honey
    and spice
valkryf: breed of horse; a valuable steed with split toes and
    an incomparable ability to climb mountains and weather
    cold temperatures
varyshki: expensive bull leather

Vyntr'makt: winter market; outdoor markets usually established in town squares prior to the arrival of winter

Whitecloak: colloquialism for the Imperial Patrol prior to the arrival of winter

yaeger: rare Affinite whose connection is to another person's Affinity; they can sense Affinites and control one's Affinity

BREGON

gossenwal: ghostwhales

ironore: a type of rock with defensive properties mined in the Kingdom of Bregon

magek: magic, or an Affinity

magen: a wielder of magic; an Affinite

searock: a rare type of rock with absorption properties, found only in the Corshan Gulf of the Kingdom of Bregon

Sommesreven: the Night of Souls, when Bregonians commemorate the dead

wassengost: water spirits

ACKNOWLEDGMENTS

An entire trilogy done, from when I was just a Chinese kid dreaming in a big American city. To the people below, thank you for championing my growth, whether as a writer or a person:

Krista Marino, a most brilliant mind and fierce warrior who continues to lift up my voice and my stories. What an epic adventure of justice and courage we have completed. Here's to the battles we will continue to fight together in this world, with our pens as our swords. Thank you for holding my wings and encouraging me to fly.

Pete Knapp, my fearless advocate from Day One and the best partner I could ask for in this industry. Your astute insights and unwavering support have shaped my path in this field, and you continue to be a guiding light. To many more adventures of magic and whimsy!

Lydia Gregovic—thank you for bringing a sharp editorial mind and boundless enthusiasm and passion to these stories every single day. My eternal gratitude to the entire team at Random House Children's Books, whose work has breathed life into this series: thank you for finishing this journey with me.

The Park & Fine Literary Media team, including Abigail Koons, Ema Barnes, Emily Sweet, and Andrea Mai—my immense gratitude for all you have done in support of this series since the very start, and for allowing my words to be shared across oceans and continents.

My writer friends, whether you've been with me since *Blood Heir* was just a few paragraphs posted to an online forum, whether you've read all my terrible first drafts or taken the time to read my words in any shape or form, whether you've helped me survive the pandemic through virtual calls or movie nights, whether you've listened to my excitement about F1 or Chinese dramas, whether we've exchanged short texts or long emails or Instagram stories and strings of TikToks. Please know that I am so grateful for each and every one of you for continuing to inspire me.

My friends who have watched my antics since we were the coolest kids back in grade school on Hogwarts roleplay sites; who took a chance on the weird Chinese international kid who couldn't differentiate between mailboxes and trash cans in the US; who went through the trials and tribulations of forging a career in finance with me and still encouraged me in my pursuit of this dream; who have shown up for me in any shape or form— I'm so happy to call you my friends, and to continue to figure out this thing we call life together.

Mom and Dad Sin, whose strength and spirit inspire perseverance and courage against the greatest odds; Ryan, whose home provided shelter for me to complete this last leg of my trilogy; and Sherry, who manages the Empire of the Kitchens with me beneath the gracious benevolence of Her Majesty the Queen Olive.

Arielle, my best sister without whom life would be so much lonelier. From kids playing pretend to grown adults still playing pretend, there is no one who is a more kindred soul. I'm so proud of everything you are and everything you have achieved, and I know you will only go on to do bigger and better things. 姐姐 is always here for you. And the Growlithes will reign supreme across their ever-expanding empire.

妈妈爸爸，感谢你们一直以来对我无限的支持。从小到大，家庭完美的环境和你们对我们的全面培养能够让我们伸开翅膀飞得更高、更远。这只是我找到自己道路的最开始，我会不断的努力，像你们一样打造出一片自己的小天地。"欲穷千里目，更上一层楼。"

Clement, who's been through it all with me, who loves and supports me unconditionally, and who always puts me first (except for when you steal all my snacks). Thank you for being there for me at the start and end of each day, whether I'm happy or sad, tired or mad; for listening to all my chattering and complaints; for picking up chores when I was too busy writing; for being my partner through life. Finding you was the best thing that happened to me. I'm beyond grateful we get to write our happily ever after together.

Last but not least, to my readers, those who have been on this journey with me since before *Blood Heir* came out, those who have discovered and ardently championed this series throughout, and those who have just crossed the finish line with Ana and Ramson and Linn and Kaïs and the entire crew to their Happily Ever After: you make this series, and you are the reason Ana & co.'s stories live on. It has always been a dream of mine to share words of hope, of love, of friendship, of courage and adventure—and if you have found a home within my books, thank you, from the bottom of my heart, for sharing this dream with me.

ABOUT THE AUTHOR

Amélie Wen Zhao was born in Paris and grew up in Beijing in an international community. Her multicultural upbringing instilled in her a deep love of global affairs and cross-cultural perspectives. She seeks to bring this passion to her stories, crafting characters from kingdoms in different corners of the world. She attended college in New York City, where she now lives. Amélie is the author of the Blood Heir series: *Blood Heir, Red Tigress,* and *Crimson Reign.*

ameliezhao.com